WALK

THE

VANISHED

EARTH

WALK

THE

VANISHED

EARTH

ERIN SWAN

VIKING

VIKING
An imprint of Penguin Random House LLC
penguinrandomhouse.com

Grateful acknowledgment is made for permission to reprint the following:

Tracy K. Smith, excerpt from "The Universe: Original Motion Picture Soundtrack" from *Life on Mars*. Copyright © 2011 by Tracy K. Smith. Reprinted with the permission of The Permissions Company, LLC on behalf of Graywolf Press, Minneapolis, Minnesota, graywolfpress.org.

Text selection from page 106 from *Little House on the Prairie* by Laura Ingalls Wilder, illustrated by: Garth Williams. Text copyright © 1935, 1963 Little House Heritage Trust. Pictures copyright © 1953 by Garth Williams, copyright © renewed 1981 by Garth Williams. Used by permission of HarperCollins Publishers.

LIBRARY OF CONGRESS CATALOGING-IN-PUBLICATION DATA
Names: Swan, Erin, 1975– author.
Title: Walk the vanished earth : a novel / Erin Swan.
Description: [New York] : Viking, [2022]
Identifiers: LCCN 2021040792 (print) | LCCN 2021040793 (ebook) | ISBN 9780593299333 (hardcover) | ISBN 9780593299340 (ebook)
Subjects: LCGFT: Fiction.
Classification: LCC PS3619.W35257 W35 2022 (print) | LCC PS3619.W35257 (ebook) | DDC 813/.6—dc23/eng/20211018
LC record available at https://lccn.loc.gov/2021040792
LC ebook record available at https://lccn.loc.gov/2021040793

Printed in the United States of America
1st Printing

BOOK DESIGN BY LUCIA BERNARD

This book is for Pete

So much for us. So much for the flags we bored

Into planets dry as chalk, for the tin cans we filled with fire
And rode like cowboys into all we tried to tame. Listen:

The dark we've only ever imagined now audible, thrumming,
Marbled with static like gristly meat. A chorus of engines churns.

Silence taunts: a dare. Everything that disappears
Disappears as if returning somewhere.

Tracy K. Smith, "The Universe: Original Motion Picture Soundtrack"

Good weather never lasts forever on this earth.

Laura Ingalls Wilder, *Little House on the Prairie*

SAMSON

KANSAS PRAIRIE, 1873

Wind through the curly buffalo grass. Hot sun on his hat. A faint irritation of flies. He surveys the plain, humped with woolly beasts. He has shot twelve today: two bulls, nine cows, one calf. A respectable haul, though not his best. Burroughs and Masters have already bent to work, sawing off tongues, stripping hides. Soon he will join them. The afternoon stinks of dropped dung and blood and his own sweat. He mops his face with his handkerchief, wonders when his beard will grow. He would like to shave with the others, squatting by the chipped mirror at dawn, his breath fogging the glass.

He considers the cow closest to his feet, ponders her final moments. Neither Masters nor Burroughs believes in animal sentience, but he imagines their minds as small campfires within their matted heads. They would crackle and glow, cast off sparks. Riding close during a hunt, he has seen their eyes, brimming with a sorrow he recognizes. When he shoots, each orb's light dims slowly, a fire winking out toward morn.

A bleat draws his attention. The calf has risen. It totters on wobbly legs among the carcasses. He has shot it in the shoulder, missing its heart. He does not raise his rifle. The time for such sound has passed. He strides forward, flies clouding his face, and draws his bowie knife. The calf stands still. It considers him with human eyes. He kneels, collars the calf's neck with his arm, tilts its snout toward the sky. Its dense scent recalls his boyhood by the stove in Liverpool: his siblings in a heap, the flames dying for want of coal. A swift slice opens its throat. He pictures the child its skin will warm. The calf drops to its knees, keels onto its side. Breath huffs from its muzzle. The light fades from its pupils.

He stands up. Masters and Burroughs have made short work. Four creatures remain. He tackles them, hacking through the thick skin and tugging the hides from the bodies. He carves out hams and tongues, abandons the rest. Their wagon can carry only so much weight; he must take what will profit him. The reek of voided bowels envelops him. He tugs his bandanna over his nose.

In town, he will purchase new overalls and a shirt. Possibly a pair of boots. His own are rotten with blood, their soles cracked from the long spring. The prairie takes time to thaw, the snowmelt to evaporate. It's hard to remember the icy winter now on this August day. Sweat stiffens his clothes. If the hides and hams and tongues fetch enough, he can do more than buy new clothes. He can visit a dance hall in Dodge City. Maybe she will be there. The one named Daisy, with hair red as his own, the base of her throat the single soft spot in town.

Daisy has never laughed at his ear. A solid lump against his skull. Liquefied like tallow, hardened to a scar. The skin around it shiny, with a bald patch where the hair won't grow. When he chooses, he can summon its precise scent, sizzling against the stovetop. The weight of his father's hand atop his skull. He might have understood if his father were drunk, but it was dawn, his eyes rimmed red from insomnia, not whiskey. His father shoveled the last coal into the stove and let its iron sides heat. Samson feigned sleep, watching through parted lids, but his father wasn't fooled. How quickly he grabbed him and pressed him down. Tomorrow, his father said, you'll go to work.

For two years he worked the docks. The vast ships sliding from shore stirred a thirst no water could quench. At their journey's end, he imagined the land he'd begun seeing nightly in his dreams: an immense dry plain, a man walking across it. I will be that man, he promised himself.

At fifteen he sold his father's sole treasure—a gold pocket watch filched from his own father's corpse back in Kerry—traded the thirty-five pounds for a ticket, and boarded a steam ship west. At Castle Garden in New York, he registered with his first name alone, relinquishing his father's with a simple negligence of the pen. Samson he kept for his mother's sake. She had insisted it meant power, particularly with his long hair. Nonetheless, he lasted a mere week before chopping the hair off. In this New World, he told himself, he would be a new man.

With the previous weeks' labor, they've enough hides now, stretched and dried in the sun. Tonight, they will sup on roasted jackrabbit and boiled beans. He will listen to the howl of wolves, and a prickle will pass from his arms to his heart. The sky, as always, will overwhelm him with stars. He will sleep to the sound of his fellows farting and snoring and grunting from bad dreams. In the morning, he will watch Burroughs and Masters scrape their chins raw in the early light and hope his twenty-first birthday will award him such bristles. Once the fresh hides dry, they will pack up camp for town, leaving broken stems where they slept, a blackened ring from their fire.

By year's end, his pockets should be richly lined. As 1873 folds into '74, he will be able to make an offer. A ring for Daisy, a wagon to Texas, a farm of his own. Together they might raise a son, a boy who could walk the furrows alongside him, casting seed into the rich brown soil of this country he has chosen, for himself and for all the generations to come. He has not planted seeds before, but he would like to do so. What a joy it must be to see that pioneering green stem, poking its head from the earth.

MOON

MARS, 2073

Once I had a family. It was a family of three: Uncle One, Uncle Two, and me. The Uncles called me Moon, and they loved me as their own. They fed me dust, sang me to sleep, took turns carrying me on their backs. When I entered my second year, they taught me to walk, and I learned the joy of putting one foot before the other. Keep your eyes on the horizon, Uncle Two instructed. That's it.

We had no fixed home. Ever since I could remember, we had traveled. Once I could stand on my own two feet, I toddled beside the Uncles, doing my best to keep up. We marched across red dunes, along mountain ridges, into valleys striated with stone. We examined pebbles, cliff faces, the shades of yellow in the sky. At first, I took our nomadic existence on faith. This is what we do. We walk. But when I entered my sixth year, I thought to ask why.

We were crossing a vast plain, the Uncles eager to discover its end, but at my question, they stopped. I saw us clearly then. The Uncles tall and thin and pale, their hearts pulsing purple through their translucent chests, and I beside them, smaller and darker, rough hair sprouting from my head, my own heart mercifully hidden. We were the only living things I had ever known. Around us nothing but the plain's vastness and the big sky, which looked terribly empty. That is what made me ask. That emptiness.

Uncle One's white eyes widened with surprise. Surely you know, he said. Our mission is knowledge. We must learn about our sandstorms and sunsets, our oxygen and gravity. We must learn our red soil, how it shifts under us, how it hardens. We must learn our planet so that we understand our place in the universe.

But why? I asked again.

We need to see where we are, he replied, so we can see where we will go next.

And where is that? I asked.

Patience, Uncle One said. We will know when we get there.

And so, we continued. We crossed that plain and discovered its end. After that, more plains, more mountains, more valleys. Through the days we traveled, subsisting on soil and air, the Uncles teaching me what they could, studying what they didn't know. With the arrival of each long twilight, I lay down with my head in Uncle One's lap and listened to Uncle Two's stories.

Uncle Two raised me on tales of my namesake and the rock around which it revolved. He told me the Moon was cold and vacant, but Earth was not. It teems with life, he said. Uncles and Moons? I asked, for I couldn't fathom anything else. Yes, he affirmed. Night had fallen, and he pointed at the twinkling light he called Earth. It swarms with us, he said. Giant white Uncles with big bald heads and little brown Moons like you, with legs that never tire and eyes crystalline as the ice at our poles.

Is that where we will go next? I asked. To meet the Uncles and Moons? The thought woke me up. I saw again the empty sky over the empty plain, and something rippled in my chest, as though emptiness itself were running its fingers over my ribs. Tell me more, I demanded. Try to sleep, Uncle Two said.

But in the years to come, Uncle Two did tell me more. He spun stories about the Uncles and Moons who populated Earth, about their loves and contests and wars. He told me they ate dust and drank air as we did, but they also built houses—What are houses? I asked, and so he told me that too—and drafted laws and tried to keep track of history.

I had no way of knowing Uncle Two was really talking about humans and their civilization. How could I have understood he was using humans to teach me about my own future? I couldn't have seen what he and Uncle One were planning. Over the years, we climbed the tremendous expanse of Olympus Mons and dipped into the canyons of Valles Marineris and tramped the length of the Hellas basin. We watched the sun come and go, watched our own two underwhelming moons— Phobos and Deimos—shuffle across the firmament.

This is this, Uncle Two told me as we walked, and that is that. I bubbled with questions, but I didn't ask the right ones. I assumed the Uncles had named those places, as I believed they had named Earth. I didn't wonder who had originally affixed such titles, didn't think to ask from whom or from what we had sprung.

Then one day something changed.

IN MY FOURTEENTH YEAR, when my hair had begun to coil and my hips to curve, we three discovered something that was neither dune nor boulder nor stony outcropping. In morning's raw light we saw it: a white dome swelling from the ground, red granules clinging to its sides, partially buried in sand. Even so, it loomed against the landscape. By then, I thought I had seen everything. This was new. The thrill of discovery made me skip as we approached.

Calm yourself, Uncle One admonished.

What is this place? I asked him, but he wouldn't answer.

His normally blank eyes looked misty, as mine felt when sadness gripped me. Certain things spawned this sadness: a rebuff from Uncle Two, a low note in the wind, how that plain had seemed to stretch into infinity. But Uncle One's feeling sad didn't seem possible. He felt only determination to keep walking, keep learning.

I turned to Uncle Two. Where did it come from? I asked.

Oh. He sounded distant. Some things just appear. As you did.

He stared at the white sphere against the red rocks. It was huge, more bulbous than the Uncles' heads and much taller than they. I thought of the houses on Earth that Uncle Two had described. You could fit a lot of us inside there, I thought.

Uncle Two turned to Uncle One. A look passed between them. Uncle One nodded.

How did they know this was here? I thought. But then I remembered Uncle One's words years ago on that wide plain. This dome was our next step. We had been headed here all along.

As though he had heard my thoughts, Uncle One settled his gaze on me.

Moon, he said, it is time we took you home.

WE FOUND AN ENTRANCE to the dome, half obscured by dune. Uncle One dug the dirt away. Then he took hold of the portal's edges and pried it open. I winced at the sharp noise. One by one, we entered. The hatchway was so low the Uncles had to stoop. Just inside was another entrance, sealed. That's a door, Uncle One told me. Then he wrenched its edges apart, revealing a dark tunnel.

Some light trickled in from outside but illuminated little. The air was dense with strange smells, odors other than dust. They made me think of my damp brown crevices, my sweat and saliva and heat. A chord within me hummed, as though my body recognized an affinity with this place.

Don't be afraid, Uncle Two told me. Then both Uncles entered the tunnel. They seemed utterly confident striding into the shadows. I couldn't imagine what was in there, but I wanted to find out. I followed them, stepping cautiously on the slippery surface, so different from the terrain I had known. As I inched through the gloom, the tunnel curved and the smells grew stronger, denser, more alive. I felt as if I were walking into my own self. I remembered Uncle Two's stories about Earth, how it swarmed with life. My breath quickened.

The tunnel ended abruptly at another door. A thin seam of light gleamed through a crack. Uncle One tore it fully open, and there we were, inside the dome. Thick heat enveloped me. It was so bright my eyes had difficulty adjusting. I rubbed them until my vision cleared. Uncle Two's stories hadn't included what now spread before me. I didn't own words for what I beheld. Uncle Two began to point, naming what I saw.

The color is green, he told me. That is new for you. Pink you might recognize. You know brown and white. He gestured at my sturdy body with its umber coloring, then his gangly pale limbs. I suppose purple is familiar too, he mused. He glanced down to where his heart's dark muscle pulsed under his skin.

The green is for the leaves, he continued, brown for the trunks. Those are trees, Moon. The pink and purple and white are flowers. Look. He sounded gleeful. Some are yellow and some are blue, he said. Green also belongs to the vines and shrubs and weeds. They are plants and plants make oxygen. That's why it smells so different in here. He squeezed my hand. This dome holds a forest, as alive as you or I. See how delicate the flowers are, how tough the vines. See how high the trees reach? They are constantly seeking light. He paused and cocked his head at Uncle One. How is everything still living? he asked. And the electricity on?

Solar power, Uncle One replied. It's linked to an irrigation system too. He pointed upward. The panels are embedded in the dome.

Uncle Two tilted his head back and then nodded in admiration. How ingenious.

I suppose they weren't entirely stupid, Uncle One said.

Who are *they*? I asked.

Oh. Uncle Two waved me off. The great they, he said. The omniscient they.

He pulled me into the forest. We waded into a patch of flowers. Around us clustered plant after plant, shrubs and trees and weeds. High above us curved the dome, glittering with what Uncle One had called solar panels. The colors were so vibrant my head had begun to hurt, the air so sticky I found it hard to inhale. I wanted desperately to like it. This is the next step, I told myself. We are here. Breathe.

Look at this, Uncle Two urged. He pointed at one flower. See those petals, he said, more yellow than our sky? That is a black-eyed Susan.

How do you know their names? I asked him.

We were here once. Like Uncle One's, his eyes grew misty.

They did know it was here, I thought. They brought us here on purpose.

You and Uncle One? I asked.

You too, child. He pulled me against him in a quick hug. We were all here.

I stood there incredulous. Why can't I recall this?

He bent down to brush a bloom's frail pink petals with his palm. You were only a few days old when we left, he said. You wouldn't remember.

I searched for Uncle One, but he had meandered into the forest. I could see him between the trunks, stopping now and then to scrutinize something. His heart appeared to be pumping more quickly. Everything he found seemed to enthrall him, but my initial wonder was ebbing. It must have been the smell. The fumes in that place were overpowering. Fetid and cloying, with an underlying stench that reminded me of the time we witnessed a star wink out forever. Death. That's what it stank like.

THE DOME was not only a dome. The Uncles showed me what lay under the surface. Uncle Two opened a hatch in the dome's floor. That is a ladder, he said to me. Climb down. I clambered down it to another tunnel, and the Uncles followed. I was relieved to escape the dome's damp decay. From the first tunnel, we walked into another. Then another. The tunnels were brightly lit, but a layer of dust coated everything. This comforted me. We hadn't left the dunes entirely behind.

The tunnels led to small enclosed spaces Uncle Two called pods. Some were already open, but others were still sealed. Uncle One pried those apart. These were for sleeping, Uncle Two informed me. He gestured at an oblong object nearly the same size as I was. It looked softer than anything I'd known. That's a bed, he said. He picked something even softer off the floor and tucked it over the bed. That's a blanket, he told me.

And this? I held up something gray I'd found in a corner. It had limbs and a torso, but seemed more like a discarded skin than a body. When I held it against me, I saw it didn't quite match my height. On the front flashed something that looked like a star, but red.

Oh. Uncle Two snatched it from me. That's a rag. For cleaning. He swiped it across a surface to pick up dirt.

Put that down, Uncle One told his brother. Let's go, he said and stalked off.

Uncle Two dropped the rag and followed him. I scampered to keep up. The underground tunnels arced higher than the entrance had. The Uncles didn't have to bend much.

Teach me more, I called after them.

At another pod, I caught up with them. I didn't know what all the square spaces and lights were for, but the lingering scent gave me a clue. It didn't smell like the soil we ate, but it made me hungry. This is the eating pod, I announced.

Yes, said Uncle Two. You're learning.

Look at this. Uncle One waved us over. He was leaning over a white basin. He turned what he called a handle, and something almost familiar poured out. It was wet like my sweat but silvery and fluid as the trail of a shooting star. That's water, he proclaimed.

By morning's end, we had cataloged the entire place. Aboveground the dome with its mysterious forest and high paneled ceiling. Belowground the network of tunnels and ladders and pods. We had found five sleeping pods, one eating pod, and one with multiple handles that spewed water, where Uncle One said we'd begin excreting. We also found a pod filled with flat square things that shone in the artificial light. Those are screens, Uncle Two said, but couldn't—or wouldn't—explain what they were for.

Uncle Two had spent years answering my questions, but he seemed impatient or preoccupied or both. He kept conferring with Uncle One, who was determined as ever, tearing open the entrance to each pod and marching in to right tilted objects or brush dust from surfaces. Despite my excitement, I felt an odd foreboding. The next step, I thought, watching Uncle One shake a blanket over a bed. I had assumed our future would be among the cliffs and clouds I had come to love. In my wildest dreams, I had imagined we might go to Earth. Yet we had ended up here, where I couldn't even see the sky.

The last pod Uncle One pried open contained piles of dirt sprouting things I presumed were more trees. No, corrected Uncle Two. Those are potatoes. His patience had returned. For this I was grateful. I needed the Uncles. I didn't know how I would learn anything without them.

THAT NIGHT I COULDN'T SLEEP. My pod was narrow and stuffy. The quiet of it pressed upon me. I missed the Uncles' warmth, their bony backs against mine, their white eyes peacefully closed. My own eyes kept opening. I kept thinking about the dome, its overwhelming colors and damp stench. I missed the glittering dark above, the nighttime winds, the firm pillow of a boulder under my head.

I could have gotten up, climbed the ladder, navigated the dark tunnel to the broken hatchway. I could have returned to the world I had known. But I didn't. I didn't want to leave the Uncles.

Resolutely, I closed my eyes. They popped back open. The bed was short and horribly soft. I rolled off it and finally managed to fall asleep on the floor.

UNCLE ONE ANNOUNCED our traveling had finished. Is this our future? I asked. Indeed it is, he said triumphantly. He insisted we would make a home there. The Uncles shook out blankets, swept away dust, yanked dead flowers up by their roots. Mostly I sulked, lying flat on my pod's floor or moping around the tunnels. I had wanted to know what would happen next. I had thought we might meet other Uncles, other Moons. But we were stuck inside a place cluttered with plants and blankets and water. Nothing that could speak to me.

Uncle Two tried to keep me engaged. He kept dragging me to the dome to teach me words. Eucalyptus. Mountain laurel. Pine. But I had trouble paying attention. All that green disgusted me. It was too wet, too alive, and too dead at the same time. The plants remained mute, as silent—I realized—as our planet itself.

Then Uncle One said we would eat the potatoes instead of dust. More nutritious, he insisted. We tried them some days after our arrival. Even Uncle One gagged. He covered it up quickly. So did Uncle Two. They polished off their potatoes without complaint, but I could see how they clutched their stomachs afterward. Now you, Uncle One insisted. Dutifully I picked mine up. I managed one bite. It was moist and mealy, different from dirt's dry crunch. I had to excuse myself to vomit, another novel sensation. As I heaved over the basin in the excreting pod, I sensed Uncle Two behind me. He pulled my long hair back and rubbed my shoulders until the cramping eased. I leaned against him, and he rested his chin on my head.

Why do we have to eat potatoes? I asked. Why can't we eat dust?

We must consume what we grow. Uncle One says we have to, Uncle Two replied. He says we're civilized now.

What is civilized? Is it bad?

He made a sound, but I didn't know what it meant. I asked Uncle One the same thing, he said. He told me it doesn't have to be.

Tell me when we can go outside again, I said.

Soon, Moon. He nuzzled my hair. When Uncle One says we can.

I pushed myself away. Why must we do what he says?

He's family. Uncle Two shrugged. We have no choice.

I TRIED TO ENTERTAIN MYSELF. I folded and refolded my blanket. I poked at the potatoes in the underground garden. I visited the pod with the things Uncle Two had called screens. The screens marched in rows along the pod's perimeter. They were the length of my forearm, the width of my two hands. Each one was resting on a surface and tilted slightly back against the wall. The screens' faces were black and shiny and blank. I picked one up. My own face stared back at me, reflected in the surface. I had not seen it before, and the sight delighted me. I liked my smooth cheeks and wide mouth, how proudly my nose arched. I liked how my features moved, how expressive they were. The Uncles' faces were blank as the screens. They couldn't smile or frown or cry as I could. I don't know how I learned, because no one existed to teach me.

My eyes were pale blue as the snowdrops in the dome, but clear too. Like ice, I thought, remembering how Uncle Two had described them. I turned my mouth up, turned it down, grinned with all my teeth. "Speak to me," I told my reflection.

The sound startled me. I had used my out-loud voice, the one I hardly used, and never used with the Uncles. I half expected a voice to respond, but the screen was a dead thing, another object in a place full of objects. A strange thought flickered. How did all this simply appear? Uncle Two had said the dome had appeared as I had, as he and Uncle One had. We had sprung into life, popped into existence with bones and skin and fingernails intact. So had our planet. If Uncle Two could be trusted, so had Earth, the galaxy, everything. But the screen was different. It was neither rock nor grain of sand. It was not even a tree. Its edges were too regular and measured, its construction too carefully planned. What if someone *had* planned it, as Uncle One had planned our arrival at the dome?

I tucked the screen under my arm and went in search of Uncle Two. I found him in the eating pod, polishing surfaces with a torn piece of rag. It was the piece with the star on it. As he cleaned, it flashed red.

I held out the screen. Where did this come from? I asked.

Uncle Two continued wiping the counters. It was a daily task. A light sediment kept settling, blown in through the hatchways we had left gaping. Does it work? he asked, not looking up.

It doesn't do anything, I said. What should it do?

He put the rag down and took the screen. If I can fix it, I will show you what it does, okay?

Okay. I was annoyed Uncle Two had taken the screen. I had wanted to know where it'd come from, but he had dodged my question. I yearned for our traveling days, when the Uncles would tell me anything I wanted to know.

You're bored, Uncle Two said. He laid a palm to my cheek. You need something to do. Come. Uncle One has a job for you.

UNCLE ONE WANTED ME to plant more flowers. He said there weren't enough to keep the place going. Going for what? I asked, but neither Uncle answered. When Uncle Two brought me to the dome to begin planting, I tried another tactic. What do the flowers do? I asked.

They make oxygen, he said. We're losing too much through the doors.

Can't you close the doors?

Too damaged, he replied.

But who cares if we're losing oxygen? I asked. We don't need much.

We don't, but somebody might.

Somebody? I asked. Are the Uncles and Moons coming here?

My heart sped up. If that were so, staying wouldn't be so bad.

Oh, my dear child. Don't get ahead of yourself. He shook his head and his chin wobbled.

His new diet was making him plump. Despite his initial distaste, he had begun gorging on potatoes, eating three times what Uncle One did.

I hadn't realized how quickly he could transform. In a few days, his belly had grown round and squishy, his chin doubled.

Let us focus on the flowers, he said. Here comes Uncle One.

Uncle One was approaching with a handful of tiny pebbles. These are seeds, he said. His hard eyes alighted on me. Kneel in the dirt, he told me. Push each seed into the ground. Add water. Repeat. He turned to Uncle Two. Help me prune the eucalyptus trees. They're growing ragged.

I did as Uncle One commanded. I knelt and began poking seeds into the soil. The swampy smell seemed less repulsive. I was growing used to it. Maybe there was hope. More flowers, I thought. More oxygen. Enough for anybody who comes.

The Uncles left me there and walked toward another section of the forest, Uncle One's strides sharp and decisive beside Uncle Two's new shuffle. They had shut their minds to me and I could no longer hear them, but I could tell they were talking from the intent way they were staring at each other.

I wanted to know what they were saying, why we had come, when the others might arrive. Frustration filled me. I jammed another seed into the dirt. They'd stopped telling me anything.

AT THAT EVENING'S MEAL, Uncle One watched me eat. Uncle Two had prepared the food—plucked potatoes from the underground garden and plunked them on the table—so I did my best to be polite, though the texture still made me want to vomit. I had almost finished nibbling when Uncle One picked up his potato and demolished it in a single bite.

You're getting older, he told me. He wiped his lips with one long-fingered hand. Then he reached out the same hand and touched me on the chest, right where the flesh had begun to swell under the nipples. Something quivered within me. I didn't like it. I placed the rest of my potato on the table.

I could tell by the set of Uncle Two's shoulders he didn't like it either. That's not what we agreed on, he told his brother.

You're right, Uncle One said. He settled back in his seat and laid both hands on the table where I could see them. Moon, I apologize. You have been ours so long I forget you belong to yourself.

I could feel where he'd touched me. I crossed my arms over my chest. Why are we here? I demanded. Are we expecting somebody?

Uncle Two turned to Uncle One. We should tell her, he said. We've waited long enough.

Uncle One nodded, his face expressionless.

Remember? Uncle Two began. My stories about Earth?

I kept my arms crossed. Since we'd come to the dome, he hadn't told me any stories.

About the Uncles and Moons who live there? he prompted.

I perked up.

Your Uncle and I have been thinking about those stories.

I have too, I thought. I liked those stories, I said.

They were good stories, Uncle Two agreed. But what if they could be real? What if we could make our own world here? He leaned forward. Moon, imagine that. An entire civilization.

Civilization, I said. Would it be bad?

Of course not, Uncle Two said. It would be magnificent. We could fill this place with Uncles and Moons, with black-eyed Susans and pine trees and oxygen for all. You could have friends, others like you. He considered me. You must be tired of us. Your old Uncles with their minds full of dreams. Neither of us knows what it's like to be a Moon.

Think about having another female to talk to, someone young, someone who understands you. It could be good.

I considered this. Someone to talk to. That *would* be good.

Then why did we travel so long? I asked. If we could have just come here?

We needed to know what was possible, Uncle One interjected. How much life this planet could sustain. We decided to return here. In case we needed more oxygen.

Are they coming here? I asked. The Uncles and Moons from Earth?

Look at yourself, Moon, Uncle One said. His voice softened. How mature you've grown. You're no longer a child. You're in your fourteenth year. You could be a mother.

At the word *mother*, I felt a rush of anger. I had thought they were finally telling me the truth, but here he was, speaking in riddles.

What's a mother? I asked, but the Uncles merely stared at me. I don't understand, I said, my anger rising. You said our mission was knowledge. Why are you teaching me nothing?

Patience, Uncle One said. You will learn.

I'm tired of being patient, I said.

I left my unfinished potato where it was and stomped off to my pod, where I sprawled on the floor as usual and stared at the ceiling. I tried to ignore Uncle Two's instructions and not think. But the thoughts crept in. I thought about mothers and what they could be. I thought about more Uncles. More Moons. A dome teeming with life. The Uncles had raised me as their own, but Uncle Two was right. They weren't my friends. How would it feel to have someone like me there? Another female with a body like mine. Someone whose bones ached with new growth, who could speak out loud, with a voice I could hear. Someone I could talk to.

I MUST HAVE SLEPT, because I woke to Uncle Two settling his bulk beside me on the floor.

I've brought you a gift, he said.

What's a gift? I mumbled sleepily.

Something you give.

It was the screen he had taken from me. I figured it out, he said. Solar power. I charged it this afternoon. He tapped it, and it illuminated. It was still blank, but bright with light. I thought it might cheer you up.

He tapped it again, and colorful shapes leaped across the screen. Those are cartoons, he said. They are entertaining.

I watched them for a while, but could make no sense of them. More colors, I thought. No faces like mine. No sound. Disappointed, I laid it down.

Uncle Two watched me but didn't protest my indifference.

What's a mother? I asked again.

Uncle Two turned his attention to the ceiling. He didn't look at me when he spoke. Someone who makes someone else, he said.

Could a mother make a friend? I asked.

A mother could make many friends, he said. Many Moons.

Does it hurt? I asked. Making someone else?

This seemed to catch him off guard. He hesitated, then nodded. It does, he said.

I don't like pain, I said. I recalled learning to walk, how often I'd skinned my knees.

Nobody does. Uncle Two squeezed my hand in sympathy.

We could go to Earth instead, I offered. We could visit the Moons there. The Uncles too.

Oh, little one, Uncle Two said gently. Those stories I told you about

Earth. His mouth's edges relaxed. They were fabrications. Neither Uncles nor Moons ever lived on Earth. Many other things used to live there, but not anymore. Now it holds only water.

Why? I asked. What happened?

Sometimes things die out. He sighed. Earth is emptier than this planet. No creatures like you. No Uncles. No families or armies or houses. Just a rock spinning through space.

I don't like emptiness, I said. It makes me feel. I paused. I don't know what it's called.

Lonely, Uncle Two said.

I cuddled into him. I liked how soft he had become. At least I have you, I said.

And I have you, he replied. But what does Uncle One have?

Then he should be a mother, I said. If he wants company so badly.

He's male. He can't be a mother. That task, my dear, is up to you.

Mothers have to be female? I asked.

So say the laws of nature.

Do I have a choice? I turned onto my back, separating myself from him.

I have spoken to Uncle One, he said. He wants the best for us, but also the best for you. He will force you into nothing. In the meantime, try to keep busy. He picked up the screen and put it back in my hands. I only showed you a fraction of what's in here. I believe it is filled with knowledge.

Knowledge? I gripped the screen. But where did this come from? I asked.

Earth, Uncle Two said. A long time ago.

Before everything died?

Before everything died. He stood up. In my pod's nighttime dark, his head glowed round and white as the dome itself. It was hard to tell in the shadows, but it seemed he was trying to smile. Ask it something, he said. I believe sometimes they give answers. Then he left.

I picked up the screen and studied its flat surface. The vivid shapes had disappeared, but bright light still illuminated its surface. I could no longer see my reflection.

Answers, I thought.

I tried tapping it as Uncle Two had, but the colorful shapes returned. I tapped again and they disappeared. I ran my fingers up its surface, then down, then side to side. Other shapes appeared, black lines on white. I didn't know what they meant. I swiped again and they vanished. I held the screen up to my face and did what I had before. I opened my mouth. I cleared my throat, and then I spoke to it.

"What's a mother?" I asked the screen aloud.

At the sound of my voice, the screen's light pulsed. My breath caught.

"I miss her," another voice said back at me. "I didn't think I would miss her so much."

I bolted upright. Not once in my short life had I heard an out-loud voice other than my own. This one was quiet, but very much there. I had longed for someone to talk to me, and now someone—or something—was. I couldn't believe it. My heart was thumping wildly.

I clutched the screen in desperation, afraid the voice would slip away. "Who are you talking about?" I asked it. My mouth was so dry I could barely get the words out.

"My mother," it replied. "I used to think I'd be relieved when she was dead. That's messed up, I know. But she was such a pain in the butt. Now I dream about her all the time."

I hunched over the screen and spoke directly into it. "But who are you? Are you real?"

I waited, eager, breathless, every muscle taut. I thought for sure the voice would respond. But as I watched, the screen's light faded. I heard a vague hum, then nothing. The screen went black.

"No," I said aloud. "Wait. Come back."

I shook the screen and tapped it and spoke to it, but nothing happened. Come on, I urged and shook it again. In frustration, I almost threw it across the room, but stopped myself. I couldn't risk breaking it. Maybe I could charge it again, with solar power, as Uncle Two had. I needed to know what that voice was. If it was real or part of the screen. Where it had come from. To whom or to what it belonged. It had spoken of a mother. It could tell me what that was. I could learn what the Uncles wanted me to become. I thought of the enormous plain where I had learned about emptiness, how alone the Uncles and I had seemed in all that space.

You're not alone, I told myself. Not anymore.

ALL THROUGH THAT LONG NIGHT I lay wide-eyed, thinking of what I had learned and what I had yet to know. By the time I heard the Uncles shuffling awake in their own pods, my resolve had formed. I didn't have to busy myself poking at potatoes or folding blankets. I had work to do.

Uncle Two had said a mother was someone who made someone else. The voice from the screen had a mother, and so someone else had made it. I had to get the screen working again. I needed to find that voice. I needed to know where it had come from. Because if it had a mother, an origin other than dust and light, then maybe I did too. The Uncles wanted me for their civilization. They wanted me to make them Uncles and Moons, to experience pain so others might live. They hoped I could build their future.

But wait, I would tell them. I must learn first about my past.

BEA

KANSAS CITY, 1975

In the summer of 1975, a girl walks alone up a continent. Out of the desert she has trekked, through canyons mournful with echoes, over a mountain crest skimmed by snow. At first the big sky terrified her, but no more. When night comes, she beds down in thickets like a deer, tucking her worn dress around her knees and watching the moon drag itself across the stars. Now she traverses a plain from one horizon to the next, the sun a searing white disk. Through this plain runs a road, bits of concrete yanked upward by some invisible hand. She stumbles over them in her semblance of shoes: tire treads under kitchen sponges, twine to bind it together.

She owns no knowledge of the year and little of the past. Much is a tangle. Grass at its roots. Her hair. The days before the fire. She can recall its great red roar, but not much else. At times she sees things: a door closing, a woman's brown fingers gentling a glass, the creased white face of a man. Then she blinks. Behind her the road. Before her the same.

She counts the lights and the darks. The dark has come 104 times since her journey began. For light, this dawn marks 105. She knows her name but little more. Upon waking she whispers it, sounding its chord against her heart's thrum.

"Bea," she tells herself, "keep walking."

The past is a haze, but the future is clear. She knows where she's going. She is heading north. A pack drags from her shoulders. In railway yards and abandoned warehouses, she has found detritus ready for cobbling, tumbled the boards and metal, the plastic and wire into this pack. With these things, she will build a shelter among the pines. Then a house. A village. From her small hands, another civilization will rise from the empty earth. She will people it with giants, a new breed not yet seen.

Her belly has grown heavy too, the brown skin stretched thin. Now and then, a series of kicks. She knows what's inside. A creature that will emerge enormous, the first of its kind. It will tower over her, and it will be hers, the one to carve a path through the wilderness, to make the dream incarnate. It will create others, an army of giants, and with its kindred, it will take over this blasted place.

"You will own this," she tells it, tapping her taut dome. "Together, we will build anew."

AHEAD, she glimpses a shadow. It looks like smoke from a fire, and she grows cold. But then she sees it's something else. It is a town, and in towns there are scraps for scavenging. She used to fear towns too, choked as they were with pale people who stared. But she needed the food they held. She learned to dart in, and then dart out, skipping free of any words the people hurled, any hands that grabbed.

Through dry weeds she approaches this new town, palms cupping her stomach. Perhaps she will find some boots with sturdy soles. Memory pokes and prods. She knew someone who wore such boots. She can picture his feet, clad in their clumsy leather blocks. But when she grabs at this memory, it crumbles to ash. All else is darkness.

The town is the biggest one she has encountered. At its fringes she hesitates, her heart a skittish animal in her chest, and then pushes on. She needs supplies. With midday pressing its hot hand down, she heads up the broad streets. She passes brick warehouses too defunct to hold anything useful, squat bungalows, gray lots with walls and windows looming on three sides. The street corners bristle with lettered signs and glass-topped posts and lights red, then green. Outside a gas station so sharp with reek it stings her nose, she sees one stalled truck with a faded *Pepsi* in curlicues across its door. More sun-bleached lots. Bigger houses, each with a metal box, numbered and square. In the distance, a few dull towers like fingers pointing in accusation.

The town appears empty, but as she walks deeper into it, she sees cars trundling along the cracked streets. White men pilot them, some slouched low, some with eyes that shift to watch her passage. These men wear shiny shirts striped or spotted, their printed caps pulled down. Their wide vehicles are so low they nearly scrape the ground. At first, she is frightened. She expects them to stop and leap out, to reach for her with hard and grasping hands. But they don't. They let her walk with her pack and her tangled black hair and her lilac dress with its ragged hem. They look at her, look away. They push their cars onward through the fissured streets. They are losing their strength. They are fading away. Or maybe they spot the future she dreams for herself, the proud paunch she pushes into the day. No room will remain for these men once the giants have their way.

The plains have faded behind her, concrete closed in. She must find what she needs and get back to her road. At one doorway she pauses. She scans the metal sign overhead, red letters scrolled on white: GROCERY CIGARETTES COLD BEER. Inside a vague scent of food. Hunger ripples through her. She craves corn. Peas packed tight in a tin. Beets for their sweet taste, the stain they'll bleed on her tongue.

Inside she finds shelves weighted with boxes and cans. A counter up front, dense shadows in back. From the ceiling fly strips dangle, spotted with carcasses. The place is quiet save for a screen behind the counter, blaring sound. On it two faces are talking. This feels familiar. She creeps closer and cocks her head. One is talking about crime and cities. She hears Detroit, New York, but doesn't understand what that means. The other face mentions war, a word she knows. Veterans, he says, hundreds have come back damaged.

"The war has ended," argues the first. "We must focus on problems at home."

"But the war *has* come home," insists the second.

The other face begins saying something about money and rockets and missions, but she blocks her ears. She has no time for the hopes of men. Your day is dead, she wants to tell them. Stop talking.

Down the middle aisle, she finds what she seeks. A shelf of cans stacked high. A few she drops into her pack. Peas and beets and corn, those sweet kernels that'll pop between her teeth. She slides her pack onto her shoulders and picks up a small box. On it a white hand motions toward a bowl of sticky-looking noodles. The hand has two eyes, a mouth, and a round red nose. *Hamburger Helper*, she reads.

In the building's back, a door slams. Footsteps. A shape coalesces, gathers itself into a man. He looks fat and mean, with sparse wet hair combed over his skull.

"Hey, you little bum," he says. "You gonna pay for that?"

She drops the box and runs. Past cereal colored with cartoon faces, milk curdling in cartons, sacks of flour and sugar.

"I ain't no welfare office," the man shouts, but she's gone.

She sprints until pain stitches her side. Below a great green sign shouting ALIVE WITH PLEASURE! She stops to catch her breath. Then she fishes a sharp tool and a tin of corn from her pack. She cracks it open

34

and drinks down the juice, the corn, the juice. Her giant kicks and curls within her. The sun has deepened its burn.

She drops the can and continues walking. The tire treads on her feet have cracked through. Again, memory flickers. A man's two feet planted on a porch, a doorway framing them. Dust films his boots. Sharp and smoky smells, like plants left to wither in the sand. From somewhere an animal barks, a rough *cough cough*, and pain jolts her stomach. The image fades. It is time to discard her shoes altogether. Time to accept the inevitability of calluses. Every inch of her is hardening to scar.

HER NAKED SOLES PIERCED and sore, she walks as deep into the town as she dares. She has found food and now must find metal and wire. More plastic. More wood. Perhaps a cradled palm of water. At one house she pauses, remembering another place with rivulets of wire in the walls, easily torn free. She recalls nuts and bolts tumbled in a drawer, a handful of nails, a plank that fit perfectly inside her pack. To build her village, she's going to need all the materials she can find.

The street is barren, the house's parched lawn bare. She pads toward the door. No locks. She expected dust and plaster, desiccation from disuse, but the house's interior stinks of lemons, and sun sparkles through the windows. She creeps from room to room, stopping to scrabble at the walls, but finds no wire, no scraps to salvage. This house cannot be trusted, but no house truly can. They are bound to go up in smoke.

She walks through rooms and doorways. Carpeted floors she can't pry apart. Brown and orange furniture too heavy to lift. That unpleasant lemon scent. Nothing useful. Nothing to gather.

She turns to leave, but stops. A white man stands in her way. Two men. Three. Their hands and faces choke the air. She staggers back.

One grabs at her pack. She clutches the straps. He snatches it away. Her wire and metal, that perfect plank of wood. Without them, she cannot build her village. She cannot tend her giants tall. She lunges toward him, but another catches her and wraps her tight.

"Check out this crazy kid," he says.

His breath smells like meat. A memory drifts upward. A plate of venison, rich purple and glistening. That is the only meat she has eaten. She used to hate the taste of it.

"Where did she come from?" asks the one with her pack.

"Came in through the door like she owned the place," says the third. He has a flat ruddy face, square at its temples, a blue *Pabst* riding high on his cap.

"Look at her tummy," says the one holding her. "Where do you reckon the daddy is?"

"Can't be too far. Bet there's a vagrant in your bushes, waiting for his girlfriend. Guess he likes them young."

"Fucking hippies," says the first. "Lucky we swung by for that hammer."

The man holding her laughs, and his grip loosens. She twists in his arms, pushes him away, spots a gap between their bodies. Like a deer kicking clear from the hunter, she bolts for the doorway. She will not be dragged down, snagged in their snares. She will break free. The doorway's pulsing light. The great and open road. Space, pines, tomorrows awaiting her in the north. Her giant slipping and sliding with each stride.

"Yes," her giant whispers. "Yes."

On the threshold they catch her. Her swollen stomach, her knotted hair, her love of trash so singular and attuned. Her dreams of gigantic men. She, who has known nothing big, only her tiny self in a world she'd hoped was gone.

They grab her at the door, one foot toward freedom.

On her they lay their hands. Her, they bear away.

PSYCHIATRIC EVALUATION—PREPARATORY NOTES

PSYCHIATRIC CENTER of KANSAS CITY—
CHILDREN'S DIVISION

> Dr. James Edward Carson
> Patient: *B (full name unknown)*
> Date of Initial Evaluation: *7/16/75*
> Case No.: *42*
> Admission Date: *7/15/75*
> Date: *7/20/75*

PURPOSE FOR EVALUATION

Patient is a young girl nearing adolescence. Though exact age currently remains unknown, my speculation would be eleven or twelve. She was found trespassing in a house in Old Westport. She was shoeless and carrying a dirty backpack, the contents of which amounted to a single can of corn, a two-by-four, and a coil of wire. The house's owner discovered her in his living room scratching at the walls. Although her physical appearance suggests Spanish-speaking heritage, the few words she spoke were in English.

In response to the patient's increasing distress, the house's owner called 911. Upon arrival, EMTs decided transferring her to us—rather than Children's Mercy Hospital—would be the most appropriate recourse. At 16:00 on July 15 she arrived at our Center and was promptly admitted. She has been allotted a bed on the girls' ward, making her our twentieth admission this year to receive inpatient services. We have filed the necessary forms with the police department so they can initiate the search for her family.

Upon initial questioning, patient has proved uncommunicative, and appears bewildered and disoriented. When asked about her background, she says nothing. When asked her name, she responds promptly with "B." No individuals have come forward to claim the patient as a friend or member of their family. It is conceivable she is a runaway, leaving her relations with no knowledge of her whereabouts, and therefore no means by which to locate her. However, it can also be speculated that she is entirely alone.

Patient is extremely thin and appears more malnourished than is usual with runaways, as though she has experienced long-term nutritional deficits. Based on the state of her teeth, one can assume a history of serious neglect. Her hair is a solid impenetrable mat. For the purposes of sanitation, it will be shaved this afternoon and her body treated for scabies and other parasites common to indigents.

Patient is also pregnant. When asked about her condition and its origins, she has been unresponsive. We have made arrangements with General Hospital for prenatal visits and eventual delivery. Her first appointment with the obstetrician occurred two days after her arrival, during which she was described as subdued and withdrawn. The report states she is somewhere between thirty and thirty-two weeks into her pregnancy, which leaves her approximately a month before the birth.

Patient's eye movements are rapid and her physical unease pronounced. When doors close, she jumps. At one point during questioning, she shrank down in her seat and covered her head with her arms, as though expecting attack.

Further examination and observation required for proper evaluation and eventual diagnosis.

Preliminary results were reported in the patient's progress notes on 7/16/75. The current report will supplement and elaborate upon those preliminary findings.

THIS PLACE IS WHITE and cold. Rows of beds with sheets tucked in. Gated windows. Girls with faces like shreds torn from paper. Even the food is white: potatoes, pasta, bread. Gone are her beets and her peas, her pack with its wood and wire, her dreams of the north.

She tells no one about the north. She tells no one anything. She keeps her lips pressed tight. She has done this before. She knows how to be silent and still, like a creature crouching low in the grass before a storm. This place is a fortress with no chance of escape. Each door is sealed, each window secure. The captors are white too—shirts, pants, coats—except their faces and hands, which are browner than hers. A few have skin to match their clothes. Their mouths spit question after question.

To their interrogations, she says her name but nothing more. Eventually they stop asking and shave her head. Then they strip off her dress with its purple flowers. They take water and a brush, a cake of soap, and rub her body red. They sheathe it in a stiff starched gown whose fabric matches their own. When she stares at a square of polished steel, her image scares her. She has become a ghost, an echo of what she thought herself to be.

She tries not to show her fear. She follows their orders. Maybe they will let her go. Obedience, she knows, can have its reward. She wakes when told, sleeps when directed. Into her mouth she spoons the potatoes, folds the bread, pops the pills they proffer in miniature cups. She stands in line for inspection, lets her nails get clipped, her body turned this way and that. When they tell her it is night, she beds down in the echoing room. The other girls moan, but she keeps her whimpers clutched within.

In daytime, she allows herself to be bundled into a vehicle that speeds. Blue and green streak past the windows, but she does not try to run. She bides her time. When the vehicle stops, she climbs out and follows them into another building. In a room with steel tables and loud machines, they instruct her to strip, don another gown, sit. They jab her with sticks: one for her ears, another for her throat, a needle for her arm. Mostly they examine her belly. It holds great fascination for them. Its size, its weight, its hum. It is a sun and they the planets, circling dumbly around.

One shows her a screen with a black-and-white shape swirling in slow motion. She lies flat on his table, another cold tool pressed to her skin. The room smells sharp, too clean. She misses the scent of dirt.

"Look," he tells her when she turns her head away. "That's your baby. A healthy baby boy."

She studies the wall. I have no baby, she wants to tell him. I have a giant. He will grind you into dust.

A door clicks and another enters, but she does not look. She can smell his presence. Coffee and sleepless nights. She has met this one before. He has blue eyes that smile when his mouth does not.

"Dr. Carson," says the first. "I thought you'd be waiting at the center. Why didn't you send the orderlies?"

"I needed an escape from the routine. How is our patient today?" he asks. "Still docile?"

"Sure, she's quiet," the other replies. "But she won't acknowledge her pregnancy. See how she stares at the wall? She doesn't seem ready."

"Who is ever ready?" says the other. She can tell by his voice that his mouth is smiling, maybe his blue eyes too. "She needs time. It's only been a few days."

How many days she does not know. She cannot count the lights and the darks, because the light doesn't fade. It has eclipsed everything. The mountains, the plains, the vaulted sky. The promise of snow sweeping down from the north.

"She's due in a month," says the one. He has lifted the chilly wand from her skin, but she feels no warmer. "Has your team decided yet what will be done with the child?"

Maybe they think she cannot hear them. Resolutely, she examines the wall. Cloth rustling, a waft of coffee, a snap. The blue-eyed one has turned off the screen. She turns her head and blinks up at him.

"Hi," he says to her, as though they are just meeting. She likes how his eyes crinkle at the edges. They are older than his face, with its unlined brow and rounded chin. Carson, she thinks. He turns back to the other. "I've called a meeting this afternoon. We'll discuss it then."

"Let me know what you decide. We can deliver the baby here at the hospital, but we're not a nursery." His voice is as thin and hard as his shoulders. He has held nothing soft in his life. "If we can't find her family, it'll have to be placed in a home. Likely they'll assign it to foster care. Adoption, if it's lucky."

Carson trades her one gown for another, and hands her a piece of green candy on a stick. It tastes like the apples she found once. The candy she got yesterday was red and too sweet. "We'll discuss it in the meeting."

The air tightens. The first one leaves the room.

"Bea." Carson holds out a hand. She slips her fingers into his, hops off the table. "Let's get you back to the center."

CARSON LEADS HER to a room with his name printed on the door. His room is green, not white. He has filled it with plants. Here is earth's damp and private smell, roots digging into soil, fresh fronds tender at their tips. Her road was dry—desert, mountains, plains, even the forests—but one day she found herself stepping through a patch of living woods. It had rained and the ground was soft, the air thick and warm and wet. Carson's room smells like that forest. She stands in the doorway and breathes.

"A man can't live without growing things," he says.

She thinks he will ask questions, but he doesn't. He offers her a chair and a cup of water. The cup is paper, similar to the ones they put her pills in, but bigger. For a while Carson doesn't speak. He busies himself watering his plants, wiping their leaves with a cloth, massaging their dirt with his fingers. Then he turns on some music.

She doesn't like that. She stands up too quickly, spilling her water.

"No music?" he asks. "I thought everybody loved the Temptations. Guess I'm showing my age. Would you prefer something else? Disco? The Jackson 5?"

She frowns, whips her head one way, then the other. The music hurts her chest. He turns it off. The day she walked through the forest, she stopped to dig at the ground. She wanted to know what was in there. Her hands upturned earthworms, pink and roiling, a confusion of shapes. The music made her feel like that. She can't sit back down. She is restless, wandering around his office. If she could climb the walls, she would.

"Want to look outside?" he asks.

Her face must say yes, because he opens the blinds.

"Come see," he says. "It's not much of a view, but at least I've got one."

She sidles up beside him and peeks out. No plains, no desert, no whispering wind. Only scattered trees, a flat lot of dead stone. Tan cars too large, their grins toothy and sinister. A man wearing a sharp-collared shirt and brown trousers walks by, thick glasses hiding his eyes. No women. A bushy-tailed animal runs up a trunk.

"You'd think it would be too hot for squirrels, but they don't seem to care," says Carson. "T. S. Eliot said April is the cruelest month, but I think it's July. Especially in Kansas City. Or maybe it's August. Tomorrow's the first. Can you believe that?" Carson is a handsbreadth away. She can smell his exhaustion. "I swore I would move away. I thought about running to Canada if they drafted me, but they didn't. So much for my escape plan." He laughs, but she hears no joy. "Now the war has ended. And we're shaking hands with the Russians in outer space." He expels a breath. "Imagine that."

There are so many things she wants to ask him. She wants to know what Kansas City is, and Canada and Russians. She wants to ask why he is here if he has the freedom to leave. If the war will come again. Why does he tell her she has a baby when she will birth a giant? She wants to know what he did with her hair, her pack, her carefully hoarded scraps. How will she build? How far has she traveled? What happened before the fire? Who were her people? When can she leave? Why can't she know who she is?

Carson is lifting her up, because she has fallen. He places her in a chair by a desk, and she drops her cheek to the wood. He's picking up the phone, talking. Her ears are ringing, her face hot and scratchy around the eyes. Her throat hurts. Her burden is kicking, curling, and then kicking again. *Out*, it insists. *I want out.*

People pour into the room. They poke her with a needle and pop a pill down her throat. *Shh*, they tell her, but their hands are rough. Carson is fading. The plants have vanished, the cup of water. She is freezing. They strap her to a table. She feels herself moving away.

"Carson," she calls. Two clear notes, one harsh, one not. "Carson."

She knows she shouldn't speak, but she cannot help herself. She needs to cry out, to be heard. Her throat makes a sound, and it is not Carson's name, but something else. The bark of a deer, that *cough cough* she has heard before. Again, she sees a plate of venison, not on a table, but on a floor, and she hears laughter, and it is not kind, and here come the boots of a man she knows but does not know, and a brown-skinned woman too, with a sour pouch for a mouth and a heart so red she can see it through her dress, and she wants everything to burn. The man, the woman, the plate of meat, the house. Even the sound of the man's laughter. She will set this world on fire.

SHE WAKES TO A CHORUS. Night has come and the others are singing. Each girl's throat is tilted, sounding its mournful song. She wonders how they've collected in this room. She imagines the fires they've fled, the roads they've traveled. The miles they logged before the journey vanished under their feet.

She tries to sit up, but cannot. Her limbs strain against straps. She makes a sound and knows it is the cough of a deer. In her mind she sees hooves, little and light, tripping away across sand. She has no recollection of how she reached this bed, only of a darkness that lasted and lasted. In that darkness something burned. She felt it deep inside her skin. She is as scorched as the desert she fled. In her mouth is an iron taste. She tries to spit. A thin drool trickles. Her whole body is singing with fire.

IN THE MORNING, they bring her to Carson.

"Bea," he says when she enters. She could weep for the soft sound of it.

She says his name over and over, but he doesn't shush her. He helps her to a chair. No pills, no needles. Fronds green and hopeful. The fragrance of soaked earth. And like a miracle, a perfect paper cup.

"Drink," he says.

His eyes are shadowed, the scent of coffee bitter.

"Don't worry." He hands her another cup of water. She's already drunk the first. She gulps this one too. "The baby's fine. I had them check it immediately."

My giant, she thinks. That broil within her, that tumult of hands and feet. She has no name for this creature they say will be a boy. To her he is simply the First, the giant. Giants need no names.

"Carson," she says again.

"Bea," he replies. They are two animals, sounding their concerns.

She stares at her hands, resting on her stomach's mound. They are still hers, brown and blunt and broken-nailed, but they are softening back to their former selves, as gentle as when she first set out. Once so tender, outside they turned dry, then cracked. She yearns for her road. It stretches beyond these sterile rooms, the gray stone lot, the gnarled trunks with their lonely squirrels. Beyond the town with its lemon-yellow houses. Out there lies her place. She needs to reach the north.

"Bea," Carson says. "You're going to have to talk to me. You need to tell me what happened to you before you came here. You have to at least try. We can't help you if you don't."

She studies her hands, focusing on a phrase she can touch, a collection of words she can somehow feel. *Talk to me.*

"We believe you can speak. We've had selective mutes before. But we can't force you to talk. You must make the choice yourself."

Under her palms her stomach is hard. Within it her giant has fallen asleep. She can feel his great weight pushing against her spine.

"Your baby is due in two weeks. Possibly less."

She stares out the window. Sparse green, stone, squirrels.

"They're going to take him away from you."

She snaps her face toward his.

"If you cannot prove you are fit to take care of him. Yes. They will take him away. Put him in foster care. It's what they do. The days of orphanages and boys' homes are gone. Another family might adopt him. Bea, listen."

He crouches beside her chair so their eyes are level. She does not know what foster care is, but she can sense it is nothing good.

"You have to prove to them you can be his mother. Your obstetrician has advised the child be taken from you at birth. My team is listening. You're under my care, but I am one man. I cannot argue the rules of the state. If you want to keep him, you have to show them you are capable."

Black rings circle his irises. His eyes are earths composed of seas.

"Please understand. This is why you have to speak to me. So much is at stake."

Eventually she nods. They will not take her giant away.

"We'll start at the beginning," he says.

EXCEPT SHE CANNOT START at the beginning, because she does not know it. She knows the road, and before that, the fire. She communicates this as best she can. It is the next day, an afternoon that stretches without metal tables or needles or pills. They are in his office again. She tries to tell him what she knows, but he shakes his head.

"Slow down," he says. "One word at a time." The crinkles at his eyes' edges smile, but she doesn't know why.

She continues. *FIRE*, he writes on his paper pad. *ROAD.* Then he lifts his eyebrows, expecting more. She tries again. *DESERT*, he writes, then nothing.

"Bea." He stands up, lays his paper to the side, pulls from his desk other things. More paper, a box of sticks in vivid hues. "Let's try something else." He places the paper and colored sticks in front of her. "Draw what you know."

She understands. This she can do. Carefully she draws her road, shading it black and jagged at the edges. Across the paper's top she rubs the violent blue sky. She plants stunted trees by the roadside and then moves on to the prairie. She shapes herself, two feet on the road, her gut's greatness pushed toward the paper's end. Behind her, she scrawls the fire with reds and oranges and deep shadows. The colored sticks break as she presses down.

"Progress," Carson says. He does not seem angry at the damaged sticks.

As she draws, she remembers. She has done this before, sketched onto flat surfaces, scratching into the night, though not with such colors. The memory is gray and black and white, but pleasing. It feels good to carve out her pictures. The layers settle into place like sediment in the ground. She can smell stove grease, a snuffed candle, tousled hair she knows is hers. Snores rumbling from another room. Her own room is small and dark, its ceiling low, its walls narrow. The sheets piled in its center smell like her. With a bent and rusted nail, she scratches her images into the room's floor. A man's two boots. A globed glass, lip prints smearing its edge. An animal's head, with a child's eyes and a deer's antlers. Its mouth opens and it speaks. Cough, it says.

"Bea," Carson is saying. "It's okay." His hand is on her shoulder, which is shaking. She has torn the paper to pieces, thrown them every which way. They have fallen onto his plants like snow. She wants the north.

"We can stop here for today." He is gathering up the snapped sticks and shredded paper. "Let's not rush it." And then, as if he knows what she wants to say, he lays his palm against her stomach. His hand is warm and flat, and though she senses he means no harm, she is afraid. "Your baby will be fine."

When he pulls his hand away, it leaves an imprint. Hot and splayed. The deer coughs. Somewhere in the desert a man is walking toward her. She can hear his boots, even in the sand. She can see his eyes glimmer, even in the dark.

MOON

MARS, 2073

The world had not vanished. Outside the dome, our red planet continued its cycles. Each morning, the sun bloomed in a blue halo. Our two moons circled, Phobos seeming to rise in the west, Deimos dragging behind. Wind rippled sand across the dunes. Meteor showers blazed the night. But I no longer missed it. I was busy.

Each day rolled into the next, filled with tasks. I woke, ate my morning potato, pushed seeds into the soil. Midday potato, more seeds. Evening meal, no stories. I didn't care. I didn't need stories. I had the screen.

Uncle Two had showed me how to charge it. He'd hooked it to a cable in the dome. See? He'd pointed upward. The cable stretches to the solar panels. The sun feeds the panels, the panels feed the cable, the cable feeds the screen. A bit clumsy, but sufficient.

Uncle One had been kneeling nearby, pruning roses. He'd turned when he'd seen what we were doing. Why are you tinkering with that old thing? he'd asked.

Knowledge, I'd announced.

Cartoons, Uncle Two had said quickly. Moon needs entertainment.

Suit yourself. Uncle One had turned back to his roses. But keep planting. Some of these flowers are dying.

He'd pointed to the snowdrops. They had indeed wilted. I'd dropped to my knees and shoved more seeds into the ground. Already a few shoots were poking upward. Don't grow too quickly, I'd whispered to them. We don't need oxygen. Not yet. I need time.

DURING THE DAYTIME I left the screen hooked up to solar power. Each night I unhooked it, retreated to my pod, and placed it in my lap. I was certain I would find that voice again, the one that had spoken to me of its mother. The very thought made my skin prickle with anticipation. "Talk to me," I begged the screen. I waited, breath held. The moment stretched into another, then into another. I exhaled. I tried again. "Please." I shook the screen. "Where are you?" The screen was fully charged, bright and active, but it was silent. I'll find it again, I assured myself. I have to.

In the meantime, I experimented with swiping and tapping and clicking. At first, I found more cartoons. They annoyed me, because they made no sense. Things with big eyes and strange faces jumped and ran about and waved their arms. No noise. I swiped them off the screen.

I discovered that if I tapped a certain way, small shapes popped onto the screen. If I clicked these shapes, other shapes appeared. Mostly these shapes were black squiggles on a white background. I squinted, turned the screen this way and that, but could decipher nothing. I kept clicking. Eventually I discovered images. My mouth swung open. I had never seen a replication of something else. I'd only seen the originals: moon, sky, rock, tree. The Uncles. My own feet. But the images showed objects in miniature. Trees. Flowers. The dome from the outside, a white bulb against red sand. The dome from the inside, plotted in sections as though someone had thought it through piece by piece.

I didn't understand why these images existed. Why have replicas when one already had the real thing? Nonetheless, I kept clicking. Roses and snowdrops, mountain laurel and pine trees. The dimensions of the eating pod, our sleeping pods. The tunnels. The doors. All the junk of the dome and what lay beneath it.

Every so often, I would talk to the screen. "Hey," I would call, "hey, hey, hey." I thought if I kept at it, the voice would respond. But the screen no longer seemed capable of sound. I miss her, I remembered the voice saying, so I tried that too. "I miss you," I said into the screen. "Come back."

UNCLE ONE AND UNCLE TWO watched me closely, but said nothing further about their plans to build a civilization. I was relieved. I needed more time with the screen. Before I became a mother, I needed to know what that was.

Let her think, I heard Uncle Two tell his brother one afternoon in the dome. I was planting nearby, and turned when I heard them, for they had forgotten to shut their minds to me.

We can't hold back much longer, Uncle One replied. This is urgent.

His face looked tired and ill. The bones were more pronounced, and his white eyes had a purple tinge. Like a bruise, I thought. He'd gotten sick once before, from dust in the Hellas basin. Too much radiation perhaps. But he seemed sicker now. His heightened pallor struck me. Maybe he didn't just bring us here to build a civilization, I thought. Maybe he needed a place to rest.

Uncle Two seemed poised to respond, but he saw me looking at them and stopped. You're doing a wonderful job, he called out instead. Keep that oxygen flowing.

I took another seed and pressed it into the dirt.

ONE AFTERNOON, the routine broke. I was kneeling in the dome as usual, dusting off the dahlia leaves, when I felt something slippery between my thighs. I touched it and my hand came away red. I remembered the day I had sliced my palm on a rock's thin edge, how brightly the cut had glistened against the dunes.

I'm bleeding, I called to Uncle Two.

He was bending over the mountain laurel to examine some browning blossoms, but straightened immediately when he heard me. Are you hurt? he asked, waddling over.

I don't think so. I turned my hand back and forth to examine it. It's just kind of messy.

He pulled some burdock leaves off a plant and handed them to me. Stanch it with this, he said. I need to tell Uncle One. Stay here.

I tucked the leaves between my legs and waited. In a moment Uncle One was striding through the trees, Uncle Two trailing behind. Uncle One's face had a strange glow to it, an effervescence I had not seen before. He didn't look ill or tired anymore. He looked elated. My blood thrilled him.

Moon, he said once he'd reached me. We are so proud of you.

Under his towering gaze, I felt quite diminished. But I haven't done anything, I said.

You've done more than you know. He turned to Uncle Two. It's time.

Uncle Two's shoulders slumped. It's time, he echoed.

Time for what? I asked.

Come. Uncle Two beckoned. Let's get you settled in your pod.

His next words made me shiver. You'll need some rest before, he said.

Before what? I asked, but neither Uncle answered me.

UNCLE TWO HADN'T VISITED my pod since the night he gave me the screen. When he entered, he picked it up. Has this kept you company? he asked.

I nodded enthusiastically. Oh yes, I said. I have learned so much.

A haze settled on his eyes, as though he were remembering something. He blinked, and it disappeared. And what have you learned? he asked.

I stopped to think. What had I learned? I thought about the cartoons, the black squiggles, the miniature images of things I had already seen. I'm not sure, I said. I've learned that cartoons are stupid.

Are they? Uncle One tapped the screen, and it lit up.

He settled his plump body on my bed and gestured for me to join him. We sat cross-legged, our knees touching. I found comfort in that. I hadn't found the voice again, but I had Uncle Two. That was something.

Uncle Two tapped the screen a few times. The things he called cartoons appeared, the same figures zipping across the screen. That's odd, he said and poked at the screen. There's supposed to be sound. Ah, he said. You have turned down the volume. He pushed one side of the screen, and the cartoons blared into life. They were very loud.

But I've learned nothing from these, I protested over the din.

You can learn from anything, Uncle Two shouted back. He pressed the screen again, and the sound decreased. Now, he said. Pay attention. His finger followed one of the figures. This is an animal, he said. It is neither Uncle nor Moon. It is a rabbit.

Is it real? I asked.

A simulation, he said, but yes, animals are real. Or were. See that one? That is a duck. And that, a pig.

As we watched, I became absorbed in the antics of the rabbit, the pig, the duck: a panoply of creatures I had not considered possible.

What's that, I kept asking. For each question, Uncle Two had an answer. That's a river, he said. A meadow. A farm. Look there. You recognize those. They are trees.

But where are they? What is this place? I asked, not tearing my eyes from the screen. The duck was spluttering in a way that reminded me of myself in the dome's wet air.

Earth, he said.

I leaned closer. The rabbit was sneaking up behind a being that looked a bit like the Uncles. Short, but with the same big bald head. There's nothing there except water, I protested.

This is the life it used to hold. See that creature. He pointed at the figure that looked like him. That's a human. They lived on Earth. I believe they called him Elmer Fudd.

Were all the humans Elmer Fudd? I asked.

He grunted, perhaps with amusement. Of course not, he said. They had their own names. Like I am Uncle Two and my brother is Uncle One. Look. He touched the screen a few times. This one will make you laugh, he said.

He was right. I laughed so hard tears sprang to my eyes. How absurd to see that stunted figure skittering across our dunes under our wispy sky. He wore what Uncle Two called a helmet and carried something named a gun, and he looked angrier than I got when the Uncles spoke in riddles. Watching his tiny tantrums, I wondered if this was how I appeared to the Uncles when I lost my temper. To them I was a small thing too, stomping my feet in the red sand. I stopped laughing. It didn't seem funny anymore.

Am I a Marvin? I asked Uncle Two.

He hadn't noticed the change in my mood. He was still swaying back and forth, jowls shaking. You're certainly a Martian, he replied. That's what our planet is called. Mars.

I sat back, stunned. Uncle Two had taught me many things, but not the name of where we lived. I hadn't questioned that. I had accepted that our home was our home. It hadn't needed a specific name.

Look at this one, Uncle Two said. Another cartoon. I believe that creature is called a deer.

It doesn't look very strong, I said.

It's a baby, as you once were. Uncle Two pointed. Here comes another. That's its mother.

We both went silent. We watched the mother deer approach the baby deer. We watched them walk through a forest like the one in the dome, but with something white blanketing the ground. We watched them bend to nibble grass. Then something terrible happened. The mother got scared. She and the baby began to run. A loud noise. A flash of light. The mother disappeared.

She died, I said.

She did, Uncle Two replied.

Do you think she bled? I asked.

I imagine so, he said.

Why am I bleeding?

Uncle Two's eyes shifted away. All mothers bleed, Moon.

But I'm not a mother, I protested. Am I?

The blood will arrive each month, Uncle Two said. You'll get used to it. Does it hurt?

I felt a dull ache, but that was it. I shook my head. Already the blood was subsiding.

I heard a voice, I said. In the screen.

A voice? Uncle Two said. Interesting. He studied the baby deer in the cartoon. It was tottering on its weak legs, calling in vain for its mother. With a swipe of his fat finger, he made it disappear. What kind of voice?

I don't know, I said. A female voice? It sounded like mine. I paused. When I speak aloud. I can do that, you know. Speak aloud. Like the cartoons can.

I did not know that. Uncle Two's eyes darkened, as though with pain. Perhaps he was hurt I had been keeping secrets.

I want to find the voice again, I said. Can you show me?

Possibly. He tapped at the screen. These things did have out-loud voices. Simulated ones. That's why I said to ask it questions. You could ask it something and it would tell you. The voices were usually female. I'm not sure why. That must have been what you heard.

Oh, I said. Disappointment flooded me. How keenly I had wanted that voice to be real.

He fiddled with the screen. What is the level of gravity on Mars? he asked it.

Mars, I thought. My planet. My home.

I waited, tense with anticipation. Even if the voice weren't real, it could tell me something. Except nothing responded to Uncle Two.

The feature must be broken, he said. A shame.

Then can you teach me? I asked. About mothers? The baby deer had one, I said. I swallowed, nervous about what I wanted to ask. Did I? I ventured.

Uncle Two looked suddenly drained of energy. As Uncle One had before, he seemed old and sick and weary. His skin appeared gray, but that could have been the pod's lighting.

Are you okay? I asked.

A touch tired, he said. I could use a nap. He straightened, and his skin lost its gray tone. I watched his heart thumping in his chest. It seemed normal.

Uncle Two, I prompted. Can you teach me?

Uncle Two shook his head. Uncle One says no. Not yet. And so, I must wait, he said. But here. He passed the screen back to me. Click this icon, he said.

I did. A figure appeared. It resembled the Elmer Fudd, but was taller and straighter. Its body looked almost like mine. Same coiled hair. Same rounded hips. Same swellings on the chest. Its skin looked thinner, though, more fragile. Its limbs seemed flimsy too. This thing couldn't survive here, I thought. It couldn't walk the dunes as I can.

Uncle Two stood up to leave. That, my dear Moon, is a female human. They called it a woman. Its younger counterpart they called a girl. Keep clicking, he said. The images won't tell you everything, but they will answer some of your questions. And remember.

I turned from the screen to look up at him. Yes?

We will need an answer from you too. And soon.

Then he left me in my pod with the screen, the woman's figure stark upon it. I understand now what he was doing. Uncle Two wanted me to learn what might happen if I accepted their plan for the dome. He wanted to warn me.

This—he was trying to say—is what happens to mothers.

BEA

KANSAS CITY, 1975

PSYCHIATRIC EVALUATION—PREPARATORY NOTES (CONT.)

PSYCHIATRIC CENTER of KANSAS CITY—
CHILDREN'S DIVISION

> Dr. James Edward Carson
> Patient: *Bea (surname unknown)*
> Date of Initial Evaluation: *7/16/75*
> Case No.: *42*
> Admission Date: *7/15/75*
> Date: *8/7/75*

Background information

CLAIMANT DETAILS

Anecdotal: Patient has now been at the Center for three weeks. Since her arrival on the fifteenth, she has been obedient, submitting to the routines of our Center without apparent complaint. A week ago, her behavior changed. When brought into my office, she became visibly upset, pacing around the room and moving her arms in abrupt gestures, as though she were pushing something away. Patient then fell down and went into convulsions. Fearing injury to her and the fetus, I collected her from the floor, at which point her convulsions ceased and she allowed herself to be led to my chair.

I called for the orderlies and stayed beside her until they arrived. As they wheeled her away, her physical movements became frantic. At this juncture she said my name, twice. This was one of the few words she had so far uttered during her time at the Center. Her utterance of my name was followed by a sort of guttural bark.

Despite her distress at the time, this episode seems to have marked a change for the better. She now speaks to me of her own volition during afternoon sessions in my office. The issue now is the fragmented composition of her speech. While I can discern exact words (*road, desert, fire*), she often interrupts these words with a variety of coughs and barks. I am reminded of the mythos of the feral child, but while I doubt our patient was in actuality raised by wolves or some other animal, it is feasible her childhood did not include substantial social interaction. This could even point to a youth spent in isolation, perhaps to the extreme. This may serve as a clue for locating her origins and the whereabouts of her family.

It is interesting, however, to note our patient can apparently spell and even read. The first day of our communication, she wrote out her name for me. It is not a simple "B" but rather "Bea," an actual moniker. She did not supply me with her family name, which perhaps she does not know, or does not wish to reveal.

For this case, I have subscribed to the recent technique of "creative expression therapy." The paper and crayons supplied by the department have been of tremendous assistance with our patient, as she has been attempting to illustrate her thoughts when verbalizing them becomes too challenging.

Bea's initial drawings were basic: visual depictions of the words she said. She drew herself—pregnant—on a road through a variety of landscapes, walking away from a fire. Recently she has begun adding other images to her drawings. Chief among them is a pair of boots, drawn out of proportion to the rest of her etchings. In the background, she has been sketching a multitude of drinking glasses—some tumblers, some wineglasses, some empty, others filled with dark liquid—and a strange figure, half deer and half child. Occasionally she will outline a black rectangle, shading in its center a small brown face, a face I presume is hers. Other times she will draw a single bright yellow line, like a ray of sun.

The boots seem to cause her the most pronounced distress. As she sketches them, she will jerk upright, start from her seat, and do a quick turn around the room before settling back to her drawing. Sometimes she will become so agitated she will snap the crayons into numerous pieces. When this occurs, I take the paper away and attempt to divert her with conversation. She appears most interested when I ruminate upon our recent war. Her expression grows alert, and her eyes, which are usually heavy-lidded from the medication, widen with interest. Since we began our meetings, her comfort with the spoken word has increased remarkably. She also becomes engaged when discussing the future of her fetus. I worry that once it is born and remanded into state custody, she will lose this engagement. We are still considering methods to handle this potential complication.

PRESENTING PROBLEMS AND RELEVANT BACKGROUND HISTORY (LEADING TO ASSESSMENT)

Due to lack of information, background history remains unverified. However, it is clear the patient is in need of strict supervision. It is evident she possesses significant psychological complications that demand treatment. The fact that she is a pregnant girl in early pubescence is enough to require medical and psychological attention. The conditions in which she was found, not to mention her behavior, make this even more pressing.

The police investigation has unearthed potentially useful missing child reports. Three in particular seem of note, as all three reference a fire and two a girl whose name begins with *B*. One details the disappearance of Bernadette García, age twelve, from her home in Santa Fe, New Mexico, who reportedly left for a party but did not return. The second is for the presumed child of Robert Samson, a deer hunter outside Socorro, New Mexico. Neighbors had not known he possessed a daughter, but they reported seeing a young girl outside his home on the night he died. When police could not locate her, they filed a missing person report. The third describes the disappearance of Beatrice Santamaria of Tucson, Arizona, who may have absconded with vagrants she met a few weeks before she vanished.

In each instance, there was a fire. Bernadette set one in her bedroom wastebasket, when she touched a match to her English homework before jumping into her older friend's car; Mr. Samson's unnamed daughter was seen walking away after a house fire claimed both his life and that of an unidentified woman; and Beatrice's disappearance coincided with a minor conflagration in Catalina Park off Fourth Avenue, a blaze that consumed a patch of grass and a single aloe plant but no human lives.

I am particularly drawn to the presumed daughter of Robert Samson, as not only does Mr. Samson's occupation as a deer hunter seem a clue to the sounds Bea is prone to, but the situation of this particular girl appears to most closely match my theory regarding seclusion from society. If the neighbors did not know she existed, it is possible she was kept entirely inside, denied access to others and the benefits of social interaction. Cases such as these are not unknown.

With this information, I believe I can attempt additional methods that may prove successful.

PAST PSYCHIATRIC/PSYCHOLOGICAL HISTORY

Though the peculiar nature of her origins makes this difficult to verify, it may be safe to assume she has not experienced psychological or psychiatric treatment before the present moment.

PAST RELEVANT MEDICAL HISTORY

As with previous psychological treatment, our patient's prior interactions with medical examiners may have been limited, if not absent altogether. Although our research into her background may prove otherwise, the state of her teeth appears to assert that neither physicians nor dentists were a staple of her childhood.

Alcohol and drug history

Speculations: Though Bea has not shown definite signs of alcohol or drug dependence, it is significant to note that her drawings often include depictions of wineglasses.

If the images she has been sketching are of her parents—they seem to point toward this conclusion—then the woman who might be her mother is often shown with a glass either in hand or nearby. If her mother was dependent on alcohol, our patient is statistically likely to develop these traits as she matures.

Furthermore, since her admittance to our Center on July 15, Bea has been exceptionally eager for her medication, not spurning it as so many other patients initially attempt to do. In fact, according to our nurses, she displays the addict's eagerness when accepting her daily dose. This behavior suggests our patient is no stranger to prescribed substances. However, if she has not previously experienced professional medical treatment, the question arises how she gained access to such substances.

Anecdotal: As a minor experiment yesterday, I offered her water not in her usual paper cup, but in one of the smaller ones used to distribute medication. Instantly her expression brightened and she lifted her eyes to my own. "Poison?" she asked. If she believes her medication is poisonous, why would she be so eager to ingest it?

FAMILY HISTORY: GARCÍA OR SAMSON OR SANTAMARIA

Initial diagnosis

Although numerous facts must still be retrieved, a partial diagnosis can be made. Based on her drawings and the fragmented element to her recollections, it appears our patient is experiencing a form of dissociative amnesia, wherein the mind erases certain traumatic events from memory. Retrieval of such memories is risky, as it could damage her increasing psychological stability. However, much could be gained if I were able to recover her memories in a fashion that would be therapeutic and not additionally traumatic.

It is also clear that our patient is a selective mute, though it remains to be seen whether this can be further qualified as traumatic mutism. At this stage in her treatment, it is evident that she continues to suffer from some language processing issues, as despite her recent progress, she still tends to interrupt her speech with barks and coughs. Once I have established further trust with her, I will ask permission for a language specialist to assist me in her treatment.

Current medications and dosages

In response to her behavior when admitted, I prescribed a mild dose of Thorazine, which she has been taking regularly since her admittance. After her attack a week ago, I decided to administer a stronger dose in an effort to ameliorate her temporary hysteria. She has since regained equilibrium, and I have resumed her original dosage. If the creative expression therapy proves successful, I plan to eventually supplant Thorazine with Valium. Though her release from our Center is quite likely a number of months, if not years, distant, once it is approved, I will advise she remain on this medication until her condition stabilizes further.

SPEAKING IS NOT EASY, but Carson is patient. When she grows tired of talking, he has her draw. Today he takes two soft objects from a room with a door.

"Try these," he says.

They have the fur and faces of animals, but their eyes are white with black dots in the center, like no creature she has seen. She spends time gazing into these eyes, but can see nothing.

"You can play with them," he suggests. "Move them around. What would they do? What would they say to each other?"

She tilts her head to the side. Animals cannot speak in the way he means.

"Or you can just hold them." He gets up and returns to the narrow room. She sees the two objects he brings back and she gets up. She does a quick turn from wall to wall, and then returns to her seat.

"No," she says, as clearly as she can. She shakes her head. One object is a woman. The other is a man. The woman wears a dress and her eyes are buttons. The man wears something blue from shoulders to ankles. On his feet are two big boots. They are pointed at the tips, not square, but she knows them.

"No," she repeats, and stands up.

"Bea," Carson says, and lifts his hand. This is his signal that she must calm down. It is something he has discussed, something to which, with a nod, she has agreed. But she is tired of calming down.

"No." She throws the false animals at the window. They need to crawl outside and join the squirrels. But the window is closed. She hunkers down, squeezing her head. Within swells a tumult, the tangle of earthworms, pink and writhing, in damp dirt. The worms are her insides, and her insides are the worms, and she needs to spit them up, for they are choking her. She spits and spits, but cannot dislodge them. Then Carson is here, with his paper cup of water.

"Drink," he tells her. She does. Soothed, she clambers back in her chair and burrows her arms against her slumbering giant.

"We'll stop here for today." He puts away the two animals and the woman and the man, but she can sense them in that room, clamoring to get out. She cannot tell whether he is trying to make her feel better or worse. Sometimes his eyes seem too blue, his mouth too careful.

"No," she says. She doesn't want to stop. She has something to say. "Paper," she tells him. She makes the motions of drawing. She uses a word he's taught her. "Please."

He takes out the paper, the colored sticks, clears a space on his desk.

"Thank you," she says.

These words are rules they have worked on. It is important to be polite, he has told her. You have a better chance of getting what you want.

She draws what she sees in her head, what has been there all along. First, she draws the woman, because she frightens her less. Her face brown as Bea's own, her eyes in shadow, her mouth pursed around her grief like a treasure she must keep. Her hand with its half-full glass, the other on her red and beating heart. She has known this woman. When she looks at her, hot things twist together, and she wants to shout and cry and whisper the woman's name. Except she doesn't know her name, only her voice, brittle as her black hair. The woman is humming a tune, many tunes, and Bea knows none are about love.

The man she draws next. It is easier than she thought. His arms are clothed in red, his legs in blue, his boots tremendous. Drawing him feels simple, because she is simply afraid. Her animal coughs in the dark, and the hairs rise on her arms. But when she tries to draw his face, she cannot finish it. She sketches his white cheeks with their deep lines, but when she reaches his eyes, she starts to shake. They are Carson's eyes, too kind, too blue. She lays her head upon the desk.

On other days, she would have shouted, torn up paper, fallen to the floor. But she does not feel wild, just tired. She does not crave the road or the plains. She craves warmth and darkness. She wants to be her giant, sheltered in an unlit place. She wants two palms cupping her. A dim cave with walls and ceiling close. A nest of sheets that smell like her. She could curl up in a spot like this, and go to sleep.

ANOTHER AFTERNOON. The sun slanting outside Carson's window tells her it is late. It is yellow and makes her chest hurt, like the music did. She is sitting in her chair, sketching her pictures, but she can't stop looking at the sun. Thick and curdled. Butter, egg yolks, a glob of fat quivering in a sink.

"Bea," says Carson. "It's okay. You don't have to draw anymore."

She has broken a crayon again. The yellow one. Cornsilk, it is called. Its letters are black against its paper casing. She's snapped it into three pieces. Me, him, and her, she thinks.

"Would you like to stop?"

"I want to stop." She is careful to keep her voice slow, each syllable measured.

Carson understands. "Shall we attempt a different route?"

Route is a word she knows. On her journey she avoided anything marked Route, choosing instead the humbler paths, weeds poking through concrete cracks.

But he doesn't mention a road. He goes to the room with the door. She is afraid he will bring out the man and the woman again, force her to gaze into the woman's button eyes, to consider the man's boots, the painful points at their tips. But he takes out cards, white squares splotched with black shapes.

He splays them on his desk. "What do you see?"

She sees black on white. Loops and swirls and blotches. She tries to tell him this, but she cannot find the words.

"I'll show you." He picks one up and examines it, flips it so she can see. "It's a dog chasing a ball. Look." His finger traces its outline. "There is its nose, and its paws, and its tail. There is the ball." He points to a separate splotch, connected to the rest by a skinny black line. "The dog is chasing it. See its tongue flopping from its mouth? That is one happy dog."

This is strange. Carson has always told her the truth. She has known by his face. But he is being false. He sees no dog in that black mark. She will show him how it's done. She leans forward and picks up a new card. On it towers her giant, as she knew he would. His legs tall and true, his face a stern square against the white. She tells Carson who he is.

His brow wrinkles. "A giant? Is that how he seemed to you?" His eyes turn sad. "Of course. You would've been so small." He shakes his head. "A child alone in the dark." He laces his fingers together as he does when he wants to think.

She lets him, waiting in her chair, stealing glances at her giant, framed on the white card. Today he feels lighter within her, more like a promise than a burden. She can picture him walking among the pines, how his head will reach the treetops. He will be strong, but also kind.

His feet kick. She must prove herself to these men. I can be this, she tells them, though she utters no sound. I can care for creatures bequeathed to me. Let me take him where he needs to be.

Carson's fingers unlace.

"Bea, I'm not sure this is a good idea, but maybe it is time. I don't know." He breathes. Once in. Once out. "I'm going to show you some pictures." With a wave he dismisses the white cards with their black blotches. "Not those. Real pictures. You have to promise you'll remain calm."

Another promise. She does not nod.

"I think this may help you. There is so much we don't know, so many ways in which we could assist you if we did. Think of your memory like a thread that has become knotted. You are untangling it, but it is still kinked up." He clenches his hand to demonstrate. "But I can help you. I have found a key. It will help unknot you."

Me, him, her. She eyes the fragments of the Cornsilk crayon, still on the desk. Boots in the night, a grumble of snores. Old fat in the air. Sorrow and dust. Put her in a dark place. Tuck her in nested sheets. Let her be safe and sound. Let her dream her quiet dreams.

"Bea." Carson leans forward. She smells his coffee, his grief, his exhaustion. "You have to trust me." He pauses. "You cannot face your trauma if you don't know what it is. I am offering you the truth."

She wants to refuse, but she cannot. Her neck is too stiff and sore. She sits, rigid with fear, while Carson opens a desk drawer and pulls out three pieces of paper.

"Look," he says.

Though she does not want to, though she can hear her deer coughing its fear and loneliness infinite as the sky, she looks. Two of the pictures show empty faces. The third shows a man. She knew it would be him. *Clomp* come his boots, loud even in sand. His eyes bright firelights. His rough hands cupping her face.

Robert Samson, reads the name under the picture.

Not once did she breathe his name. The Father. That is what she called him. The man who named himself her father. And the woman beside him, the one not in the picture, not in any pictures, the phantom who hid her sorrow in songs, her love in a glass too deep and sweet. She knows to call her Mama. For it is she. The Mama who loved her Bea.

The Bea that could've been me, Mama would say, her palm easing the hair off her face. The Bea I will never be.

She gets up, hunting, searching, scraping at the walls. One plant she tips over. Two. The second pot shatters, its dirt scattered, its roots laid bare. She needs fire. Its lick and sip. Carson has hidden it. Matches. A lighter. Two sticks to rub together. Scratch, they will say, and with red flames they will speak.

She hears her name. Carson is calling her name. She has no time for him. He has tricked her. She should have kept her tongue stilled in her mouth. She should have been the tiny critters she glimpsed on the plains, the ones that crouched low to avoid storms.

She wrenches out desk drawers, rakes her nails down walls, claws open the narrow room and rips the big-booted man to pieces. Litters him across the floor. Fire is how you fight a war. The land of men peopled no more.

Cough, says her animal. *Set this world ablaze.*

Footsteps. The evil squeak of wheels. They come again to drag her away.

HER NAME IS BEA. Alone she whispers it. She needs some sound to pierce the dark. In her closet, the shadows need puncturing. In the evening Mama will grant her a yellow circle of lamplight. Together they will pore over Mama's papers, the books and journals Mama uses to teach her.

This is a boy, a ball, a balloon. Say *B*. That's you, Bea. This is a tree, a pine. They live in the north. This is a cactus. Two syllables. *Cac-tus*. They live outside, where you can't go. See this picture? Yes, she does look like you. See her cracked hands? The pickax did that. The shovel too. I didn't want that for me, so I walked away. I headed north. Say *B* for boy, for ball, for Bea. You will be the Bea I could not be.

A fragment snatched from time. Then Mama will be herself again. Her mouth a fist, her fingers on her glass's stem. Playing her records, warbling song after song. Mama's eyes darting to the door, seeking the step of the man who named himself her father. He will not come until dawn. He will roam the desert, and when he returns, he will lay his face not next to Mama's, but to Bea's.

Her name she knows, and Mama, and the Father. She knows her closet and the windows shuttered thick and how teeth can wear through sheets if she gnaws hard enough. She knows the sensation of a nail between her fingers, scratching her pictures into the floor. She knows the smell of their house, which has never been hers. Grease and wine and sorrow and dust. Sinks that never learn soap. She knows darkness and lamplight and one slice of sun a day, when the Father cracks the door, letting her crawl catlike to rest her face in its beam.

She knows what outside looks like, the narrow edge she can glimpse through the door's crack. Scents of cactus and mesquite on the dry breeze. A wooden rack strung with deer, snouts aimed at the earth. She remembers the one that arrived kicking, coughing its fury to the heavens, until the Father pointed his rifle and knocked it down. She learned their language then, let their coughs and barks roll off her tongue. She knows their taste, a purple that lingers on her lips. She knows the way their eyes can shine.

She knows Mama and she knows the Father. She knows what she reads in Mama's books and what she peeks on the flickering screen, the times she creeps up beside Mama asleep. People tinny and distant behind the gray glass. A house among pines, a mother scolding her son. Laughing women on a cart, skimming over white sand called snow. She likes the crisp look of it, how clean it seems. In the north, says a voice, there's snow. In the north, it says, the trees grow tall as giants. She remembers Mama saying she headed north. I too, Bea thinks, will head north.

One night the Father comes home early and catches her staring at the screen. There are battered faces, men with metal hats yanked low, a chatter of something he calls guns.

That's the war, he says. He unlaces one big boot and lets it fall to the floor. Men fighting their battles. His lip lifts in scorn. My father claimed Americans were men of honor, that they only fought wars for freedom. He laughs. The great freedom to buy and sell and be God-fearing Christians and rape this land dry. We should've left it to the Indians.

She studies his face. It is leathered where hers is tender. Why don't you fight? she asks.

His thick fingers in thick laces, removing his other boot. Little Bea, he says. You think I'd fight for this country? I've seen what they do, what my father did. He killed the buffalo. He wiped this country clean. Then he turned this nation's soil to ash. My father, the Dust Bowl. His very hands a bowl full of dust. No.

You and me, he says, we'll make our own path. We can do better than my father did, than these soldiers are. Napalming babies. Shooting water buffalo and dumping them in the village well. These American men. He laughs, and it is a cold sound. Let them fight their battles, he says. Our war is here.

His second shoe falls to the floor. With a snort, Mama wakes up.

Go to sleep, she insists, though whether she means she or the Father, they cannot tell.

She has learned her sounds from Mama and the Father, from the black-and-white screen she studies and the books they pore over, the paper rags Mama brought before Bea was Bea. Sometimes she tries her voice at song, humming snippets to herself in late morning, when Mama and the Father burble their snores. The songs are from records and the records are from Mama, who carried them crammed in her pack with her books and papers and hopes of tomorrows to the north. Mama has trekked from another desert farther south than their own.

I walked through the lonely night, Mama says, and fetched up here, where I had you. My Bea who was destined to be. Her palm smoothing her hair.

Mama's eyes are black and brittle in the weak light. Her hands are as soft and useless as Bea's own. For so long they have been circling each other in this place. She and her. Her and she. Mama and the Bea.

From Mama she has learned no love for sugar, has settled for beets from a can, perhaps a lick of honey on a spoon. Mama gets her own sweets from the bottles she leaves empty by the door. She says the desert that birthed her stripped sugar from her tongue. Says everything tastes like sand.

Who were your people? she asks Mama on one of their lamp-lit nights.

I am from no people, Mama replies, and her face closes like a door.

What about the Father? she asks then. Who were his people?

Your father was a deer, Mama says, with antlers this wide. She stretches her arms to show her. He came from the east, leaped all the way here.

Bea tries asking more, but Mama has turned to her glass. Soon she will be sleeping. At dawn Bea asks the Father, when he crashes into the house, blood thick on his boots.

A deer? He snorts. It's your Mama who's the deer. I found her in the desert, meant first to shoot her, but her beauty took my breath away. I roped her firm and fast and true, and brought her here to kick those hooves up at home. I taught her to be cow, not deer. How good she's been to me.

She's from no people, Bea adds.

He laughs. No. Your mama comes from a proud line of starving silver miners in Zacatecas. She used to cry for her mother's courtyard, how the sun slanted through the lemon tree. I stopped all that. Cows don't cry, I told her. He laughs again. My little Mexican cow. She's lucky I found her. Kept her safe from prying eyes all these years. Without me, she'd be shipped back to the mines.

On this truth she chews. What was Mama hoping for, the day she set heel to road, leaving her people behind? With her records and books, her longing for something more. Instead, she found the Father, or he found her. She seemed a deer, but he named her a cow, noosed her neck and brought her home. Locked her up in the dark, where one day she birthed Bea.

In her closet she's grown, infant to girl, tucking her fists against her belly to stop its growls. Whispering Mama's songs to herself in the day's shadowed grip. Listening to pots slamming when the Father comes home. I'm not hungry, damn it, I just want to eat. Soup burning on the stove. Fat's stench, dark with blood and brine. A spoon clacking a bowl. The record player's whir. One song after another, not one of them about love.

Love is for children, the Father says. And you—leveling his finger at her—are child no more.

The Father has no time for children. He speaks of giants. At dawn he breathes it, while Mama sleeps her sweaty sleep and the sun pulses at the door, waiting its turn. There'll be a new breed, he says. When ours is done. A race of giants, men bigger than men. They'll make this world right. The government's shipped men to the moon, you know. But our giants? They'll go beyond that. They'll travel to the stars themselves.

The Father says she will spawn it. Time for you to marry, he tells her. He picks his teeth, inspects his fingernail after. Studies her with his coarse and grainy eyes, bright blue. Marry somebody tall, he says. New breed has got to be tall.

Except no one exists for her to marry. Only Mama and the Father know she's there. Nestled in her sheets. Hidden away.

I'm done hunkering in the dirt, the Father says. His eyes alight on her scrawny self. Let us grow tall as the tallest tree, he tells her. Let our giants take over this earth.

At times she dreams of poison, though she knows it is no dream. The Father with his pinch of powder in her soup, the hour it comes time for sleep. Meat filming her teeth, that bitter tang underneath. Her eyes grow dense, her tongue unwieldy. But he is right. It is better to sleep. The Father is kind. He wants it easy, wants her to feel nothing, no push and tear.

With morning stretched into noon, she wakes. Mama in the bath-room, hunched and heaving over the dirty bowl. Needle spinning on the record player, static on the screen. Old fat in the air, sorrow and dust. A scatter of papers, not one about love.

Bea looks at the Father, still sleeping. His lidded eyes, his bristled cheek pillowed next to hers. She counts each hair on his head, runs her finger along his jaw. His lips tremble with each breath. How she adores him in this moment. Each thread of hair, each vein in each fragile lid, each rough finger on each rough hand. This man who has named him-self her Father. This man who will help her build anew.

One night the war comes home. Mama in the kitchen, tearing pots from the walls, pans from their hooks. Bea in her closet, peering through the open door, her swelled stomach pressing its cheek to the floor. What have you done to her? Mama rips a shutter down, lets the forbidden moon stream through. She's only twelve. She's your *daughter*.

My father is a deer, Bea whispers.

The Father's eyes are brined and mocking, the red eclipsing his blue. He laughs when Mama breaks a glass and presses its jagged edge to his throat. He waves her away like a fly. We must remake this world, he tells her. We need a new breed. It's how we fight our war.

Mama lunges again. Rakes her nails along his jaw. You. Her voice low and terrible, the guttural bark of a beast roaming free in the night.

My father is a deer, Bea says again.

Then Mama has her bottle, not wine, but the clear liquid that knocks her sideways when she drinks. The bottle is full, and Mama has a match, and she is lighting a rag that spouts from its throat. Bea knows fire from books, the screen, the stove's low flame, but not like this. It is beautiful. Watching Mama with her fire, she wants it for her own. Bea crawls out of her closet, stands up, legs strong beneath her.

She looks at the Father, braced and grinning, and thinks, I don't need you anymore. Your task is done. She looks at Mama, her face alight with fire, and thinks, I will be the Bea you could never be.

The Father was right. Their war is here. She against him, him against her, she against she. Mama, the Father, and the Bea. Gnarling each other's throats, stripping them to the bone. She knows the truth. Fire is how you fight a war.

She wrestles it from Mama. Her bottle, its rag, its match. The floor blazes quickly, the walls, the roof that has blocked out the sky. The Father's mouth in its terrible O. Mama's black and broken hair. Her heart so red it becomes its own element, burning away in the dark. Deer coughing their hatred in the desert, under those cold and indifferent stars.

From the burning house she steps. She turns her back on the fire, and she walks away, hefting within her small body the dreams of her father, curled in the shape of a baby. She strides through deserts, mountains, plains, only to end up in a sterile room with pain galloping through her.

Within her splits a seam. Water and blood and fire and ash. Voices whispering, urging her to be anything but Bea. Her giant is fighting free.

PSYCHIATRIC EVALUATION—OFFICIAL REPORT (EXCERPT)

PSYCHIATRIC CENTER of KANSAS CITY—
CHILDREN'S DIVISION

Dr. James Edward Carson
Patient: *Bea Samson*
Date of Initial Evaluation: *7/16/75*
Case No.: *42*
Admission Date: *7/15/75*
Date of Report: *9/7/75*

Anecdotal: Last night, more than two weeks after her expected due date, Bea Samson went into labor. The orderlies heard her scream and discovered her water had broken. She was taken immediately to General Hospital, where she was given an epidural and admitted to the delivery room. At 10:30 p.m., in response to her escalating distress, the medical staff determined a caesarean section was necessary and administered a general anesthetic. At 11:00 p.m. the obstetrician successfully delivered her infant, a male weighing a mere 5 lb., 6 oz., his slight weight a logical result of the mother's age and physical condition. The infant was promptly removed from the delivery room and deposited in the hospital nursery, where he will await placement in an appropriate situation.

Summary of previous tests or assessments

1. Creative expression therapy (potentially beneficial)
2. Role play (unsuccessful)
3. Rorschach tests (a red herring)
4. Behavioral therapy (hopeful)

PERSONALITY ASSESSMENT

Patient is a selective mute who vacillates between obedience and violent, even potentially dangerous, behavior, especially when placed under restraints. She often seems confused and bewildered by her surroundings, showing symptoms common to schizophrenics. Additionally, she suffers from fear of social contact and anxiety when approached by staff. No relationships with her fellow patients have yet been observed.

Mental state examination (MSE)

See attached document for results on the following: appearance; psychomotor behavior; mood and affect; speech; cognition; and thought patterns.

Formulation/summary

Based on clinical observations and assessments, it is evident this patient faces numerous psychological obstacles. While she possesses basic cognitive functioning, her struggles with memory and communication point to more complicated malfunctions than are usual in patients suffering from trauma. While attempts at memory retrieval showed initial promise, efforts have been temporarily halted due to changes in the patient's condition.

Four weeks prior to this report, patient fell into a near catatonic state, interrupted briefly the night she gave birth. While she is mostly compliant with the physical routines of our Center, she is largely unresponsive in both facial expression and verbal communication, although the latter was previously progressing.

Although we expect this to be a relatively temporary state, a stricter regimen of medication is necessary to assist the patient in regaining some measure of equilibrium.

Diagnosis

Axis I: Schizophrenia with temporary catatonic symptoms (moderate to severe; early onset); General Anxiety Disorder related to trauma (severe); Selective Mutism (moderate to severe); Language Processing Disorder (moderate)

Axis II: Schizoid Personality Disorder (moderate); Dissociative Amnesia (recurring)

Axis III: None

Axis IV: Childhood malnutrition; extreme seclusion; probable sexual abuse; physical neglect

Axis V: CGAS—40

Risk assessment

Patient is not currently deemed a physical risk to herself or others. However, given her earlier behavior, this could change once her catatonia decreases. Her newborn is under the custody of Children's Welfare, and, at this time, it is impossible to determine what effect the infant's removal will have on the patient's psychological condition.

Treatment plan

A continued course of Thorazine has been prescribed, with a daily oral dosage of 200 mg. Given her current state, decreasing it to Valium does not seem a viable course at present.

When the patient emerges from her catatonia, cognitive behavioral therapy will be provided to address her amnesiac and trauma-related disorders. Once she is stabilized, group therapy will also be added to her daily schedule, and she will be assigned a language specialist.

In the short term, patient's prognosis appears hopeful. If her schizophrenic and trauma-related symptoms decrease, it is possible her amnesia and language processing issues can be treated. The goal is to improve these symptoms within the span of two to three months. A time frame of six months to a year is expected for a decrease in psychotic behavior and an increase in positive social interaction.

In the long term, the prognosis also appears positive. The goal is to assist the patient with deinstitutionalization, with a recommended time frame of approximately six years. At this time the patient will turn eighteen, approximately, since information on her exact birth date remains elusive. Within this time frame, the expectation is to move the patient from our Center to a halfway house, where she will be offered vocational training and assistance with life skills so that she may eventually move to a residence of her own and, in a best-case scenario, become self-sufficient by the time she becomes a legal adult. Her various disorders notwithstanding, she may eventually become a productive member of society.

In the most optimistic scenario, patient will recover sufficiently to remain outside the institution, but also to be reunited with her son and even achieve full custody. Much depends on her treatment in the months and years to come, and on the correct administration of the methods prescribed.

SAMSON

TEXAS PANHANDLE, 1935

The boy won't come to church. Samson sits in the truck with his wife, waiting. From the dooryard, the boy stares back. He's donned his overalls, not his Sunday shirt. Even from this distance, his eyes look cold.

"He's stubborn," his wife says. "Boys are."

But Samson knows different. It's not a fourteen-year-old's orneriness. The boy isn't right. There's a slyness to him as he slinks out of sight around a corner. Hands in his pockets like he's hiding something. As their truck jounces away on the rutted road, Samson resists the urge to glance back. It wouldn't surprise him to find the entire farm burned down on his return. The boy's done things before. Killed a chicken for the fun of it. Knocked a fence pole down to let the hogs escape.

"I don't like it," he says. "We should have forced him."

His wife folds her hands in her lap. Her gloves, he notices, have been mended too often. Her profile in the April sunshine is young. Not the cherub he married, but a girl still. That dimple in her chin. Her hat's straw brim latticing shadow over her nose. And he a man over eighty. What has he done to earn such wealth? This wife, their frame house, the wheat he's hewn from the earth. I could die happy, he thinks, if not for the boy.

As they near town, other trucks join them, rumbling in from the farms beyond. The men in ironed shirts, hanging arms out the cab windows. The women in cotton dresses, pastel with spring colors like his wife's. In most truck beds, a gaggle of towheaded children. They do not speak of the past, these good men and women, but for some it lingers in their eyes. His head, seared with an ancient scar, speaks where his own eyes do not.

In the church parking lot, Mrs. Ernst approaches. "A morning straight from God," she chirps. "Will you be joining us at the picnic afterward?"

"We might," says his wife. "Depends on the boy."

"Left him at home again?" Her voice drops. "How's he getting on?"

Mrs. Ernst has a broad German face, not unlike that of Samson's wife. It's possible our people fought in the Great War, Samson thinks. Funny how here we get on. He swings the truck door shut. Rust blossoms by the handle. And the driver's seat is torn. He hopes the wheat will be better this season. Last year's soil was so thin and dry that many seeds just blew away.

"Nothing easy about a son," replies his wife.

Samson senses both women trying not to look at him. "Best find a spot inside," he says.

The sermon is brief. We are the flock, the pastor remarks. Put on earth to graze this land. As they bend their heads for prayer, Samson thinks of that June afternoon over fifty years ago when his first son—seven-year-old Charles, son of Daisy—disappeared while pasturing the cows.

Samson should have known it was coming. He'd seen it in a dream. His son standing in their field, and then winking out, suddenly, like a light. Nothing left but grass. Samson saw many things in dreams. Daisy going into labor before she'd even told him she was pregnant. His own self striding across the Kansas prairie before he'd stepped foot in America. When these things finally happened, he felt no shock, for he'd already lived them.

With Charles it was different. The shock hit quick and cold. It was like his dream, but different. The field was not entirely empty. Two calves had been killed, their bellies gutted of their mothers' milk. He had heard tales, stories passed down, but he'd thought the Comanche had settled onto reservations, the kidnappings subsided. The year was 1882. The buffalo were gone. From east to west, the continent glistened with railroads. Nonetheless, his son had disappeared.

He'd heard sometimes the stolen children would return. One story told of a boy who returned a grown man, calling himself a name nobody in town could pronounce and refusing to sit at table for meals. Instead, this man would take horses from the paddock, ride them bareback past the settlement and into the plains. He'd return with small animals—squirrels, prairie dogs, jackrabbits—and chew them raw. According to the story, his hair was uncut, crawling with lice.

But no matter, Samson told himself, how his son might return. He wanted him back. He tried bartering, tried contacting the fragmented Comanche bands to trade, government soldiers to assist, but in vain. Counterraids availed nothing. The boy was gone.

A man should not live to see such things, he thought then. Look at him now at eighty-two. His hands on the prayer book timeworn as trees. At home a second son nothing like the first.

They attend the church picnic because his wife wants to. As they spread their horse blanket among the others on the lawn outside, he's glad they did. Crocuses are poking through the dirt. The breeze puffs the sweet smell of manure across the fields. Sun a benediction upon them. Mr. Becker has ridden his sorrel mare in, and the sound of the animal chomping grass by the hitching post sends a keen thrill through

Samson's bones. Limber yet in the knees, he sits cross-legged on the blanket with his wife, gorging on Mrs. Ernst's red potato salad and the Tuckers' pullets, fried to crispness in a vat of oil. In his wife's hand, a plate overflows with beans. The pastor walks among his people, offering sips of lemonade from a tin cup.

The picnic ends too soon. The townspeople and farmers roll up their blankets. Samson helps wash dishes by the pump. His wife trades dessert recipes with a neighbor. If it weren't Sunday and everything closed, he'd purchase more seeds at the general store. He needs a bumper crop this harvest. Please God—he sends up his own small prayer—let the dust storms stay to the north. This isn't New York. He need not fear the banks. He owns his farm, the money it brings. But the news from Oklahoma has troubled him. The storms are getting closer. I need to get this boy grown, he thinks. I need to get him gone.

They return to a quiet house. He counts the chickens in the yard, the hogs in their pen. The two cows are grazing at the field's far end. His aging horse—named Butler for the solicitous way he offers his neck for pats—stands knock-kneed in his stall. When they step inside, he notices what's different. It is God's day, a day to rest, to do no work. Yet the boy has cleaned the house, scrubbed the floors, shined the windows. He's even spread a fresh gingham cloth on the table.

"On a Sunday," his wife grumbles. "Isn't that like him?"

"At least he did it," Samson says. He doesn't like it though. On their ride home, a stiff wind picked up and a cloud passed in front of the sun. Something strange floats on the air, beautiful morning regardless.

I'm too old, he tells himself. I should have died with Daisy. Sixty years later and he cannot shake the sight of her mouth in anguished rictus, how the birth room's stench recalled the buffalo he once butchered on the plains. He can still hear the wail of his newborn son, the child doomed to disappear.

Hard on this thought's heels, a blush of shame. You lived to raise your first son, and now this one, he tells himself. You lived to marry this wife. It's God's day. Do not ask for more.

His wife finds the boy up in his room. "Robert H. Samson," he hears her cry. "What are you doing?"

Fear lances through Samson. He sprints up the stairs like a man in his prime and finds them staring each other down. He expected a broken heirloom, perhaps their tabby cat strangled. Instead, he finds a satchel stuffed with clothes.

"I'm leaving," the boy says.

"You're fourteen," Samson replies.

"You left at fourteen." His eyes challenge his father's.

"Fifteen." At the recollection, a shudder passes through him. "And my father was a monster. Am I like that?"

"You're not anything," the boy says. "I just want to leave."

"But haven't we provided?" asks his wife. "Haven't we given you all?"

"It's not you. I keep having this dream." The boy points out the window to the north. "Something's coming," he says. "Something awful. I don't want to be here when it arrives."

He stops. If Samson didn't know better, he'd swear the boy was afraid. He doesn't dare look at his wife. He keeps his eyes locked on his second son. Before it grayed, his own hair used to flame red, but the boy boasts his grandfather's black locks. That same nasty pucker to his mouth. Samson feels his father's hand again, pressing his skull to the stove.

"Go," he says.

His wife catches her breath. Samson is still looking at the boy, but he pictures her breasts straining the fabric of her Sunday dress. Tonight, he thinks, I'll turn the lamp down and pull her close. It's been too long since I've circled her waist with my hands. The month they met, he bedded her. Married her a week later, though not from duty. She's been good to him, this plump German girl. Arriving in his life after so many empty years. So valiantly she's strived to fill the hole his other family left.

The boy hefts his satchel in hand and takes his straw hat from the quilted bed. On his face a flicker, but it can't be sadness. This boy of his has shown neither sadness nor joy, nor much in between. Perhaps a sliver of glee the afternoon he killed that chicken. Twelve years old and smashing a rock down. You wanted it dead he told Samson when he ran outside. Now we can eat it.

"Where will you go?" his wife asks.

"Somewhere different," the boy replies. "Somewhere new."

FROM THEIR SON'S BEDROOM in the frame house they built for his birth, they listen to him descend the stairs. Through the store-bought glass pane, between the muslin curtains the boy's mother stitched while pregnant, they watch him walk away. Down the potholed road, between the dun fields spotted with fresh green growth, Robert Henry Samson walks toward the woman he will someday capture in the desert, the daughter he will make his vessel, the fire that will burn him to the ground.

Beneath the Texas sky brilliant with light, this boy vanishes from his father's life. As his second son dwindles to a point, Samson's emotion builds. Even that evening, when the terrible dust storms of April 14 boil in black clouds from the north, when half their farm—one cow, three hogs, nearly all the chickens and twelve inches of soil—blows away toward the west, never to return, he cannot stanch the feeling. Relief, like a torrent of rain within.

In the storm's black belly, Samson pulls his wife close. Grit filling their ears, their nostrils, their throats. The clean cloth blown from the table, the curtains from their rods. Butler the horse neighing bloody murder in the barn. Samson clutches his wife's girlish body to his own, the one that lived through the last century and too far into this one. "Let him wreak his destruction elsewhere," he shouts above the wind. "Let him go."

He cannot see the future, how merrily his wife will sweep the dust from their kitchen, how they will make do with a smaller farm, how a decade later he will die an old man's peaceful death. I have been a boon to this earth, he will tell himself before dying. I have planted a bounty and watched it grow.

For now, the storm obscures this future. Samson thinks they are ruined, that the dust will spell their end. Nonetheless he feels relief, for the boy who settled on their home like a blight upon the land has walked west, never to return.

My son—he thinks, bending his head in grateful prayer—is gone.

PAUL

KANSAS CITY, 1993–2017

BEGINNING

Paul is an orphan until the day after his eighteenth birthday.

Then a letter arrives, and he has a mother.

A life in foster homes has taught him to notice details. He had to pick up on them: the Ross father, whose eyes would blink in two short bursts the moment before he lost his temper; the Burnsides' tabby cat, which would tolerate caresses solely on its left ear; the teenaged Murphy son, who would delay a pummeling if you offered him a secret.

The letter's paper is thick, creamy white, and smells of flowers. Paul does not know enough about flowers to identify the type, but he thinks something purple, maybe red. A typewriter has stamped the words; he can tell by the round edges, the deep indent where the keys have punched. The envelope, however, is handwritten. The return address is Bee's Flower Shop on Thirty-Ninth and Troost. His own address—Paul Smith, Cherry Street Hall, University of Missouri-Kansas City—spikes upward, as though written by a jerky, insistent hand. He does not understand the necessity for addresses, because he found it not in the mailroom, but slipped under the door of his dorm suite. The envelope bears no stamp.

Once he has logged the letter's details, he reads the words.

Somewhere, he registers his heart's pounding.

His mother is Bea Samson. She lives in a halfway house on

Thirty-Sixth Street near Prospect Avenue. At the bottom, the house's street number. Beside it, a scrawled signature: *JEC.*

He folds it—one side, then the other—and slips it back in the envelope, which he has slit precisely along its seam with a pencil's point. He places it inside his desk and gets up.

In the common area, his suite mates are eating Ruffles potato chips and watching *The Simpsons.* The year is 1993, the month September, the time 9:00 a.m. Paul is in his first year studying engineering on a state scholarship, and so far, college is like a foster home: unfamiliar rooms, a strange routine, the habits of other people rubbing up against his own. He has not made friends with his suite mates yet, though despite the fact it's been only a week, they all seem to have grown close with one another. One is Bengali, one Senegalese. They assumed he was a fellow immigrant until he spoke. When he did, the one from Senegal looked startled. "I thought Americans were tall," he said.

They do not register his passage behind the couch. He does not tell them about the letter.

I am not an orphan, he thinks as he pushes open the front door.

Paul does not know how he feels, only that he feels something. It takes shape as a throbbing behind his eyes. He squeezes them shut, but the sensation does not disappear.

He is early for his ten o'clock class. He takes a seat in Scofield Hall among the circle of folding chairs. The room is empty. The air conditioner hums. He fills the time erecting a small tower with his blade-sharpened pencils and a series of paper clips. When the door opens to admit his classmates, he allows it to topple.

A halfway house, he thinks. Halfway from where?

The class is expository writing. The teacher is instructing them in definition essays, where they must expand on the definition of a concept. Their choices are family, home, love, and war. He lingered on the first three choices, but has chosen the last one. War is a mystery, but he is a good researcher. The key, as with most things, lies in the details.

He has lived in five different foster homes. He remembers the floors—gray linoleum, orange carpet, plywood splotched with paint—for all the time he spent studying them. A few of the foster parents took interest in him, prodded him with questions. Others ignored him, set microwaved Swanson dinners on the table and turned away. Usually, he shared space with other children, other wards of the state. Between homes, he bunked in the institution, a series of pale yellow halls whose orderliness comforted him.

The writing instructor provides them ten minutes to write freely about their chosen topic. He uses the time to describe the Murphy boy in Home Number Four, who shipped off to Desert Storm and left a profound silence Paul tried, and failed, to fill. He didn't miss that home when he left, but he missed the mother's face, for its sorrow and intensity. When the ten minutes have elapsed, he lays his pencil alongside his yellow legal pad and reads what he has written. He is uncertain whether he has written about war. When the instructor calls for volunteers to share, he does not raise his hand.

After expository writing, he attends his remaining classes—chemistry and calculus—taking dutiful notes in exact lines on his legal pad, responding to questions when prompted. In chemistry, they are reviewing concepts he learned in high school, and he is bored, though he does not let this show. In calculus, he fits numbers and symbols together with precision and is deeply satisfied with the results.

Numbers please him, but buildings dominate his dreams. He spent his boyhood constructing tiny edifices from matchsticks and pushpins and shreds of cardboard. At first, he demolished them when moving homes, but then began hiding them in apartment corners, or attics and basements if possible. Minuscule bridges and towers litter three foster homes in Kansas City. He wants to be an architect, but he won a scholarship for engineering, his second choice.

"You can change your major," his adviser told him on their first meeting. She peered at him over the rims of her thick glasses. "There is plenty of time."

He nodded and agreed, but doubt plagues him. Change, a force he can neither predict nor control, has always happened *to* him. He does not understand how to make it happen for himself.

AT THE DAY'S END, he walks across the hot humming lawns and past the stately stone buildings of campus to check the bus schedule. A Frisbee narrowly misses his head. He waves off the apology from a young woman in a Benetton tank top and scans the schedule posted at the stop. He can take a bus up Troost and another east. Campus authorities have warned freshmen away from that neighborhood, but he has learned to discount such cautions.

The bus arrives and the door folds open. The driver eyes him as he drops his fare in the slot. He knows what the driver is thinking, because people have thought it before.

I'm eighteen, he wants to tell him, but does not. He takes a seat in front, sitting as erect as possible. He wishes he had worn something more adult—a button-down perhaps—rather than his polo with its imitation Izod alligator stitched haphazardly to the breast. He is exactly five feet tall.

Poor nutrition as a baby, one foster mother had told him with confidence. It happens.

In class photos, the teachers stood him squarely in the front, because he would block no faces. With every move from school to school, home to home, he abandoned friends he would not see again. He is not a virgin, but pain—physical or otherwise—has marked each sexual encounter. He likes numbers and columns because they organize the world. At 3:00 a.m. most nights, he wakes sweating from dreams of a faceless man walking through a desert he has never seen.

On the bus, he imagines his mother. She will be plump and gray, and she will hold out her arms to him. She will be thin and dark, and her eyes will slide away when he arrives. She will be brown like he is, and she will smell like the graphite in pencils, a metallic scent he loves. She will call him *son*. She will call him Paul. She will call him her own.

When he was a child, he thought a great deal about his parents. When he pictured them, they were holding hands. They had his skin color and his thick black hair, the same arch to their noses. In his mind, they spent a lot of time at the dinner table, passing food back and forth. Though nobody told him as much, he assumed they were dead. He imagined a car accident, a mugging gone awry, cancer. He imagined them dying together, not separately.

Other foster children had dead parents too, but some had parents who were alive. They were addicted to heroin, or they had done bad things and gone to prison, from where they wrote short notes to their children promising Disney trips or days at the beach, which was very far away. These children would show their notes to Paul, proof that they were loved.

He is curious what it would feel like to claim love for one's own. When he was twelve, one family came close to adopting him. Their names were Betsy and Leopold Steinhoff, and in 1939 their parents had shipped them from Germany to London with the Kindertransport. Leopold had kept his name, but Betsy, once Gretchen, had changed hers when she reached London. They had met there, grown up, married, and applied for visas to America, where the past would never catch up to them. They chose Kansas City because it was called the Gateway to the West. They liked the idea of living in a portal to somewhere else. They seemed much older than they were and they wanted something to love. They said they loved Paul because he, too, was alone. *And different like we are*, said Leopold.

The system allotted Paul a trial period, after which the Steinhoffs would make their final decision. All he had to do was behave and he would be theirs. He made it until the last day. Then he took Betsy Steinhoff's single photo of her mother and tore it into small pieces, which he placed on her pillow in a series of concentric circles. Afterward sleep eluded him, but he told himself he didn't regret it. He didn't want to be theirs. He didn't want to be anybody's. He wanted, in that pure moment when he tore the first shred from the photo, to be left completely alone.

The bus deposits him on Prospect Avenue. He will need to walk the rest. He does not know if his mother will be home. He does not know how halfway houses work. He does not know if he wants her to be there. His head is throbbing again and his stomach hurts. He should not have eaten tuna casserole at the dining hall.

Paul walks down Thirty-Sixth Street through a neighborhood drowsing in dusty quiet. His white Keds pad softly on the rutted asphalt. With their stone porches and corniced windows, the houses retain a semblance of old beauty, despite their peeling paint and weedy yards. In one house, a bedsheet curtain twitches and a woman peeks out, before dismissing him with a proud flick of the chin. His head continues to pulse, thumping in time with his footsteps. The weather has grown muggy. A thunderstorm is building to the east; he can see the clouds piling up, sense the electricity in the air. Once he saw a tornado. It passed so close to his room in the Burnside home he felt the walls shake around him. Ever since, he has paid strict attention to the sky, hoping for another.

The rain has not yet begun when he reaches the halfway house. He expected a building like the one that housed him between placements: a grim edifice built in the sixties, pale yellow with ocher trim, wobbly windows that jammed. But this is a house with lilac paint and cedar boughs shielding its front porch. A bright green fern hangs from a hook by the door.

"You're here to see Bea," says the white woman who answers his knock. She is fat and friendly, with greasy hair and a lazy smile. She is wearing a yellowed *Flashdance* shirt, a possible relic from a Salvation Army bin. Her movements are sluggish. Paul assumes drugs or medication or both. "He said you would come. There's tea in the pot on the stove. Right down the hall."

He does not ask who "he" is. It must be JEC. He enters the house, then the kitchen. A fragrance of black tea. Jasmine, perhaps oolong. Two black men sit at the linoleum table, one in overalls, the other in beige trousers and a blue shirt. Their faces are gaunt and they look very tired. They do not seem surprised to see him. They offer him tea—definitely jasmine—that he accepts and drinks quickly, although it is hot and burns his tongue.

The fat woman reappears in the doorway. "Bea won't come down. Don't worry," she says to his look of alarm, "she tends not to. You'll have to go up. First door on the left."

"Take her a cup of tea." The man in the overalls hands him a steaming mug. "She likes tea."

The throbbing behind Paul's eyes intensifies. He carries the mug up the stairs, careful not to spill. The wallpaper looks Victorian, a flocked print. The stairs are carpeted, his footfalls muffled. A pang strikes him, and he recognizes it as regret. For the first time, he wants to return to Betsy Steinhoff's room and paste her mother's photo back together piece by piece. He cannot recall the cruelty with which he tore it up.

He reaches the top step and follows the woman's directions to the room on the left. The door is open. He wants to hesitate, but does not. He steps inside.

The room he enters is long and dark and smells of paint. The blinds are closed, but he can make out murals on the walls, great blasts of red and orange, with antlers sprouting haphazardly from human figures and big boots and what seem to be wineglasses. By the far wall, a woman's body flickers in the dim light. Her left arm swipes up and down in long fluid strokes, her hand clutching a brush. She is painting a figure whose head reaches to the ceiling.

"Hello," Paul says, because he does not know what else to do.

The woman does not turn immediately. She finishes painting. The figure is completely black, silhouetted against a fiery background. Its massive head bears no face. She lays the brush on the sheet below her, and turns around.

She is he, but female. She is no taller than his five feet, and her face looks like a child's. She is wearing a shapeless gray dress and her feet are bare. She has his black hair and brown eyes and the same hands he has often cursed for their delicacy. They could be brother and sister.

Her body is quiet. She takes a seat on a folding chair before he registers her moving. She gestures to another chair, and he sits. He hands her the tea, and she drinks it immediately, like he did.

After that, they sit and watch each other for a long time. Though he has sought his entire life to remain unnoticed, her gaze does not bother him. The throbbing behind his eyes has morphed to pounding, and he knows he will return to the dorm with a migraine and have to skip his classes tomorrow, spend a day in the dark.

When he feels the urge to speak, he does so without embarrassment.

"I have been waiting for you," he says. Its truth startles him. "Where have you been?"

She stands and walks to him. Her toenails are blackened with dirt, her naked feet bent and knuckled as a ballet dancer's. They are the feet of someone who has been walking a long time. She kneels and takes his head between her hands. She smells like acrylic paint and tea and something he might call sadness, might call joy.

When she speaks, her voice is rusty.

"I have been in a fortress," she says. She clears her throat and the next words emerge crisp as snow. "But now I am free."

WHEN PAUL LEAVES the halfway house, despite the relentless pain in his head, he wants to shout with glee. He wants to run, but does not. He measures his steps—right, left, right, left—to the bus stop on Prospect Avenue. The blocks are run-down but peaceful, houses tilting over scuffed lawns dotted with toys and barbecue drums. Ferns and ficus adorn the porches, and oaks cast their shadows over the parked Fords and Chevrolets. A few children are riding bikes down the one-way streets. As they stream by, one hollers, "Look out, mister," and he hops out of the way, heartened by their frenzied pedaling, the casual way they glide past stop signs. A man grilling meat in his driveway lifts his hand as Paul passes. He waves back.

The thunderstorm has come and gone. He heard it while in the room with his mother. Both of them felt its electricity along their arms. They held them out parallel and admired how tiny hairs rose on their forearms.

"You're a giant," his mother told him after the storm subsided.

"Not me," he said. "I couldn't even make the JV basketball team."

But she shook her head and placed her finger in the center of his chest.

"We will be new with you," she said, and though he didn't believe her, his lungs expanded as though he'd gulped a tremendous breath.

As a child, he was laughed off every team—basketball, soccer, even Ping-Pong. As an adolescent, he wore knockoff Converse and tried dyeing his hair with food coloring when his classmates were using Manic Panic. Other than his knack with numbers and skill constructing tiny towers, his sole talent is identifying the personalities of a house's inhabitants by the odor of Campbell's soup in the air: chicken noodle means kind, vegetable overprotective, tomato angry.

A giant? A man to make the world new? Not he.

A bus arrives and hauls him to another, which ferries him back to the dorm. His suite mates have finished classes and are watching *The Simpsons* again, though they have progressed from potato chips to pizza and beer. They offer him a can, so he accepts a Miller Lite and a seat on the couch beside them. He presses the can's cool cylinder to his burning brow and thinks of the desert.

"The desert knows you," his mother told him at the halfway house. "And you know it."

"I've never been there," he told her, but thought instantly of his dreams. The desert in his dreams was either too hot or too cold, but always felt familiar.

"The man will walk out of the sand," she said. "He will show you his face."

"How do you know about the man?" Paul asked, startled.

"I dream him too," his mother said. "We all will." After that, she said no more.

On the couch in his suite, Paul takes the cold can from his forehead and pops its top.

"Pizza?" asks his Senegalese roommate. He is six feet tall and has evenly spaced teeth that look yellow and strong. His name is Ahadmadoul, shortened to Ahmadou. He is also studying to be an engineer.

A few hours ago, Paul would have said yes and eaten it without thinking, wiping his plate clean with the crust. But now he shakes his head.

"No, thanks." He pats his stomach, pushing it out to seem full. "I've already eaten."

"Have you been researching at the library?" Ahmadou asks. Their Bengali roommate is laughing at Bart Simpson and not listening to their conversation.

"Something like that." He presses his fingers to his temples and rubs.

"If you have got a headache, I have some pills. Vicodin. Very potent."

"I'll be okay," Paul says, and realizes it's true.

HIS MIGRAINE IS GONE the next day. He attends his classes, nodding at the instructors and crafting plans in his head. He will move out of the dorm and into a cheap one-bedroom apartment near the university. His mother will take the bedroom and he will sleep on the couch, which he will buy at Goodwill or find discarded by the campus dumpsters. He will get a part-time job so his mother does not have to work. She will stay at home and paint while he goes to class and layers sandwiches at Subway or bags autumn leaves for the rich people in the Country Club District. At night, they will listen to his Nirvana CDs and eat Top Ramen and she will tell him stories about his past. She will tell him who his father was, where he came from. He will change his surname from the generic Smith to his mother's. Samson, a title with power.

During Introduction to Engineering, he pencils these plans on his yellow legal pad. The lecturer's voice dims to a dull drone in his ears. The migraine has not returned, but his eyes occasionally tingle, as though waves of electricity are coursing through them.

Halfway houses are for addicts. Other foster children spoke of them, waiting for their parents to emerge. He used to picture them as dots on a line, halfway between Before and After. The parents either went forward to the After or back to the Before to start the cycle again. Halfway houses are also for the insane. *The mentally ill*, he corrects himself. His mother could be an addict. His mother could be mentally ill. He is not sure which. He is not sure it matters.

Either way he will take care of her. He imagines himself gently prying the needle from her hand. He imagines holding her arms while she rages or mopping up her tears when depression takes hold.

At lunch he refuses the dining hall's tuna casserole and baked beans, selecting bread rolls and oranges instead. He could pack these items for a journey. They would be easy to carry.

I am a giant, he thinks, standing in the cashier line. I have places to go.

In that moment before he swipes his card, the dining hall din clattering around him, he feels himself grow a little taller.

HE HAS NOT VISITED his mother since the day he received the letter; classes and assignments have monopolized his time. On Friday his schedule is clear and so he boards the bus, then the other.

The house is shabbier than he remembers it. The porch sags behind its stone columns, and the leaves of the fern have browned at the tips. A broken Crock-Pot sits discarded by the steps. The upstairs windows wink in the sun. It is early September, but blazingly hot. He hopes to see his mother's face at one of these windows, but he does not.

The person who answers the door is neither fat nor jolly. He has a gray face and white hair hanging over his eyes. At Paul's question, he jams his thumb upward at the stairs and grunts. The two men are missing from the kitchen and there is no scent of tea.

The door to his mother's room is closed. He knocks and, when no one answers, tries the knob. It opens easily onto chaos.

Black paint splashes the murals, and the shades are in tatters. Both chairs have been kicked over, and one is missing a leg. In the patchy light he can see his mother, curled under her metal bedstead. Her eyes are open and shining.

The evening before shipping out, the Murphy boy threw a tantrum. He shouted obscenities at his mother and put his fist through a wall. After that, much screaming ensued, from the boy, the mother, the father. Paul took refuge in his room, but later, once the shouting had stopped and the boy banged out the door and into the night, he emerged and helped the father patch the wall.

This time he cannot take refuge. This chaos is his.

He drops to his knees and reaches out a hand. She does not take it. "What happened?" he asks. She does not answer.

He surveys the mess. He doesn't know where to begin. The room reeks of acrylic paint. When he tries to dismantle the tattered shades, thinking he'll find a way to replace them, a loud cough from under the bed makes him jump. It sounds again. *Cough cough.* His mother has shrunk farther back into the shadows. He can hear her muttering something, but he cannot make out the words. She coughs again, and the throbbing returns behind his eyes, rhythmic and insistent.

"Please," he says through the pain. Then: "Mother."

He has called her this only in his mind, and it sounds stupid said aloud, a word too formal for its meaning. Paul begins to cry in a way he does not recognize. Loud sobs with deep indrawn breaths, no melody about it. He wishes he had a yellow legal pad and a perfectly sharpened pencil. He wishes he had an equation to untangle, a series of molecules to fit together, a tower to design.

When his weeping slows, he wipes his face with his hands and then wipes his hands on his jeans. His T-shirt is soaked with sweat. In the midst of his outburst, he longed to feel a tug on his pants. Perhaps a gentle hand on his arm. He thought his sobbing would bring his mother out into the light, but she is still under the bed. Her muttering has ceased and the room, except for a siren wailing outside, is silent.

He goes downstairs to the kitchen and finds the two men from before. When he enters, they stare at him without recognition. The fat woman does not materialize.

He pours a glass of water and brings it to his mother, but she won't emerge. It was morning when he arrived. The shadows lengthen while he waits. In late afternoon he leaves, placing the water glass under the bed with her. As he shuts the door, he can hear her drinking it as an animal would, with large messy swipes of her tongue.

BEE'S FLOWER SHOP might be closed, but he does not wait. He remembers the address from the envelope slipped under his door. He gets on a bus. The lopsided houses pass in a blur. Another storm is encroaching, this time from the west, perhaps blown off the peaks of the Rockies, hundreds of miles distant. He thinks of the Steinhoffs, who dreamed of a land so large they could forget the past. America has never seemed like that to him. Through his boyhood he felt locked in place, an orphan who did not belong, anchored in the center of a hostile continent.

This has changed. He has a mother. He belongs, at least with her. No matter how many times she coughs in the dark, no matter how broken she proves herself to be, he will not relinquish that.

The bus deposits him on a corner flanked by a dry cleaner's, a Citgo station, a vacant storefront, and a brick box with a picture window and glass door. On the west side, a stone church rises above the sparse, squat buildings. Bee's Flower Shop inhabits the brick building. Vibrant blooms crowd its window and obscure its interior. Paul spots purple and red blossoms, and remembers the letter's thick paper between his fingers. The hot afternoon presses against him. A Chevrolet pulls into the flower shop's parking lot, and a black woman with an aristocratic arch to her eyebrows emerges, hauls a trash bag stuffed with clothes across the avenue to the cleaners. She and Paul appear to be the only human beings in existence.

Bee's Flower Shop is not closed, but as he approaches, a hand is reaching from inside to flip the Open sign over. A face peers out at him. The face is a man's: middle-aged, white, with the brightest blue eyes he's seen. The face does not smile when he sees Paul, but the eyes do, crinkling at the edges. Paul opens the door.

"Hello," he says, and Paul thinks maybe he has met this man before.

"Are you closing?" Paul asks.

"I can wait." The man's eyes do not lose their smile. "Please come in."

The shop smells of flowers and coffee. A pot burbles behind the cash register. A can of Maxwell House sits to the side. On the counter lies an array of round red flowers and a pair of scissors. This man must spend the evenings here, snipping stems in solitude.

"Dahlias." The man gestures at the crimson flowers. "Perfect for a lover. What can I get you?" He turns to the glass cooler. "How about some irises? Purple seems a recent favorite."

Paul doesn't know how to begin. "I'll take some roses," he says finally.

"How many?"

"Five?"

The man begins pulling roses from their buckets. "Baby's breath? Ferns?" he calls over his shoulder.

"Why not?"

The shop is cramped and green and comfortable. A faint fragrance of cigarette smoke laces the air. He examines it while the man arranges the bouquet. Then he examines the man. White buttoned shirt, tan trousers, hands with tapered elegant fingers. Brown hair flopped across his brow. He appears to be the same age as two of Paul's instructors. Both are Vietnam vets; they pause often in their lectures to reference the war. Paul thinks of his definition essay for expository writing, its first sentence: War is an armed conflict between two or more opposing forces. He doubts this man could tell him something he could use. He cannot imagine this man on a battlefield. He has the studied air of an artist or a scholar. He exudes sleeplessness. It must be the scent of coffee.

Paul wonders how this elegant man ended up here. To open a flower shop on Troost makes no sense. From what he's heard, even the remaining shopkeepers in the business district farther north see little traffic. Surely no one would stop here to buy flowers. Maybe this man is punishing himself for some past crime, choosing exile to this lonely intersection as a form of atonement. He considers what the man could have done before, what connection he holds with his mother. JEC.

The man completes the bouquet and wraps it in paper.

"How much do I owe you?" Paul digs in his pocket.

"Consider it a gift." He holds out the roses. "How is she doing?"

Paul knows exactly whom he means. He lifts his shoulders an inch higher. "Not well."

"I am sorry to hear it." In his voice, Paul detects truth. "It's her first time out."

Paul takes the roses and lays them on the counter. "She said she was in a fortress."

"She spoke to you? Ah." The man picks up a dahlia and snips its stem. "That is a good sign. Her speaking."

His mother curled under the bed, her eyes shining. Her tongue's wet sound in the water glass. That animal cough.

"What did she mean, a fortress?" Paul asks. He feels he can ask this man anything.

"I imagine she means the hospital." The man does not look up. "I was her doctor. Her psychiatrist. For a time."

"She was in a mental hospital."

"Yes."

"She's not a junkie."

"No." The man holds out one fine-boned hand. "My name is James."

Paul grasps the man's hand, which clings to his own a fraction too long. "Pleased to meet you," Paul says, and he is. This man is a link to his mother, to her past. The *J* stands for James. The *E* and *C*, for what?

"I left years ago," James says. "Resigned. A few months after your birth, in fact." He cuts another flower. "You look very much like her." His gaze travels from the dahlias back to Paul.

Paul allows James to examine him.

"My letter clearly found you." James's scissors have stilled, frozen in the act of cutting. Paul watches them, waiting for the snip. "It took some research. I am pleased it reached you."

"But why write to me?" After a lifetime living in quiet corners, Paul cannot understand why someone would take the time to find him.

"I apologize." James returns to his flowers. The scissors slice together. The stem falls. "This must be quite overwhelming for you. And I've been intrusive, to stare. I have known your mother many years, but have not seen her for much of your life."

"Because you resigned."

"I wasn't good for her. In the end, I wasn't good for anybody. Flowers are easy. They just need water and light to grow."

Hope pricks at Paul. This man has known his mother a long time. He can offer Paul information. "Did you know my father?" he asks.

James looks up. "I didn't meet him. But I knew of him."

"Who was he?"

"Someone your mother needs to forget." He turns back to the flowers. "Please don't ask her about him."

But I want to, Paul thinks with frustration. He remembers his mother's shining eyes, her animal cough. "What did he do?"

"I made a mistake once, talking to her about him. Maybe if I hadn't . . ." James smiles as though in apology. "You have seen the results."

"How did you know they released her?" Paul asks.

"One of her companions in the halfway house used to be my patient. The big woman with the nice smile." James puts the scissors down. "I had hoped your mother would be released earlier, but I was no longer her doctor. I gave up my rights to expect such things. She's been out a month. Her housemate told me they secured her a job in a supermarket. Bagging groceries." James opens the glass cooler and sinks the dahlias into a bucket filled with water. "I've heard the routine has been good for her."

Paul tries to picture his mother in a supermarket, a Price Chopper or Piggly Wiggly, placing egg cartons and celery and Cheerios into paper bags, but he cannot reconcile his image of her with what James has said. In his mind, she rips the bags to pieces, hurls the eggs at customers, howls down the meat aisle, escapes out a back door.

"Have you spoken with her?" Paul asks. "Do you visit her?"

"Alas, no." James turns from the flower cooler, his face impassive. "As I said, I wasn't good for her."

Paul feels as though he should offer James something in exchange for what he's given him. He wouldn't have a mother without this man.

He wouldn't know she exists. "I could give her your regards?" he says. "The next time I see her."

James's eyes change, lose their artifice. They are naked and afraid and alone. "Please do."

"I will," Paul says.

"Paul." His name sounds oddly familiar in James's mouth. Paul senses he has uttered it many times before. "I am glad to see you looking well. This cannot be easy for you. And don't worry." He smiles. "Your mother is resilient. She will handle this world better than it might seem right now."

"I hope so." Paul picks up his roses and turns toward the door. "Would you like me to keep this open?"

"No," he says. "Close it."

As Paul shuts the shop's door behind him, he senses the man's eyes on his back. He gifts his bouquet to a woman in sweatpants dozing at the bus stop. When he places the roses beside her, she opens bloodshot eyes and nods, as though they've met. He returns the nod, and warmth suffuses his body. Then he takes a bus back to what is no longer his home.

WHEN HE RETURNS to the lilac house the next day, his mother is gone.

"She couldn't," the fat woman says. Today her eyes are brighter, but not by much. "Not today."

No sign exists of the other man, tired and unhappy, white hair over his gray face. The two black men are back at the kitchen table, playing cards. Paul can see them from the doorway, though he does not enter.

"Did she return to the hospital?" He thinks of the room upstairs, smeared with her paint. Maybe they've already repainted it. Something innocuous, he thinks, white or ivory or cream. Even so, her drawings—the black, the red, the orange—would seep through.

"Oh, them." The woman pushes a hank of hair out of her eyes. "They don't want her. I'm surprised they kept her as long as they did. The seventies wasn't too kind to us folks. Frank and George in there?" She jerks her head toward the kitchen. "Booted them out fifteen years ago. Ejected me once I hit eighteen. Lucky they don't run these houses like they run the wards. Don't know where we'd go."

He does not understand what he is hearing. "But where is she?" A knot has clenched in his stomach.

She shrugs. "She'll come back. Most do."

"I'll find her."

"She found you."

"Someone did."

"She's lucky." She is missing three teeth, way in the back. He can see the gaps when she grins. "To have somebody."

She closes the door gently in his face.

He walks to Prospect Avenue, glances east, then west. No thunderstorms are building. The sky is glassy, arced over a continent that spent his life rejecting him. He thinks of his essay for expository writing. He will revise the first sentence. *War*, he will write, *is a struggle to retain what one loves.* He thinks of his mother—somewhere, wandering—and the throbbing returns behind his eyes. This time he welcomes it, because he recognizes it for what it is. It is not sorrow. It is a deep and abiding happiness. He has a mother now. He has a place, if he can find her, to call his own.

MIDDLE

The water captivates Paul. Muddy and terrifying, it rises, and then rises again, an unstoppable force. It swirls down streets, eddies around buildings, chokes houses to their rafters. The month is August, the year 2005, New Orleans submerged. Paul cannot look away. He remains glued to the television, his torso strained forward. His body sits on his couch in his carpeted house in Kansas City, Missouri, but his mind is elsewhere, adrift in the flooded Louisiana streets.

His birthday is eight days away, then six, then two. New Orleans does not drain. On the news, a parade of images: two men paddling furiously down Annunciation Street, their boat heaped with cabbages; an ancient woman on a rooftop, her dining room table and chairs beside her; a German shepherd at an attic window, its throat presumably too sore from barking to utter sound.

Paul is thirty years old, a car insurance salesman. He has a two-story house and a wife who keeps it violently clean. He follows consistent routines. But now he cannot sleep. He slips from the cool ivory sheets and pads downstairs, turns the TV on low. Relief efforts have intensified. The president has finally galvanized his forces. Helicopters whir over the swimming streets, blades rippling the surface, ladders lowered for children and old men. Still, many are left behind. Paul thinks about the dogs and cats, the ones not drowned, expecting their owners' return. Clouds bruise the southern skies. Talk of more rain.

In the mornings he drives from his home in Brookside to his job, but he cannot concentrate on work. As intended, he graduated in 1997 with an engineering degree, but accepted the first position offered. Now he sells auto insurance in a Westport office complex down the street from where the Oregon, California, and Santa Fe Trails once crossed. At this crossroads an Irish pub offers happy hour ten-cent wings and dollar Michelob drafts, but once it was a general store selling gunpowder and salt pork to families heading across Kansas and beyond. Paul's cubicle looks out onto a parking lot where covered wagons must have stood, where women in gingham bonnets must have peered west, fearful of the dangers to come.

The insurance office has become a hive, buzzing with activity. Sales are up in the wake of the hurricane; his phone rings and rings. His manager and the other salesmen are pleased, but Paul doesn't care about cars. His mind is on buildings, their vulnerability to disaster. What if, he wonders, one could lift a city above water? He imagines stilts, intricate scaffolds. Instead of logging calls to potential customers, he drafts his ideas onto printer paper, rough blueprints over which he crouches when colleagues pass his cubicle. He uses the same pencils he's had since college, newly sharpened; their scratching brings him satisfaction deep and quiet as water. On the news the experts talk of levees and dams, methods to keep floods out, but Paul is unconvinced. He pictures a city in air, a metropolis impervious to catastrophe.

He remembers the tornado he witnessed in childhood, the thrill— electric as a shock—that passed through him. That was when he lived with the Burnside family in a trailer on the city's margins, with a view of Missouri farmland. He can still see the tornado pitch black against the alfalfa field, its dark cylinder like an indifferent finger touching the earth.

He wanted to run toward it, to acknowledge its power to obliterate. He imagined it sweeping across the city, wiping out the crumbling suburbs, the derelict jazz district, the abandoned downtown. It would pick up the World War I monument and fling it aside. It would decimate Union Station. It would wrench the railroad tracks from the city's center and crumple them into balls to be tossed away.

Penciling his visions, shoulders pained from hunching, Paul envisions a future where humans could adapt to their environment instead of molding it to fit them. American history, with its slaughter of people and animals, its perpetual pushback against the wilderness, has not seen such a place. His mother's words—Make the world—ring in his ears, and he bends with fresh fury to the page.

The hurricane is not the only force dictating Paul's ideas. He has other reasons to think of tomorrow. He has his mother Bea. She did not vanish in 1993. She still lives in the halfway house near Prospect, a ten-minute drive from his neighborhood. She still has her job bagging groceries at the Piggly Wiggly. To Paul's surprise, she has rarely missed a day of work.

The first afternoon she disappeared, Paul walked in widening concentric circles until he found her standing in a vacant lot on the Paseo, rubbing her elbows and muttering about snow. When she saw him, her eyes flashed. "The man is coming," she said. "Do not run." He calmed her, led her to the bus stop, helped her board when it arrived. She sat rocking in a window seat, humming to herself.

Now when she's missing, he knows where to find her. Sometimes she is muttering about the north and snow, sometimes about the man in the desert. When she sees him, she becomes obedient, easily led. He helps her into his Subaru, buckles her in. On the way home, she often sings quietly, but Paul cannot recognize the songs. She's always ready for her shift the next day.

He must think of the future for his mother, but also for his wife. Her name is Eva, and she is three years older and six inches taller than he. They met in 1999 at a gallery opening he stumbled into. He was drawn to her olive skin and blunt speech. "Little man," she said when she saw him examining a photograph. "You must join me at this bistro nearby. I need to feed you and help you grow." To his surprise, he found himself laughing. "Show me the way," he said.

An art critic with a taste for oysters and red wine, Eva is the only woman who's accepted him for what he is. Not just his stature, but his tremendous girth. Their first night in her Crossroads loft she unpeeled his blue polo and beige trousers, not flinching, as so many had done, at the size of his cock, the single gigantic part of him. Instead, she took it in her hands, her mouth, and then with the smooth slipping of a shadow, into her body. One year later, he married her and settled her into the house he'd bought: a three-bedroom in placid Brookside with a lawn, garage, bunnies in the bushes.

Their first night of marriage, he turned to her in the dark. "Why did you marry me?" he asked. In their lovemaking, they had tossed the covers off, and he could see the blurred outline of his feet, farther from the bed's end than hers. "I'm so much shorter than you," he said. "And so ordinary."

Eva laughed, a full-throated sound. "Paul," she said. "My small Paul." She nuzzled his neck. "I can't tell you how tired I was of those art men. Those critics. Even the artists. Everybody was a posture, a statue. You are your own true shape." With that, she clambered onto him and they began to move again, in tandem, in the dark, in their quiet house on their quiet block. When they had finished, she collapsed onto him and whispered in his ear, "With you, I feel safe."

Now she bustles around cleaning while he watches the news on the plastic-wrapped leather sofa. Windex for glass, Pledge for wood, Febreze daily in each room. Chemicals jam the space under their kitchen sink. "We don't want stains," Eva asserted when they bought the furniture. She covered the couches and chairs in plastic, the kitchen shelves in contact paper, the mattresses in zippered cases. Paul could not understand it—her loft had retained its bare wood and unadorned bed—but he did not contradict her. It seemed to make her happy; she hummed as she encased their home. When they'd married, she had stopped writing art reviews. She'd said she wanted to try other things, but neither the printmaking nor quilting nor knitting circles stuck. Cleaning did.

It is Sunday, the fourth of September, a quarter to noon. More coverage of New Orleans. A few hours before, police fired shots on a bridge at the city's margins. Men are dead. The TV screen shows their faces, one old, one young, both black. There is a girl too, others. The cameras pan over bloodstained concrete, a blur of faces. Witnesses admit these clashes between cops and civilians are nothing new, but their faces look shocked, their eyes stunned and glassy. Paul also feels stunned, his stomach leaden. This planet exhausts him.

Eva is spritzing the windows, but turns when she hears the report. "Don't watch." She gestures with the Windex bottle. "It'll give you more nightmares."

Paul twitches his shoulders in irritation. He sometimes wakes screaming, but does not tell her what he dreams. That man walking through the desert has nothing to do with the news. Soon Eva will pester him to switch the TV off. "I'm fine," he says. Eva is hovering behind him, concern emanating from her in waves. Paul gives in and turns the TV off. "What shall we have for dinner?" he asks.

"I got broccoli rabe from the Price Chopper. I'm making pasta and sauce. My grandmother's recipe." Her response doesn't surprise him.

Eva's family came from a crumbling Sicilian town named Porto Empedocle, where they'd learned a deep appreciation for food.

Paul wonders what it would feel like to own such secure knowledge of one's family. The last time his mother disappeared, the police picked her up at Eighteenth and Vine, more than two miles from the halfway house. Believing her homeless, they signed her into a shelter for the night. At 1:00 a.m. she called him from the pay phone. A single word—"Come"—and he sat up. Abandoning his sleeping wife, he sped in his beige Subaru to the shelter, but had to wait until dawn to sign her out. She emerged clear-eyed into the morning and hummed another sad tune he didn't know on the ride home.

Paul and Eva have known each other six years and been married for five, but he has not yet told her about his mother. He doesn't know how she'll react. Eva is so clean and careful, Bea anything but. The times he must hunt his mother down, he tells Eva it's a work emergency. He's not sure she believes him, but she has yet to question it.

That night sleep eludes him again. He slips from his bed but does not turn on the TV. Instead, he pads down to the basement, a wallpapered room where Eva used to attempt her various projects. He clicks on the single bulb. On a long table in the basement's center, scraps remain—a few squeezed and dried-out paints, a ball of wool with knitting needles protruding. He's surprised Eva has not scrubbed this room, swept these things away. He sets them aside, clearing a wide space for himself. He has no materials beyond the drawings he's brought home from his office. These he splays across the table. The only noises are the papers' rustle and the house's vague hum.

He tries to look at his drawings objectively, the way a city planner might. He tilts his heads, squints his eyes, examines his work. Lattices and ladders, rope swings and towers. The sketches are amateurish and childlike. Even ridiculous. He has penciled images one might find in a picture book about imaginary places. No cities resemble these. He thinks of downtown Minneapolis with its network of enclosed walkways, Toronto and Albany with their tunnels between buildings; in each instance, the goal is to protect inhabitants from the severe winters. To adapt themselves to the world, not it to them.

It is the same, but not the same. He cannot quite pinpoint why. Perhaps because in those places, life continues as normal, even with the winters raging outside. In his settlement too, life would continue, but it would be different. His city's inhabitants would be kinder, more considerate. Black and white and brown would commune. Police would not gun down men asking for help. Children would not be locked away in institutions. Neighbors would take in orphans as their own.

He peers at his drawings again. "I'm an idiot," he says aloud.

A place like this would never work. Still, he loves what his blueprints represent. He surveys the materials Eva has abandoned. A couple of paintbrushes, knitting needles, wool. Under the dim basement bulb, he collects these items and works with them, bending, snipping, tying. An hour later, he has a structure. It is fragile, absurdly precarious, but it stands. The semblance of two scaffolds, a woolen bridge knotted between. His nascent city in air. Fantastical as a picture book.

IN THE MORNING, he tells Eva he would like to donate two hundred dollars to the relief efforts in New Orleans.

"Why?" She is buttering a Thomas' English muffin for him and seems distracted by the falling crumbs.

"Why wouldn't I?" He glances at the clock. He has ten minutes before he must leave for work.

"Because it's your money. Because you've worked for it."

"Precisely."

Eva swipes up the crumbs with a Lysol disposable cloth. As soon as he eats the English muffin, Eva wipes his face with a Wet-Nap, as though he's a child. His city, Paul decides, will have no chemicals.

She crosses her arms. "New Orleans is not our city. Besides, we can't afford it."

"But we can. Eva, my dear." He moves close. She is wearing flats, and his nose is level with her neck. She smells stringent as the yellow bars of soap they provided at the institution. "We make a good living. Why not share?"

"But the government." She runs a lacquered nail along the counter as though checking for crumbs. "Aren't they helping?"

"Some." He nuzzles her ear with his forehead and feels her tense. It is slight, barely noticeable, but the strain is there. He steps away. "I don't think we can depend on the government. How have they helped us?"

"They gave you a childhood. Anywhere else—India, say—you would have been out on the streets."

"I could send less. How about one hundred?"

"That's a lot of money. Think of the future."

"This is the future." He thinks of his creation downstairs, the bridges woven of wool.

"I know." She pulls another Lysol cloth free and wipes the counter again. "I'm pregnant."

It's like a movie. He's too surprised to speak.

Eva speaks for him. "I'm six weeks in. I've only known for two."

His jaw unlatches. "Why didn't you tell me right away?"

"Oh, Paul." Her face turns tender. "I wanted to. I've been so excited about it. It was like it was Christmas, and I was hiding your present. But I needed to be sure." She steps on the trash can's pedal and drops the cloth inside. "So much has seemed uncertain recently. I wanted at least one thing to be definite. Even at six weeks, it's risky to say. But I had to.

So." She throws her arm wide. "Now I can offer it to you. Your early Christmas gift. I can't know for sure, but I think it's a girl."

"Wow." The only sufficient word.

She will have a child. *He* will have a child. Maybe a girl. Female like his wife. Like his mother. What if? His sight blurs. He remembers his mother the second time he saw her. Crouched under the bed, barking her strange sound. Her tongue's swipes in the water glass. He pictures Eva cradling their newborn. What if when the baby cries, she sounds like Bea? What if when she drinks, she does it on all fours?

"Are you okay?" Eva touches his arm.

He manages a smile. "I'm okay. Wonderful, in fact. Eva, this is stupendous."

"You understand now?" she asks. "About the money?"

"I do."

A ray of sun from the window has hit Eva's head, illuminating her thick hair. It is dense and black and alive in the bright light. To think they are creating someone who will sprout such wonder from her own head. An entire human being. Paul pushes his first thought away. Their daughter—if the baby is indeed a daughter—will not be his mother. She will be her own person. She has to be. She has to be better than the terrible world.

There is a way to be certain. He needs to make his mother a part of his life. Eva needs to know what they're up against. A child does not originate from nothing. If their daughter is to have any hope for the future, she will have to know where she came from. He feels something crackling to life in his chest.

"Eva," he says. "I want you to meet someone."

"Who? For what?" She rests a hand against the counter, as though to brace herself.

"On Sunday. We're free then, right?"

"What does this have to do with the baby?"

"Nothing," he says, but this is not true. "You just need to meet this person."

He hopes his mother hasn't left for the vacant lot. He hopes she'll be there when they arrive. If he's lucky, she will have combed her hair, done something about her teeth. On one of his monthly visits, he brought her toothbrushes and toothpaste, instructed her on how to use them, but she refuses to remember. Her teeth are blackened nubs; some are missing. Nonetheless, her smile is dazzling. When she showers it on him, he cannot look away.

"Paul. Tell me who it is." Eva's tone is curt. Her previous warmth has evaporated.

"Somebody important to me." He takes a breath. "A family member."

Her eyes widen. "You have no family."

"I have you."

"You know what I mean."

"I found somebody. Recently." This is not exactly true, but true enough. He presses on. "I've been wanting you two to meet." He pauses. "It's my mother. I've found my mother."

"Oh." Her face relaxes. "Your mother." She stands still, as though considering this new information. Then a grin splits her face wide. "Holy shit, Paul. That's something. How did you find her?"

"The internet is an amazing thing."

"This is exciting." She touches his arm, slides her hand up and down. They lean into each other and stand there for a long time, breathing into each other's skin. Eva, Paul thinks. My wife, my own. To have any family at all feels like a miracle.

Eventually, Eva pulls back. Her face is soft with something, but he's not sure exactly what. Relief or joy or love. Or all three. "How incredible," she says, and it sounds sincere, a deep and solid note. "I had no idea. I thought you were all alone."

"So did I."

"And now our child will have two grandmothers. Like everybody else."

At this, his resolve falters, but just for a minute. Who cares if one of those grandmothers is a little nuts? The planet itself is more than a little nuts.

They look at each other. Then Eva gathers her long hair into a knot, preparing for her daily scouring of the house.

"I can't wait," she says.

"When you meet her." Paul clears his throat. "Keep an open mind. She's had a hard life."

"My little man, so have you." She pecks him on the cheek. "I promise, I'll have the most open mind. I'm just excited you have a mother."

"So am I." Despite his fears, Paul's heart swells. His two families will meet. Disorder and order. His mother and his wife. His daughter's life will be different from his. She will not have to blunder blindly through her childhood, cut off from what came before. She will know her past. She will have a family, people who can show her who she is, who she has yet to be.

A WEEK PASSES. New Orleans has begun to dry out. Some houses have been salvaged, some missing people found. Authorities are investigating the shooting on Danziger Bridge. The number of dead, though, continues to rise. Without consulting Eva again, Paul has donated one hundred dollars to the Red Cross. He has also visited the basement twice more. The scaffold is evolving, more paintbrushes erected, more bridges strung. At work he is foggy from lack of sleep, but his colleagues are too distracted by the insurance boom to notice.

Sunday arrives. Paul and Eva drive east toward Troost. All morning Eva has seemed eager and excited. She applied lipstick and zipped up her best linen dress from Ann Taylor. As they enter the neighborhood, however, her bright face sags. At first, Paul does not understand. Then he does. Through her eyes he sees the cracked asphalt and boarded up shop fronts, the few corner stores with iron grilles over their windows and grizzled men outside, nodding over their paper-bagged forties. She did not expect his mother to live in such a place.

"The mayor's done a lot here," he says. "Cleaned up the streets. Funded new businesses." Paul points through her window. "See that flower shop? They have dahlias for sale. I'll buy you some before we leave." Eva does not look at Bee's Flower Shop.

"Careful," she says. "The light's red."

A knock at Paul's window startles them. Paul turns and sees a man's face, black and seamed, his eyes rheumy, his hand holding a bottle of water. One dollar, he mouths through the glass. Around his neck a cardboard sign: *Vietnam Vet Please Help.*

Paul fishes in his pocket. "Thirsty?" he asks Eva. He unrolls his window and hands the man two bills. "Just one bottle," he insists when the man offers two. "Keep the change."

"You're funny," Eva tells him as the light flips green and Paul hits the gas pedal. "Offering an extra dollar."

"Why not?" Paul says. It feels good to have extra money to give.

"You don't consider the future, do you?" Eva takes the bottle from Paul and sips.

"I do." Paul accepts the water back. It is cool and sweet. "What would it look like without kindness?"

They park outside the lilac house and walk up the stairs. The fat woman answers the door. She's wearing a voluminous Adidas track suit with a broken zipper and a stain on the chest.

"Bea's not here," the woman tells them. "Hasn't been for weeks."

At first, he doesn't understand. "But she's not gone," Paul says. "She can't be. I just saw her on the Paseo. Not long ago."

"Long enough, I reckon." The woman's bleary eyes wander past them. "Our Bea has found her mission."

"What are you talking about?" Paul asks.

"Who is Bea?" asks Eva. "Is that your mother?"

"Go to Troost and Thirty-Ninth," the woman says. "Next to that flower shop. Clapboard house. Second floor. Our patient," she says with a wink, "has become a doctor." And with that, the woman shuts the door.

"Paul." Eva plucks at his sleeve. "Tell me what's happening."

"I'm not sure myself," he replies. "Let's go to that house."

Back in the car, they retrace their route. Paul finds the clapboard house and parks his car by the weeds outside. To make Eva happy, he secures his Club to the steering wheel.

He puts his hand on his wife's knee. "We've known each other six years. I love you, Eva. I really do. I want you to know everything about me. With the baby coming, it's important."

Her knee warms under his touch, and her eyes darken. He remembers her when they met, how easily she took his body into her own, how graciously she accepted him into her life.

"Let's go," he says, and opens his door.

The air hums with heat. The street is deserted. Somewhere the agitated burr of flies. He surveys the house. It is white and dirty, the first-floor windows naked, the second floor shaded with tattered blinds. He has a wife. A mother. In-laws. Soon he will have a child of his own. As a young boy shuffling from one foster home to another, he didn't dare dream such riches.

At first nobody answers the doorbell, but then the buzzer sounds and the door swings open when he pushes, revealing an ordinary hallway carpeted in gray. A flight of stairs to the top. The top floor stinks of cigarettes, a bleak odor that reminds Paul of the Murphy house. The same airlessness. He fights the urge to cough. The door opens before he can knock.

He has not seen James in twelve years. James has changed. His tapered fingers and scholarly air remain, but he has grown stooped and shrunken, his height diminished. His eyes—bleared and yellow, the blue faded—are nearly even with Paul's forehead. They take in Eva without comment, but Paul sees the smile in them and knows his wife is welcome.

"Come in," James says, and in his voice, Paul hears the rattle of bones.

"I'm not sure I understand," says Paul, but doesn't know how to continue.

James latches the door behind them. "She knew you were coming." He looks bemused. "Sometimes I think she knows everything."

Paul scans the apartment, noting the slouched furniture, the wood paneling, the pack of American Spirits on the coffee table, an overflowing ashtray beside it. There are no murals, but his mother's paintings are here, miniaturized and notched into frames adorning the walls. One red. One blue. One depicting a starburst high in the corner. At the far end, one in black and white: what appears to be a woman, cradling a child nearly as tall as she. Plants hang from numerous hooks, lending their damp fragrance to the cancerous air. On the windowsills sit potted orchids, geraniums, ivy. Paul doesn't know how they flourish in this shaded room, but they do.

With a strange stab, Paul realizes Bea lives here too. But why?

"Where is she?" Paul asks.

James opens his mouth, but begins coughing before he can answer. The coughs are hollow and racking. When they abate, he pulls out a handkerchief and spits a gob of blood into it.

"She's here." He slips the wadded handkerchief into his pocket. "She's been quite impressive, our Bea. She has taken extraordinarily good care of me. But please do introduce me to our guest." He turns to Eva.

Eva's face is unreadable. She holds out her palm. "I'm Eva. Paul's wife. And you?" Her smile is tentative. Paul wonders what she is thinking.

James clasps her hand in his own. "James Edward Carson. Former psychiatrist. Current aficionado of green and growing things. Current invalid as well." He squeezes Eva's hand, then lets it go. "It is a peculiar experience, owing my salvation to the one I once dreamed of saving."

Then Paul understands. "She's living here because she's taking care of you."

"Indeed," James says. "She just knew. One afternoon she arrived on my doorstep like the Good Witch of the North. She waved her wand and poof! I felt so much better."

James's expression looks beatific, saintly, as though Bea's presence has exalted him. Paul's chest lurches. He thinks of his long, lonely years in foster care. All those TV dinners and dirty carpets and cast-off Matchbox cars, the quiet ways in which the world told him he was unloved. He remembers his mother the second time he visited her, how she hid under the bed and didn't hold him when he cried.

Fuck you, he thinks, but isn't sure to whom he is speaking, whether it is Bea or James or himself, for believing his mother might someday enter his family, whole and healthy and sane. How could she choose to coddle someone who isn't even her son?

A low grunt makes them turn. Bea is here. She is hovering in the doorway to what Paul presumes is her bedroom. He had assumed her position as caretaker would have changed her, made her look more adult, more polished. But she is herself: her hair is its usual rat's nest, her dress stained, her eyes immortal.

A shiver runs through him. Someone is walking toward him through the dark, someone he does not want to see. In his dream last night, he saw the man's shape coalescing in the desert night, and then he was on the lip of a continent, the ocean swirling behind him, and he could pick out one star above. It was red.

"Paul?" says Eva, and in her voice's quaver he hears fear.

"This is Bea." His chest tightens. "My mother."

Eva's composure is impressive. She neither flinches nor crumbles. She does not collapse dramatically onto the couch. When she speaks, the fear has vanished. "I am very pleased to meet you. I see the resemblance."

Eva holds out her hand, and to Paul's immense surprise, Bea takes it. She gives Eva's hand one firm shake. "It is a pleasure to meet you," Bea says. The syllables are separate, each one a careful enunciation. She has been practicing, Paul thinks. But for what? She couldn't have known Eva was coming. Or was James correct? Does Bea, in fact, know everything?

James coughs into one hand in what Paul assumes he intends as a polite interruption, but once begun, it cannot be stopped. He doubles over, his body trembling. The noise is awful, as though his lungs are tearing free from his chest. He pulls out his handkerchief, hawks and spits. Once. Twice. The scent of rot. When he stands, his face is waxy, his eyes bloodshot.

"Would anyone like some tea?" he asks. "I have Twinings Earl Grey."

Paul wonders what they do at night, his mother and this dying man, if they ever make dinner or watch *The Office* or play Scrabble. If they've been to the movies, to baseball games at Kauffman Stadium, to art openings at the Kemper Museum. It cannot always be like this: fraught with tension, embedded with import.

"Tea would be lovely. Let me help." Eva follows James into the kitchen. Paul can hear her mellow voice, offering her assistance. It used to remind him of gold, if such metal had a sound.

Paul and Bea gaze at each other. He wants to ask her why. Why devote herself to James, this man who should have protected her, but didn't? Why doctor a man who couldn't be a proper doctor for her?

A long moment passes. From the kitchen come teacups tinkling, a kettle's whine.

His mother breaks the silence. "Follow the red star."

Paul's skin prickles. He sees the star from his dream, and though it resembles fire, he feels certain it is cold. He wants to push the image away, but he can't. He drops into a rose-colored chair. It smells of James, his lungs' decay. In the kitchen, the kettle's whine reaches its peak, and then unwinds. The scent of Earl Grey cuts through the layers of plants and smoke. A detail to which he clings.

"We're back," announces Eva. She is carrying a laden tray, James behind her. Who is this woman, Paul thinks, who has bound herself to me? I can't offer her the safety she craves. How could I have thought my family could be normal?

James's face points toward the bedroom. "It seems we have lost her. A shame."

Paul turns. His mother is gone. Again. Exhaustion overwhelms him. He feels as he did when watching the coverage of the bridge shooting. This third rock from the sun, too burdensome to bear.

"I'll get her." Eva sets down the tray and, before Paul can stop her, marches into the bedroom. She utters no exclamation, but when she returns, the blood has drained from her face. "She's under the bed," she announces. "She's making this weird sound. How do we help her?"

James runs a hand through his thinning hair. A few strands lift and float free. Paul sees the skull grinning through his skin. "We can't," James says. "We must let it run its course."

"But how can she take care of you," Eva asks, "if she needs so much help herself?"

"She needs less than you might think," James replies. "She has become quite adept at the mundane particulars. I've even begun sending her on my shopping expeditions. It's a little embarrassing I can no longer manage myself, but I am learning to leave shame behind."

"So why this?" Eva presses. "Why now?"

"Hard to say. Things trigger her. It could be anything from a strong emotion to the way the sun slants through the window." He looks at Paul. "Don't take it personally. Now." He turns to the tea tray. "Do you prefer lemon or cream?"

"Actually," Eva says. "We have to go. I just remembered. My parents are coming for dinner. I have to prepare."

Paul exhales with relief. He is so tired. Tired of this house, the rot from James's lungs, his mother. He needs to escape this house of death and reach the sanitized safety of their Brookside home. He will plop himself on the couch, pop open a Sprite, watch *Jeopardy!* He will forget his mother's world exists. No more prophecies. No more animal grunts. You never took care of me, he thinks. Why must I care for you?

"Please do come again," James says at the door. "She struggles," he tells Eva. "Life for her has not been kind. And yet." His face opens. "She persists. She should be a lesson for us all."

"Thank you for the tea," Eva manages.

"Our door is open," he says to Paul, and before Paul can stop him, James embraces him.

James's body is light as a husk. Any moment it could blow away.

As they leave, Paul hears it. That animal cough, harsher and lonelier than James's death rattle. His mother on all fours under the furniture, barking her truest sound. Goodbye, he imagines his mother is telling him.

IN THE CAR they are silent. He wants to touch Eva's bare knees, but senses he can't. After the complex smells of his mother's home, the vanilla air freshener is calming. He breathes in and out, in and out as he pilots them home.

When they reach their neighborhood, Eva visibly relaxes. He does too. Here is the quaint wooden shopping district with its dime store and CVS, its Price Chopper, its café where Eva meets friends for brunch. Here is their house with its tan siding, its tended lawn. When they step out of the car, the scent of watered grass and gardenias greets them. A rabbit munching clover takes flight at their approach, its white tail flicking.

Once they are inside, Eva cleans the entire place, top to bottom. He has not seen her move with such speed before. He thinks of the Tasmanian devil in those cartoons. He waits on the plastic-sheathed couch until she has finished. He does not turn on the TV to watch the news. He does not do anything. At 3:00 p.m., Eva lays down her cloths and spray bottles and calls her parents to invite them over for dinner. After she begins cooking the sauce, its fragrance snakes through the chemicals—Lysol, Tilex, Febreze, Pledge, Windex, Clorox, names he imagines his wife chants as a witch chants her spells—but cannot dislodge them.

That night, they feast on the food of her homeland, her innocent father and mother presiding over the dishes. Eva's parents speak to each other gently, their faces open in the overhead light. Her mother offers the semolina bread to her father, and their fingers brush. Paul cannot help his envy. To have parents like this.

Paul eats nearly nothing. Eva devours three plates of pasta, two hunks of bread, a heaping of salad, and an entire artichoke down to its tender heart. She has still not spoken to him about their visit. She waits until her parents have departed and bedtime arrives, once they are under the flowered coverlet in their air-conditioned room.

"Has no one noticed how young she is?" She has switched off the light, and her voice rises disembodied in the darkness.

Paul does not need to ask whom she is talking about. "She doesn't really age."

"She looks twelve."

"You think so?"

"Not over forty. But that's impossible if she's your mother. She would've been a kid when she had you."

He knows his mother looks young, but he has not thought of it like this before. In the dark, he sees that man from his dreams, walking out of the desert. He has yet to see the man's face. "I'm sure she's older than that. Nearly fifty, I imagine." He wants to believe it. But if Eva is right and his mother is actually under forty, how much more that says about her, about his family. He stretches his arms behind his head. "What did you think of James?"

"That smelly old man?" She huffs. "I can't believe she moved in with him."

"Yeah," he admits. "Neither can I."

"He's an enabler. That woman." He notices she does not call her his mother. "She shouldn't be his nurse. She's mentally ill. She needs to be in a home."

The gloom is oppressive. He considers snapping the light on.

Eva shifts. "I need to pee." Eva's silhouette rises and floats into the bathroom. When she emerges, she smells like soap and hand lotion, a light cottony scent. "By the way, that money? That you wanted to send about the hurricane? Go ahead and send it. Two hundred is fine."

He is too startled to breathe. He does not want to break the spell.

"I couldn't stand it if we lost this house," she says. "Tornadoes destroy towns in Kansas and Missouri all the time. I can't imagine what we would do. Where we would go. And with this baby." She leaves the sentence unfinished.

She snuggles deeper under the coverlet. Her toes brush his, sending a tingle up his shins to his thighs to his groin. Her hands smell of cotton, but from her nightgown's neck wafts her real fragrance. Roses and musk. He senses if he places a hand on her stomach, her breast, she will respond. He slides one hand across the mattress, then the other. Her back still faces him, but under his touch, her legs part and then, as she turns, her lips. She is warm and slippery and soft. The door is shut, the air-conditioning cranked high, their skin under the sheets pulsing with heat. In their embrace Paul is a giant. As their bodies meet, part, meet again, he hears his mother's voice.

Head out, she says. Follow the red star.

SEPTEMBER PASSES. Most of October. Paul has not driven to the vacant lot nor to the clapboard house. He keeps thinking about what Eva said. How young Bea seems.

His work in the basement brings relief, the single activity that does. From a craft store he has purchased balsa wood, Super Glue, and a delicate X-Acto knife, its blade keen and precise. The nights he wakes from his terrible dreams, he pads to the basement, switches on the bare bulb, and works. So far, he has constructed one city block, its towers lifted high on stilts, its skyline intricate and soaring. One midnight Eva opens the door to the basement and picks her way down the stairs. He expects her to question his activities, to show surprise, but she doesn't.

"So, this is what you've been doing," she says with a smile. She brings him a glass of water with ice and lemon and brushes her lips to his hair. "It's beautiful," she says, and then leaves him to his toils.

Since their visit to his mother, Eva has been very careful with him. It's not pity Paul senses, but a tender concern, as though she now understands the depths of who he is. They make love most nights, her agile limbs enfolding him. Her body is slowly, perceptibly swelling. Her nipples have darkened, her morning sickness come and gone. At times he'll catch her watching him and then examining the walls and doors as though testing their safety. She urges him to send another hundred dollars to the Red Cross.

October ends with their casting candy to the neighborhood children. Eva loves the costumes. "An astronaut," she marvels at the trick-or-treaters. "A monster." November comes, the first and then the second, a Wednesday cold with drizzle. Evening has descended and Paul is outside tossing their Halloween jack-o'-lantern into the trash when he hears the phone ring. His heart leaps, then sinks, and he is not sure why he is running inside the house. When he picks up the phone, he understands.

"My giant." His mother's voice is even clearer than when she greeted Eva. It's the voice of an adult, a woman in control. He cannot picture her on the other end.

"Come to the hospital," she says, and there it is. An odd tilt to her voice, as though her words are slightly off center. It is Bea after all. "The hospital nearest me," she says. "It is time."

James, he thinks. Then she hangs up.

He almost doesn't go. Forget James. Forget Bea. But it's his mother. How long did he wait for her to appear in his desolate life? He can't abandon her now, not even if she's abandoned him.

He knows the hospital she means. He's passed it driving over Troost toward her halfway house. "James is dying," he tells Eva. "I'm going to the hospital."

"Let me come," Eva says, already reaching for her coat.

"Stay here," Paul replies. "Keep the baby safe. I'll be fine." He kisses her forehead, and she trails a finger along his chin.

"My small Paul," she says. "Sometimes you are so tall."

Outside the night air is crisp with oncoming frost. Paul climbs into his Subaru, buckles his seat belt, starts the ignition. As he drives, he remembers his initial flight toward Bea, after James's letter arrived.

The hospital is little more than a clinic, its facade mildewed, its interior odorous with disinfectant and sewage. Gurneys, laden with humans in various stages of distress, choke its corridors. Most eyes are shut, but those open plead with him as he passes. Despite the squalor, Paul feels at home here. He is no stranger to institutions. Among the ordered schedules and muted colors, safety exists.

At the information desk, he asks for James Edward Carson. A black woman with a profile aquiline as his own directs him to a room on the second floor. When he arrives, two nurses—both, he believes, West African—are stripping the bed.

"Oh," says one when he inquires. "I will summon the doctor."

He waits an hour, sitting on a plastic chair while the nurses dismantle the room, bundling the stained sheets, unhooking tubes, clicking off machines. By the time the doctor arrives, they have rolled in a new patient, an ashen man no more than a skeleton. He wheezes as they lift him onto the mattress, and Paul thinks of the teakettle in James's kitchen, its prolonged and painful whine.

"I am Dr. Leigh," the doctor tells Paul. "And to whom am I speaking?"

"I'm Paul." He pauses. "His friend."

"Let's go into the hallway." The doctor's skin is light brown, his features softer than Paul's. He does not introduce himself, does not shake Paul's hand. His mind is elsewhere, the back of his long coat unwrinkled. This man is too busy to sit down.

Dr. Leigh keeps it brief. They admitted James a week ago due to difficulty breathing. The tumor had begun to restrict his airways. His cancer was too advanced for surgery. They made him as comfortable as they could. In the end, he suffocated.

Paul's grief is deep and dry. He sees James as he initially encountered him: letters typed on a creamy white page, words that smelled like flowers, that offered him a family he didn't know he had. James was a man who loved his mother. Paul's resentment dissipates. Who is he, to deny this sick man attention from a woman he'd fought to save?

"Was there a woman with him?" he asks.

"Yes." Dr. Leigh consults his clipboard. "Bea Samson." His eyes light up. "Quite a personage. So refined and articulate. The nurses adored her. Sometimes, in moments of distress, the family is rather—" His expression grows apologetic. "Uninterested in the social conventions. But Ms. Samson had impeccable manners. One of our nurses— she reads a lot—called her a great lady."

"Are you sure?" Paul is certain he has the wrong person. "Was her hair brushed?" It's a stupid question, but once asked, he can't take it back.

The doctor lifts his eyebrows. "Of course." He emits a low chuckle, as though at the oddness of the question. "In a neat bun, if I can remember. Those tailored suits she wore. Truly, she was like someone out of a Victorian novel. Oh." He rummages in his pocket. "She left this for you." He holds out a key. "The key to her house?"

"Thanks." Paul clenches it, feeling the metal dig into his palm. "But where is she?" Paul watches a woman wheeled past on a gurney. No sheet covers her, and he can see both her feet have been severed, her ankles bandaged. "She phoned me maybe two hours ago."

"She left immediately after we called time of death."

The doctor's words land with a thud. She's gone. Again. He will go to the vacant lot. She will be there or at the house. That's why she left him the key. She wants him to let himself in, to feel welcome. She still wants him in her life.

SHE IS NOWHERE. The lot is truly vacant, emptied of her, the schizophrenics, the crackheads and junkies. So too is the house. He unlocks the front door, then the apartment, but finds nothing. The home his mother shared with James remains how he saw it last: choked with plants and cigarette smoke, her paintings on the walls. The plants, however, have begun to die.

One of her paintings is sitting upright on the couch. It's the one depicting the woman with the giant infant. She must have left it for him. But why? When he peeks into her bedroom, he finds her gray dress, stained and torn, discarded on the mattress as though she tore it off in a hurry.

He cannot quell the anger that rises within him. To have known her and lost her. To have known her and yet not known anything about her. He was wrong. His own child will not know her past. The frustration this brings is too much. He picks the painting up from the couch and throws it to the floor, shattering its glass. He hates how gently the woman is cradling her giant baby.

He thinks of Bea cradling James in his last hours, tenderly mopping his face with a cloth. She became an adult for him, a woman in a proper suit and shoes, hair neatly combed. That's what she was practicing for. Her years bagging groceries, her handshake with Eva. All of it was part of that practice. If she could do that, why didn't she do it for Paul? She clearly had the capability to use when she needed. Maybe she learned how to act like that in the hospital, or while working at the Piggly Wiggly. Or possibly James taught her. Paul pictures her at the corner store, sliding dollar bills across the counter in exchange for Twinings tea and American Spirits. Chirping a cheerful goodbye as she jingled the bell on her way out the door.

She never showed this side of herself to Paul. With him, she crawled under the bed and coughed like a deer. She wandered into vacant lots and mumbled about the desert and sang sad songs he didn't know. She told him to follow the red star, but left before she told him what that meant.

Paul looks at the giant baby in the painting. Bea insisted Paul was a giant, but what did she know? He's just a man. A car insurance salesman, five feet tall in pleated pants. A man without a father, and now without a mother.

He leaves the painting where it has fallen. He places the key on the coffee table and does not lock the door behind him. Nothing in that house has value.

On the sidewalk, he pauses. He sees his mother out there, wherever she is. At first, he pictures her as he's known her: knotted hair, ragged dress, blackened grin. But that isn't right. If he believes the doctor's words, she has changed. In order to survive her journey, she has morphed into a grown-up. She is wearing a dark blue suit with a long skirt, her black hair smoothed into a knot at her neck's base. Shoes with laces and short square heels encase her feet. She does not buy a bus ticket or rent a car or stick her thumb out for a ride. She walks along the highway, away from the city that is no longer hers, that maybe never was. She is walking north or to the desert or in an entirely different direction. Perhaps she is looking for the red star.

He climbs into his car. Waiting at home are his wife and child, yet unborn. Perhaps a girl. He doesn't know how he will raise a girl in this awful place. Panic flutters his heart. He starts the engine and pulls away.

Back at home, he walks straight to the basement and sits at the table. His model city rises before him. He considers destroying it, wiping the table clean with one sweep of his arm. He recalls another painting his mother left behind in the apartment, not the one with the giant. This one was a tiny square swirled with blue, like wind or water. In its bottom corner an even tinier man, looking up.

That's me, he thinks. But what am I looking up at?

With Bea gone, he cannot know, will possibly never know. And maybe that's okay. He can have his life with Eva in their squeaky-clean house. He can buy deodorant at the CVS with coupons he gets in the mail. They can raise their child with two sane grandparents from a poverty-stricken Sicilian town, good people who know the value of reality. He can drive his Subaru to his job and spend the day keeping other car owners safe. In the evenings he can sit at this table and work on his model, and it can be just that: a model. Before bedtime, he will quaff a couple American beers—Budweiser or Miller Genuine Draft—and watch *Law & Order: SVU* and then go to bed. He will try his best to snore through the night, keeping at bay all dreams of faceless men in the desert.

As he picks up a piece of balsa wood and a tube of glue, Paul cannot help wondering how long his mother will travel. If she will return someday to claim him, once again, for her own.

Paul is worried. His daughter Kay has stopped coming home on time. She is eleven, the year 2017, the school semester recently begun. When Eva asks her where she's been, she says with friends. When Paul asks her, the same. But she is never smiling when she finally walks through the door; her face is clouded, her eyes downcast. Hers is not the face of a girl who has spent the afternoon at the mall or watching Netflix in a class-mate's basement. She reminds Paul of his preteen self: furtive, abashed, exuding a miasma of solitude. He wonders whether she is being bullied.

One autumn night, he tries asking her. When Kay opens the back door to the kitchen, Paul is waiting. "Have other kids—" he begins.

"No," she says. "They haven't."

Since Kay began speaking, she's been able to finish his sentences. Paul merely has to begin a thought before she rounds it out with words. But this is a sentence he needs to complete.

He tries again. "When I was a boy—"

"You were tortured mercilessly. I know. Everybody was." She pushes long strands of hair impatiently behind her ears. Much to his chagrin, she dyed her glorious red tresses black two weeks ago, on his forty-second birthday. "And you were short. So, it was worse."

He raises himself to his full height. He is convinced he has grown an inch since he hit forty, but under his daughter's withering gaze, this certainty wavers.

"I survived," he says.

"So will I."

Kay takes a soda from the fridge—a Diet Coke, Eva's choice—pops the top, and drinks, her eyes glued to her cell phone. Then she leaves the kitchen. Paul can hear her upstairs in her room. She is pacing, a preoccupation since childhood. The floorboards under the carpet emit their familiar creak. Maybe she is talking too. He cannot be sure.

Paul does not know what his daughter is thinking. This pains him deeply. When she was smaller, she used to help him work on his model wooden city in the basement. She would sit on his lap, her head's crown wafting Johnson's shampoo and applesauce, a singe to it as though her fiery hair possessed the ability to burn. Often, when Eva summoned them upstairs for supper, they would not hear her.

When Kay grew bigger, Paul hauled in a chair from a sidewalk sale one block over. Kay would perch in this chair and glue sticks of wood and prattle words, acquisitions gleaned from dictionaries and television and books like *The House on Mango Street* and *Anne of Green Gables*. *Prolix. Spartan. Scope.*

Eva signed her up for early SATs the previous spring, but she vanished when it came time to go, returned later the same day with AirPods stuck in her ears. Eva was too furious to speak, so she sent Paul to talk to her. When he asked Kay where she got the money for them, she said she found it. The next day he checked her room, hoping for clues to her behavior, and noticed an entire row of books missing from her shelf. Gone were the Brontës and Adichie and Cisneros. Gone her set of Gary Soto's titles, read at the tender age of seven. Gone the Magic Tree House, *A Wrinkle in Time*, her stack of Little House books, literature on which she had cut her teeth as other children did on plastic rings. She seemed to be shedding language. Recently he'd noticed a change in her vocabulary. No more *simulacrum*. No more *jejune*. Only *yes. Maybe. No. Huh. I don't know.*

The same month she stopped visiting the basement. Without her presence, Paul stopped too. A year has passed since he's worked on his tiny metropolis. In the house's bowels it waits—a mélange of turrets and bridges and archways, structures lifted high above the tabletop—covered in dust.

Paul takes a canned protein shake for himself and brings it to the living room, where he plumps down on the couch and sips it, thinking of growth. Kay is nearing her mother's height, a respectable five feet six inches. On family outings—to restaurants, miniature golf, water parks—people eye them strangely. Once, on a trip to Disney World, a ticket seller asked Eva if she wanted two children's fares for a roller coaster.

"I'm a full-grown man," Paul shouted, gesturing to his spreading crow's-feet.

The vendor apologized, but didn't seem to care.

Paul turns on the TV. The news brings no relief: drought in California, 8.2 earthquake in Mexico, a smog alert in Beijing so extreme the Chinese government is urging citizens to say inside. Texas and Florida are still reeling from Hurricanes Harvey and Irma, entire islands in the Caribbean obliterated. Another storm is swirling toward Puerto Rico. The ice caps, as usual, are melting. The regular litany of horrors. Nature wreaking havoc across the globe. Inept governments pushing weakly against it.

Paul remembers his alarm when the hurricane flooded New Orleans. The grief he felt then now seems obsolete and useless. He has donated funds to Houston and the island of Barbuda but has done so mechanically, a click on a screen. Such efforts are Band-Aids, not surgery, not a cure. If a city like his model one could exist, there could be hope, but he knows that's a fantasy. He takes another sip of protein shake. The back door opens. Eva is home from yoga.

She appears in the doorway. At forty-five, Eva is more beautiful than ever. Gray streaks her black hair, lending her a striking look. She wears no makeup, and her olive skin is burnished and glowing. Her body in its navy Lululemon pants is taut, her arms and calves sculpted with muscle. She has not written art reviews in years, but she carries herself as though she is her own piece of art, waiting to be admired.

Her yoga and lunch-date and shopping friends often remark on her beauty. They are envious. Looking at her, Paul glows with pride. He remembers the days after Hurricane Katrina, after Eva met his mother, when her belly was swelling with Kay. Her tender concern for him. Her need for his body's safety. He wants to pull her close, bury himself in her loveliness.

"Is Kay home yet?" Eva asks. She picks up an apple and crunches into it with her perfect teeth.

"She's upstairs," Paul replies. "I'm worried about her." He sits up straighter. He doesn't know why he chose belted gray trousers for today. They make him look distinctly middle-aged.

Eva takes another bite, chews, swallows. "So am I," she says.

"I tried talking to her." He lifts his hands and then drops them. A gesture of futility. "She'll be a teenager soon. People warned us."

"She's like a teenager now," Eva says. "Have you noticed? She's so precocious, so self-contained." Her eyes twinkle at Paul. "We have raised an adult, not a child."

"Indeed," he says, thinking of how quickly Kay learned to read. "An adult who keeps everything to herself."

Eva finishes her apple and wraps the core neatly in a napkin. She disappears into the kitchen. Paul hears the trash can open and close. She reappears.

"I've made a doctor's appointment for her," she says. "This Saturday at three."

"She already went to the doctor for her school physical."

"This is with a psychiatrist."

Paul thinks immediately of James, the one psychiatrist he's known. James professed to have his mother's best interests at heart, but years ago, in the flower shop, he'd admitted to Paul that he'd failed her. That maybe he was the reason Bea hid under the bed and emitted her animal sounds. Paul's stomach grows cold.

He does not know what has happened to his mother. Since she vanished, he has heard nothing from her. He tries to believe that she is alive, she has found her destination. His anger at her disappearance has not abated. At times he feels it will choke him.

"Why a psychiatrist?" he asks his wife. "You think Kay needs one?"

"With her family history, why wouldn't I?"

"Your parents are fine." He can hear his own doubt. He clears his throat. "So are we."

"Paul." Eva's face softens. She moves toward the couch, sinks down beside him. "I know you miss your mother."

Do I? he thinks, but does not say.

In the years since his mother disappeared, they have spoken of her carefully, only in the dark, when Paul has woken from his nightmares. I'm afraid she'll come back, he told Eva once. So am I, his wife admitted.

Now Eva takes both of his hands. Her own are supple with antiaging creams, each nail filed and lacquered. His hands look like a child's in hers.

"Our daughter is special." She presses his fingers. With this he cannot argue. "The way she speaks. Her abilities with language. She read *The Wizard of Oz* before she hit first grade. And now look at her. She seems so much older than eleven. Think of who she might become when she's twenty."

Eva leans forward and kisses him. Her face is close, her breath light with spearmint. Then it recedes. "I would hate to see your mother's genes take over."

But Bea. A half-formed thought. The Bea that is he. These are not his thoughts. The Bea that will be she.

He pulls his hands from hers and stands up. "Our daughter will be fine," he says.

"Yes." Eva stands too. Her gaze is a steady beam. "She will."

On the TV, the news has changed. No more natural disasters. Another shooting on the Paseo. Paul reaches for the remote and turns it off.

"I'll make dinner tonight," he says. This is not usual. Eva is the one who roasts the chickens, browns the casseroles. So easily, he realizes, they have fallen into their roles. For all his talk of a different society, how thoroughly he has slotted himself into this one.

THE DAY OF HER APPOINTMENT, Kay is waiting by the car when Paul emerges, pulling on his windbreaker. She's yanked her hair into a ponytail, and her face's pale angles gleam in the autumn sun. More and more she resembles his mother, but with a difference, something he cannot put his finger on. He has thought perhaps because she is taller or because her skin is white. But today he sees it. Her eyes. That's what is different. His mother's eyes were a child's. Kay's belong to a woman grown.

"You don't have to tell the doctor anything," Paul says as they climb into the car.

Eva is locking the house, her back turned.

"Whatever," says Kay. She's staring at her cell phone again, but seems to be scrolling, not texting. He would feel so much better if she were using it for communication. He doesn't want to think she's as lonely as he was.

Paul and Eva have dressed in suits for the occasion, but Kay's wearing jeans and a black hoodie, her feet in Converse. With a pang, Paul remembers the Converse his high school classmates wore. His own shoes were knockoffs and no-names, whatever the institution or foster parents granted him. In class, he used to hide his feet under his desk.

"I don't mean to belabor the point." He maneuvers in the driver's seat to look at her behind him. She has put her cell phone away and is studying the driveway, the trees, the perfectly clipped lawn browned by September. *Belabor.* A word two years ago she would have loved. "But you can keep some things to yourself."

"You don't trust doctors." Kay's breath mists the window. She does not turn.

"No." He thinks of James, the precise way he snipped stems from dahlias. No. He doesn't trust doctors.

"But I can." Kay breathes on the window and draws a star in the condensation. "I don't have to be like you."

The car door unlatches, and Eva slides in. "Let's go," she says to Paul. "We don't want to be late."

ON THE WAY HOME, Kay seems less tense. She has unstrung her hair from its ponytail, and it falls loosely around her face. She does not stare out the window. She talks to her mother about school. Paul learns she's recently joined the soccer team, something he wouldn't have predicted. She's getting Bs instead of her usual As, but *no big,* she says, and he wants to believe her. In her hand, a carefully folded prescription. They are on their way to the drugstore to fill it.

"Depression," the psychiatrist told them during their consultation. He had already seen Kay, talked with her behind a closed door for their allotted hour. "Some anxiety. A touch of insomnia. Normal in kids her age. I've prescribed a mild dose of Wellbutrin. She'll be fine."

At the mention of Wellbutrin, Eva nodded with approval.

Paul's head grew light with fear. He didn't want to give her medication, but Eva was right. Kay needed help. And this could work. His daughter had seemed almost cheerful when she'd emerged from the psychiatrist's office.

"Any symptoms of schizophrenia?" Paul asked the doctor. He felt Eva tense beside him. He thought of his mother, how she'd drunk water from a glass like a dog. He didn't know if she was schizophrenic, if one could classify her, but this was the single word he owned to describe it.

At this question, the psychiatrist shook his head. "No. I wouldn't say that." He glanced at his notes. "I see." Eva had filled out the forms, written *schizophrenia, grandmother* in the family history section. "We will set up regular appointments, monitor her. But at this stage . . ." Again, a shake of his head. "She is an average eleven-year-old girl in the twenty-first century. Anxiety is quite common in those her age."

"Is her anxiety related to school?" Paul asked. "I've been worried about bullying."

"Bullying?" The psychiatrist raised his eyebrows. "She said nothing about that. No." A slight smile curled his mouth. "It seems she is worried about the future. So many of her peers are. Climate change. What, in our day, they called global warming. It seems your daughter is afraid the world will end."

Eva laughed at that, waved it away. "The medication will help?" she asked.

"It should," the psychiatrist assured her. "In the meantime, try to distract her. Encourage a new hobby. Keep her mind off the future."

Paul nodded along with Eva, but now, piloting his family back to Brookside, Paul also feels it. Fear of the future. He recalls the tornado of his youth, tapping its casual finger to the ground. The submerged streets of New Orleans. The earth fissuring in Mexico. His daughter is stepping out into this world. His hands shake on the steering wheel, and the car lurches left.

"Paul," Eva cries.

He yanks the wheel right, stabilizes the car.

"Don't kill us," Kay says from the back. "I want to see if these happy pills work first."

THAT NIGHT PAUL DREAMS of the desert again. The plain is sand, dotted with small cacti clinging close to the soil. It is night and the stars are isolated red fires. Behind him, the sand crunches. Paul knows he'll see a man in boots, walking toward him. A coyote yips, followed by another, and another. Paul turns, but there is no man. And no coyotes are making that sound. It is his mother, and she is walking toward him, and she is smiling her blackened grin.

He wakes without screaming, too scared to move. Eva is warm beside him, laden with her rosy musk and the tang of the cleaning agents to which she still subscribes. When his breathing slows, he stretches one leg, then the other. Slowly, not waking his wife, he crawls from bed. He will go to the basement, he thinks, he will work on his model. He has missed the quiet solace of gluing together pieces of wood, of erecting what he has envisioned in his head.

When he reaches the basement steps, he pauses. The light is already on. Someone is down there. He can hear a body moving through the space.

"Hey," he calls down the steps.

"It's me," replies his daughter. "Don't be mad."

He pads down a few steps before he sees it. His city, his entire intricate metropolis on which he has spent years, is gone. It has been destroyed. Smashed to bits. The table upended. Kay is standing to one side, breathing heavily, her hands and forearms spotted with blood from where the wood must have scratched her.

"I had a bad dream," she says.

Paul sinks down onto the bottom step. "So did I."

"I'm tired of this dream. I'm tired of how it makes me feel." Her eyes are black in the dim light. Her mouth the fist of old age. Her slim self looms tall in the short room.

He surveys the wreckage, trying to feel anger. But he can't. What he feels is relief.

"Please don't be mad," she says again.

Her hair and eyes are shadows against her white skin. They are both wearing pajamas from the Gap, hers with flowers, his plaid, both Eva's choices. Paul thinks how absurd their conventional garb is against such a stage.

"I thought you were being bullied at school," he says. "Sometimes—"

"That happens," she finishes. "No. The kids at school are fine. I'm just tired."

Paul remembers what the doctor told him. Kay is not afraid of other people. She is afraid of the end of the world. He wants to ask her about this but doesn't know how.

"Maybe the medication will help?" he offers instead.

"I hope it kills these fucking dreams," she says.

Her words hover between them. What did you dream about? Paul wants to ask. Was it the desert or something else? He sees the man in the night, hears his boots. He thinks of the hurricane bearing down on Puerto Rico, imagines the citizens steeling themselves against it. When he first began his city, he thought it could become reality, that humans could really live that way. Even when he told himself it was just a model—a fantasy—it was in the back of his mind, that someday he would build it for real. But Kay is right. It's time to kill that fucking dream.

"I'm sorry." Kay's tone softens. "I don't want to see that man in the desert anymore."

She shares my dreams, Paul thinks with a start. At first this affinity comforts him, but then he shivers. How irresponsible he's been to make this child, this girl doomed to the same nightmares that have plagued him, that plagued his mother.

"I don't want to dream of this city anymore either. I don't want to be your hope for the future." Kay's lip trembles. Paul thinks she will cry, but she doesn't. "I don't want to be anything."

If this were a film, he thinks, his daughter would take this moment to sweep past him up the stairs and slam her bedroom door. They wouldn't speak for days. Then she'd pack a bag and run away.

But this doesn't happen. Kay stays with him in the basement and helps him clean up her mess. Paul fetches a Glad trash bag, the same kind he uses to collect autumn leaves. Together they sweep up the wreckage: the mangled turrets, the splinters, the frail rope bridges twined out of yarn. They ball up his ancient blueprints and gather the graphite pencils with their points ground down. Kay rights the table, wipes it down with paper towels and her mother's Lysol. He switches off the light before they climb the stairs.

Outside, they startle an animal on their way to dump the trash bag.

Something dark and humped. He cannot see what it is. As it skitters away into the bushes, it cries out, and he pictures his mother as she appeared in his dream. Go away, he tells her memory. Leave me alone.

EVA GRIEVES FOR HIS broken city.

"It was so beautiful," she says, her expression forlorn. Morning has come and she is standing in the basement, surveying the barren space.

"It's all right," Paul says.

"You were happy working here." Eva leans into him, her hair brushing his head. "My little man." Her old pet name for him, furred with love. "What will you do now when the nightmares come?"

He is grateful for Eva. When they married, she said she loved him because he was ordinary and safe. Then she met his mother, about whom nothing was ordinary. How that must have frightened her. Paul sees it clearly. With her manic cleaning and rigid schedules, Eva has been attempting to order the chaos that threatens him. Yes, he thinks. Keep me here. Keep me safe.

"I'm a grown man," Paul says. He remembers the ticket vendor at Disney World, the kids laughing in gym class as he aimed a ball at a hoop, the bus drivers nervously watching him navigate the high first step, each person who has noticed his height before noticing him. "I'll survive."

They trudge upstairs to the living room. Eva sits on the couch. "She needs a punishment."

Kay is upstairs sleeping. She does not know yet that her mother knows what she did.

"Does she?" He pictures his tall daughter in the squat basement, the desperation in her eyes when she talked of her dreams. Again, he feels the rush of relief when he saw what she'd done.

"She destroyed your art." Eva crosses her legs, begins swinging her foot. "If that had happened to any of the artists I used to review, there'd be punishment. Litigation."

"I don't think we need to sue her." Paul laughs, but it lacks luster.

"We can restrict her reading. For a week."

"She doesn't read anymore."

Eva's shoulders droop. "I know."

"She doesn't do anything anymore. Except join the soccer team."

"We could prohibit that."

Above their heads a floorboard creaks. Kay is awake and walking. Paul eyes the ceiling, thinking of his daughter up there, pacing. He hopes her sleep was black and dreamless. Eva's gaze follows his. Together they listen to their daughter map out her boundaries with her feet.

"Maybe," Eva says, "your sadness will be punishment enough." She pats the cushion beside her. "Come sit."

He sits, and she takes his head, bends it toward her, holds him close to her body's richness. "Don't you think it's time," she says, "to give up your job?"

"Why would I?" he mumbles into her shoulder.

"Because you hate it."

"Do I?" Paul asks, but he knows she's right. Building his dream city kept it at bay, but that city is gone.

"You want to build things. You're good at it. That model you made was incredible."

He pictures the office at the insurance company: cramped cubicles, men in shirts, the clock's dull thud marking time. He sees his wrecked model, with its ridiculous bridges toppled. If he built it again, he would make it different. Sturdier. More sensible. "You're right. I do want to build things."

"You could apply to graduate school. I could go back to work. Kay's old enough now."

Paul pulls away from his wife. Her expression is earnest, her hands clutching his.

"Don't look at me like that," she says. "You want to. Don't question it. Besides, I miss working. I miss art."

"I didn't know."

She laughs, tipping her head back to display her golden throat. "Neither did I. But I do." Her face darkens. "This life is shit, Paul. The least we can do is create some measure of beauty."

The creaking over their heads stops. A door opens. Footsteps on stairs. Kay enters the living room. Her hair is red again. She's dyed it back to its true color. Its fire lights the room.

"Can I get your Amazon password?" she asks. "There's a book I want."

THEY PUNISH KAY by restricting her access to their Amazon account, but it doesn't matter. She goes to the public library and gets the book anyway. *The Dream of a Common Language* by Adrienne Rich. Paul sneaks a look at the first page, where the line breaks surprise him. Before this, she has read chapter books, novels, comics. Poetry is new.

"Why this genre?" he asks her one morning before school.

"It keeps the dreams away," she says, but says no more.

In the evenings Paul can hear her upstairs, pacing. She reads while she walks. He has seen her as he's passed her room on the way to the bathroom. She paces and reads and mutters the words to herself. As they cook dinner together, Eva and Paul listen to the floorboards and smile at each other.

"She's going to be okay," Eva says. She has recently begun baking bread, and the newest loaf is nearly ready. When she cracks the oven door to check, its fragrance permeates the kitchen.

Paul uses a wooden spoon to taste the potato leek soup they are making. "Has she been taking the Wellbutrin?" he asks.

Eva's face brightens. "She has. I think it's working."

"I don't love her taking medication."

"It's 2017. You can't make it without a little help." The lines on Eva's face have softened. She hums as she helps him stir the soup, as she checks every so often on her bread.

She is relieved, Paul sees, that they've steered their daughter clear of his mother's fate. Maybe, Paul thinks, he is relieved too.

The weeks that follow his model city's obliteration are, despite everything, happy. Kay finishes the Rich book, takes out another: *Diving into the Wreck*. Then another. As September rolls into October and the leaves on their quiet street quietly flame, she moves on to other poets. Sharon Olds. Sylvia Plath. Yusef Komunyakaa. Pablo Neruda. Tagore. As wildfires scorch northern California, she reads poems by Martín Espada and Tracy K. Smith, and though their words save no one in Sonoma, Paul believes they might be saving his daughter. He does not know these poets, but as his daughter speeds through their books and her face relaxes more each day, he is moved to action.

He takes Eva's advice. He applies to graduate programs in architecture. He has no credentials beyond his undergraduate degree and years of service at the auto insurance company. His chances are slim. Nonetheless, he fills out each application in his painstaking print, types the essays with Kay's help, tracks down former professors for recommendations, submits payment for the application fees. He will receive responses in the spring. Until then, he must wait.

He does not quit his job. Eva has reached out to her former colleagues in the art world, has begun writing a review here, another there.

But it's not enough to live on. They still need his paycheck. Each morning he wakes at seven, pulls on his muted clothes with their plain buttons, and drives his new beige Subaru—the same as the old one—to his office.

The weeks roll forward. Electricity returns to isolated spots in storm-ravaged Puerto Rico. Fires sweep through California once more, blackening the southern hills. After the fires, mudslides. Houses and people are buried voiceless under earth. And yet their own home in Kansas City remains standing. Over beef Wellington one night, Kay calmly takes out a book and, without preamble, reads a Gwendolyn Brooks poem. It's long, but her voice hitches on a single line about the tantrums that lurk inside adults. At these words, grief rises in Paul like a flood. He has not dreamed of the desert since the night he found Kay in the basement, his imagination in splinters at her feet. He wants to believe he's left such visions behind.

LIFE APPEARS NORMAL. Then, less than a week before Christmas, the tips of each continent flood. Okinawa. Hong Kong. The southern shore of Bangladesh. Singapore. One beach in Madagascar. The Cape of Good Hope. The Orkneys. Sicily. Gibraltar. Tierra del Fuego. The Galapagos Islands. On North America's West Coast, the California coastline and Vancouver. In the east, Campobello Island in Canada. The Outer Banks of North Carolina. At Long Island's fingertip, Montauk. Strangely, not Florida.

Paul hears it on the news, driving to work. The day is Wednesday, the date December 20. For years scientists have sent warnings. Global warming, Kay's psychiatrist called it. Climate change. But these floods are not extreme. The sea level has risen a couple of feet, no more. No buildings are submerged. No deaths. Flood, asserts one newscaster, seems too dramatic a term. The others argue. They predict high waves, dangerous tides, society's end. The poles, they insist, have melted. No, the newscaster continues, a little extra water does not spell apocalypse. Remember Hurricane Katrina, he says. Remember the 2004 tsunami? Fukushima? Harvey and Irma and Maria? We survived those. We'll survive again.

Yes, Paul assures himself. We'll be fine. He thinks of Eva, waving away the diagnosis of Kay's anxiety. The end of the world? He turns off the news. Ridiculous.

But when he gets to work, a package is waiting on his desk. No return address. His heart begins thudding. He slits the tape, the box, unravels the tissue paper. Inside is a painting. One of his mother's. It's almost identical to one she left behind in the apartment she shared with James before she disappeared. It's not the woman with the enormous baby. It's small and swirled with blue, as though the painting itself has flooded. In the bottom left corner, a tiny man staring up.

Paul's first thought is She's still alive. Close behind that, another. No, he thinks. I won't let the water catch me. He pictures Kay, starting awake from another nightmare. I won't let it catch my daughter.

Without telling anyone, Paul leaves the office with the painting under his arm. His earlier complacence has evaporated. He was lying to himself when he heard the news. He knows his mother's painting tells the truth. The floods will get worse, if not now, then soon. He has to escape. He has to leave the city. Kansas City is nowhere near a coast, but he's not thinking rationally. He climbs into his Subaru and screeches it out of the parking lot. He has to get his family.

He speeds down a few blocks before pulling the car into a Shell station. He needs to fill up the tank. He wishes he had jugs to get more fuel. He walks into the convenience store and buys their entire supply of water. Poland Spring, Dasani, Aquafina. The acned teen behind the counter eyes his miscellaneous collection—twelve ounces and liters and gallons, sports caps and screw tops—suspiciously.

"A storm is coming," he says. How stupid he's been to think he could escape it. Wind and water, the paint swirled blue on blue. His mother knew. She's always known. He remembers what James said. Sometimes I think she knows everything.

The cashier gapes at him as she rings up bottle after bottle. He shuttles them by the armload to his trunk. On his last trip, she points at the tinny TV above her head.

"Weather forecast is clear," she says.

"Everything will change," he says. The prophecy sounds as dumb as his comment about a storm, but in his gut, he knows its truth. The cashier shakes her head.

"Crazy as fuck," he hears her mutter as he jangles through the door.

The roads seem more congested than usual. His brain is blurring, filled with static. He needs to collect people, he thinks. Together they can flee. He checks his cell phone, but it's dead. He forgot to charge it. He can't call anyone. Eva's parents live in Grain Valley. It isn't far. He can drive there within the hour, bundle them into his car, zoom home. And then. And then. He doesn't know.

Follow the red star, his mother told him.

He peers through the windshield, but the sky is white with frost, the sun a pale disk behind a wisp of cloud. Dirty snow clumps on the lawns, rises in piles at intersections. Autumn has vanished and with it the color red. He'll get his in-laws, gather Kay from school, phone Eva. Convene them in his living room. As a family, they'll decide what to do.

He zips down side streets, tailgates slow drivers, drums his fingers on the wheel at stoplights. When he reaches the ramp to I-70, he speeds onto it with an audible sigh. He didn't realize he was holding his breath. He swerves from lane to lane, seeking the speediest path.

The sky is growing whiter. Perhaps it will snow. In other parts of the planet this could mean rain. Choked with glacial melt, the sea has no room for it. An overfilled bowl, Paul thinks, remembering a distant science experiment in school.

Kansas City will be fine, he tries telling himself.

He is safely through the city and onto the open highway when it happens. A slight miscalculation, perhaps his, perhaps the towering Freihofer's truck's, veering on his right. Their noses touch, part, touch again. Something jars him from behind. A silver wall rises before him, glass and chrome. A flicker of human faces. The bleached sky overhead.

His body loosens, his big feet on their stunted legs floating free from the pedals. His arms extend, his fingers splaying like stars. For an instant, the universe expands, a glittering field of possibility. He has never felt so tall.

I am a giant, he thinks.

Then he is falling. He mourns his descent with howls, and they are not human, and even as his body meets earth, he sees his mother crouched under the bed, hears her cries, and he is soothed. He crumples into asphalt and glass and another's body, and the pain is unreal.

This is where darkness comes, he thinks. But he does not black out.

Somewhere metal is screeching against metal. The reek of spilled fuel. Smoke in his nostrils, though he sees no fire. He has fallen against a body from another car. It seems sucked dry of blood, the face turned mercifully away. He can feel each part of himself: scraped arms, forehead sliced by the windshield, his fingertips sensitive and singing. His cock curled in his beige trousers, oddly hardening. Pain. He cannot, however, feel his legs.

The metal stops screeching. He smells fresh water. A puddle laps his cheek. The bottles in his trunk have burst. A low whine, then a shriek. Sirens. White sneakers wade through the wreckage toward him. He can see their thick soles, their laces, the scrim of athletic sock between shoe and pant leg.

"Bring a tourniquet," the voice above shouts. "Bring two."

A face levels with his. It is brown and gentle as his mother's on her good days.

"You're awake," the face says, and Paul blinks in response. The face turns. "Bring a tranquilizer too," it shouts.

"I'm fine," Paul manages to say. He sounds small, and he is back in the Burnsides' trailer, watching the tornado finger the alfalfa field. "You don't need to worry about me." He struggles to sit up, but a hand presses him down. "I can walk home."

"We'll get you fixed up," the face says. "Don't exert yourself."

Another set of shoes appears, and something cold slides into his arm.

"The stars are out," Paul tells the two faces. "But only one is red."

ONE MOMENT HE IS LYING on the highway. The next he's in bed. Between each moment, no dreams. He opens his eyes, closes them, opens them. Neither the ceiling nor the heavy coverlet is his. He smells hand sanitizer and leaky bowels. Urine. Applesauce. This last recalls Kay, the scent of her toddler head. She is not here. Eva is not here.

This is hell, he thinks, but then a nurse walks in.

"How nice to see you awake," she says. She checks his heart, his blood pressure, presses switches on the machine by his bed. Flicks the IV bag with a painted nail. Tubes sprout from his body, some with clear liquid, some with red, yellow. He cannot lift his head, then he can. The mattress below his waist looks flat.

"The doctor is with a patient in the next room," the nurse says. She is white, her accent Canadian. From the north. Perhaps she knows his mother. "Let me get him."

Paul wants to protest—I need no doctor—but she is gone, the curtain swaying behind her. Someone has taped a Santa above his bed. Part of Santa's beard has peeled off, and his bag of toys looks faded. Paul remembers it was December, but he has no idea whether Christmas has come and gone. He doesn't know why he's worrying about Christmas.

Metal screeches and he winces, but it is only the doctor, pushing back the curtain on its steel rings. His skin is dark brown, his hair carefully oiled and parted. Paul thinks he could be from South Asia, India, or Bangladesh. He wonders whether this man's homeland has flooded.

The doctor runs through his pleasantries. Then he places his hand on the mattress where Paul's legs should be. "The EMTs were efficient," he says. "They kept you from bleeding out. We hoped to reattach them, but I'm afraid they were badly damaged in the accident."

The doctor takes off his glasses to polish them, and in his stunned state, Paul wonders whether he learned this from a movie. He wishes he had glasses of his own to fiddle with. All he has are these tubes. He runs a finger along his IV. Where the needle enters his arm a bruise has blossomed, faded purple with a green tinge. He does not want to ask how long he has been here. He wants to know where his legs are, but he doesn't want to ask this either.

"How many cars?" he manages.

The doctor looks up, slides his glasses back on. "Five."

"Who lived?"

"Everybody."

Paul sees the body he landed on, leached of blood. Somehow it got up. It walked away.

"Have my wife and daughter been here?" he asks.

"Each day since you arrived." The doctor—Ahmed says his tag— smiles, but then seems to decide against it and coughs into one hand.

Paul realizes the doctor is nervous. He doesn't know how Paul will react. Any moment he could start screaming, demanding his legs.

"Where are they now?"

"In the cafeteria, taking a break. The nurse urged them to."

"Can someone get them?" Paul asks. His heart leaps at the thought.

"I'll tell the desk to page the cafeteria." Dr. Ahmed stands to go. "Many people have lived without their limbs. The field of prosthetics has taken a tremendous leap." His mouth twitches. "Do forgive my pun."

Paul glances away from the doctor and sees it. The painting. The tiny blue one his mother sent him at work. Someone has propped it on the bedside table. He assumed it got crushed in the accident, but here it is. He peers closer. Beneath the blue is something black. He didn't notice it before. Very faintly, under all that blue paint is a black outline. A silhouette. It's his model, his fantastical metropolis, the one he thought Kay had destroyed forever. His mother knew about his model. Of course she did. She has painted it. A city floating in water.

"How do I work the remote?" Paul asks. "I want to see the news."

"The news?" Dr. Ahmed's face ripples, as though a tremor has passed through it. "I don't think that's a good idea."

"I know." And he does. He picks up the remote attached to his bed. "Do I press this button here?"

A simple push does it. The screen flickers to life. With another polite cough the doctor leaves, pulling the curtain behind him. Paul knows what he'll see before he sees it. The bottom of the TV screen tells him it is December 24, but nobody is talking about Christmas. They are talking about the weather.

A hurricane. Two. Three. Four. Bigger storms than any seen before. More violent. In the days Paul has slept, Earth's shape has shifted. New York is the most obvious. Chennai in South India. The Maldives. New Orleans. Nobody is calling it a loss. It must seem too immense, too sudden.

The newscasters offer no more predictions of doom. They don't want to say it. The experts are asserting survival. We can make it through this, they say. The governments are sending supplies. Food. Bandages. Boats. The tides will relent. The cities will be salvaged. Civilization will stagger on.

In his rumpled hospital bed in the center of North America, Paul struggles with his new body until he can sit up. The space his legs used to inhabit feels huge, but he feels no shorter. Quite the opposite.

He is a giant. His mother was right.

He pictures her, too young—yes, Eva spoke truly, she was too young—bearing his body to its denouement. How it must have split her when he entered this life. How she survived that, he does not know. But she did. With sudden and bounding strength, he realizes he can survive his transformation too.

Down the hall he can hear his wife and daughter, murmuring their anxiety. His wife, who has always supported him. His daughter, who will be a poet. No more can she flee her dreams. No more can he. He is nothing if not his dreams. He knows that now.

"Do you think he'll know us?" he can hear them whispering. "What will we say?" Each sound is magnified: the instruments pinging, the nurses' shoes squeaking, a patient retching his lunch into a pail.

On the TV, a reporter is interviewing a refugee in Baton Rouge. "Everything's gone," the refugee says. Mascara streaks her face, and her eyes are those of a ghost. "New Orleans has drowned. It's not like Katrina. This is for good." The reporter turns toward the screen, chirps something about drainage.

Paul clicks the TV off. He has seen enough. He thinks of his model city, the water he imagined beneath it. The stilts, the bridges, the tenacity of its citizens. It was a fantasy, but no more. Now, it will be real.

Yes, he thinks. It is time.

MOON

MARS, 2073

Time had spiraled inward. Days had passed. Or only hours. I didn't know how long I had been sitting with the screen, studying its images. I kept clicking from one to the next, my heart alternately speeding up with excitement and slowing down with dread. I wondered when the Uncles would call me for our mealtime potato, how I would stomach it. Maybe they wouldn't summon me. Maybe they had given up on me. She won't do it, they were telling each other. We should never have asked.

I didn't know if I *would* do it. Become a mother. Generate more Uncles and Moons. Part of me wanted to. The images of female humans—women, I corrected myself—had shown me what it looked like. The seed in the body, perceptibly swelling. How it would sprout ears and nose and fingers. How eventually it would emerge, unfurl like a plant, continue growing. That seemed magical. Magnificent, as Uncle Two had promised our civilization would be.

But then what? I didn't know. Would I water it, as the irrigation system watered the forest? Would I feed it dust or potatoes? Would it talk to me? If I talked to it, would it listen? I placed my palms on my belly, imagining it swollen, ready to burst. Except I wouldn't pop open. The images had taught me that. The Uncles and Moons would slide out between my legs. But no, I thought. That's not possible.

I circled back to the first image Uncle Two had shown me. Begin again, I told myself. Study each step. You have to know what you're getting into.

WHEN I FINALLY STEPPED OUT of my pod, my eyes were squinty and raw. The harsh light in the tunnel blinded me. I had to creep along the walls to keep my balance.

By the time I reached the eating pod, my sight had cleared. Uncle One and Uncle Two were seated at the table, leaning toward each other in intense communication. They moved apart when I entered. Their skin seemed gray and flaky, and their heads heavy on their necks. I wondered if they had been sitting at the table the whole time.

Moon, said Uncle Two. We have missed you.

How many days have passed? I asked.

Three, said Uncle One. His tone twanged with impatience.

He is tired of waiting, I thought.

Have you found your answers? Uncle Two asked.

Some, I replied. But tell me. I pointed at my midsection. How does the Moon get in here?

This child. Uncle One rolled his eyes to the ceiling. You said she'd learn everything, he said to Uncle Two. Yet here she comes with her ceaseless questions. Listen. I take this thing out. He pointed at the pouch between his legs. And eject the seed. It's simple.

I eyed him warily, unsure what he meant.

Brother. Uncle Two touched Uncle One's arm. You are frightening her.

Uncle One's tone softened. Don't worry, he told me. They have equipment here for insemination. It'll be painless. I won't even have to touch you.

Do you need more time to think? Uncle Two asked me.

We have no time, Uncle One said. You know that.

But we do, I protested. I haven't completed my fourteenth year. The women in the images look older than I do.

They are human, Uncle One said. They are different. We don't know how long we— He stopped. Moon. Think about us. Think about this planet. In all our travels, did you see anybody else?

No, I said.

No, he confirmed. Uncle Two has told you about Earth?

Many things used to live here, I repeated. Now it holds only water.

Precisely. Uncle One picked up my hand and pressed it to the translucent membrane in his chest. I felt the steady thump of his heart. We are all that remains, he said gently. We must try to make more of us.

But why? I asked. Why go to such effort to continue this?

As though to amplify the nothingness between them, Uncle One spread his hands wide. What else is there? he asked in return.

I looked directly at him, staring into the white depths of his eyes. I saw the three of us on the empty plain we had crossed in my sixth year. It stretched ocher and unending to all horizons, our thin atmosphere an insufficient dome above, and beyond that the stars: frigid, indifferent, long dead. I recalled how I had banged on the screen, yelled at it, begged it to speak to me.

I swallowed my doubts. I nodded.

Okay, I said. We can try.

BEFORE TODDLING OFF TO SLEEP, Uncle Two embraced me, but did not look at me.

I am fortunate, he said. To have you.

What will it be like—I wondered, watching him shuffle toward his pod—to have a Moon of my own?

I retreated to my own pod and curled up on the floor with the screen, its light the only illumination. I could hear Uncle One pacing away down the tunnel. His excitement felt physical, a low hum in the air.

I began clicking, flipping through images of human women and cartoon rabbits and rhododendron and pine trees and the eating pod, our sleeping pods, one tunnel after another. I had found some answers. The Uncles had given me more. Yet I was missing a piece. I did not know the Moon who had made me. I did not know my mother.

I swiped all the images off the screen, clearing it until it glowed blank and white. "Please," I said to the blankness. I knew it would do no good. I was tired of asking. But I couldn't stop. Even if I found only the simulated voice Uncle Two had mentioned, it might tell me something. Who made me? I would ask it. And where did she go?

"Please," I repeated. "Talk to me."

To my utter shock, the screen pulsed, as it had before.

"I'm talking," said the voice. "I've been talking. Why haven't you been listening?"

I sat straight up. Blood rushed to my face. My cheeks felt hot. My ears were ringing. I felt very far away and yet very close. I couldn't believe it had worked. The voice sounded louder and more alert, less melancholy than it had, but it was the same one. Caught off guard, I didn't remember the questions I'd had. Instead I said, "Tell me what you've been talking about."

"All kinds of things. You can say anything to a computer, right?"

What's a computer? I wanted to ask, but was afraid to interrupt.

"For a while, I was pretending you weren't some bot, but my mother, come back from the dead. I could finally tell you the things I wanted to."

I leaned closer, breath quickening. "What does one tell a mother?"

"Not a lot when they're alive." The voice lowered. "I wish I'd told her everything."

"What did you want to tell her?"

"I wanted to say I liked the wrinkles around her eyes. And how fifty-whatever is too young to die. How she could pester me to comb my hair. She could demand I eat my dandelion greens and I wouldn't care."

I knew what dandelions were. We had them in the dome. If the voice were a simulation, it might know that. But its cadences sounded too natural. Could it be real? That made no sense, not if Uncle One were right. Not if we were the only ones left.

"What else?" I prompted. I needed the voice to keep talking.

"I wanted to be a better daughter." Its tone turned flat. "A girl she could admire."

A girl. Uncle Two had said female humans could be girls. But this couldn't be a human. This was a simulation. It was the only explanation.

"You're a *she*," I said. Uncle Two had said the voices were usually female.

"Obviously," the voice said. *She*, I corrected myself. "I know you're not my mother," she said. "I'm not stupid. But I wish you were. I could tell you I'm sorry. That I left you to die alone. I was scared. I had to leave the tent. Please understand. I'm sorry it was cancer and not an animal that killed you. I know you wanted to die on a hunt, not in your bed like an old lady."

Sorrow threaded through the voice. I knew that emotion. I recalled emptiness tapping its fingers across my chest.

I was wrong, I thought. This can't be a simulation.

Maybe this was another Moon. What if she were here, on this planet? What if there were other Uncles too? Uncle One had said nobody else existed, but what did he know? If other Moons and Uncles lived here, I wouldn't have to do what I'd promised. In the morning I could confront Uncle One and say no.

I was pressing the screen so hard my fingers had begun to ache. I wanted to jump up and run around my pod, yelling at the top of my out-loud voice. But I remained still. I didn't want to lose the connection. "What's cancer?"

"A stupid disease I read about in my mom's medical book. If it even was cancer. We don't have doctors to tell for sure. But I knew it. I saw how stiff she was. She couldn't stand tall anymore. She kept complaining about her ribs. Except they didn't seem broken. I bet it had gotten into her bones."

I knew the voice's owner was sad, but I was happy. This girl—whatever she was—remembered her mother. *That* is what a mother is, I thought. Someone who does not truly vanish after they're gone. This girl was lucky. She knew where she had come from.

"Tell me more about your mother," I said.

"What's the point? She's dead and gone, my lady, dead and gone." Humor crept into her voice. "They stage plays here. They're *obsessed* with Shakespeare. My mom used to make fun of it. She said it was cliché. But I kind of like it. It breaks up the days. I know all of *Hamlet* by heart. Or whatever they pass as *Hamlet*. My mother said they've screwed up the words. Old Joe in Tent Number Five has a copy but he hoards it as though it's gold. Not that gold has value anymore."

I had so many questions. What's a tent? What's a Hamlet? What's gold? But I didn't want to overwhelm her. Instead, I settled for a broader question. "What does have value," I asked, "where you are?"

"The present, I suppose. The big today. What we will eat. How we will find it. What the weather will bring. Will we have blizzards in

August or droughts in December? That's what we care about. Do you know about weather?"

"I know about dust storms," I said. I didn't know what a blizzard was. Or a drought. We didn't have those. She can't be on this planet, I thought. Then where?

"Dust storms," she echoed. "We have them too."

"What else do you care about?" I felt as I did with Uncle Two, pleading for information.

"We care about our tents. The mountains. We like singing around the big fire."

"Fire?"

"Computers don't know about fire? It's red and orange, bluish green at the center? You throw sticks in it and it burns them up?"

I stored this away. I could ask Uncle Two about it later. "What else?"

"We like animals and plants," she continued. "We've named the children after plants. My name's Ivy, by the way. Of course, we value children, because we don't have many. Maybe you know that. I'm one of ten kids, and there are lots more adults than that, most pretty old. Like, over forty years. Makes it hard to have families. People get jealous. I think they resented me and Mom, for how we stayed together."

The owner of the voice had lightened her tone. Ivy. I tried to picture her, but all I could imagine was actual ivy, the tendrils we grew in the dome. "Family," I repeated, because that was familiar. "Do you value that?"

"Not really," she said. "Couples merge and fall apart. Fathers drift away. Sometimes mothers too. My mom stayed with me until she died. She said she was done traveling, that she had already journeyed too far."

"Fathers?" I prompted. "What are they?"

"Who cares?" A laugh rang through the screen. "I don't have one.

Or I did, but I don't know who he was. Mom wouldn't tell me. I used to think it was the man who had joined our tent."

"Who was that?" My entire body was straining toward the screen. I had never spoken so much before, not to the dunes, not to the sky, not to myself. More and more I felt I wasn't talking to another Moon, but to something else. A human? But that wasn't possible.

"You know what's funny?" she said. "I don't know who he was. He kept changing his name. He said names were tricks, another way the colonizers could pin you down. He yelled a lot about the railroads and how he'd built them. Or his grandfathers had built them. Or something."

I couldn't follow what she was saying. I felt dizzy trying to keep up.

"We all thought he was loony," she continued, "even my mother. But she liked him. They would stay up all night talking about the lost world. He was super old, so he knew what it was like before the floods."

"Floods?"

"Water, water everywhere, but not a drop to drink." She sounded as though she were smiling. "Sorry for all the quotes. We like poetry here. It's, like, our thing."

"I know about water." I wanted to contribute, even if I didn't know what poetry or railroads were. "You turn a handle and it comes out," I said, pleased with my knowledge.

"The Great Mother must have pulled a big-ass handle then, because from what my mom used to say, the Earth has *changed*."

I was so surprised I stood up. "You know about Earth?"

"Um, yeah?" Ivy sounded confused or mocking or both. "Don't you?"

"I know nobody lives there," I said. "Not anymore."

"What magic mushrooms have you been eating?" Ivy laughed. "I live here. *Everybody* lives here."

"You're making that up," I said. "You're telling stories."

But I knew she was telling the truth. The cartoons had come from Earth. So had the screen. Ivy could have too. She might be long dead, her voice stored in the screen for years. Except that wasn't right. She was talking to me. We were exchanging words. This voice was neither simulation nor recording. Ivy was real.

"Believe me or not," she said. "But lots of folks live on Earth."

"I don't," I said. I was pacing from one end of my pod to the other, clutching the screen.

"Yeah," Ivy said, "but you're a bot. You live in the computer. You're not alive."

"I am alive."

It was Ivy's turn to sound startled. "What?"

"Yes."

"So, where do you live if not on Earth?"

"Mars." I said the name with pride. My planet, I thought. My home.

"Huh." A pause. "You're sure?"

I laughed and it felt good. "I'm sure."

A long silence ensued. Eventually, I asked, "Are you still there?"

"Just processing," Ivy replied. "It's not every day you talk to a Martian, you know." She sounded as though she were smiling. What would that be like, to see someone else smile? "It's too weird," she said. "That man I told you about? My mom's boyfriend? He used to talk about Mars."

"What did he say?" I had stopped pacing and begun to skip in circles around my pod. Alive, said these skips. Alive, alive, alive. I wasn't thinking about Uncle One anymore, what I had promised him. I was thinking about Ivy.

"He gave me this device. The one I'm talking to you with. He stole it from where he used to live. Someplace way up north. Called the Rescue or the Refuge or something. He said they kicked him out because he knew too much. I told you he was cuckoo." She laughed. "Anyway, I used to watch him tinker with it, hooking it up to our generator and searching for one of the signals that still float by. When my mom died, he walked south. But before he left, he gave it to me. He taught me how to work it."

I thought of Uncle Two showing me the cartoons. "And?"

"And I found something," she continued. "He said he'd been trying for years to get information. He'd tapped into the system up north. Eventually he snagged something."

Something appeared on the screen. Black squiggles on white. They looked exactly like the ones I had found, the marks that made no sense. My breath caught.

"It's only a fragment," she said. "Which is super annoying. But look at the first sentence. 'This morning, we landed on the red planet.' That's your planet."

"But what is it?"

"Like a diary or something. Do you know who wrote it?"

"I don't know what that is." I stopped skipping. A dim anger pulsed within. Now Ivy was speaking in riddles as Uncle One had, expecting me to understand. "Wrote."

"Oh." Ivy paused. "You can't write? Can you read? What does the next sentence say?"

"I don't understand. But look." I fiddled with the screen until the same images appeared, the black marks I had discovered and then ignored. "I found the same thing."

"Show me," Ivy said. "Click that green square so I can see your screen."

I followed her instructions until our screens mirrored each other. Lines of black marks. Except where hers ended, mine continued, screen after screen of squiggles on a white background.

"Holy moly," she breathed. "You must have the whole thing. The entire diary."

"But what are *you*?" I wanted the screen to show me a face, but I could only see the black marks, side by side. "You're clearly not an Uncle. Are you a Moon?"

"Ha. You're right. I'm definitely not an uncle. But maybe I could be a moon? That's a fun idea. Much better than being an eleven-year-old girl with a dead mom and a tent to myself."

"You live on Earth. Are you a human?"

"Well, I'm not a deer or anything," she said.

I pictured that wobbly-legged creature crying for its mother. No, I thought. You're stronger than that.

"Listen," Ivy said. "I have an idea. I want to know what this thing says. My mom's boyfriend spoke of a mission, but wouldn't tell me much. We could read this diary together. I could teach you how."

I thought of Uncle One. Knowledge is our mission, he'd said.

I repeated his words. "We must see where we are now, to know where we will go next."

"You sound like Mom," Ivy said. "This is history, she'd tell me. You can't ignore it. Now." She scrolled her screen to its top. "Let's begin."

KAISER

NEW ORLEANS / THE FLOATING CITY,
2027

DAY ONE

One morning at Council, Pa said we would begin a chronicle of our time in the Floating City. He looked at each of us in turn: Thatcher, Gandhi, Mussolini, Roosevelt, and me. All the members of the Council, who gathered each morning to talk through matters of the city. Every Council member will write one, Pa said. He must have seen the uncertainty on my face because he said, Even you, Kaiser. We are the keepers of history.

The rest of us looked at each other, doubt clouding our faces. Six of us served on the Council, with Pa acting head. As his daughter, I was de facto adviser. Thatcher had wiry gray hair and might have been thirty or fifty or seventy, and had quite large front teeth. Because of her accent, we thought she was Russian, but she wouldn't discuss it. Gandhi was American, blond and blue-eyed, strangely plump despite our spare diet. She must have found a candy supply somewhere and was squatting over it like a magpie with its jewels. Mussolini's family had originally come from Haiti. *But then an earthquake*, he said with a shake of his head. His skin was dark and shiny, the whites of his eyes so yellowed he appeared ancient, though he was only twenty-five. Roosevelt was in his early fifties, the same age as Pa. He was Dominican—born and bred, he asserted with pride—and had fluffy brown curls and liked to argue with

Mussolini about the pronunciation of *perejil*, which was a favorite joke with them.

I asked them once why it was funny, but Roosevelt wouldn't tell. Read your Danticat, he said. I left my books behind, I protested. Then go write a poem, he said, about borders and boundaries and hatreds. It's your story too. He paused to spit. Your nation's tale.

But when Pa said we would write histories, Roosevelt laughed. History is dead, he said. Look at us. My name's Roosevelt, for fuck's sake. Didn't we agree the past is irrelevant? But Pa shook his head. Their past may be, Pa said, but ours is not. When we are gone, how will the children know what came before?

Roosevelt leaned forward, rubbing his hands on his knees. We were circled in the tower of St. Louis Cathedral, a foot of bare boards between each of us. In our cramped quarters—there in our flooded city, where dry ground was limited—we treasured personal space. Roosevelt's movements made us uneasy. Lately he had seemed irritable, erratic in his gestures, disagreeing with the Council's decisions. The day before he had balked at Pa's idea to plant petunias on our rooftops. What's the use? he asked. They can't feed us. But Pa insisted. Beauty is necessary, he said. You're living a fantasy, Roosevelt told him but stopped arguing.

At the mention of children, Roosevelt's irritation returned. How do we know our kids will survive? he demanded. How does anybody? Pa countered. When writing history, an element of faith is essential. The others slowly nodded. Where will we get the paper? asked Mussolini. Where we get everything, Pa replied. We find it. We keep it dry. Pens too. We can start the search this evening. For now, I have a supply.

He opened his rucksack, scavenged long ago from an attic on Dauphine. With a triumphant flourish, he pulled out a block of printer paper in plastic wrapping and six ballpoint pens, one for each of us, including him. Kaiser and I found these in the Old Opera House, he said, in a filing cabinet. He nodded at me to acknowledge our collusion, and the others mimicked him with a deferential bend to their necks. I recognized the paper and pens, but when I'd wrestled open that metal cabinet, I wasn't sure what he'd wanted them for.

Let me help you, I said, and reached to tear the paper open. I didn't want him to damage his fingertips. Pa's hands we took seriously. He was our architect, his business our city's shape, his hands the tools that crafted it.

I had not touched paper in some time and had forgotten how smooth it felt. I used to write my poetry in notebooks, but they grew scarce early on. After that I began painting my poems on the walls. Over time my words had littered the Quarter's top floors.

Pa created a small ceremony, handing the paper and pens around. Though Roosevelt still seemed agitated, he relented when offered his. We're shouting into the void, he muttered. But he took it. What do we write? asked Mussolini, and Thatcher said, Yes, how will we start? Pa surveyed us, each of us cross-legged except he, for he sat squarely on his stumps, and though we were a sorry sort—Mussolini wearing a plastic trash bag for a shirt, Roosevelt a series of child's ponchos stitched together—under his gaze we felt quite grand. The keepers of history, I thought, my earlier doubt dissipating. I liked the way it sounded.

Start however you want, Pa said. There are no rules here.

There are plenty of rules, Roosevelt mumbled, but we ignored him.

Forget narrative, Pa told us. The former ways of thinking are gone. Start in the middle. Or at the end. Gandhi looked up from her blank paper. But we don't know the end, she said. At twenty-three, she was two years older than I was, but Pa was gentler with her. She had a child's voice, all bells, and she wore a locket with two sides. On one, Cinderella. On the other, Jesus, his hands spread wide in benediction.

Start simpler, Pa told her, his tone softening. Describe your sleeping place. Or a friend. Or, he said with a wry grin, the weather. The stained-glass windows obscured our view, but we didn't have to look. We knew what we'd see, for every day we saw the same. Sunshine from a cloudless sky. In midafternoon thunderheads rolling up from the sea. A torrent. A deluge. In the evening, sunset sparking the sodden air, illuminating each droplet a brilliant orange. At night starlight. At regular intervals the moon. Candlelight pinpricking the Quarter at suppertime, blackness beyond. Beneath us the constant slosh and splash of brackish water.

I'll start at the beginning, Gandhi said. She was sitting beside me, and I saw her scrawl at the top of her page, *Once upon a time God said to Paul.* Her letters emerged fat and round, her *i*'s dotted with circles, carefully shaded. I longed to cross out her sentence, but I didn't. She could choose what she wrote. Pa had said. Still, I didn't like it. God has nothing to do with it, I wanted to tell her. We did this to ourselves.

THAT AFTERNOON I TRIED. I sat on my balcony with my ream of paper, pen in hand. By Council's end it had seemed easy. Write a history. I would sound like a textbook. Authoritative. Commanding. Like the ones I read in middle school, with their maps and illustrations and declarative chapter headings. Grand Expeditions. Colonial Conquest. A Path to Revolution.

I bent over and scratched a few words. *The Flood. A Family's Journey. First Days.* But what I'd hoped would sound grandiose looked stupid on the page. I tried another heading. *Society Building.* Then I scribbled each word out.

I was a poet, not a historian. I knew how to string together images, feelings, impressions, not the logical progression of events. Cause and effect. This, then that. I couldn't, like Gandhi, start at the beginning.

Once upon a time, I could have written, Pa and I took a bus ride south, then a boat. Or, once upon a time my father's legs were sheared off with surgical precision when his Subaru collided with a bread truck, two sedans, a Smart car, and a convertible. Or, once we lived in a tree-shaded neighborhood in Kansas City and my mother, who was very beautiful and very angry, scrubbed our house until it glittered. Once she and Pa argued about a city flooded with filthy water. Once she refused to accompany us south. Once we left her behind.

That was the problem. I had too many ways to start. Pa had been unrealistic in his expectations. He should have realized history couldn't be written in the present moment. One had to see the end to recognize the beginning.

I put down my pen. I couldn't write a history, not then. Instead I rocked in my chair, contemplating my world. My balcony was one in a string of balconies. Its railing was wrought iron, its floor laid with maroon tiles, the grout between them splotched with mold. From its ceiling of warped wooden boards dangled a motionless fan, its blades rusted through. The balcony was attached to a Creole Townhouse, not to be confused with a Cottage or Shotgun or Double Gallery. Those others were too low to be of use. Our Townhouse boasted pine boards, polished oak, glass wavy with age. In other buildings—along Canal, on the other side of North Rampart—the glass was bulletproof. That was a necessity before our Flood, Pa said, but the city is safe now.

The wood of my rocking chair was fat with moisture, its veneer sticky under my elbows. Another rocker waited to my left, in case of visitors. Behind me lay our sleeping place. My camping mat was gray, Pa's black. We each possessed a plastic shower curtain for privacy. In our shared space, we kept a collection of jugs for rainwater, two candleholders, the can of house paint I used for my poems. The walls were burgundy, chipped here and there to reveal pale blue, and underneath that, ugly yellow. The walls told their own history, each layer a remnant of a different generation, those who had lived in New Orleans before it became the Floating City nine years ago.

Our fellow Council members lived in other Townhouses nearby. Thatcher and Mussolini also had camping mats, but Roosevelt owned a foam mattress encased in pee-proof plastic (he was prone to night terrors), Gandhi a feather bed so mildewed I didn't know how she slept on it. Each space held a jumble of jugs, candleholders, scavenged clothes, folded neatly by some, scattered wildly by others. Wellingtons and rubber sandals, not all of them matching. My own Wellies were one purple, one with daisies. The purple one fit better. The other was too loose and flopped when I walked.

In front of me stretched what was, once upon a time, Jackson Square. Pa had told me about Jackson Square. During the first Flood in 2005, he'd studied this city. In the old days, he said, which were not so old, ice cream vendors and fire jugglers filled this square. It had a grassy park with a fountain and a statue of Andrew Jackson on a horse. Oak and banana trees. Beaming tourists. Spare-changers and trash-pickers. Once a year, a festival of beads.

But no longer. The square had become water. Muddy and opaque, it lapped at the Townhouses, reaching high as the first-floor ceilings. It had submerged the square's paving stones, the park, the fountain. From its surface rose the crowns of dead oak trees, branches waterlogged and drooping. Jackson reared from the modest whitecaps, doffing his rusty hat, his horse's majestic leap cresting the surface. The morning sun skimmed the water's top layer like cream from milk, and evaporated it. The afternoon storms replenished it.

Does the Gulf of Mexico drain? Pa had asked in early days, when questions of salvation abounded. No, we'd replied. This is our element now, he'd said. We are the Gulf, the sea with which it merges, the ocean. The majority of our globe is liquid, he'd reminded us. We cannot escape it.

The streets were also water. The entire city. The bayous farther south. The fringes of Mississippi, Alabama. Florida, surprisingly, did not flood. They must have sold their soul to the devil, Roosevelt said, to earn reprieve. Levees and sandbags, Thatcher retorted with a flick of her gray head. Why didn't they think of that in the north? Roosevelt replied. They could have saved New York.

Occasionally a wanderer would come rowing across the waves, carrying tales of distant lands. One of the first travelers told us that inland everything was normal. You've got roads and stoplights and grocery stores and the stock market in a new place—Louisville, Kentucky, can you believe that?—and Old Navy selling shitty clothes from poor countries and the news at six and sports bars and bowling lanes. He paused, bobbing in his boat beneath our balcony. Everything's how it used to be. More or less, he finished.

If everything was normal, why did you leave? Pa asked.

Why wouldn't I? said the wanderer. He was wearing a massive straw hat against the sun and held a backpack stuffed with dehydrated hiking foods he had offered as gifts for safe harbor. I was bored, he said. I had to get out of there.

He stayed with us. Most of the others who followed did too. They had reason to. In the Floating City we were left alone. The outside world—the one where people rolled oversized balls into wooden pins, where the time for drowning your sorrows was called happy hour—wanted nothing to do with us. We owned no resources, no oil, no fields of grain. Our rooftop gardens produced just enough tomatoes and squash and beans for us, a meager community of one hundred people. We could not export our small mealy potatoes, our greedily hoarded boxes of oatmeal, cans of beans, tins of condensed milk. Nor would we have wanted to. We had sweated enough foraging to know their value.

The inland society did not know we had Pa the great architect.

Kaiser the poet. The skilled gardeners Mussolini and Thatcher. Gandhi the songwriter. The valiant sailor Roosevelt, a man who could navigate treacherous whirlpools to glean supplies from far-flung outposts. Once he'd rowed as far as the airport and returned laden with Kind bars and Johnnie Walker and duty-free perfume, secreted in a storage room on the top floor, where the water hadn't reached. We were the Council members, the ones who ruled without ruling. A different type of government, Pa called us, one not seen before.

Pa had a chiseled face and dense black hair I cut regularly with a bowl and big shears. His arms were very strong, because they had to be, because he had no legs. Unlike the other men, he was beardless. Each morning he scraped his face with a straight razor and rarely nicked.

I was much paler than Pa, and I burned easily, so I kept covered with breezy long-sleeved shirts. Pa said I looked a lot like his mother. You have her mouth, he told me. And her forehead. But your skin color is different. I think she came from Mexico, he said. Or farther south. I actually don't know. Where did I get my red hair? I asked. He shrugged. From my father maybe? I'm not sure. I never met him. He shook his head. I'm sorry. I wish I knew more. But I do know you have your own mother's eyes, he added.

I always hated when he said that. I was glad that in the Floating City I owned no mirror. I didn't want to be reminded of my mother. She had refused to follow us. In unguarded moments, I still saw her face as our bus pulled away. Her dry eyes. Her hand that didn't lift to wave.

When the Council had first banded together, we decided we needed new names for our new lives. My name sounded stupid to me. Kay was a sullen preteen I no longer recognized. She was the girl who'd raged when her father ordered her to leave Kansas City, the child who'd pressed her nose to the bus window, watching her world recede. Upon our arrival that girl had vanished. On the boat across Lake Pontchartrain, she'd tossed her cell phone and bottle of prescription pills into the depths. She of soccer practice and slammed doors and Wellbutrin had no place in the Floating City.

Pa felt the same. He admitted he hated the name Paul, always had. A name from foster care, he assumed, from the state he never trusted. Call me Samson, he insisted. We tried, but it didn't stick. Instead, we christened him Pa, because he was the father of our city.

In a fit of silliness, the rest of us decided to name ourselves after former leaders. Because history is bullshit, Roosevelt said, and we agreed. That's how I became Kaiser, though I would lead no wars. Other titles were tossed around. Trotsky seemed too suspect. Ho Chi Minh too wordy. Obama too recent, and also, still alive. We drew the line at Hitler. Eventually, Thatcher and Mussolini chose leaders they mistrusted, Roosevelt and Gandhi ones they respected.

The rest of the community laughed at us, but over time their names changed too. Rachel from Oklahoma became Rotgut, for the rancid liquor she fermented from our discarded squash skins and potato peels. Micah from Tremé morphed to Michelangelo, because he began painting the apartments with elaborate murals. Sophia from Magazine Street became Porcupine, for her personality, Henrique from Metairie Harbinger, for how he watched the skies. Isosceles and Rhombus, for their shapes. Lily and Rose, for their sweetness. We took comfort in the notion that our former identities existed solely in forgotten records. With our invented names, nobody could find us. We would not—not ever, shouted Rotgut when she'd imbibed too much—have to reclaim our discarded selves.

WHILE I SAT on my balcony failing to write my history, the afternoon storm arrived, pounding on my balcony roof. When it had passed, I heard Pa calling me. Kaiser, he said. Not gentle like he said Gandhi's name, but deeper, weightier. He was inside on his camping mat. It was time for our evening expedition. He needed another shirt, and I needed a new paintbrush. If the rest of the Council members were to continue their stories, they needed more paper and pens.

Hey, Pa, I called back. Hey, he replied. To us, that meant *love.* I went inside and hid my empty pages under my camping mat. I slid on my Wellies, the purple and the loose. Then I picked Pa up and eased him into my backpack and buckled him tight so he wouldn't slip as I crossed the swaying rope bridges between buildings, or swung from cables where bridges had seemed too tame. We owned a rowboat, a canoe, and a kayak—most Floating City denizens did—but Pa and I favored flying over paddling.

Once he was buckled, I heaved him onto my shoulders and he wrapped his arms around my neck and I thought, despite myself, of my mother. Then I stepped back out on the balcony and grabbed the cable we'd hooked there. And we were off.

DAY TWO

The morning after the Council began their histories, they read aloud what they'd written. Thatcher and Mussolini had described their gardens, which made sense. They used to be landscapers in the city's parks, and they missed the earth. They'd written of how they'd gathered soil from the Quarter's houseplants, dove deep to dig river sludge, purified it and dried it and composted it and shoveled it into troughs, sprinkled it with seeds snatched from second-floor shops, peppered it with cuttings from window-ledge gardens. Mussolini had devoted an entire page to his peach trees on the Preservation Hall rooftop, Thatcher a long paragraph to her mushroom experiment on Toulouse.

Gandhi had written a story from the Bible, with Pa as both Adam and Jesus. There was a lot of God said, Pa said, and a lot of begetting, though in the near decade since the Flood, two babies had been born in our city and only one lived. We were respectful and did not laugh. Gandhi had come from Georgia, and her parents had been tent-revival evangelists. Though she was a mere thirteen when our planet changed, they drove her to the fringes of Lake Pontchartrain and launched her out in a canoe lined with marsh grass, dreaming addled dreams of Moses. Why not closer to home? we asked. They said my destiny lay here, she replied.

Roosevelt's history accounted his now legendary voyage to the air-port: the exact dimensions of his rowboat, wind shifts, compass points, dangers (riptides, water snakes, a sudden squall earlier than usual) that beset him. He'd written it like a captain's log, with precise times and terse sentences. Roosevelt had loved *Star Trek* as a kid. He said he'd always wanted to keep a log like Captain Kirk's.

Pa had written about me. I was both flattered and embarrassed, and I shifted uncomfortably as he read it aloud. I felt like the Council members were watching for my reaction. I did my best to keep my face bland. He'd written it like a fairy tale, though I was no princess. I was the knight, with a mythical sword and a helmet over my red hair, who'd traveled to a far-off kingdom to fight a dragon. No maiden, no damsel in distress. Just me and the dragon facing off on a desert plain. At the point where he'd left off, I'd laid down my sword and was making friends with the dragon. It didn't seem much like a history, but he was Pa, so he could do what he liked.

Sentimental drivel, Roosevelt grumbled after Pa read it, but the rest of us clapped.

When my turn came, I mumbled that I wasn't ready to share.

After that, Pa passed around the additional paper and pens we'd discovered in a second cabinet at the Old Opera House. He hummed a Buddhist chant, then Nirvana's "All Apologies," and bowed his head as he offered the supplies. We bowed back and took the items and finished our meeting with an accounting of our food stores (new tomato crop; five nearly ripe peaches; a bounty of potatoes; a handful of remaining Kind bars from Roosevelt's expedition; chickens doing well in their coops on Bourbon Street, eggs might be ready soon; maybe a few roasting hens for the New Year, Pa has two lighters still that work; and so on) and other news.

I reported on Rhombus, who'd gotten sick from eating catfish speared from the muddy currents—something we knew not to do, but did anyway—but who seemed to be recuperating with a strict spinach cleanse. Thatcher informed us Rotgut's batch would be ready soon and said we should organize a communal gathering in its honor. Pa suggested our own rooftop, but Roosevelt insisted we'd need more space than that. He proposed we include the other roofs surrounding the square. We thought this a fine idea. Gandhi sang a mangled hymn from her childhood, plugging in random phrases from the Bible where she'd forgotten the words, and then a song of her own, about the birds she missed. After that we said adieu and dispersed for our midday meal, the writing of history, evening expeditions for me and Pa and Roosevelt and Gandhi, gardening for the other two.

THAT DAY, I didn't even attempt to write my history. I sat on my balcony, rocking and waiting for the afternoon storm. So that Pa would think I was working on it, I kept the paper in my lap. When the wind picked up, I had to hold the sheaf down so it wouldn't blow away. I must have noticed how much harder the rain hit, how long it took to die down, how much higher the water level had risen when it had ceased. But possibly I didn't. We had been there almost ten years. I had grown accustomed to storms: what they took, what they left behind.

A storm had brought us to the Floating City. At the end of 2017, a hurricane had flooded it. Other hurricanes had decimated other cities. Those storms were nothing like the ones that had come before, the Katrinas and Harveys and Marias. The earlier hurricanes had caused widespread destruction, had flooded cities to their rooftops, but it had been temporary. The ones that struck in December of 2017 were gigantic, vicious, sudden. Nobody saw them coming. The floods they caused were permanent. We lost cities and towns, entire coastlines. People began calling it Year of the Storms. Then 2018 arrived with even bigger hurricanes. That became Year of the Collapse.

It would've been logical to avoid the floods, but Pa insisted we go meet them. He had his heart set on New Orleans. We can build a different society in the ruins, he argued. We can make the world. My mother refused, citing dirt and disease and food deficits. I love you, she'd told Pa, but I can't go with you. I cannot walk toward death with my arms open. I can't believe you're doing this, she spat at him. I've tried so hard to keep you safe.

She begged me to stay with her, but I had no choice. I left Kansas City because Pa did. We shared the same nighttime dream, one in which a faceless man walked toward us through a desert. We were father and daughter. We were linked. I couldn't escape that. By the time Pa and I had packed our bags, my mother had sealed her face to me. Go, she told me. Break my heart. Then she'd turned away with another spritz of Lysol.

Pa and I took a bus as far south as we could. It was the end of April 2018. The globe had changed shape. I had just turned twelve. In Baton Rouge we rented a speedboat we knew we wouldn't return, and chopped through the waves to reach this place. We arrived under the guise of rescue workers, hauling supplies (gallons of water, stacked cans of spaghetti and Spam and diced carrots), but we didn't intend to leave.

Most people fled, absconding on government boats with family photographs clutched to their chests and army surplus blankets swaddling their shoulders. Soon after, in a whir of helicopters, the Red Cross and FEMA left too. A few citizens remained because they trusted Pa. They admired the rooftop extensions and rope bridges and rainwater barrels he was designing. A few more arrived, summoned, as we had been, by hopes for a different life.

One year passed. Two. Three. We did what Pa wanted: we made the world as he dreamed it. We were happy. At the time I assumed we would stay forever.

DAY THREE

The day after the Council shared their histories, a stranger came to town.

At dawn he arrived, before our morning meal of squash pulp and shredded potato. I woke to him calling below our balcony. Hello, he called, good people? His voice reminded me of a train whistle: reedy and thin, but persistent. I pulled on a blouse and my camouflage trousers, mended and mended again. I stepped onto the balcony. When I saw the sun's rays glazing the water to gold, my blood sang. This is our place. We have earned it.

Another hello drifted up. It was the most quotidian of greetings, but in it I sensed movement. I saw the man in my recurring dream, marching across the sand. I pictured the clouds that tumbled in for afternoon showers. I felt it. Something was coming.

Hello, I called back. I swung my head over the railing for a good look.

He was old. Too old for voyaging. He had sinewy arms and hollow cheeks and a neck that looked like our chickens'. A shock of white hair pointed in myriad directions. His eyes were so brown they seemed black. I could not understand how he'd reached us. Before the Flood, Lake Pontchartrain had stretched over twenty miles wide. Now it was wider. Our other wanderers had been young and fit, able to navigate those miles. This man didn't look strong enough. He was bobbing in a kayak, no food supplies evident. Not even a hat against the sun. His skin was red and peeling. Where patches had flaked off, it was whiter than my own. I could have broken his arms in two.

How old are you? I asked.

Old enough to be your grandfather, looks like. Maybe twice over.

Aren't you tired?

Not anymore, he said, now that I've seen you. Like a tall glass of water on a hot day.

Dirtbag, I thought. We'd had a few creeps who assumed no laws existed there, but Pa wouldn't have it. He didn't forbid it—he insisted we'd left rules behind—but nobody could freeze you out like Pa. Eventually, those men had taken their predilections elsewhere. Probably Florida, Roosevelt said. He'd lived there after he left DR, not Miami or the Keys, but smack-dab in the middle, so he swore he'd earned the right to scorn it. Not slander if it's true, he said.

I'll get my father, I told our visitor.

I left the old pervert sloshing around in the waves and went inside. Pa was awake, blinking up at our ceiling, which mildew had filmed a light and pleasant green. In the Floating City, one learned to live with damp.

I had a dream, he said.

My breath caught. I looked into his eyes and told myself, Kaiser, breathe.

Was it him? I asked. We didn't need to specify whom. Never could we see his face. Always we could hear his boots. I could have outlined his exact shape in the dark.

It was you, he replied. You were walking away from me.

The desert? I asked.

It was too dark to see, he said, but I knew he was lying. It was always the desert. Sometimes the sand was red.

Someone is here, I said. I jerked my head back toward the balcony. A wanderer.

Have you offered him water? Pa asked.

I will, I said. A tall glass of water, the man had called me. I felt a prickle of irritation. I said I'd get you, I told Pa.

Let me prepare, Pa said.

I helped him sit up on his stumps and brought him the razor. I fetched him a cup of water from our jug, and filled another for the visitor.

Breakfast? I asked, but he shook his head. Later, he said.

Pa was wearing his shorts with the legs pinned up, but not his shirt, and I marveled at how big he seemed. When I was a child, he was a very small man. After he visited my school for open house, my shithead classmates used to laugh their asses off each time the teacher mentioned our parents. Small Paul, they'd jeer, pointing at me. I'd lock myself in a bathroom and saw my arm with a pair of left-handed scissors I'd had since kindergarten, but this didn't make it hurt less. Look at him now, I wanted to tell them. They'd be adults too, but were probably still in Kansas City, managing used car dealerships and pretending the perimeters of their continent hadn't vanished under water.

I left Pa to his ablutions and took the cup of water outside to our visitor, where I'd left him, seated in his kayak with our city's backdrop behind him: Jackson and his rearing horse, the grimed facade of St. Louis Cathedral, the circle of Townhouses, their roofs sprouting tomatoes and beans and rain barrels, their balconies webbed with bridges.

I handed the glass down to him, and he clutched it greedily.

Funny, isn't it? the man said, after he'd downed the water. To feel thirsty surrounded by this?

He dipped his hand in the currents, Mississippi and Gulf mingled. Dark brown, gritty, swimming with parasites. When we'd arrived, we'd looted the hospital for antibiotics: creams and salves, pills and injections. Pa knew we'd need them. Nearly a decade later, the expiration dates were a joke, but they still seemed to work.

I wouldn't do that, I told the man. Not if you have any abrasions.

He lifted his hand and surveyed it. Even from the balcony, I could see his age spots, the gnarled veins. Nope, he said. No cuts. His black eyes turned to me. They seemed too sharp for such an old man. What do you do for drinking water? he asked.

Rain.

Can't be too clean.

Nothing is.

No, he said. His teeth were whole, square, white. He'd come from a place with dentists.

Pa rolled out behind me on his platform. Lily and Rose, who grew up in Kolkata, had suggested its design, a plank of wood with four Rollerblade wheels attached. They said the legless beggars used them in the Sealdah railway station. Less cumbersome than a wheelchair. It was a good idea. I couldn't carry Pa everywhere.

Welcome to the Floating City, Pa called down to our visitor. We have food and water and we can offer you a sleeping place in one of our salvaged apartments. We expect you to follow the Council's guidelines and help gather resources. Artists, in particular, are welcome, so if you can sing or draw or write, please do. Do you have a name?

The man grinned. It looked like a death mask, teeth in a skull. I thought of apes, how I learned in fifth-grade biology that, for them, smiling could mean aggression.

I'm David, said the man. His smile vanished when he spoke.

Would you like to keep or change it? Pa asked. You have that option.

I've had it so long I might as well keep it, he said.

I'm Pa, said Pa, and this is Kaiser, gesturing at me. Are you here to stay or to see? he asked. Citizen or tourist?

David used his paddle to brace his kayak against our balcony. The water was especially choppy. To stay, he replied. I've traveled rather a long way to find you.

Pa invited our visitor to join our morning meal. I lowered the rope ladder, and the man tied his kayak to our railing and climbed up, more deftly than I expected. Close up, he seemed less ancient. He smelled like cedar, an aroma I remembered from the wood chips in which Mother packed our winter clothes. It made me miss trees.

Over breakfast, David told us he came from the north.

Canada? I asked.

Yes. Over the border from North Dakota.

Why here? Pa asked.

David scooped another mouthful of squash from the communal bowl. He swallowed before speaking, the tendons in his neck stretching. I heard stories, he said. Of a magical place. I wanted to see if they were true.

We have no magic here, Pa said softly, but I could hear his impatience. He liked to say we were doing what we could have been doing all along. This is simply society how it should be lived.

This squash is delicious, David said, scooping out more. I tried a raw food diet once, he said, but nothing tasted this good.

We cook sometimes, Pa said. If it's meat.

Alligator?

No. Too scarce. Not enough land for them to crawl onto.

Fish?

Pa shook his head. Too polluted. We've got some chickens. That's all.

David lifted his eyes from his food. How the hell did you get chickens out here?

You'd be surprised what people kept, Pa said. And where they kept them. We found an entire attic full of chicken coops over on Bourbon. Relocated them to the roof so they could get some air.

Amazing, said David. His eyes drifted around our room. How did this man with his perfect white teeth regard our moldy shower curtains and piles of ragged clothes?

Pa pushed the bowl of potatoes closer to our visitor, and David dug his fingers into them. Watching him lick his hands clean, I wondered what he'd eaten on his journey. He looked ravenous. Like he could devour our city and ask for more.

HALF OF THE COUNCIL accepted our visitor. Two years had passed since the last one, a woman from Biloxi who reported their watery city had collapsed, but refused to say how. Thatcher said she didn't mind fresh company. Mussolini agreed, but Roosevelt didn't.

He rocked back and forth, rubbing his knees. Why won't he change his name? he asked.

Some don't, Pa said.

Most do, said Roosevelt. We could call him Columbus.

Mussolini laughed. That's funny, he said.

What if he brings diseases? Gandhi asked. What if he has polio?

Don't be dumb, I said. We're vaccinated.

Kaiser, Pa said warningly. He didn't like it when I lost patience with Gandhi.

Estrella's not, Gandhi said. She was talking about the baby who had lived. She was three years old and belonged to Lily, who wouldn't identify the father. We knew it was Rhombus—everybody except Isosceles did—but said nothing, because it would have broken Isosceles's heart.

They were our Bert and Ernie, down to the separate beds. Rhombus pretended not to see how Isosceles pined after him.

Precisely, said Roosevelt. Estrella's not immune. And we don't know what else he might be infected with. We have to consider our children. I saw him, you know. When he arrived. He came kayaking up St. Ann Street, talking on a radio. Who could he have been talking to? What does he want here? He could be from the government. He could be here to evacuate us. I don't like it.

Then Roosevelt broke our unwritten code and stood up. He'd fractured our circle. He walked to the stained-glass window and pressed his face against a scarlet pane. I don't like it, he repeated.

You don't have to like it, Pa said.

Roosevelt's shoulders drew in. He'd been a boxer in both DR and Florida, and he had the body of a middleweight, even with the lean food. When his shirt was off, you could trace the outline of each muscle beneath the skin.

What's the point of anybody coming here? He asked it so quietly we could barely hear him. When it's all coming to an end?

DAY FOUR

The next morning, we took a break from our histories to discuss water levels. The rains seemed to be worsening. The previous day's storm hadn't let up until dark. Roosevelt said he'd take measurements on ten buildings in the Quarter. The discussion appeared to subdue him. I remembered what he'd said in our last meeting.

Our city can't end, I thought. Can it?

After Council meeting, I left Pa at home and swung across the Quarter to check on Michelangelo. I wanted to see how he was adjusting to his new roommate. Pa had offered David a sleeping place with Michelangelo, on the top floor of the Lalaurie mansion over on Royal. The mansion was one of the tallest buildings in the Quarter and therefore among the best preserved, its flocked wallpaper barely curled and the horsehair sofas springy, if not quite dry. Despite this, only Michelangelo wanted it. The others claimed ghosts, wouldn't go near the place. They killed our people, Rhombus told Michelangelo. Tortured them in that room you covet. Chained them in the attic. One of Delphine Lalaurie's slaves jumped off that roof just to escape her.

But Michelangelo told him to check his history. That house burned, he told Rhombus. This one is a reconstruction. Nothing haunted here.

He took one of the sofas for his bed and spent eight years painting the ceiling with his namesake's *Creation of Adam*, making both God and his first man black. When he finished, he invited Rhombus to see his mural, but at the last minute, Rhombus balked, claiming he'd heard a cry from the third-floor window.

WHEN I REACHED MICHELANGELO'S MANSION, he was brooding. Like me, he valued solitude. We could exist in the same room—he fine-tuning a mural and me slopping my poetry in wild wet arcs—in comfortable silence. I used to write neatly, but that took time and neck-cramping precision. After the intricacies of Council meetings, it was a pleasure to splash my words where they wanted to go.

I could understand why he was grouchy about his new roommate, but I didn't like him like that. He acted as petulant as a child. I was twenty-one, too young to worry about children. I preferred him painting, or swinging from balconies, or bringing Pa presents, like the gift of ossified chocolate he'd offered a few days prior at the evening meal he sometimes shared with us. Or when he was with me, just me, and he whispered in my ear words that didn't belong in any history, and sometimes the rain drummed on his roof when I arrived in the afternoon, and the city, with everybody else asleep, belonged to us.

I haven't seen you in days, he said when I climbed through his French window. His top floor was higher than most, but Pa had designed a slanted bridge especially for him.

I've been busy, I replied.

You'll not want to speak loudly. Michelangelo jutted his chin toward the next room. Someone in there was snoring. David. The master is sleeping, said Michelangelo.

He was definitely in a mood. I turned to leave, but he stepped closer and wrapped his arms around me. In his embrace, I could feel his softening. Stay, he said. We'll be quiet.

And we were. Once we'd been friends who wove bridges and strung cables, who joyfully stormed department stores for supplies, but by then we had become lovers, though *love* was not a word we ever spoke.

Afterward we lay cramped together on his sofa, the horsehair pricking my skin, and talked of the visitor.

He's taken my space, Michelangelo said.

His body, on top of mine, stiffened. His dick hardened against my thigh, and I slid out from under him. I didn't want him to distract me with more sex. His face saddened, the lines around his mouth deepening. He'd come from Tremé, and he'd lived seven years longer than I had, and it showed. You don't know what it was like, he'd insist when I tried to talk of the past.

Pa told him to move in, I said. I pulled on my blouse and trousers. He had no choice, I told him. Pa is Head.

I brought Michelangelo a damp cloth to clean off, and as I watched him wipe down, I realized I'd forgotten the same for myself. Between my thighs was sticky. I'd have to change clothes later, soak the old ones in a tub of rainwater on the roof. It was time to do laundry anyway. I didn't want babies—not yet—but I wasn't worried about pregnancy. I kept careful track of my cycles. That week was safe.

I'm tired of the Council, Michelangelo said.

He pulled on his cut-offs and T-shirt. The shirt had a faded *Nirvana* across the front. A gift from Pa. You're getting serious, Pa had said to me the last time Michelangelo had joined us for supper. All is temporary, I'd replied, and retired to my mat.

Roosevelt feels the same, I said to Michelangelo. I think so anyway. He's been arguing with everything we discuss.

We heard noises from the next room. A shuffling of sheets. Springs. David's sleeping space was a proper bedroom, with a massive mildewed four-poster. Michelangelo had chosen his sofa over that bed. Too grand for me, he'd said.

We paused, listening. David's snoring had stopped. I wondered if he'd heard everything. I wondered if I cared.

I should go, I said. Midday meal. Afternoon storm. Pa will need me for expedition.

Michelangelo was pulling on one rubber sandal, but when I said this, he stopped. What the father says goes, he teased.

Yes. I stood there, challenging him with my eyes. No lover could shake my loyalty to Pa. Don't worry about the visitor, I continued.

He's an old white dude, he said, who has taken up residence in my house. We know what comes next.

The old rules are dead, I replied. Pa said.

Your father has nice ideas. Come here.

And because he was a beautiful man who made me feel good and his face was suffused with feeling and something in me wanted David to hear us, I did. Michelangelo smelled like me and like himself, sweat so sharp it reminded me of pain, and as we kissed goodbye, I heard his voice in my head. You don't know, Kaiser. You don't even know.

PA INVITED DAVID TO EVENING MEAL. On our expedition, Pa made me swoop over to the Lalaurie mansion to slide the invitation under his window. David was gone, possibly off exploring. Michelangelo was also missing, out on his own expedition. Sometimes he would join Pa and me. Mostly he traveled alone.

Shall I invite Michelangelo? Pa asked, but I shook my head.

I saw him already, I said. I didn't say what I was thinking, that we should leave him alone. With his roommate gone for an hour, he'd want some space. Besides, I didn't think he'd want to share anything more with the man who had invaded his home.

When David arrived at our window, I was surprised. He was dressed up. Just a buttoned shirt, but more than most of us bothered with. Only Rose liked fancy clothes. She owned a closet jammed with vintage dresses, some from Civil War days, assiduously gathered over the years from attics and second-floor shops.

David's shirt seemed to please Pa. Though he professed relief over our current freedom, I think sometimes he missed his ironed polo shirts and glossy loafers.

You look quite respectable, Pa told him. David thanked him and joined us on the floor.

Pa had cracked three precious eggs into three individual bowls for us to sip. While we ate, the rain thundered on the roof. Afternoon storm should have finished by then, but it hadn't. Sipping at my egg, I wondered how much higher the water might rise.

We had finished our egg bowls and the snap beans and the ubiquitous squash, and we were sitting around, Pa picking his teeth, me staring out the window at the rain, when David asked, Where are your books? He gestured at our floor, piled with jugs and clothes, at our bare shelves.

Why do you think we'd have books? I asked.

Because you're a writer.

Poet, I corrected.

And keeper of history, Pa said.

To this, I said nothing.

Writers have books, David said. His shirt, crisp upon his arrival, had wilted in the damp.

I don't read books, I said. I left them behind.

Their story was done, Pa said. We needed a new one.

Besides, I said. I wasn't reading stories anymore. Only poetry. Stories tired me out.

The thing is. David fumbled in the shoulder bag he'd brought. I've brought you a gift. I was hoping you'd want it.

He pulled it out. A book. My book. Adrienne Rich's *The Dream of a Common Language*. I recognized it immediately. The cover was partially torn off, the pages dog-eared from use. A library copy, borrowed and never returned. When I snatched it—rudely, I admit—from his hand, the inside cover verified it. Kay Samson, someone (*me*) had written in felt-tip pen, *Kansas City, 2017*. I had borrowed it months before Pa's accident, when we lived in a square house on a square block and I was so terrified that the man in my nightmares would come to life that I relinquished narratives and picked up poetry instead.

Where did you get this? I asked.

From your house, said David, his face unreadable. You'd be surprised how much is the same. But the internet's down, at least for the time being, so I looked up your address in a phone book.

The internet's down. Pa's voice sounded flat and final.

But how did you even know our address? I asked.

David turned from Pa to me. I'd heard stories, he said.

What do you mean? I asked.

People tell tales, he said. About this place and the people who run it. A crippled man and his daughter.

Pa's not a cripple, I insisted.

David bent his head in what I assumed was apology. These are the stories they tell, he said. What I heard impressed me. I wanted to meet you.

Other cities exist, I said. You could've gone there.

Not so many. David maneuvered his eyes from me to Pa, then back again. I don't suppose, he said, you've heard about New York.

Pa spoke up. Yes. We've heard.

A shame. David bent his head again.

We don't eat people here, I said.

No. He lifted his head. You don't. The problem is—he leaned forward—the coastal communities have vanished.

Not all of them, Pa said. He was rocking on his stumps. He reminded me of Roosevelt.

Yes, all of them. David swiped his hand sideways, as though to illustrate their disappearance. Biloxi and Mobile you know about, he said. Their people have come to you.

I nodded. I remembered our last visitor. I knew something about Biloxi.

The eastern coast too, I'm afraid, David said. The west we lost immediately—you know that. He looked at us, but we shook our heads. We hadn't known about the west. Ah, said David, straightening. This is difficult.

Go on, I said.

A few cities in the east persisted, he said, some smaller towns too. Humble communities like yours. Self-sustaining. Rooftop gardens. Councils and rules. Peopled by those who wanted to shirk the grid.

It's a good life, Pa interrupted.

I won't argue, David said. As I mentioned, I admire you. This is why I came.

What about Florida? I asked. I realized I was rubbing my knees. I thought of Roosevelt again and hoped he would visit after David left. Occasionally he would swing by my balcony after evening meal and we would sit in the dark, slapping mosquitoes and saying nothing. I wanted his quiet presence in the dark. I wanted his anger.

Florida? David lifted his thick lids in surprise. Why ask?

They're still dry, I said. They made a pact with the devil.

David's mouth tightened. This is more difficult than I thought, he said. Who has been bringing you these stories?

Wanderers, I said. Like you.

An extended game of telephone. David laughed, but not happily. Florida's gone, he said. A tsunami submerged it two years ago. From Miami to Jacksonville. Pensacola. The entire state.

We don't have tsunamis in America, I said, though I knew it sounded stupid. Of course we had them. By then we had everything.

Earthquake, 9.5 on the Richter scale, off the coast of Haiti. David offered an apologetic look, but I questioned how sorry he felt. Something told me he was enjoying this, despite all the tragedy. Haiti disappeared too, he said. The rest of Hispaniola. Much of the Caribbean, in fact.

I thought of Mussolini and Roosevelt, how they would mourn their homelands. Maybe they already had. Maybe they knew more than I did.

I'm sorry, David said.

For some time, we sat without speaking, the rain thundering on the roof, the chopping of the waves reaching us through our closed French doors. The wind was rocking the chairs wildly on the balcony. In his mansion on Royal, Michelangelo would be painting, or singing the songs of his youth. There used to be marches, he'd told me, parades through Tremé. Any occasion would warrant it, he'd said. Births, deaths, christenings. A saint's day. A day to honor war's veterans. There would be instruments. There would be song. When he told me this, he was naked. We had just made love and I was naked too, and he belted out a song and swept me to my feet and we danced on his bare boards, his God and his Adam sole witnesses to our glee.

The rain began to lessen, but the wind still roared.

Was our house empty? Pa asked.

I didn't need to look at him to know what he was thinking.

Nobody there, David said. Some cobwebs. Some books. Not unusual, considering the situation. There'd been a fire.

David looked like he wanted to add more, but Pa's face had closed.

He didn't want to learn what had happened to Kansas City. It must have been lurking in the back of his mind, that if our experiment failed, we could return home. Part of him must have hoped my mother would still be there, waiting with a warm word and a bar of soap to scrub him clean.

I examined the book in my hands. But why go out of your way to get this? I asked.

David smiled his death's head grin. I wanted you to trust me.

But why? I persisted. Why would it matter if we trusted you?

Kaiser. Pa held up his hand to signal our conversation's end. He lifted himself onto his roller board and began clearing dishes. David's cup held some water, but Pa took it away. He piled the dishes by the door. We'd wash them on the roof in the morning. I could tell by his shoulders' stance that he was thinking about my mother. David's visit had unburied too much.

Pa turned to our visitor. Would you like Kaiser to row you home? he asked.

I can make it on my own, David said. Your network of bridges is quite impressive.

You admire them also, Pa said.

I do. David untangled his legs and stood up.

I stood too. Pa, though no higher than our waists, didn't seem small. He remained balanced on his board, bracing it with his arms.

As though ours had been a normal dinner party, we said polite good-byes. I had my book, Rich's *Common Language*, under my arm. I didn't yet know if I would read it. I didn't like how many memories David had stirred up. When he left, I slammed the door after him and wished—wickedly—that the winds howled him back to his stolen home. That the bridges swayed under his feet.

DAY FIVE

We used our next Council meeting to talk again about the rain.

Water's up six inches, Roosevelt reported. He'd been out at dawn measuring the levels and was sweating from exertion, curls plastered to his temples. He was agitated again.

The sun will burn it off, Gandhi said blithely. She'd brought her history, the sole member to do so, and seemed eager to share it. When not speaking she hummed, though I couldn't tell if it was a hymn or a song of her own. I hoped she would sing the one about birds. I hadn't realized how much I would miss sparrows. Seagulls were all we had.

Surely not six inches, said Thatcher. How could it rain so much in a few hours?

Here you ask this? said Roosevelt. His arm's violent sweep indicated the miles of flooded blocks beyond our stained-glass windows.

But so soon? Thatcher's question was a wail. It hasn't even been ten years.

I thought we had more time, added Mussolini.

Maybe we do, said Pa.

Bullshit, Roosevelt interrupted. The end has come. And us, sitting pretty.

He shifted as though to stand, but I laid my hand on his knee to still him. We exchanged a glance. Roosevelt had been my first, five years before, when I was sixteen and dying to know a man. He'd been a gentle lover and I'd felt fortunate, lying in his arms afterward while he whimpered in his sleep. I would have stayed with him, but Pa had insisted he was too old. We were still friends.

How do you know? asked Gandhi. Did you have a dream?

I don't need dreams to tell me the truth, Roosevelt said. Watch the skies. Ask Harbinger. He'll tell you how the clouds have changed.

Can I share my history now? Gandhi asked.

Please, said Pa. We could use a happy tale. His voice grew whispery, and I wondered why he hadn't loved anybody since my mother. Gandhi was unlikely, but so was everything.

Gandhi read her new installment, but it was no happy tale. The air in our tower prickled, and my skin chilled. I imagined the others felt the same, because Roosevelt was leaning forward, his hands frozen on his knees, and Thatcher looked like she was holding her breath and Mussolini was slowly shaking his head. Even Pa seemed nervous, a rarity for him, who had lost his mother and his legs and his wife and still woke each day with a smile for me.

Gandhi's history told the story of a visitor, a stranger who came to town. He arrived by sea with tales of distant lands and gifts for the town's leaders, and he took a haunted house for his home and a poet for his bed. He insinuated himself in their lives and their hearts, and when he left, he stole something from them they could not retrieve. Gandhi's story wasn't biblical until the end, when she described the horrors that followed his departure. Red rain. Fire. Floods.

I told you, Roosevelt said. That man is a sign. The end is coming.

He stood up, breaking our circle again.

You need to sit down, Mussolini told him.

But Roosevelt would not. We've heard this story before, he said.

You've heard this story before, he told Mussolini. I keep seeing him in his kayak, babbling on his radio. The next thing we know he'll be selling us diseased blankets or forcing us to pronounce a word we cannot.

Roosevelt, Pa said, and Roosevelt considered him for a long moment before sitting back down.

It's true, he told Pa. Think of the rain. It's too much to be coincidence.

I don't understand, Thatcher said, though I could tell she did. I had seen her face when Gandhi read her history. We've had visitors before, she continued.

His visit is different, Roosevelt said. I know it.

Roosevelt's right, I said. Surprised eyes turned to me. I rarely talked in Council. I was Pa's carrier, his right hand, but more listener than speaker. I don't trust David's arrival either, I said. Tell them about the book, I urged Pa. But Pa shook his head. I wanted to press it, but didn't.

In the end, we let the issue lie. We were too worried to discuss it further. Even Roosevelt relented, but I could hear him muttering as we descended the tower stairs to the water level. For fuck's sake, he said when we reached the bottom and noticed the stairs ended two steps sooner than we remembered. Mussolini and Thatcher climbed back up to the next floor and lowered themselves from the windows into their boat, but Roosevelt, Gandhi, and I waded through the extra water to ours.

Pa tensed as I stepped into the risen currents, and I remembered the first time I swung him onto my shoulders, when we'd disembarked in Baton Rouge and realized we'd have to leave his wheelchair behind. The doctors had offered him prosthetics, but he'd refused, asserting he'd found his true form. You'll ride with me, I'd said. I'd emptied my pack on the bus station floor and lifted him into it. We must have made a funny sight, but nobody had seemed to notice. With the emergency just begun, the Baton Rouge station had been loud and frantic, choked with jostling people, their faces stretched wide with panic.

I wondered what it looked like a decade later. Probably placid. Patient people waiting for their buses. The past was a wound sealed over.

THAT AFTERNOON I TRAVELED by bridge and cable to the Lalaurie mansion.

Hello, I called, rapping on the panes. I could see Michelangelo's empty couch, a folded blanket. I cracked the door open, and God glowered at me from the ceiling. Usually Michelangelo was there. We didn't expedition in the afternoon, for fear of storms.

Hello, called David's reedy voice. He appeared in the doorway between rooms. He was wearing his buttoned shirt from the night before. It looked crisp again. Had he brought a fucking iron with him? I wondered. And a generator?

Where has he gone? I asked. I could feel my body's hunger. I needed to find Michelangelo. If we were going to lose our Floating City to another flood, I wanted each moment to last.

The Superdome.

That's far.

He took his boat.

I sat down on Michelangelo's couch. David remained in the doorway. He seemed completely at ease. Columbus, I thought, what a perfect name.

He's good on the water, I said. He'll make it before afternoon storm.

He said you could meet him there.

David shifted from left foot to right. I smelled cedarwood, light and fragrant over the usual stink of mold. I stood up and moved closer to him. He was tall, but so was I. Our gazes were nearly level. Up close, his eyes seemed kinder, twinkles deep within their darkness. His body radiated warmth. I had not been close to anything dry in a very long time.

I'll go now, I said. Before the storm.

It might be dangerous, he offered. You could wait.

His wizened face appeared open, but I doubted his candor as I'd doubted his sorrow when relating the horrors of the world beyond our city. I remembered Gandhi's history about the stranger who would bring gifts for the town's leaders, who would take a haunted house for his own. It was true about the house. And he had brought me a book. But he'd gifted nothing to Pa, and he certainly wouldn't take a poet for his bed. I stepped backward.

I think I can make it, I said. Before the rain hits.

Suit yourself, David said.

He watched me cross the room and clamber back through the French doors. If he'd thought a mere book would make me trust him, he'd been wrong.

I SWUNG TO MY TOWNHOUSE to collect my boat, hoping the storm would wait. Maybe, I thought as I paddled toward the Superdome, the rains wouldn't overwhelm us. Maybe we could keep our city after all.

We tended to stay away from places west of Canal. The structures were tall and mostly dry and therefore good for expeditions, but they were cavernous and dark. Gandhi and Rhombus talked of ghosts. I simply did not like the way my footsteps sounded in the vacant towers. We used to worry it would be like New York; we would shiver with fear stepping into those shadowy rooms, creeping up the pitch-black stairwells, questioning what hand would snake out to grab us, what teeth would flash in the dark. But this fear had proved empty. Except for us, the city had disgorged its people. We remained blessedly alone.

At the beginning we had traveled across Canal frequently, mostly for supplies from the medical centers, battling our fears for necessity's sake. The last time I'd been west of Canal had been three years before with Roosevelt, when Estrella had needed food because Lily's milk had dried up. I remembered our winding course through the glowering buildings, how loudly our canoes had spoken in the silence. Our glee when we'd unearthed a box of powdered milk high and dry on a top shelf at the Family Dollar. How we'd been too cowed by the quiet to shout our relief.

Boating up Canal toward the Superdome felt the same, except I was alone, switching my paddle left, right, left. The handful of unbroken windows winked at me in the vanishing sunlight. The clouds were looming, the tropical heat dense and wet. The city smelled like ancient mud and future rain. I could smell myself too, my musty sweat. I needed a rain barrel bath, a comb through my hair.

The Superdome rose up past Canal and Tulane, on the other side of Poydras. I had seen it shortly after we arrived in the city. Pa and I had stopped at Tulane Medical Center and filled our rowboat with antibiotic creams and pills and bandages, any antiseptics we could find. Then we'd rowed over to the Superdome. That's where it happened, Pa had said. What? I asked, though I knew he was talking about the first Flood. Where civilization nearly broke down, he said, but didn't. His voice in my ear was softer than when he spoke to Gandhi. They managed to stay human, he said. Did they? I asked, because my sixth-grade social studies teacher had told me different. Yes, he insisted. They did.

I was twelve by then and so overwhelmed by the way my life had changed that I sat gaping at the white dome. I thought of the people inside in 2005, and how it must have felt knowing any second the lights could wink out—toilets blocked, food dwindling—and I was grateful they hadn't tried it again. When the second Flood hit, the government had known better. The 2017 hurricanes had struck in rapid succession, leaving little time to prepare, but at least they hadn't cautioned anyone to take shelter within the cities. Get out, they said. Most did.

The Superdome looked more or less as it had during our previous visit. Still white but smeared with mud, a few more holes in the roof. I'd brought my kayak, and I was able to get inside and weave through the doors and halls and gates to reach the open field. A scrim of water covered the turf, bobbing with plastic: soda cups, shopping bags, sunglasses. Rows of seats circled the field, erect and patient, as though anticipating the next game. A lightning flash lit the gloom. Through the holes in the roof, rain began to fall. The storm had arrived.

In the field's center, Michelangelo sat swaying in his kayak. He liked open spaces. Often, I would find him on his roof among the tangled pea vines and strawberries, shouting his Tremé songs to the sky. My heart quivered. I would miss him if I left. If the rains continued like they had, we would all have to go.

I called, Hello, across the water. He turned and waved. I paddled closer.

You need to comb your hair, he said.

I touched the knots and considered the time it would take to pick a comb's teeth through the mess. Roosevelt might help me later. When I was a kid, Pa had done this for me. Combing was a father's job, not a mother's. My mother used to yank the brush straight down and scold me when I cried.

Why have you come here? I asked.

He pointed upward, tilting his head so his neck gleamed. See up there? he said. That ceiling? Imagine what we could do.

The ceiling's black squares shimmered vaguely. Unlit bulbs dangled on long cables. I felt what Pa must have when he was small and the universe had arced unknown above him.

The Sistine Chapel is nothing to this, Michelangelo said. Kaiser, give me a line.

He would say this when he wanted poetry, usually after we had loved each other, when we lay breathing on his prickly couch. He would want it in whispers, in his ear. In the Superdome, he insisted I shout it.

Fill this space with your words, he urged.

I chose a line I'd painted in Lily and Rose's sleeping place. I'd written it before David's arrival. This seemed important. A relic from the time before our lives began to change.

The marching boots march still. My lungs expanded with the words.

More, said Michelangelo.

A man in the dark. Shouting felt good.

More.

You, too, will see your own face in the glass. I was trembling.

More.

And be afraid.

Yes. His voice was hushed.

You, too, will hunker alone in his shadow / Sense the antlers / Sprouting from your head.

More, Michelangelo whispered.

There is no more, I said. That's the whole poem.

Now, he said, spreading his arms wide. Picture it scrawled up there in giant letters.

Nobody will see it, I said. I paddled closer. Not when this place is gone.

It doesn't matter, he said. He reached to pull my kayak alongside his. Someday our children, or our children's children, will return. They will come to see what their parents built.

I surveyed the ceiling. What if Estrella's generation is the last?

Michelangelo laughed. Why are you so gloomy?

I've been thinking, I said quietly. About children. They don't seem like a good idea. We wouldn't be able to make them strong enough. I turned my eyes toward him. The water's rising, you know.

Have faith, Kaiser. We do not die out so easy.

Maybe we should.

To this, he had no reply. I looked back up at the ceiling.

You'll have to build a big fucking scaffold, I said. He took hold of my left hand. I liked the way he rubbed my fingers. One. Then another.

We can do that, he said. I'll ask your father. He can design it.

I detached my hand. It felt too good. He has things on his mind, I said.

The rain, he said. He phrased it as a statement, not a question.

We paused, listening to the sky sobbing overhead, feeling its drops pelt our faces.

I thought of you, he murmured, when the storm hit last night. That man. He paused to take a breath. That man came in with a smile and a straight collar. I don't trust him, Michelangelo said. I hear him after dark, talking on his radio. How many batteries did he bring for that thing? And to whom can he be speaking? I peeked through the doors, but he was in bed, behind the curtains. I could see nothing.

He'll be gone soon, I said. I grabbed his hand again, but he didn't rub my fingers.

Men like him come only to take, Michelangelo agreed. They don't come to stay.

When the storm finished, we left. I had tucked my book in my trousers' waistband, and it was rubbing against my back. As we kayaked through the echoing wreckage of the Superdome, I pondered plucking it out and casting it into the water, but I did not.

The words I had shouted to the ceiling returned to me—*a man in the dark*—and I decided I'd written enough about my dreams. I was tired of the desert, that man, his boots. Surely, I could write something new. *The Floating City*, I would call my next series. I would talk about Jackson Square and Pa's bridges and the way Michelangelo's arm strained as he painted. So much existed to lyricize. I swiveled my kayak to exit the dome, and Rich's book jabbed my back again.

I was no historian, I thought, but I could still be a poet.

I INVITED MICHELANGELO to evening meal, but he didn't come. Neither did David. Pa and I ate alone. No eggs this time. Squash and potatoes. Again. The rainwater in my cup tasted dull.

Is Rotgut's batch ready? I asked.

Pa swallowed and reached for more. I think so, he replied. I spoke to Thatcher and Mussolini. They have a few peaches. Plenty of potatoes.

At the mention of potatoes, I shuddered, but tried not to show it.

I said we could roast them.

I perked up. I hadn't eaten cooked food in months. We didn't build fires often. The damp made it difficult.

Roosevelt found an iron fire pit, Pa said, over on Esplanade. Not so rusted. I have those lighters. It's a special occasion. We'll find something dry to burn. I offered our rooftop and the ones next door. We can invite everybody.

How soon? I asked.

Tomorrow night, Pa said. He lifted himself onto his board and took our empty dishes, began stacking them by the door. When he returned, he took my face in his hands.

Hey, I said.

Hey.

That was our signal. Bedtime. Hey meant *love*, but it also meant *good night*, and sometimes *remember*.

I pulled his shower curtain closed for him so he could blink at the ceiling or sketch designs, feeling the page in the dark. I wondered if he was still writing his history, if any of them were.

I couldn't sleep, so I went out to rock on my balcony. After a bit, Roosevelt arrived and took his place in the other rocker. I had washed my hair that evening on the roof, but not yet brushed it. He took a comb and, strand by careful strand, untangled it.

Kaiser, he said, I'm afraid our dream is dead. I am too, I thought, but didn't say it aloud. I took his rough paw in my own and we sat there rocking in the dark. Out across the water, the wind picked up.

DAY SIX

In the wee hours of the morning, Pa had a visitor. He didn't knock. I woke to a rustle beyond my curtain. The rain had come and gone. Outside the waves lapped. I peeped out and saw a man's dark shape. I knew him by his cedar smell. David was crouching by my father's bedside. He must have come in through our French doors as though he owned the place. His arm slid back the curtain. I could make out Pa's velvet outline. He was sitting up. He did not shout his alarm, did not seem startled. They whispered together, but the waves were lapping and the blood was rushing in my ears, and I could not hear what they said. After a couple of minutes, David withdrew and left.

I must have slept, because I had a dream. The man with no face. The desert. He smelled like cedarwood. I woke to anger, not fear.

Son of a bitch, I said too loud and woke up Pa.

He parted his curtain. Kaiser, he said. That man came.

I know. I don't like it.

He says he has a proposal for us, Pa said.

I don't want to hear it, I said.

Kaiser. Pa's voice was soft. I don't think we have a choice. The future won't wait.

Oars splashed outside. Roosevelt was circling the square again, checking water levels.

When's he going to tell us? At Council? I imagined how Roosevelt would react if David joined our circle.

No. The proposal is solely for us, Pa said. He says it's something gigantic.

But we have all the giants we need. I laid a hand on Pa's forearm.

Pa placed his hand over mine. That's what I told him, he said.

AT COUNCIL, we did not talk about water. We talked about homebrew and potatoes, fire pits and rooftops. We arranged our communal gathering for sunset when, weather willing, the skies would clear. Roosevelt said he'd tour the Quarter in his canoe to ring the party bell, which was a cowbell, which was a lot of fun. Last time we'd held a celebration, I had rung the bell while Roosevelt rowed. I loved the whoops from inside the Townhouses, the ecstatic shouts from our citizens. They spent their days sowing and hoeing and scavenging the dying city for what decayed gifts it could offer. They always welcomed a party. I offered to accompany Roosevelt again, but Pa said we had other plans. Oh right, I thought. David.

After we'd planned our party, I presumed the others would share histories.

Is anybody still writing? I asked.

They shook their heads. My paper got wet, Thatcher said. Mine too, said Mussolini. What's the point? grumbled Roosevelt. Mine's just a fantasy, Pa admitted, to which Roosevelt muttered, No surprise there. But Gandhi said yes, she was keeping hers. More predictions of doom? I asked. No, she replied. In my history we've left this planet behind.

That can't be history, it hasn't happened, I said, my voice sharp.

I was angry because Pa had spoken to David alone. Because he hadn't woken me up. Because David hadn't told me about his forthcoming proposal. I should have heard about it first. I was the one who'd greeted him when he arrived in the Floating City. I thought he owed me something for that.

But Gandhi didn't sense my irritation. Time is a spiral, she said, her blue eyes glassy, her smile beatific as a saint's.

You're a fucking idiot, I told her. Then I stood up, snapping our circle.

Kaiser, said Pa. Sit down.

I'm going home, I said. I'll meet you there.

I stomped down the stairs and into the standing water and waded to the windows to our boat. I tried not to think how Pa would get home. Roosevelt would bring him, I told myself. And shortly thereafter he did, rowing him across the square to our balcony. You forgot something, Roosevelt said, handing Pa up to me. Grudgingly I leaned over the railing to grab Pa's arms and, with Roosevelt's help, grapple him to safety.

Once I'd lifted him over the railing, Pa fixed his eyes on me.

Don't act like a child, he said.

Then you should've let me be one, I retorted. That shut him up.

We sat on the balcony in silence until David appeared, his kayak bumping against our railings. I stopped rocking in my chair, Pa on his stumps. Pa put a polite smile on his face and called out a welcome.

I lowered the rope ladder, and David climbed up. He was wearing another buttoned shirt, this one pale blue, also crisp and clean. He probably did have an iron. And a generator. He'd probably brought lots of stuff, hidden in his kayak where we couldn't see.

Let us circle inside, Pa said. The rains will arrive shortly.

I carried him in. David followed. We sat on the floor, facing each other.

We'll break bread, Pa said. He took our can of Spam from the food box.

We were saving that, I said, which wasn't true. The can was left over from our stint as rescue workers. We had deemed it too old to eat.

I'm not here to demolish your supplies, David said.

Yeah, right, I thought.

Here in the Floating City we have manners, Pa said. He peeled off the tin's top and slid the quivering cube onto a plate. He took a knife and divided it into three equal pieces. Or mostly equal. David's piece looked slightly bigger. The Spam didn't seem rotten. My stomach rumbled. I'd been living off vegetables too long.

We each took a bite. Saliva flooded my mouth, but the sensation was hunger, not nausea. I gobbled the rest, as did Pa. David chewed his thoughtfully, glancing from me to Pa and back again.

When our plates were clean, Pa cleared his throat. Your proposal, he said.

Yes, David replied. Bear with me. It will sound strange.

Everything is strange, Pa said.

So it is. David licked his lips, removing a fleck of Spam from his mouth's corner. I want you to leave the Floating City, he said. I want you to come with me.

I felt a dull thud of recognition. I had known he would say something like this. The portents existed: my nightmares, Gandhi's history, David's arrival in conjunction with the rain.

You want us to go to Canada? I asked. He nodded. How would we get there? I asked.

Boat, said David. Then van. I've parked mine in Baton Rouge.

Say we come with you. I watched David's expression and there it was: a flash of excitement. Could we fly? I asked. Do people do that? It was hard to imagine the age of airplanes, runways, delays that sent businessmen raging.

Some do. David's head tilted. If they have money.

Do you? I asked, thinking of his crisp shirts, his radio.

He cleared his throat. I need your help, he said. With the project.

What project? I asked.

David spread his hands wide, as though in offering. A project to make the world, he said. He sounded sheepish, as if the statement's grandiosity embarrassed him.

What kind of world? Pa asked. His face had lost color. He'd always been the one who said he would make the world.

A world beyond the stars, David replied. We have exhausted this planet. I believe it is time to look farther afield.

I remembered Gandhi's history, and goose bumps rose along my arms. A world beyond the stars, I thought.

But why us? asked Pa.

I need an architect, David said. Someone who can design structures.

And me? I leaned forward. I thought of the rising water levels, the increased frequency of storms. The rains are coming, I thought, and this man has plans. Big plans. Suddenly I didn't care about the Floating City, what we had worked so hard to build. I just wanted out.

For a long moment he considered me. I stared at his dry hands, his body like a stick of wood. There would be trees in Canada. Pines. Oak. Cedar.

We also need a poet, he said. Someone to keep us human.

It took me a moment to realize he'd switched from *I* to *we*.

Since when has anybody cared about that? Pa asked.

We're trying to, David said. We're building something huge. The society we create will be better than any of this. He gestured toward the square, where rain had begun to fall.

The Floating City is incredible, I snapped, my loyalty returning.

Yes, David agreed. But it won't last.

No, said Pa. It won't.

His words stopped me cold. I had thought only I was doubting. And yet here Pa was, acknowledging how unstable his experiment had grown. That must have been why he'd stopped writing his fairy tale. He'd recognized it for what it was.

The storm had begun, clouds boiling outside, wind rattling the panes. We sat in silence, listening to water pelt water. Somewhere, thunder. I hoped Michelangelo was safe in his haunted house, watercoloring the windows, charcoaling the floor. I didn't like thinking of him alone in the Superdome, measuring it with his arms to see how wide the scaffolding must be.

Does your project have a name? Pa eventually asked.

Red Star, David said.

The air prickled, like it had when Gandhi read her history.

Where did you get a name like that? Pa asked. His face looked pale. I remembered, after his accident, Pa babbling in his sleep about a red star.

David's sheepishness returned. This will sound ridiculous, he said. I heard it in a dream.

What kind of dream? Pa and I shared a look. We knew about dreams.

I met a woman in the forest, David said. She had uncombed hair and a gleam in her eyes. She spoke to me without speaking. She told me to follow the red star.

A woman once told me to follow the red star, Pa said. Sorrow etched his face. I did. It brought me here.

Believe it or not, that makes sense, David continued. She was the one who gave me your name. Paul Samson, she said. Find the giant.

And you believed this dream? I asked. Enough to track us here?

Honestly, I wouldn't have, David said, if it weren't for the legend we have up there. People in the north talk about a mythical being—half woman, half deer—who wanders the woods and sings sad songs no one can name. They say she is not just a wanderer but a queen. They say after days in the forest, she goes home to a palace among the trees. According to the legend, she is leader of an entire community deep in the woods, that she rules with a firm, fair hand. Some people have gone off, hoping to join this community. They say it's magnificent.

David chuckled. It's just a story, he said, but the woman in my dream reminded me of it. And when I looked up Paul Samson, he was a real person with an address on Walnut Street in Kansas City. I've believed crazier things. Things have gotten damn weird recently.

That sounds like a bunch of bullshit, I said.

Maybe it is, he said. But I had to try. And I've found you, so the dream held some truth.

We're having a party later, I said. I guess we should invite you.

Thank you. David smiled. But my roommate has already done so.

He did? I asked.

He says we must attempt friendship, even in troubled times. Or especially in troubled times. He also said that I would come whether I was invited or not. He said he should freely offer me what I would take regardless.

Pa had regained his color, but still seemed jumpy. I couldn't categorize his expression when David had talked about the woman in the forest. It could have been fear or excitement or anger. It could have been all three.

Kaiser? Pa asked. Do you still have that book David brought?

I do, I replied, feeling it poke me in the back. I reached around to pull it free.

Will you read something to us? Pa asked. I remember how you used to pace around your room reading this book.

The memory warmed me. I had felt like I had to scratch the words into my brain, like everything depended on it. I suddenly regretted leaving my books behind. I opened the dog-eared copy to its most visited page: "The Origins and History of Consciousness." I began to read.

When I'd finished the poem and we three sat breathing, I thought of a line from the poem's beginning, a line about each person in a particular room having lived through a crisis. How perfect to read these words in the year 2027, as our continent dropped piece by piece into the sea.

My mind turned to another poem in the book, whose last line speaks of love and intelligence. Reading it as a kid, I used to believe that was how I wanted to be when I grew old enough to think about love. And maybe, I told myself, sitting in that rain-battered room with my father and a man who might be a pervert or our savior or both, I had done this. I had learned to love with all my intelligence.

I studied David, who was studying Pa. Perhaps I could be the poet for Red Star. I could be the one to keep it human. Stranger things had happened.

AFTER DAVID LEFT, Pa and I spoke.

What did he mean? I asked. About the red star? Does he want us to go into outer space?

I don't know. Pa looked toward the window. The rain had grown stronger.

Do we leave? I asked.

We have to, Pa said.

But this is your dream, I said.

Pa sat up straighter. The Floating City is one step, he said. There's another.

And another after that? I asked.

He stared down at the abrupt space where his legs ended and the floor began. Not for me.

For me? I thought of Pa's nightmare, me walking away from him through the desert.

Maybe, he said. I can't see that far. I've wanted. He paused. I've wanted so much for you, Kaiser. So did your mother. I suppose in the end we wanted different things.

At the mention of my mother, I felt the usual hum of anger, but with a new undertone of grief. Our house in Kansas City was empty. There'd been a fire. I realized I had also assumed we might return. I had thought I might see my mother again. Now she was gone for good.

You've done right by me, Pa said. I hope I've done right by you. If you ever have children of your own, you'll know.

Not likely, I said. I thought of what I'd told Michelangelo. This is no world for children, I added.

It could be. He lifted his bright eyes to mine. I think there's time to make it right.

If we go with David?

If we go with David. See what we can see. Beyond the stars.

We sat in silence for a few minutes, the plate emptied of Spam between us.

Wouldn't it be something—I sighed dramatically, my body slumping—to be ordinary? To have no visions? No dreams? No guests in our city shouting doom?

Yes, Pa agreed. That would be nice.

THAT EVENING WE HAD OUR PARTY. We waited until the rain had subsided. Then our community bounded out in its ragtag beauty to play. They came swinging toward our rooftop on cables, swaying across the bridges Pa had designed, clambering up the ladders Roosevelt and

Michelangelo and I had knotted with cord and wire and bedsheets stripped from sodden mattresses.

They came bearing tomatoes and snap beans, strawberries and squash. Hoarded canisters of crackers, rock hard with age. Tins of tuna, retained since the Floating City's inception. Rose arrived as an antebellum dream, tremendous pink skirts dragging from her waist, yellowed lace scratching her brown throat. Her sister Lily trailed behind in borrowed blue satin, one arm cupping Estrella, who wore an ivory christening dress, smudged at the hem. Rhombus and Isosceles arrived holding hands, which swelled our hearts with happiness. Porcupine brought Harbinger, who could not wrench his eyes from the sky. From across the Quarter straggled the rest, our citizens and wanderers, our scavengers and gardeners. Perhaps it wasn't our full one hundred, but it was a lot.

Our people, I found myself thinking as I watched them crowd our rooftop and the ones nearby. Our place.

The Council welcomed them with handshakes and invitations to the fire pit, where potatoes already smoked. David came too, with Michelangelo. I shook David's hand and pulled Michelangelo close in an embrace. Finally, Rotgut hoisted herself over the ladder and clinked her bulging sack of bottles to the roof's tarred top. The party began.

I got drunk. Gloriously and stupendously drunk. Others got drunk too. Rotgut's swill scorched throat, gut, and bowels. We bit into potatoes before they cooled. Our mouths joined our bellies in burning. What a relief, to feel fire rather than rain.

Roosevelt brought me strawberries, which he slipped into my mouth, gentle as a mother, if one had a mother nothing like mine. My mother would have spent twenty minutes rinsing the berries before dumping them in a bowl and thrusting it at me. Roosevelt must have noticed my expression, because he offered me his bottle. I offered him mine. We linked arms and shouted Gandhi's song to the stars. Cardinals, we screamed. Bluebirds.

With an elaborate flourish, Thatcher unveiled her surprise. A whole chicken, neck wrung, interior gutted, carcass swaddled in leaves from her single living banana tree. Huzzah, we shouted and lowered it onto the coals. As it roasted, its fragrance singed our nostrils and made our bellies growl. When we bit into it, we thought we'd died early and gone to heaven.

Darkness fell. Stars twinkled in the swampy night. I tried to locate the red one, but the grog I'd drunk made them all glitter alike. The fire pit became a pinpoint of light. Damp wood smoldered. Paper caught and flamed. Thatcher's penned words blackened beside Mussolini's. Roosevelt's grayed to ash. The Council had abandoned its histories.

Lily and Rhombus and Isosceles were hugging, Estrella asleep in her mother's arms. Porcupine was chuckling over her bottle, sharp lines erased from her face. Harbinger was pacing the roof's perimeters. Gandhi sat cross-legged by the pit, her locket reflecting flames, her voice her instrument. Herons, she crooned. Red-winged blackbirds. Pa and Thatcher were sharing a potato. Her face bent toward his, illuminated by flames. Huh, I thought. Not Gandhi after all.

Michelangelo appeared at my elbow. Come, he said, and we slipped downstairs.

I took him into my bed. My mouth, my neck, my thighs on fire. His body in mine. You'll paint the city to its rafters, I whispered in his ear. His scent eclipsed mine, the sweet tang of a man pure in his intent. I will, he whispered back, and beyond. When he slipped free from me, I felt the loss like a fist. He left me alone in my sleeping place and returned to the party.

A step outside. A voice in the dark. Reedy and thin. Kaiser, it called. Join me on the balcony, David said through the open door.

I pulled on my clothes and did. We sat together rocking while the celebration raged above. I could hear Gandhi singing. Or perhaps that was Rose, sobbing over a torn hem. Or Roosevelt. Maybe he had dozed off, been woken by terror. Maybe those were screams, not songs.

I don't want to leave, I told David.

But you will. He did not sound smug, only certain.

I will, I said. Pa too.

When? he asked.

Tomorrow, I said. Why wait? The rains won't stop.

You have some time, he said.

I don't care. I tipped my rocking chair back and braced myself, lifted in air. When I was a kid, I said, my mother let me wear Band-Aids for a single day. Then she'd rip them off. Say the wound needed air.

I'm glad, David said. This city doesn't suit you.

I released my chair and let it rock. I thought you admired it, I said.

I do. But not your place in it.

Anger made me sharp. What the fuck do you mean? I asked. Presumptuous asshole, I thought.

You could be great.

I am great.

Playing your explorer games with your boyfriends. His tone mocked me.

You're jealous. I wanted to kick his shins, but refrained. We have rules for visitors. Hospitality, Pa has said, defines the course of events.

Possibly, David said. I've waited a long time to meet you. You're more than I thought.

At this, I felt proud and hated myself for it.

You're a woman, he said. Not a daughter or a lover. You could be great, he repeated. You could shape what is to come.

Pa has my loyalty, I insisted.

And do you have his?

Yes, I said, though his words stirred doubt.

He tore you from your mother. Pulled you from a normal life and dragged you to a city in chaos. David stilled his chair's movement. A mere child.

I wanted another drink. I wanted to shout for Roosevelt to bring me a bottle, but feared my voice would be lost in the din. And you, I said, want to drag me too. What makes you different?

I can offer you a future.

So what? I said, but we both knew that's why Pa and I had chosen to follow.

The project is enormous, he said. You won't regret joining us. I can promise you that.

I didn't like the way *promise* sounded in his mouth. Like a contract. A paper to which I had already signed my name.

You and your father will have to make sacrifices, he continued.

As long as you aren't asking for Pa's arms too.

No. He grinned. Nothing like that. It'll be worth it, Kaiser. More than worth it.

We stopped rocking and climbed upstairs. When Roosevelt saw me, he shouted my name. Gratitude for his friendship rushed through me. He held out his bottle. I took it and drank. You too, old man, Roosevelt said and passed the bottle to David. To Columbus, he trumpeted, our esteemed invader. To Columbus, David conceded, and I knew he understood the joke. May all societies echo this one, he said. May it never rain again, Roosevelt rejoined.

The three of us drank, then Michelangelo, and Mussolini. Some were sleeping, others awake. Rotgut was snoring by the fire, which had collapsed to embers. The Biloxi woman was stuffing squash in her mouth with both hands. Pa and Thatcher were huddled by the roof's edge, his torso in her lap. He was kissing her eyelids, and I wondered how my mother would feel if she saw. I remembered her chastising me when I forgot to take my Wellbutrin. Would she chastise Pa too? Or would she not care at all?

You relinquished your right to care, I told her memory. Go away.

The night deepened. We huddled around the coals, our bottles nearly drained. Columbus and Roosevelt. Mussolini. I stared across the pit at Michelangelo. He stared back. Columbus told a tale of snow, and our hearts hungered for what we'd lost. One by one, we fell asleep, nodding off into dreams, or lack thereof.

At midnight the rains began and drove us inside. I went to bed alone, my body ablaze.

DAY SEVEN

In the bleary dawn of the next day, I could hear Thatcher and Mussolini splashing outside, gathering the Floating City's night soil from each Townhouse, depositing it in their barge, rowing it to the building on North Rampart we'd designated for disposal. They were children of the earth, those two. Such tasks did not disgust them.

Pa and I had decided to strike out early. We would not say goodbye. I broke this rule. I went to see Michelangelo. I found him outside his mansion, untethering his canoe.

The Superdome? I asked. He nodded. Can you get inside? I asked. With that canoe?

I'll manage, he said. His boat was crammed with paint cans.

You haven't built a scaffold yet, I said.

I'm starting low, over the top tier of seats. The city I paint will need a foundation.

What city will it be? I asked.

This one, he said. We will need a record.

What will the foundation be? I asked. Water and mud?

You and your father, he said.

Ah, I replied. I was standing on a balcony, he floating below. He used to shave his head with a rusty collection of Bic disposables, but they'd broken one by one, so he'd let his hair grow out. With his beard, it framed his face with a perfect circle.

You're beginning to look like Jesus, I told him.

The old rules are dead, I hear. He grinned. The old tales too.

How long will you stay? I asked.

As long as the painting takes.

And the floods?

They will wait.

Won't you be lonely? I asked. The others will leave too.

Roosevelt won't. Nor Mussolini. Not until I do. We made a pact.

I thought Roosevelt wanted out.

Michelangelo shrugged.

I leaned over the railing. So, you and Roosevelt and Mussolini will stay until the floods come. I'm going north, I said. With Columbus. Pa too.

Michelangelo ducked his head so I could not see his face. Columbus told me, he said. He told me to let you go.

He doesn't understand you.

I wouldn't keep you.

I know.

In the shadow of the Lalaurie mansion, he finished untying his canoe. I scanned the house's facade. He'd claimed this reconstructed place for his own and driven any lingering ghosts from its chambers. He'd made his own history. If anyone could survive this city, Michelangelo could. I'll write you a letter, I said.

Who the fuck writes letters anymore? he asked.

What, you expect me to text you? I said with a grin. He began to laugh, and I joined in. I felt Rotgut's brew rising in my throat and swallowed hard to calm it. He quieted too, and we stood there gazing at each other.

And how will you send it? he asked finally. By Pony Express?

Sure, I said. On a white horse.

Black, he said.

Okay.

AND THAT, MICHELANGELO, is how we said goodbye. Perhaps you remember it. I thought it would be a fitting end for this history. Six months after my first attempt, I have finally figured out how to write it. As you can see, I have started with the day Pa told us to begin a chronicle. I have called that Day One. I thought it would make sense to end it a week later, on the morning Pa and I departed the Floating City, the morning you and I said our farewell. Seven days, straight from Gandhi's Bible. She would have liked that. You can tell her, if she's still there.

Half a year has passed since we left. This morning, Pa told me it was almost Christmas. He chuckled. That old story, he said. Since Christmas is nearly here, Michelangelo, you can consider this missive a gift. You can think of it as the letter I promised you. I didn't know what else to write. We never did speak of love.

Now I have finished my history, I will package it up and get it to you. David has messengers to do his work. They're not black ponies, but they'll do. They will travel south as we—David, Pa, and I—traveled north in David's van last summer, subsisting on gas station burritos and trying not to let the weather kill us. Maybe the messengers will also hit heat waves in Nebraska, droughts in Missouri, blizzards in Arkansas. Or maybe the sun will shine the whole way.

I hope the Floating City hasn't floated you away. I hope you will know what to do with this history, my gift to you. Take it somewhere, Michelangelo. Spread our story. And when you have finished, come find me. Travel over the North Dakota border into Canada and ask for the

Northern Refuge. You will find us in the forest, buried underground in a warren of white tunnels. David will let you in. He's not the evil man I thought he was. His arrival did indeed signal a change, but not a tragic one. He simply wanted Pa and me for his project. His project to make the world.

What's funny is that we're not the only ones David brought here. He told us the other coastal communities had disappeared and that was true. He didn't tell us he got there first. Nearly eighty people live in the Northern Refuge, most of them refugees from those other flooded communities. As the water levels rose, David visited them as he would visit us. Come with me, he urged. I have a dream. And like we would, they boated over their waters, climbed into his van, and came. You should have seen our surprised faces when we arrived to discover the Northern Refuge already full of bedraggled, yet earnest, survivors. This seems strange, I said to Pa. Do we stay? We stay, he replied. We've come this far. We have no choice.

Pa and I are collaborating with David, drafting plans for the Red Star project. He's put the others to work at computer screens or in the kitchens or down on their knees scrubbing floors. Most seem content, but one man did try to foment rebellion. They did this to my ancestors, he shouted to his fellows ranged along the computer banks. This is the railroads all over again. Then go back to China, another man shouted back.

We were with David in his office and saw it on the surveillance cameras. Without a word, David got up and walked out. Pa and I watched him on the cameras. He took both those men by the arm and marched them up the ramp to the surface. He slid open the exit and threw them out into the wilderness. Red Star has no place for you, he told them. Then he shut the door.

This startled us. But we also felt relieved. We've had enough of chaos. The society we're creating is going to be different. It'll have Pa's designs and my words. A solid foundation. I've been thinking a lot about what I said to you in the Superdome. That thing about children. I was wrong. My kids won't be weak. Even if they are, they'll be able to survive. We're making a place where children can thrive. Where they don't have to fear our planet's limitations.

Pa said it best when he woke up this morning. His dream last night didn't feature the man in the desert. He'd dreamed instead of the woman from David's story. The one who is half deer, half woman. The one who roams the forest and speaks without words. He said he'd seen the community David had spoken of, that it was indeed magnificent.

Kaiser, he said, his old fierceness returned. Listen. We're going to build this world anew.

Michelangelo, when you arrive, I will tell you two secrets. One is about the project we are working on, where we're heading and what we're going to do there. One is about something else, something to do with me or, I should say, with us. I think you will want to know both things. Both are the reason I picked up this pen so many months after Pa insisted I should, why I realized our history did matter. Both are about creation. Both concern the future.

It's a trade, Michelangelo. Hear me. I give you this. You give me you. An even exchange.

Humans operate this way. They always have. I believe this time we can do it right.

MICHELANGELO

THE CARIBBEAN SEA, 2030

Michelangelo doesn't like the clouds. Above him arcs a tropical blue sky, but a black line is spreading on the horizon. As he watches, a jagged red finger darts from within. Lightning, he thinks. The air crackles with electricity and, even at this distance, his beard stands on end.

"Roosevelt," he calls. "Batten down the hatches."

"Another one?" Roosevelt crosses from the yacht's stern to the bow. Together they peer at the thunderheads building to the west.

"We should have stayed on that island."

"The storm would have hit us there too."

"But there were mangoes."

They grin at each other, remembering the laden trees, how the ripe flesh nearly burst through the skin. They brought as many with them as they could, but they couldn't eat them fast enough. In the end, they had to dump the spoiled ones overboard. Michelangelo still gets sad thinking about those red-and-gold fruits tumbling into the sea, the Caribbean so clear they could watch them sink for a long time. A waste, he thinks, like so much else.

"Go tell Mussolini," Roosevelt says. "We need to furl these sails."

Michelangelo clambers to the cabin's door. He's not as steady on his feet as Roosevelt, who seems more at home on this boat than he did in the Floating City. At night Michelangelo's dreams still pitch and roll with the water's undulations. Last night he dreamed of a red-haired woman moving under him like a wave. Kaiser, he thought upon waking, and the familiar longing plucked at his heart. He laid his palm to the slender bound book under his pillow, and recalled her words. Spread our story.

He discovers Mussolini napping in the dining nook, his squat body sprawled with abandon across the faded cushions. It's hard to imagine the yacht in its former life, crowded with retirees and grandchildren, the cushions' plaid still crisp, the nickel and wood gleaming. When they discovered it a year ago, Roosevelt crowed with delight. A Morgan, he shouted. I've always wanted one. Out of all the yachts in the harbor, it remained the most intact. Hurry, Michelangelo urged, the sea's rising.

They escaped the Floating City with their lives but little else. The others had already fled. For a single perfect year, Michelangelo and his two friends owned the city. Then the true storms arrived, with a vengeance. It was as Gandhi's history predicted: red rain, fire, floods. *I must be gone and live, or stay and die*, thought Michelangelo as they raced toward the harbor in their flimsy canoes. Kaiser would have been proud he'd retained poetry until the end.

Mussolini liked to recall those early days at sea as a marker for how far they'd come, but Michelangelo did not. This was before they learned to fish. Hunger pressed their empty stomachs against their backbones. But Michelangelo's chest felt emptier. Each grueling day on the waves, waiting for the afternoon storms to bring rainwater, he counted one more thing he'd lost. His mansion. His mural, finessed to minute and perfect detail, scrolled across the ceiling of the Superdome. The woman who'd left him to their city's fate. Kaiser.

He shakes Mussolini's foot. "Wake up. A storm is coming."

In a second, Mussolini is standing. His yellow eyes are veined red from sleep, but he moves quickly, following Michelangelo to the deck. The clouds have rolled directly overhead. Crimson flashes periodically illuminate them, revealing a sickly green underside. Roosevelt is furling the mainsail, but the jib is luffing wildly in the wind. Michelangelo and Mussolini tackle it, managing to get it down before the first rains hit.

They cram into the hold and seal the hatch behind them, but not before the rain comes. It's not the humid downpour of the tropics. These drops feel like ice. In the sudden gloom, their scared eyes find each other.

"What the fuck?" says Mussolini. Then the waves strike.

Michelangelo doesn't know how long they crouch in the cabin while the storm batters their boat. He tries to count seconds between lightning and thunder, but loses track almost immediately. The air has turned bitingly cold and they shiver in their shorts and thin T-shirts. Their bare toes lose all feeling. Everything pitches back and forth: the yacht, the cushions, their bodies. They take turns staggering to the toilet to vomit. Each time it emerges more acidic than before.

Michelangelo wipes his mouth and thinks of the wasted mangoes. During their year at sea, they've discovered a multitude of islands, usually no more than a green hump above sea level. On these outposts of dry land, they've scavenged for guavas and bananas, sometimes stumbling upon remnants of human civilization, though no humans. Once they found an entire mega-market. Its food had decayed, of course, but they found clothing, muddied by floods but wearable. Fishing poles. Sunglasses. The mother lode, Roosevelt crowed. But none of those islands boasted mangoes. They should have stayed on the last one they found. Michelangelo braces himself against the swaying wall and vomits again. His fingers have gone numb.

They sleep, or something. They slump together in a pile, these three friends who lived to watch a city die. Michelangelo can feel his companions' fetid breath on his face. Searching for heat, they burrow closer.

Sometime toward midnight, the yacht stops moving. The cold deepens. Michelangelo wakes and sleeps, wakes and sleeps. A chilly light finally flutters his eyelids open. He disentangles himself from the others and climbs to the hatch. It won't open.

"Son of a bitch," he mutters. His toes look white, as though all color has bled from his body. He rams his shoulder against the hatch. It cracks and whines, then opens. He emerges into a world of ice. Around him stretches the Caribbean, frozen solid. A puzzled-looking seagull is stalking across it, pecking feebly here and there. The deck is a slippery sheet. The furled sails glisten. The sun is rising, but it's a winter sun. Michelangelo crawls onto the deck, careful not to slip. At the railing, he peers down at the rigid sea. Beneath the ice, tropical fish are swimming. He can discern their purples and yellows, their blues and greens. There is hope, he thinks.

DURING THE ENDLESS DAYS, he clings to this. But by day five, even Roosevelt has lost his energy. They have tried to ration their food supplies, but they didn't have much to begin with. Some dried fish. A bushel of raw peanuts from another island. They'd been counting on another stretch of land soon. They hadn't reckoned on an ice storm.

They spend their time in the dining nook, telling stories. They've sealed the doors and dragged all the blankets from the berths, piled them on the floor with the plaid cushions. Mussolini has found socks stashed in one of the closets, so at least their feet have thawed. Very carefully, Roosevelt has kindled a small fire in a metal pan. They take turns tending it with wood from a busted chair and table. A few times they climb up to the deck to observe the weather. Still no change. The white sun circles the earth but emits no warmth. Michelangelo wonders how long the fish will survive. Probably a long time, he thinks. We'll likely die first.

Roosevelt tells boxing ring anecdotes and Mussolini offers winding jokes that seem to have no punch line, but which they enjoy anyway. Michelangelo shares stories from his ancestors. When he was a boy in Tremé, he watched his mother stencil a family tree on their kitchen wall. On his sixth birthday, she completed it. Each night after dinner, she would relate a tale from one member of their family. He knows each generation back to slave times. In 1832, his great-great-great-grandfather bought his freedom and his own Creole cottage near Congo Square. Nearly two hundred years later, Michelangelo was born and raised in the same house. The Flood forced him to abandon it, but he can trace each branch of that family tree in his mind.

"You are rich," Mussolini tells him. "To know your family. My past is a vacuum. I know we also used to be slaves. I know Trujillo's men killed my grandmother's sister. That is all."

"I don't know shit," Roosevelt adds. "For all I'm aware, my grandfather murdered your kin, Mussolini."

"This is why, in the Floating City, Pa wanted us to write histories," Mussolini says. "To keep track of the past."

"That man." Roosevelt smiles fondly. "What a fucking crackpot. I wonder what happened to them." He nudges Michelangelo with an elbow. "Remember Kaiser?"

At her name, Michelangelo's heart leaps. "I remember," he says.

He checks the fire. It's nearly gone out. He feeds it another stick of broken furniture. He hasn't told them about the bound book under his pillow: Kaiser's story of seven days, the one she called a history. Over two years ago, three men brought it to him. He was alone in the Superdome, painting. The men put Kaiser's history in his hands and left the way they'd come, zipping through the watery streets in an actual speedboat. He still doesn't know what to do with it. At first the prospect thrilled him. Spread our story, she'd written. Yes, he thought. Our story matters. He kept her pages safe and dry, wrapped them in plastic and stowed them beneath the cushions of his horsehair sofa. When they sailed away from the drowning city, he had it strapped to his body under his clothes. This is my chance, he thought, to share it with the world. Everybody will learn about the small man grown big, the girl who carried him on her back, the spectacular society we built on the rooftops.

But as their time on the yacht lengthened, so did his doubt. He had no way to share it. They'd encountered no people on their voyage. He could show it to Roosevelt and Mussolini, but because they knew it already, that seemed pointless. And maybe it didn't matter as much as he'd believed. The city was gone, its people scattered. Nobody would want to hear about a failed experiment. People liked success stories. Those were the narratives that mattered.

Besides, he thinks now, what kind of story was it? Just another self-centered tale by a white person who thought they knew everything. He should have left it under the mango trees on the last island. At least then it could have been useful, fertilized the trees, helped grow more fruit.

"Kaiser." Mussolini sighs. "You should have married that woman."

Despite his thoughts, Michelangelo can't help smiling. He recalls the abandon with which she splattered her poems on the walls. "She wouldn't have married me," he says. "She said the old customs were dead."

"Too bad." Roosevelt scratches his beard. "You would have had some badass kids."

Michelangelo lies down and tucks a cushion under his head. "We would have had sad kids," he says. "I bet everybody has sad kids these days."

THAT NIGHT THE ICE BREAKS. In his sleep Michelangelo hears it and starts awake. Roosevelt and Mussolini sit up too. Together, they climb the stairs and push open the hatch. The moon is new, the darkness near complete. In the sprawling mass of stars above, Michelangelo can pick out the planets. Mars is a fat red star. He wonders what it would feel like to be there, gazing out at Earth. He wonders how green their planet still looks from space. Perhaps now it's all blue.

"Listen," Roosevelt says, but he doesn't have to. The ice is booming as it breaks up. It sounds like cannons in the battles of yore.

"In the morning," Mussolini says, "we can push on."

In the morning, they do. The sea is washed clean, each wave a glittering miracle. Overhead the sun blazes tropical heat. A handful of raw peanuts and one dried mackerel remain. Maintaining hope for dry land, they share the fish around, each man taking a bite before passing it on. Their teeth gleam through their bushy beards. Wind billows the sails. When a dolphin leaps before the yacht's bow, Roosevelt shouts his excitement. "Thar she blows!" he cries. Their desperate midnights of storytelling and fire seem very far behind. It feels good to sweat again.

In late afternoon, they spot land. A green hill curves up from the sea. White houses speckle the slopes. Mussolini points. "Are those people?" he asks. From a distance the figures look small as insects, but when they squint, they can see them. Yes. People. A chance for food. For conversation. Possibly a chance for fear. Michelangelo's pulse quickens.

"Holy shit." Roosevelt consults his compass, his creased map, his compass again. "Mussolini," he whispers. Awe has hushed his voice. "We've come home."

"No."

"Yes."

"That is our island?" Mussolini asks.

"What's left of it," Roosevelt replies.

Mussolini and Roosevelt revert to childhood, kids gaping at the wide wonders of the world. Here is the land they lost, the one they assumed they'd never see again. Love for these men knifes through Michelangelo. They may have lost his birthplace to rising water, but they've found the homeland of his friends. An embattled island—pummeled by earthquakes, tsunamis, centuries of bloodshed—rising emerald green and alive from a crisp blue sea.

Michelangelo watches the island draw closer. Some of the people have noticed them. They are pointing and waving. Many seem to be smiling. The first humans they have seen in two years. This could be his opportunity. He could share Kaiser's story, tell these islanders about the Floating City, the wonders they created there. The rope bridges, the rooftop gardens, his mural that depicted it all. Maybe, in the end, it is a tale worth telling.

He focuses on the houses dotting the hills. When they dock, he might be able to claim one for his own. He didn't realize how much he's missed treading dry ground. In her story, Kaiser told him to come north. Two secrets, she wrote. Come find me. But Michelangelo isn't ready for secrets, not about her, not about the project she's working on. He certainly doesn't want to hear about David, the man who convinced her to leave. He doesn't want to hear about her future. For now, contending with his present is enough.

As the wind puffs them toward shore, Michelangelo spots one house by the beach. It looks abandoned, tattered curtains flapping in the windows. Nobody is in the yard. That house could be his. He could claim it as he did the Lalaurie mansion. This time he might not stay there alone. He could find a woman, one with black hair, no oversized dreams. Together they could make babies. He could name one Kaiser, one Pa. These kids will not be sad, for they will own this wide white beach, this expansive sky. They will not know the vanished earth, only the one they've inherited, the one that freezes and thaws and floods and burns but does not seem ready to die.

That house on the beach must have a kitchen. On its wall, he can redraw his family tree. Before he shares Kaiser's history, he will share his own. He'll do what she did, what all historians do: place his family at its center. Generations of free men and women in a nation that wanted them chained. He is now the last one standing. And he has sailed to this incredible island to spread his story.

See there, he will tell whoever will listen. He will point to each branch of the tree he's etched on the wall. Those are my people. That is my blood.

PENELOPE

MARS, 2046

May 1, 2046

This morning, we landed on the red planet. Our ship docked in the Red Star station. They must have rolled our hibernating bodies out. A technician with chopped hair woke me and cut mine off too. I watched my fat curls fall. Hair can muck up the vents, she told me. This is more hygienic. My mouth tastes like glue. My ankles are bloated with fluid. My body registers its long sleep, but my mind does not. My brain tells me that yesterday I was at the base in the Russian steppes, awaiting the launch. I had flown there on a private jet, my first time on a plane, wrenching me from the Northern Refuge, from K and Pa, everything I'd known. Today I'm millions of miles away in a station composed of interlocking pods on a rocky surface, my stomach churning in perpetual somersault. The technician weighed and measured me. I have lost five pounds and grown one inch. I hope the station's gravity is powerful enough to shrink me back to my original size. I do not like how stretched my spine feels.

This evening at a reception milling with the station's scientists, I met the other three volunteers. Agnes, Winona, Chantrea. I'm Penelope, I said, and we shook hands. We were all wearing the station's jumpsuits, gray with a red starburst on the chest. It felt bizarre to meet women with whom I had shared space for nine months. At the Russian base, they had frozen each of us in solitude and slotted us into the ship like cargo. They didn't want us to meet beforehand, maybe in case we drew battle lines, named enemies and friends. At Red Star, they promised, we would be clean, fresh, and new as babies. Is that what K would call irony?

At the reception, they offered us water, not wine. As I was sipping mine, the head of the Red Star project approached me. Gabrielle. I had seen her before only on a screen. In person her chin looked softer, her eyes gentler. She brushed my finger when offering me a cube of synthetic cheese. The dunes beyond the sealed windows are less red than I thought, but the sky more yellow. I assumed I wouldn't crave sleep again so soon, but I am so tired. Interplanetary jet lag, I guess. After I finish this first entry in the log, I will try to sleep. My duvet is crimson, my favorite color. Pa is an expert with details.

May 2, 2046

This morning they took us on a tour of the station. I was excited to see the place K and Pa had designed, but frankly, it seems rather plain. First, we watched a film in a gray auditorium. Gabrielle's face appeared on the screen, welcoming us to Red Star. With her high cheekbones, she looks like her uncle David, but with an unlined face and black hair instead of white. We could not expand this colony without help from women like you, she said. Thank you for your contributions. We've done nothing yet, whispered Agnes next to me. The screen showed footage of the station in its early days: astronauts who died from radiation poisoning, failed attempts at terraforming, ice mined from underground and liquefied. The current inhabitants posed on a dune, grinning through their helmets. The film closed with the station's anthem. I know they meant it to be an amalgamation of Earth's national songs, but it sounded like "The Star-Spangled Banner."

The real Gabrielle met us at the door. She seemed more serious than she did last night. She shook our hands brusquely. An honor, simpered the volunteer called Chantrea, to meet the head of the Red Star project. Chantrea's tight face loosened when she saw Gabrielle. You bless us, Chantrea continued, with your generosity. Then she bowed, which seemed too much, but maybe in her homeland, on the shores of the Mekong Sea, this quaint custom continues. Her fawning, however, seemed to charm Gabrielle. She must have enjoyed hearing her efforts praised. K told me Gabrielle has devoted her entire life to this project, picking up the reins when David died, traveling here when she was a mere girl to head the team.

Come, Gabrielle said. Let me show you your new home. She brought us to the mini-mill and the chicken lab. The chickens were not the genuine artifact. They'd been formed from micro-fungus, yet formed whole, yellow feet, red combs, and all. They were hanging upside down from hooks, row upon row. Why the mimicry? asked Agnes. We want this place to feel familiar, replied the lab assistant.

We continued the tour. Featureless hallways. "Laundry" room aka chemical cleaners. Hydroponic gardens with buttery lettuce. Gabrielle showed us how to position our palms to the airlocks and whoosh them open. We met the obstetrician. His hand was cold when I shook it. I didn't like the thought of him putting those hands on me, but I would have no choice. He asked who would be first. Agnes volunteered. Her spine is erect as a pine tree, her nose severe. She was born in St. Putin in the United Russian Republic, but she possesses precise English. Winona offered to go second, I third, Chantrea fourth. We'll fertilize immediately, the obstetrician said. I pictured our eggs, scooped from our bodies at the Russian base and sealed in their own tubes, sent spinning through space beside us. We will not meet them again until implantation. A funny kind of reunion.

My entire life I've been preparing for this. As a child, I craved adventure, an escape from the underground tunnels of the Northern Refuge. I pictured myself soaring into space, shot into the stars. Great, K said when I told her. We'll send you to Mars. I remember her smiling as though it were a joke, but it wasn't. They needed volunteers for this project. How delighted K was that her daughter elected to be one of them. In the old days, she told me, women didn't have many choices. Their bodies, she said, were co-opted, used for the whims of others. You will make your own decisions, she promised. Say yes, and we will launch you into the stars.

So here I am, making my own choices. I chose to come here. I have chosen to be the third volunteer implanted. I am choosing to type in this log. Soon, I will choose to go to bed.

My ankles are still swollen, my body ponderous from the return of gravitational pull. Perhaps it is shrinking back to its correct height. Even typing this log takes extra effort. I expected to feel a lot more excited, but all I want to do is sleep. I don't recall dreams from my journey through dark matter, but they must have visited. I would like to dream of K. I call her Mother in dreams, but not in life. She wasn't comfortable being a mother. Let me be myself, she would say, and I'll let you be you. Tomorrow, Gabrielle promises us, we can contact our families. It's not the same though. You can't hug someone through a screen.

May 3, 2046

We've established routines. Six a.m. wake-up. One hour of cardio on the treadmill. Breakfast is a bowl of grain boiled to a paste. Medical examinations. I met the geneticist. Why do we need you? I asked. I'm not a synthetic chicken. We must ensure the radiation does not affect you, he said. No two-headed babies, I said. Certainly not, he replied.

After examinations, thirty minutes of cardio on the elliptical. Lunch is something beige and indeterminate. In the early afternoon we study. This was K's idea. To keep the mission human, she said. We had a chance at humanity once, she would tell me, let's not blow it again. Except here we don't read literature, as I did with her. We read baby manuals. Today I learned how to offer my breast upon first contact. Do not give up, the manual encouraged, if infant refuses to latch. As though I need a lesson in perseverance.

In late afternoon we have recreation time, which translates as naptime. Then we tackle restrictive exercise, which means repetitive lifting of small weights. Dinner tonight was micro-fungus disguised as chicken breast and potatoes stained red from the mineral-fed soil in which they grow. Post-supper, we watched a film from the early century. Something in Euro, which K called French. Chantrea fell asleep, her head lolling against my shoulder.

I am also exhausted, but tonight I fear sleep. K would understand. Both she and Pa suffered from the same recurring dream. In it a faceless man would walk toward them through a desert. There were variations, but it was always a desert and they could always hear his boots, though they trod on sand. She said the dream terrified her, because she both knew and did not know what it meant. I used to think it sounded silly, but last night I had the same dream. The desert didn't look hot. It looked cold, as I know it is. I was shivering when I woke.

When we talked through the screen, I tried to tell K about it, but the connection was poor. Her face kept cutting out, her voice in patches. I miss you, we both managed, but that was it.

May 10, 2046

I have skipped days in this log. I meant to keep it daily, but at night I am so tired. My stomach is still looping from the journey here. The nausea—not to mention the dreams—makes sleep difficult. The others seem weary too. Everybody except Agnes. She is wide awake. They implanted her today. Her face glows like a candle behind paper. After she returned to our pod, Chantrea touched her stomach. I wish I were you, she said to Agnes. At dinner, Gabrielle brought Agnes actual meat. A roasted guinea pig, its skin crackling and crisp. We're experimenting with live animals, Gabrielle said. We must keep you strong, she told Agnes, protein is essential. Chantrea and Winona salivated at the sight, but I didn't like how the cook had left the head on. Its teeth were too long and yellow.

They will implant Winona next. Then me. We are special. Blessed. Nine out of ten women cannot get pregnant, they say. Our numbers have dwindled with our landmass. It seems our bodies understand the need for conservation more than we do. It doesn't matter, K used to insist. We can reclaim this place. You will save us, she would say to me. You will be the mother of thousands. We are so grateful, she added, that you've chosen this. I'm grateful that I can, I replied.

You're lucky, Gabrielle told me tonight. She had stayed with us to watch Agnes polish off the guinea pig. In a few minutes, Agnes had reduced the animal to a pile of bones. Gabrielle smiled. Her eyes are liquid brown, her skin ivory where mine is golden brown. Her shorn head makes her look like a bird. An eagle perhaps, or a falcon. Something with alert eyes and a quick bend to the neck. I wish I could do what you can, she whispered to me. Her words puffed me up with pride. I *am* lucky, I thought. I have so much to offer. When Gabrielle stood to leave, she bumped her hip against my shoulder. The flesh under my gray jump-suit hummed. Tonight, I do not fear my dreams.

May 15, 2046

During recreation time we no longer nap. Agnes and I play gin rummy. Usually I win. Agnes laughs at my small victories, how I jump up from my chair and shout my triumph. Chantrea studies us with hungry eyes. I invited her to join, but she said she preferred to watch.

Today Gabrielle swished through the airlock and joined us at the table. She watched us for a while before turning to Winona. Winona had dug wool and knitting needles out of our craft box. Already she had the beginning of a hat. Would you care for a game? Gabrielle asked her. But Winona shook her head. Card games are not for me, she said. Too much plotting.

Here. Agnes tossed her cards down. Continue for me. I need to take a nap. This is wearing me out. She patted her abdomen. Already it looked swollen. Chantrea's starved gaze trained on it. Nuns raised her, Buddhists of an ancient order who had taken up residence in the Reclaimed City of Angkor Wat. I wonder what deprivations Chantrea faced in her stony city, what hungers forced her to join this mission. I know why I joined. I did because I could, because my body was capable. How could I not pledge myself to the cause?

I wish K could see me now. All cozy with the other volunteers, playing cards with the head of the Red Star project. I want to run to K as I did when I was a kid, showing her a new word I had learned from a screen or telling her about a dream I had. I wasn't awake to know it, but I celebrated a birthday on my journey through space. I'm eighteen now. An adult. So why do I still feel like a child?

May 24, 2046

They have twinned Winona. When she arrived, she was the youngest Ojibwe of the First Nations, famous for defeating the White Pirates at the Great Lake Sea. Now the youngest of her tribe fattens within her. We do not ask who fertilizes our eggs. Perhaps Red Star technicians. Perhaps men on Earth. It doesn't matter. The infants will be ours. Gabrielle has promised this. It's part of the reason I volunteered. I admired how K had raised me on her own. I liked the idea of motherhood without a man's meddling.

After implantation, Gabrielle brought Winona a guinea pig too. Winona picked her teeth with its bones. This time the smell made me salivate. My mind believes I ate venison a month ago, but my stomach knows better. The frozen journey was so strange. It has obliterated an entire section of my life from memory. My brain feels as though it's constantly running to keep up with my body.

Last time we spoke through a screen, I asked K to tell me a story. Once a girl grew up and made her mother proud, she responded. That's no story, I protested. You're right, she admitted, it's just a fact. I'm sorry, she said, you have taken my imagination with you.

I think she meant it as a joke, but it didn't sound like one. I wonder what my father would think about me being here. His name was Michelangelo. K said he was a painter, a great artist. She knew him in the Floating City, where she and Pa had tried to build a civilization. Lucky for them, David arrived before the new floods did, and whisked them away to the Northern Refuge. K said Michelangelo stayed. To finish a masterpiece, she scoffed when I asked why. I sent him a message, she said, and told him to join us. As you can see—she gestured at our chamber, empty except for us—he didn't. K assumed he'd drowned. But he could have gone somewhere else when the floods arrived. The desert. A mountaintop. Another submerged city in need of an artist.

Winona and Agnes have begun to whisper together in English, sometimes Russian. Agnes is teaching her. They have formed a close pair, independent of us. Despite this, Chantrea follows them to watch their games. Her closed face opens when she's near them, childlike wonder illuminating it. They favor board games. Risk. Sorry! Monopoly. Relics of a dead time.

The game of Risk I find most amusing, witnessing them conquer areas that no longer exist. That's my home, I heard Chantrea tell them today. She pointed to the landmass that used to be Southeast Asia. I'm very good at climbing stairs, she said. I know how to fish too, in the Mekong Sea. And I can recognize all the faces of Buddha. Neither Agnes nor Winona looked at her. They didn't seem to hear her. They implanted Agnes only fourteen days ago, but I swear she is already showing. When she leaned back, I saw a slight swell under her jumpsuit. That must have been a trick of the light. It is too soon.

Occasionally Gabrielle stops by to play cards with me. Today she told me about her homeland, somewhere in Europe. This surprised me. I had assumed she'd been born near the Northern Refuge, as David had been. But Gabrielle said she'd never been to North America. I heard her accent then, a taut quality to her vowels. You should have seen my city, she said. In the springtime, the pear blossoms were extraordinary. This was before the Land Wars, of course. She paused. I watched her, thinking of all the children gone. If only they'd known how hard it would be to make more.

It was a beautiful city, Gabrielle said. Full of lights. What city was that? I asked. No matter, she said. It's wastelands now. Half water, half rubble. A place where missiles went to die.

Do you miss home? I asked. Do you? she asked. I miss my mother, I said, though she was sad a lot. She had a city too, I confessed. It drowned.

But we didn't, Gabrielle said. Did we? Her eyes remind me of a pool in the forest above the Northern Refuge. In autumn, leaves would fall into that pool. Shades of brown and amber and gold. I would like to see Gabrielle's eyes closed, in more than a quick blink. No, I agreed, laying down my winning cards. We did not.

May 37, 2046

Time here stretches like a rubber band. How do you measure years, I asked Gabrielle, since one here lasts two on Earth? The same, she said, but longer. We wanted to keep the years in sync, she said, so we changed the calendar. Months extended to sixty days, I said. More or less, she replied. Was that David's idea? I asked. It was mine, Gabrielle said, looking very pleased with herself. If I were her, I would congratulate myself too. It's no small feat to erect a station on Mars, even in the best of times. Gathering the resources alone must have been a tremendous undertaking. All those private donors she must have approached. She must be very persuasive, to part people from their money when so little of it exists.

I am thinking of time tonight for a reason. Tomorrow they will implant me. I, too, will be twinned. Be strong, K told me today through the screen. You are the new breed, she said, the one who will carve a path through the wilderness. You must meet your destiny. I will, I promised. You are everything I hoped you would be, she said. And more.

Next time I speak to her, I will have my own small me fattening within. K and Pa will burst with pride. When I told them I wanted to volunteer, they threw me a party with confetti and a cake. You will complete the family's cycle, Pa trumpeted. You will build the world anew. But I wasn't an architect like Pa or a poet like K. I couldn't paint masterpieces as my father could. I grew up no scientist, no geneticist or technician or interstellar botanist. I grew up a woman, nothing more. I could only offer myself.

May 38, 2046

This morning I skipped cardio and breakfast. They wheeled me from our pod in style. The scientists lined the hallways to watch my procession. Good luck, they called after me. Some reached out to touch me as I passed. I'm their rabbit's foot, their four-leafed clover. With me, this society will flourish. I expected Gabrielle in the lab, but she wasn't there. Technicians I did not recognize needled my arm and masked my face, told me to breathe. The obstetrician loomed over me, his face pitted and colorless. I saw walls and lights and smelled disinfectant, then roasting meat. The guinea pig has come, I thought, but that was a dream.

When I woke, I wasn't wearing my gray jumpsuit with its red starburst. I was wearing a white gown, like a queen. My mouth tasted like glue, a familiar sensation. I thought I'd journeyed again through the stars. Then I remembered. I pressed my stomach through the gown. A hardness to it. It grows, I thought, and flushed with pleasure.

We are so grateful to you, the obstetrician told me. Such sacrifice. Can I call my mother now? I asked. I thought of her fleeing the Floating City as the sea rose, the seed of me nestled within her. What must it have been like, to realize she was pregnant after she'd left my father behind? It hasn't been like that for me. I've known what to expect. I've done this on purpose.

But the obstetrician shook his head. Tomorrow, he promised. Today you must rest. Let's get you back to your quarters, he said. I thought of Gabrielle and my duvet, how nice it would be to draw it over our heads and cocoon us in its dark.

Later, when Gabrielle carried in my guinea pig, I meant to refuse it, but when I caught its scent, I felt such a hunger. I gobbled it down. I even sucked its skull, holding it firm by its two yellow teeth. I do not know if synthetic chicken will content me again. Agnes and Winona watched me, smiling softly with their eyes. Agnes's jumpsuit bulges. It's no trick of the light. Winona is a broad woman, so it's hard to tell, but she winces sometimes. I imagine kicks, tiny feet battering her from within. Our small new selves are as eager as we are.

Miracle children, I tell myself, grown on a miracle planet. They will fatten like potatoes in the red soil. They will take their first breaths of alien air. Their stomachs will not somersault, as mine still does, for this will be their home. Their motherland. And they its native sons.

May 45, 2046

I am sick of May. Sixty days feels longer than I assumed it would, too long for a single month. I recall that winter a decade ago, the one that would not end. It lasted ten months, followed by a brief blip of summer before the leaves dropped again. We gnawed dried venison, then little more than bark. K grew skinny and pale. Pa's muscled arms atrophied. He could no longer scoot himself around on his roller board. I was thin and tired too, but young, so I pushed him in a chair. He hated that. It was a relief when the next winter lasted only three months. I suppose this could be worse, but it's hard to tell it is spring without flowers or rain. The dunes seem more monotonous than ever. The wonder of arrival has worn off. You stare at something long enough, no matter how marvelous, and it'll get boring too.

Maybe it's the nausea, which the implantation has heightened. At least once a day I vomit. Sometimes more. Keeping it contained is a challenge. Why not total gravity? I asked Gabrielle when she arrived for our nightly card game. We do not want to forget where we are, she said. That seemed stupid. One must simply look out the windows to remember.

I tried to tell K about the nausea. I wanted to ask her advice. But the last time I contacted her, she waved it away, the choppy connection pixelating her hand as it moved. It's normal with pregnancy, she assured me. And you're the new breed, she said. You'll be fine.

Agnes and Winona have noticed my discontent. They have invited me into their games. Chantrea is jealous. I can tell. But I do not join them. I play cards with Gabrielle, and when she leaves, I retreat to my pod to lie under my duvet and not sleep. Sleep frightens me. Last night I dreamed of the desert again. I was walking through it and the sun scorched me, hot as fire. A silhouette appeared on the horizon and I felt a sadness so profound it woke me up. I was not crying, but holding my stomach, which had stopped somersaulting. Then it flipped again and I had to bolt to the bathing pod, where I threw up micro-fungus and masticated lettuce and then bile.

When I lay back down, I tried to calm myself. It's okay, I thought. Nausea is normal. The cook at the Northern Refuge used to talk about other places on Earth, places where things happened too terrible to detail. The cook was the one who told me about the Land Wars. His stories used to scare me to bits. I would run to K and bury my head in her lap. She would stroke my hair, laughing gently at me. Penelope, she would croon. Do not worry. You are safe here. We don't call it the Refuge for nothing.

I tried repeating that. You are safe here, I said aloud and rubbed my belly until I felt better.

It's not only the nausea tiring me out; it's the examinations. A parade of needles. And the tablets, each one more bitter than the last. Why so many visits? I asked the obstetrician. This is no normal venture, he said.

We want it to go well. Must he always be present? I asked, jutting my chin at the geneticist. Two-headed babies, he joked. Remember? Fine, I said, let's make this quick. And I held out my arm for another jab.

Fifteen more days, I tell myself, until May ends. I would give anything to see trees.

May 52, 2046

Agnes is sick. They have taken her away. I picture another pod, white and featureless as ours, but sparkling with sterilized instruments. A multitude of scalpels. Will they cut it from her? No, they wouldn't dare. It must survive.

After she'd gone, Chantrea lifted her chin and squared her shoulders. They will fix her, she announced. They have to. So much blood, said Winona, her eyes wide. You don't puke blood like that because of a baby. She looked to me and Chantrea in turn. Do you? No, I said, it's likely the radiation. Don't say that, Chantrea snapped, the radiation can't touch us. She'll be fine, I soothed, trying to channel K. They'll be able to implant you soon, I told Chantrea.

They had planned to implant Chantrea today, but the obstetrician said no. We must wait, he apologized, until we see the results. Originally, they'd allotted a two-week window between each implant, but that has changed. Agnes's bulge has grown very prominent. Winona is showing too. This morning when I touched my belly under the duvet, it was rock hard, with an odor of copper. I thought of the pennies kept in a jar in the Northern Refuge's museum, displayed beside the American flags and DVDs.

Last night the smell woke me up. I got out of bed and slid open my shutter. The station is so brightly lit it was difficult to see the stars, but I managed. I couldn't identify any constellations. The perspective was too different. Where was Orion, with his telltale belt? Where were his dogs?

You need to get back on the treadmill, K told me on our call today. You look a little pale. I'm not feeling too good, I reminded her. Too well, she corrected me. You're not feeling too well. You're not listening to me, I said, but we'd already lost the connection. One would think that if they could rocket five women through space and implant them with embryos and feed them cloned guinea pigs, they could have made better communication devices.

My nausea is getting worse. Will I also vomit blood? If so, it's worth it. For the mission. I think of the line of women before me, the ancestors who chose this. K and her own mother and my great-grandmother and whoever came before that. Those women who said yes. Let me grow with this seed. Let me offer my own blood and muscle to this earth. And here I am, offering myself to a new earth, a different soil. Be brave, I tell myself. I remember K's mantra. Be strong.

But it's a challenge. Tonight, I felt too sick to eat. If Gabrielle would bring me another guinea pig, I bet I could. She did arrive for dinner, but wouldn't eat anything. She said she'd already eaten. Afterward, she stayed for film time. It was an American film from the late twentieth century. I was grateful. I didn't have energy to read subtitles. Here, Gabrielle said, offering her shoulder. Rest your head. I laid my cropped curls upon her unburdened body. You are safe, I reminded myself.

May 60, 2046

We have reached the last day of May. Finally. Agnes has returned. She's not throwing up blood anymore, but she doesn't look any healthier than when they took her away. Her nose is pinched, her skin washed out.

She's says she's too tired to speak English. She and Winona huddle at the table, exchanging the few Russian words Agnes has taught her. Her midsection is enormous. We are afraid to mention it. We have no words to discuss it. We knew it would be different here, but we could not have predicted this.

K didn't answer my call this afternoon. She's busy, I tell myself. But busy with what? What did she ever have to be busy with except me?

The obstetrician and geneticist remain optimistic. Twenty-two days have passed since they implanted me. Going as planned, they chirrup when they examine me. Then they slide another needle in. They are both white with blond hair. They seem interchangeable. I can't remember their names. Bill or Bob or Brandon. It doesn't matter. I sleep heavily now and do not dream. The tang of copper weaves into my slumber. I wake with a metallic taste on my tongue. My skin looks thinner, stretched at its seams. I fear I might burst.

June 1, 2046

Agnes was too worn out this afternoon to play Risk. I'm going to lie down, she said in English and disappeared into her pod. I was left at the table with Winona and Chantrea. Join us for a game, Chantrea offered. A game of Risk, I suggested. Winona brought out the board and the colored wooden cubes. I'll be red, I offered. I'm green, Chantrea said, grabbing her pieces. Winona collected her yellow silently. Her lips looked pale. How do you feel? I asked. How do *you* feel? she countered. Nauseated, I replied.

I hoped to establish our affinity, but she turned her face away. Your move, she said. I placed my infantry onto Ontario, assuming I would provoke her into choosing the eastern United States. To see Canada and the US divided felt disconcerting. It felt even more so to see Earth with a landmass so large. Mapmakers have yet to draw the new globe's boundaries. I suppose humans will abandon it soon, at least those with money, so what's the point?

But Winona did not plop her infantry anywhere in North America. She chose Southeast Asia. Not fair, Chantrea shouted. Hush, said Winona, Agnes is sleeping. Then I'll take her land, Chantrea said. She nudged a green piece onto part of Russia. I took Western Europe on my next turn, thinking of Gabrielle. The painted blue water beside it looked harmless.

I pushed my chair back. This is stupid, I said. We can't own these places. They don't exist. What else do you suggest? asked Winona. Color rushed to her cheeks. I had not seen her angry before. Usually she is placid, her face a plain board. Should we sit around twiddling our thumbs, she asked, waiting to die? What are you talking about, I heard myself argue. Nobody's dying.

Chantrea's face knotted more tightly. Yes, she said to Winona, we're making life here. Agnes, Penelope, and I are, said Winona. You're not making anything, Winona tossed at Chantrea. Are you?

Chantrea's eyes narrowed. Winona stood up. Then I heard the kick. It was a solid thud against her body's dome. Winona's face drained and, before we could catch her, she fell backward onto the floor.

Chantrea clambered over her chair to Winona. Turn her over, she cried. Don't let her choke. She was vomiting blood, like Agnes had. We managed to roll her onto her side, and the blood arrived in gushes, one hideous wave after another. I couldn't tell if she was awake. I smelled copper and thought I'd puke too, but I didn't. I could hear her baby's feet thudding from within.

Call Brandon, Chantrea said. Who? I asked. The obstetrician, dummy, she said. Hit the button already. I scrambled to my feet, sliding in Winona's blood. Minutes later, the airlock opened and one of the blond men arrived (Brandon, I told myself, my doctor) with a team of technicians. They hoisted Winona onto a gurney. All will be well, Brandon said, beaming at us, and disappeared with the woman who should have felt like a sister, but didn't.

I wanted to make tea with Chantrea. I wanted us to hold hands, comfort each other. But she announced she was going to bed and locked herself in her pod. Fear coagulated in my throat. My stomach flipped, but it was not my stomach. It was lower down, where my new self was swimming. I touched it and felt a bump, solid and spherical as a rock from the Northern Refuge.

Pa, I whispered. K. But they weren't there. Why weren't they? K had done this before. She would know what to do. She would know how to help me. I yearned for a screen, buttons to push, anything that would summon them. This time she would pick up. She had to. But I didn't own access to the screens. I knew how to open airlocks, how to program the treadmill, how to radiate micro-fungus to warmth, but that was it. If I wanted to speak to her, a technician had to set up the screen. Gabrielle and the obstetrician had to agree. K had to answer.

My life here is so isolated. I haven't even been on the surface, walked out under that jaundiced sky. Too dangerous, Gabrielle had said when I'd asked. You want to keep me inside, I'd dared to reply. Barefoot and pregnant in the kitchen. This had made her smile.

I cleaned up Winona's blood, down on my hands and knees, with cloths and disinfectant. Already some of it had started to separate and lift, ever so slightly. Fucking Red Star, I cursed as I swabbed the floor. You could have at least given us real gravity.

When I'd finished, our pod smelled like the obstetrician's lab. Brandon. I thought of him in that lab with Winona. I wondered what he was doing with her. How he was helping her. How he would help me when my turn came.

I sat back on my heels and examined the shining floor. Why did you sign up for this? I asked myself, out loud.

I used to think I had chosen this. But did I? Or had it already been written in the stars? I missed Pa and K before, I'm not sure I do anymore. I hear K's voice, telling me I must make sacrifices. She was never really talking to me. I see that now. She was talking to herself. I am her sacrifice. She must have realized the experiment is going wrong. That's why she has stopped answering my calls. She's given me up, cut me loose. I'm on my own.

I recall Winona's fury, how she shoved her yellow Risk pieces across the map of a forgotten world. She didn't choose to come here. None of us did.

Agnes has not awoken nor Chantrea emerged from her pod. Before I retired to mine, I sat at the table for a long time, the Risk board spread out before me. My red infantry piece still squatted over Ontario. It doesn't belong to you, I told it. I plucked it up and set it aside. Nothing does.

June 5, 2046

My last log was a mess. This one will be different. We have reason to hope. Winona has returned, ruddy with health. Brandon has prescribed fresh meat each supper, which means half a guinea pig brought on a lidded tray. Room service, Winona calls it, a term I recognize from K's books. I salivate watching Winona eat. He's prescribed it for Agnes too, but she doesn't want it anymore. She nibbles the butterhead lettuce, pokes her spoon at the boiled grain paste. I'm tired, she says a lot, and goes to lie down. This is normal, Brandon tells us. She needs strength for two. So do I, I want to tell him but don't. I haven't been sick enough to earn privileges.

In fact, I feel oddly strong. Two days ago, my nausea disappeared and has not returned. The copper smell has dissipated. Now I smell meat hot on a grill. It's the guinea pig, I tell myself. I'd like to know where they keep them. Gabrielle did not show us their lab on our tour. I conjure a pod lawned in genuine grass, tumbling with furry nut-brown creatures, so multitudinous they don't notice when one of their own is taken. Last night I dreamed of such a pod. I was rolling luxuriously among them. The rank stench of beast—fur and feet and breath—rose up around me. Then I was one of them, crawling on all fours. When I woke, my skin was burning. I pulled the duvet over my head and thought of Gabrielle. When I pressed fingers to flesh, they were hers, or so I imagined. Soon I slept again.

June 7, 2046

I write late tonight. Our clock passes into its magical twenty-fifth hour. Tomorrow I will be tired. I will lag on the treadmill, my head drooping. During examination Brandon will chastise me. You have lost color, he will admonish. Get more sleep. I will nod and say yes, as I have always done. Yes to Pa. Yes to K. Yes to the Red Star project.

Tonight, I said no. Don't leave, I told Gabrielle. We were in my pod. I had asked her to help me identify Orion from my window. See, she pointed. It's there. She was right. Orion sparkled in plain sight. His three-starred belt. His hunting dogs, big and little. I don't know how I missed him, I said. There's no trick, she said. Constellations here are more or less the same. There's Phobos, I said, nodding toward the wobbly moon. It's so dull, Gabrielle said. I laughed. Orbiting three times a day, I agreed. It's a little much.

We had turned off my lights to see the sky better. She stood close to me, her body breathing under its gray jumpsuit. She smelled like clean cotton, with a faint whiff of roses. Why do you smell like flowers? I asked. She grinned. It's a surprise, she said. For when your baby is born. Tell me now, I insisted. We've built another station, she said. I visited it this afternoon. It's a marvelous place, filled with trees and flowers. Your babies can grow up there. They'll be happy. That wasn't hard, I said, to get you to tell me. She moved closer. I was never good at keeping secrets, she replied.

She touched my stomach. Does it hurt? she asked me. No, I said, not now. Any kicks? she asked. I shook my head. It's quiet in here, I said. That's when she turned to go. I reached out to pluck her sleeve. No, I said. Don't go. And she did not.

Now she sleeps. Her closed eyelids are papery, darker than her face. I have touched them, lightly. One. Then the other.

June 11, 2046

I meant to log notes last night, but I could not. I shivered too hard to tap keys. Not the duvet, not Gabrielle, not my own heat under the covers could warm me. Penelope, said Gabrielle. Do not cry. Until she said it, I didn't realize I was. How will the baby live, I wailed, without its mother? People have done it—she wiped my cheeks—for centuries. It will survive.

I did not voice my true fear. That I would not survive. The kicks began a day ago. The power of each one is indescribable. When they hit, I double over. Afterward, I am weak and trembling. All I want to do is sleep.

At breakfast yesterday I could not eat. Winona wolfed down my portion, cheeks glowing. Chantrea said, Yes, eat up. You're eating for two. It feels like three, Winona said, wiping her mouth. Maybe four. May we prosper, Chantrea said. In her tone I sensed the composure of the nuns who raised her, their serenity in the face of trouble. Agnes had not appeared, but that was normal. We assumed she was sleeping.

They found her in the afternoon. How we had heard nothing, I do not know. Brandon and Bob (or Bill) discovered her. Since she was too weak to travel to their lab, they had begun to make house calls. They arrived for their examination, called a cheerful hello to us, and clomped toward her pod. They opened the airlock and froze. From the open door poured a stench of copper. Silence. Then a wail. Not from them. Not Agnes. That was a baby. My gut clenched at the sound. By Winona's whitened lips, I could tell hers did too. Mercy, whispered Brandon. The word was an echo from an antique time, a plea for divine benevolence.

Chantrea ran to see. Winona and I hoisted our heavy selves and followed her. At the threshold, we paused. A quaint phrase rang in my head: My heart in my throat. I could not breathe.

On the bed, a portrait. A still life. Blood. Agnes. Her body torn asunder.

An infant lay on the sodden mattress. It wasn't curled up and helpless. It was splayed on its back, its eyes wide open and very white. The rest of its body was white too, but its chest was translucent. I could detect the dark thump of its heart. Its head looked abnormally large. Between its legs, a pouch covered its genitals. Not human. No, I told myself, before Chantrea started screaming. Human. It had to be. Otherwise, what was the point?

I'm still shaking. Gabrielle came last night and took me in her arms, but it didn't help. It's going to be okay, she promised, but she looked more terrified than I felt. I'm only thirty-three days in, but my skin feels stretched thin, my belly ponderous with weight. We did not speak soon enough about what was wrong, about how quickly they grow. It feels too late to speak now. Brandon and the geneticist appear unconcerned. No more needles, I told them this morning. They jabbed one in anyway. All will be well, they said. I spit in their faces. I couldn't help myself. Even that didn't ruffle them. There, there, said Brandon, swabbing the puncture. I'm not a fucking child, I told them. With another needle, they put me to sleep.

I woke in my own pod, under the duvet, alone. I thought of the games we had played. The gin rummy. The Risk. I wondered what we were hoping to win. Typing this, it occurs to me that now I am the game. Agnes lost hers. Will I lose mine too?

June 15, 2046

This morning they brought us to meet the baby. Winona stayed behind. She didn't feel well. Chantrea insisted on bringing a gift, but we had nothing appropriate. I'll bring this, she announced, and dragged her duvet from her pod. It was green, printed with daisies. I didn't expect that. I expected something angry, to match her face. Babies get cold, she said, especially without their mothers. I was too tired to protest. She dragged it down the hallway like a bridal train.

At the door Brandon stopped us. You can't bring that in, he said. It's unsanitary. Chantrea didn't argue. She piled the duvet in the hall and stepped into the antechamber, where we scrubbed and sprayed and donned head-to-toe plastic sheaths. Then we entered the nursery.

A plastic dome covered the baby, but it wasn't lying down. How can it stand already? Chantrea asked, but Brandon didn't reply. Its legs looked strong and sturdy. It was pressing its palms to the plastic. I counted the fingers. Five on each hand. This comforted me. A onesie studded with blue rocket ships covered it, but the stitches appeared strained, the leg-holes too tight.

As we crossed the room, its white eyes followed us, but its face showed no expression. I remembered its wail when they found it, but now it remained silent. It did not cry or gurgle or squeeze its eyes shut before popping them open. It watched us cross the room and when we lined up beside it, taking each other by the hand, it watched that too.

What's its name? asked Chantrea. He has none, said Brandon. We thought maybe you would like to name him. We'll call it Phobos, Chantrea said promptly. Because it's lumpy and boring. It's going to be okay, I said. I laid my hand on Chantrea's arm. Don't touch me, Chantrea said and snatched her arm away.

We're all upset, I assured her. We're just trying to help our species. Chantrea spun toward me. Does that look like our species to you? she asked. No, I agreed.

Remember there are two more, Chantrea said. She turned to Brandon. What are you going to do about Winona? Or this one, she said, pointing at me. Let them die too? Certainly not, Brandon said. I noticed he didn't look at the baby when he spoke. We are taking measures to prevent that.

What will you do? Chantrea asked. Cut them open before they burst?

Caesarean has saved many lives. Brandon tipped his head toward the baby, but still didn't look at it. Phobos? he asked. Phobos, Chantrea replied. We can name the next one Deimos, I said, if it lives. It'll live, Chantrea replied.

June 19, 2046

K hasn't answered my calls in weeks. As a palliative, I have turned to Gabrielle. Every night she visits. She doesn't speak of Red Star or the other station filled with trees or anything else in our circumscribed world. Not Agnes. Not Winona. Not the baby who is no baby, the one who looks bigger each time Brandon brings us to visit him. She does not speak of the real moon named Phobos that arcs beyond our window three times a day. We close our eyes. When we look, it's gone. In its absence, Gabrielle offers her downy limbs, the perfect curve of her torso from neck to thigh, the flick of her tongue against me. When we have worn ourselves out, she leaves.

This evening before she left, she paused. Penelope, she said. Her amber gaze sought mine. The pod smelled of us: a heavy, rich, womanly scent. I waited. The moment froze itself, and then thawed. It has been something, she said, knowing you.

I didn't know how to respond. It felt like goodbye. But where could she be going? After she left my pod, I understood. I'm the one who will be taking a trip. Agnes has already departed. Winona is next. Then it will be my turn.

It has been something knowing you, Gabrielle said. Her words touched me. She loves me, I thought. But now I'm not sure. If she meant it as goodbye, why say it so casually? Is it really that easy to let me go?

Before my time approaches, I will delete this. Initially I thought to keep this log as a testament to my experience, a kind of first-person textbook. But I've changed my mind. Forget history. No one needs a record of this.

June 24, 2046

Winona has not died. This morning they wheeled her away, her face as clenched as Chantrea's. A crust of blood rimmed her lips. Brandon returned in the afternoon and reported the C-section a success.

Deimos lives? Chantrea asked. They both do, Brandon replied. The mother is sleeping. He held out a screen to show us a video: another big bald baby with blank eyes staring at whatever was filming it. As with

Phobos, I could see straight through its skin to its heart. I didn't like watching it beat. Brandon didn't, however, offer any images of Winona. Not even a photo.

We must celebrate, Chantrea trumpeted. Join us, she said to Brandon, but he demurred. I must attend to matters, he said. I pictured him standing over Winona with his clipboard, attending to her as he would a business matter, discussing profit goals and five-year plans with the geneticist. Behind them, Deimos would be lying under his plastic dome, anticipating his future. He will grow until he can stand, until he can touch his prison with skinny fingers and question why he's enclosed. Like Phobos, he will split his onesie's seams. A baby for a day or two. No more.

I'll make a cake, Chantrea sang after Brandon had gone. She spooned grain paste into a bowl, sprinkled sweetener on top, and radiated it. When it emerged, she sliced it in two, and she and I ate, our mouths sticking with each bite. I considered our faces, plucked from different corners of the globe. We could be sisters, I thought. We are joined after all.

My time is approaching. Soon I will follow Agnes and Winona into that dread world of birth. As they did, I will bear a being not seen before. Will it be like Phobos and Deimos, staring at us as we stare at them? Or will it be in its own thing? Something entirely new.

I will not say goodbye to Gabrielle. Minus a farewell our tale could continue. Perhaps I will live. Likely I will not. But my child might. I believe it's a girl, like K and I, like the countless women who have preceded us. My daughter will grow into monster or human or both. No matter how she manifests, she will choose this star for her own. This red star, which is no star, but a planet, trapped in its orbit like any blind thing.

My single regret is K. Weeks have passed since we spoke. I wish we could talk at least once before my time comes. You would understand this, I could tell her. Any mother would. We link hands with fate, and we leap. We can't predict the story our child will tell.

MOON

MARS, 2073

A mother is a basin," I said aloud. "You fill her with water. Then you pour her out."

"But what happened to her?" Ivy asked. She tried scrolling farther down the screen, but couldn't. The diary ended there. *We can't predict the story our child will tell.* "How can that be it?"

Ivy and I had stayed up all night reading the diary we had found. Ivy had taught me to read very quickly. "You learn fast," she'd marveled. "Learning is all I've ever done," I'd replied. "I guess I'm good at it." Together we had scrolled through the screens of black type, Ivy reading one entry, I the next. We spoke each line aloud.

After we'd reached midway, Ivy whispered, "This is some freaky stuff."

"Is it?" I asked, because I knew no different. "Isn't it always like this?"

"Oh no," Ivy said. "This is new."

We kept reading. By dawn's arrival, my throat was dry, my lips cracked. For the first time, I thirsted for water rather than air. Yet I didn't leave my pod. Not to drink. Not to excrete. Not to breathe fresh air. I remained fixed to the screen, reading a story more fantastical than any Uncle Two had told me. This story didn't come from Earth, I told myself. This story belongs to Mars.

"Ivy." I paused. Toward the end of the diary, a certainty had begun to grow in me. I needed to say it out loud. "I think Penelope was my mother," I said.

"Huh." Ivy also paused. I tried to picture her expression. She was probably frowning, sunk deep in thought. "You think so?"

"I do."

"So, you're like," she said, "a medical experiment?"

"Who else could her baby be?" I replied. "She didn't give birth to the Uncles. That was Agnes and Winona." Phobos and Deimos, I thought. I had to be the third one. The other moon.

"Wait," Ivy said. "Who are the Uncles? I thought you were alone up there."

"I thought so too." The screen's light was dimming. It needed to be charged. I jumped to my feet. "Listen," I said. "I need to find her. What if she's still there, at the Red Star station?"

"But aren't you there too?" she asked. "And who the heck are the Uncles? Actually." Her voice grew curt. "I don't know anything about you."

"I'll tell you everything," I said. "I promise. First, I must find my mother."

The screen dimmed further, then grayed, then went black. I would find Ivy again later. I was confident I'd be able to. I would tell her about everything. About the dome, the station Gabrielle had built for the Red Star babies, the trees and flowers she thought would sustain them. If I found Penelope—my *mother*—I would bring her to meet Ivy.

With the screen tucked under my arm, I raced through the tunnels and up the ladder to the dome. I plugged the screen into the cable connected to the solar panels. I considered joining the Uncles for morning potato, but discarded the idea. I'll eat dust, I told myself, like it's the old days. Besides, I didn't want to see them. Uncle One would be perched at the table, impatiently drumming his fingers. He wouldn't care about Penelope or Agnes or Winona. Who was his mother to him? Uncle One had never cared about the past. He sought only the future.

I headed toward the tunnel that led outside. Already I could smell the dunes.

Moon, said Uncle Two behind me.

I turned around. He had climbed up the ladder through the hatch. He was standing beside a pine tree, leaning against it for strength. He looked sicker than ever. His thick flesh had sagged on his frame, his skin grown dulled and gray, his once-plump cheeks sucked close to the bone. Even his heart seemed to have slowed in his chest. When I return, I thought, I'll make you well.

I found a story, I said. I know about my mother. I know about yours too.

I see. Uncle Two studied me, his face drawn. I'm sorry you had to learn about that.

Why didn't you tell me? I asked. We could have saved so much time.

Are you going to the Red Star station? he asked.

I have to, I said. The thrill of it seized me. What if she's there? I asked.

Go if you must, Uncle Two said. But trust me, there's nothing to see.

I ignored this. The Uncles had been wrong about so much. And what was trust?

I'll be back for the evening potato, I told him. Goodbye, Deimos.

He managed an eerie half smile. That was never my name, he said.

Without another word, I entered the tunnel that led to the exit. My pulse quickened. I was so close. I stepped through the two hatchways and then I was outside.

Here was my world entire. A warm wind sighed across the dunes.

The air shimmered with static from the last sandstorm. Bits of dust blew toward me and clung to my cheeks. The atmosphere was so transparent I could sniff the metallic singe of space. I pulled air into my lungs and rejoiced at the absence of moisture. I walked farther out, joy filling me as sand buried my bare toes. My hard, brown body felt a part of the planet, my dark hair textured as the dirt, my breath as clean as the breeze.

I'm coming, I thought, pointing my face to the west. A little late, but I'm coming home.

I EXPECTED THE JOURNEY to take longer, but the sun had barely begun its ascent when I arrived at my destination. Something sticky with dust loomed in the landscape ahead. I remembered when we had discovered the dome. That had to be the Red Star station.

As I approached the place about which my mother had written, I wondered about my father. Penelope had had one. So had Ivy. I must have a father too. Penelope hadn't known him. He had been a sperm to her egg. That was all. But what if he wasn't a technician or her obstetrician, as she had speculated? From what I could tell from the screen, I was human enough in form, if a touch taller, but I could walk this planet rapidly and without tiring, surviving on its soil and air. And the Uncles—with their height, their oversized heads and transparent chests—were even more alien than I. Our fathers might not have been human at all. But what other possibility existed?

This thought quickened my pace. A tremendous hunger for answers filled me. I thought of Penelope with the guinea pig, how she had torn its meat from its bones. But what I saw made me stop. My eyes dampened. I hadn't cried in so long I hardly recognized the tears when they came. Around me so much dry land and arid air, and trickling from my eyes those two wet trails. Not even the Uncles could cry. The presence of my tears on that water-starved planet made me feel stranger and more alone than ever.

Uncle Two had been right. I wouldn't find anything here. The station was enormous, sprawled across the dunes. But it was a wreck. A destroyed thing, blackened and crumpled. Years of dust storms had smothered what remained; only the top half of each shriveled pod crested the surface. I considered digging down to find more, but didn't. Ivy had taught me about fire. Something had burned the station from the inside out. Nothing remained but a shell.

I approached the nearest half-buried pod and touched it. Then I plopped down in the sand and rested my head against it. I thought I heard humming and jumped, thinking some mechanism yet moved within; but then I realized it was my own blood in my ears. I'd found nothing. Only a place where the Uncles had split their mothers wide with their birth, where I probably had as well.

"All mothers bleed," I said aloud.

I didn't want to bleed. The realization struck me like a physical blow. I didn't want to be a mother. On a subconscious level, I had known this for a long time. Reading Penelope's log had confirmed it. I didn't care if the Uncles and I were the only ones left. I didn't want to be implanted with Uncle One's seed. I didn't want to be like Agnes or Winona. I didn't want to be like Penelope. She had pledged herself to her family. She had promised to continue their line. And the Red Star station had burned. Maybe she'd burned too. Maybe I'd killed her when I was born. Maybe—just maybe—she'd returned to Earth, but this seemed like a fantasy.

I knew what I would tell the Uncles. I would not say yes. I would not accept their plan. If I grew the Uncles a baby, it could kill me. It could grow up to burn the dome down. It could turn against us. Or it could walk away. It could leave me behind.

I didn't see the point. The Uncles and I were the products of a failed experiment, of a dream that grew too big.

When I got back to the dome, I would confront the Uncles. I would give them my answer.

Forget your big dreams, I would tell them.

PENELOPE

MARS, 2046

HOUR ONE

June 28, 2046

Two women trek across a desolate landscape. Their suits are stark white against the rust-colored dunes. Their big boots march forward. Their helmets amplify their breathing. Ahead the sun rises, haloed in blue. Behind them lies a blackened shell. In their noses lingers the stink of smoke, an Earth smell, one they thought they'd forgotten. The station— the place they tried so hard to call home—has exploded.

One is Penelope, the other Gabrielle. Eighty-eight days ago, Penelope arrived on this planet, tender and hopeful for what would come. She met Gabrielle, learned about love, struggled to maintain hope for the future. But a fire has destroyed the Red Star station, and they are on their own under an alien sky. They want to run, but with the stiff suits and lower gravity, it's like trying to run in a dream.

This is a story, Penelope tells herself. Something I can shape as I go. This comforts her, for stories are familiar. Her mother K raised her on stories, ones from books but also from Penelope's grandfather Pa. Follow the red star, Pa told K, because his mother had told him. But K accepted Penelope for the grand experiment, sent her hurtling through space. She meant her daughter to be the pioneer who would carve a path for their species. She raised her on tales of heroines who undertook such missions. You are the new breed, she insisted. You will bear the next generation. You will be the mother of thousands.

Penelope knew K desired victory, a satisfying denouement. She expected Penelope to birth a baby in this distant place, the mission to be a success. The other volunteers would circle her, cradling their newborns too. The station would ring with joy: streamers, confetti, the popping of champagne corks. Together they would take a stand against the shrinking birth rates on Earth. They would populate a colony on this fourth planet. They would, as Pa liked to say, make the world.

But as she trudges away from Red Star's burned station, Penelope knows she is no heroine, for heroines succeed in their quests. I have failed you, Mother, she thinks. Our family's dream is dead.

No, she imagines K replying. Have patience. And loyalty.

At the Northern Refuge, she used to spend mornings on her mother's lap poring over books. Here is Poseidon, K would tell her, who governs the seas. Here is Demeter, goddess of the harvest. And this mortal—pointing to a lonely woman weaving—is Penelope. That's me, she would cry. Loyalty and patience, her mother would assure her. They can have their rewards.

Penelope practices uttering one word with each step. Right foot, loyalty. Left foot, patience. It's a relief to focus on her feet instead of her belly. It hangs heavy, silvered with stretch marks. It threatens to split her suit wide open. Today marks the twenty-eighth of June, the year 2046. It's an innocent day, guileless as those on Earth. Except in ten more, this planet's elongated calendar will read June 38 and if the other volunteers' time is any predictor, Penelope will give birth. Or maybe before. Maybe today. She is uncharted territory.

These babies they have grown are something new.

The dream is not dead, she tells herself. The fetus lives. You have not failed, not yet.

Beside her slogs her companion, whose waistline is narrow where Penelope's juts outward. Gabrielle turns to her. Her plastic helmet magnifies her face. Penelope thinks, patience. Except she does not have to sit in one place like Odysseus's wife, weaving tapestries until her lover returns. Her lover travels with her, matching her pace to her slowed one. Loyalty, she reminds herself. It can have its reward.

How will this story end? Penelope asks the specter of her mother.

You tell me, this mother says. It's your story now.

Penelope reaches for the other woman's hand. The woman reaches back. Penelope mouths her name so she can see. Gabrielle. Gabrielle mouths something back, but she cannot tell what it is.

Their hands are clumsy in their gloves. Penelope can barely feel Gabrielle's fingers in her own. They walk forward into dawn's blinding light, leaving the wreckage behind.

HOUR TWO

June 28, 2046

The sun has arisen, the sky lightened to a hue delicate as the buttercups in the Northern Refuge. Penelope pauses, out of breath. Pain stitches up her side. She breathes in. Out. In. Out. She recalls the manuals they gave the volunteers to prepare for implantation and beyond, the ones for expectant mothers. These manuals had rules for breathing, how to moderate it when contractions began. Slowly, she tells herself, evenly. The pain's grip lessens. She thinks it can't be her time, but she's not sure. She stands still, exploring her body's sensations. She waits for a muscle clench, a kick within, wetness between her legs. Nothing. She raises a hand to signal to Gabrielle. Let's go, this hand says. They push on.

They're headed to the other station, the one Gabrielle told her about. The one intended for the babies, where Gabrielle had said they'd be happy. It's ready for occupation, Gabrielle said back at Red Star. She and Penelope were at the exit, breathless from their sprint down the hall. Hurry, Gabrielle said. She released the suits from their cages and helped Penelope with her boots before buckling her own. Penelope felt lucky it wasn't the turn of the century, when suiting up took five hours or more. Privatization, with the money it's unlocked, has brought benefits.

Penelope watched Gabrielle fumble at the airlocks. What about the others? she wanted to ask. But Gabrielle had latched their helmets in place, and they couldn't talk anymore. No time remained to locate the communication devices and thread them through their suits. Before the airlock sealed behind them, Penelope glimpsed the flames. They turned a corner like a pack of dogs, sniffing them out. Then the door whooshed shut and the other opened, onto a landscape she had seen but not yet touched. She and Gabrielle stepped out wordless as infants. Unlike infants, they did their best to run.

Penelope doesn't own language to describe the fire that demolished the station. It was. Then it wasn't. One second it was barreling down hallways, scorching the labs and the sleeping pods and the dining hall where the botanists used to sample their experiments. The next second it was gone. A single explosion, brief, too bright. Then nothing. Oxygen's absence had extinguished the flames. It left a tangle of metal and melted plastic, everybody burned alive except Penelope and Gabrielle

With each step they take, the burned station grows smaller. Soon the dunes will obscure it. Penelope tries to picture the sister station, where they're heading. We've filled it with trees and flowers, Gabrielle said. Penelope focuses on this. So much time has elapsed since she's seen trees.

Before they fled Red Star, Gabrielle turned to her. A sol's walk, she mouthed. Penelope understood. A sol meant a day. That's how long their journey would take. Not impossible, she thought then.

Now she wonders whether Gabrielle meant a day's twelve hours or the full twenty-five. This planet, with its overlong months and days. She hopes their oxygen will last. She hopes these suits insulate against more than the dawn. Nights here can freeze the soul from a body.

HOUR THREE

June 28, 2046

They are not alone. Someone is following them. Two someones. Gabrielle spots them first. Look, her mouth motions, her arm pointing. Penelope can make out two figures silhouetted against a scrim of boulders. Phobos comes into focus first. Then Deimos. They're not babies anymore. They're boys, teenagers, more than able to walk. They must have escaped the station, but Penelope doesn't know how. She thought everybody burned. It makes sense though. If anybody would escape, Phobos and Deimos would. In the brief time since their birth, they've confounded all expectations.

Babies on Mars, Penelope used to think. It'll be cute. But looking at the creatures behind her, that's the last word that comes to mind. *Monstrous* maybe. *Giant.*

Deimos and Phobos are wearing the station's gray jumpsuits, their massive heads like orbs above. They must have long since outgrown their onesies. Maybe the geneticist clothed them, or maybe they found spare suits and put them on. They're too far away for Penelope to make out the starbursts on their breasts, but she knows they're there. Here they are, the products of the Red Star project. She wonders whether

David would be proud. She imagines him still alive, his eyes brightening at the sight of Phobos and Deimos, able to survive this atmosphere with no help at all. Yes, she thinks. He would be very proud of these babies the Red Star volunteers have grown.

Phobos's and Deimos's white heads glow in the morning light. Penelope remembers the moon riding high over Earth. Her mother taught her its phases. Penelope tries to picture her in that pinpricked darkness, searching out the star that is no star—the one that burns red. Except it's not night there. It's daytime too. Gabrielle managed to align the Red Star station's longitude with the Northern Refuge so that even if their years couldn't move in tandem, their daily clocks could. The only difference is that magical extra hour, stretching time here to a fraction beyond what it used to be.

K should be awake by now. Penelope conjures her mother's red hair, wired with gray, less curly than her own. Her skin so much paler than Penelope's bronze. Her mouth that avoids laughter. Patience, her mother would instruct, and Penelope would know she was thinking of her father. The man K had left behind in the Floating City. Michelangelo. You're his, her mother would insist when Penelope questioned it. Look at your beautiful skin and hair, your sturdy shoulders. You have the same curve to your neck, the same distant look in your eyes. He would know you anywhere.

When Penelope was little, K taught her to expect him. Someday, she'd insist, he'll come galloping up on horseback with paintbrushes stuffed in his pack and my history folded against his heart. He will sing us the songs of his people, and sorrow will drop from us like snow from pines. Even as a child, Penelope pitied her. When she grew older, her mother admitted it. He's gone, she confessed. Drowned, most likely. A captain gone down with his ship.

Penelope is using these memories to distract herself. She does not want to think about the two figures behind them, the ones she and the other volunteers named after this planet's moons. She can tell Gabrielle doesn't either. They are her experiment, after all, an experiment gone wrong. Gabrielle has already resumed walking, but faster, as though to leave Phobos and Deimos behind. Penelope follows as best she can, willing herself onward.

Sweat studs her upper lip. If they were back at the station, safe under her crimson duvet, Gabrielle would lick each droplet with her tongue's tip. Then Penelope's throat. But their bodies don't matter like that anymore. They are machines that need fuel, protection from weather, solar winds, radiation. The suits offer oxygen, tubes with water and liquefied nourishment. These resources, however, are finite.

She turns. Phobos and Deimos have grown closer. She doesn't know what they want. They might not intend to hurt her. They could be following because Gabrielle knows where she's going. Or maybe they recognize in Penelope's condition what happened to their mothers. They might want to help, she thinks hopefully. But when she looks back at them, their faces show no expression at all.

Walking faster is hard. Despite her desire to keep up, her pace slows. It doesn't take long for Gabrielle to slow down too. She reaches out a glove to touch Penelope's arm, her face transmitting concern. Though her breath is rasping in her throat, Penelope smiles to reassure her.

The wreckage of the station has disappeared behind them. The other one has yet to appear. Above them Mars's moons—the real Phobos and Deimos—hover in pale silhouette. Phobos appears to speed east while Deimos dawdles, a mere pinprick, in the other direction. Within Penelope orbits her own little moon. This moon has neared fullness. It is almost ready to burst. She glances behind at the two figures following, and then up again at their namesakes. Not even in the Northern Refuge, with the infinite mystery of stars spread overhead, did the sky feel so beyond her understanding.

HOUR FOUR

June 28, 2046

Penelope has to stop. She's sweating, her legs trembling. She lowers herself onto a rock. Gabrielle doesn't notice. She keeps walking. Wait, Penelope calls, but she cannot hear. She will walk away. She will leave her behind. Phobos and Deimos will catch up, will do who knows what to her. Wait, Penelope calls again, and though she must not hear, her beloved turns. Painstakingly, Gabrielle makes her way back.

Does it hurt? Gabrielle mouths, her lips exaggerating the words.

Penelope thought she was simply tired, but with this question, she feels the baby. It is turning and spinning within. She feels it against her spine, searing a line from point to point. She cannot breathe. Then she can. In. Out. In. Out. Her body calms, unclenches. Red Star chose her for her steadiness in times of crisis. If she had been otherwise, would it have mattered that she was the daughter of K, who had helped plan the Red Star project? How badly she wants to believe she made it here on her own.

Gabrielle places her glove on Penelope's shoulder, and though Penelope cannot see her fingers, she can picture them: elegant and thin-knuckled, each fingernail a careful crescent. When they first met,

Gabrielle's serious face drew her in. Penelope had grown up in a serious place with serious people during a very serious time. Among so much that didn't, Gabrielle seemed familiar. Penelope wishes they were back under her duvet, whispering their secrets. I like your freckles, Gabrielle told her once, but would admit no more. What else do you like? Penelope wanted to ask. Why are you saving me, she wants to ask now, when you could have just saved yourself?

Gabrielle looks even more serious than her uncle David, whom K called Columbus. David is dead now. Penelope was six when he died, but she remembers his funeral. It was a grand affair. They sang "America the Beautiful" and led a procession down the central hallway. With elaborate ceremony, K hung his portrait in the great hall and garlanded it with wildflowers. Red Star was originally his project. They had to pay tribute, but Penelope doesn't remember tears. Not from her. Not from her mother. Not from anyone.

With Gabrielle's help, Penelope struggles to her feet. At this stage, most women would be anticipating the end. Hurry up, they would say. Not she. The end is what she fears.

She turns, assuming Phobos and Deimos will be right behind, but they have paused too, maybe fifteen feet away. It's an unexpectedly polite gesture, as though they are offering the women privacy. When she and Gabrielle start walking again, so do they. She notices they don't bounce lightly upon the surface as she does. This planet anchors their bodies. She shouldn't be surprised. It's theirs, after all. This blood soil, this sickly sky.

HOUR FIVE

June 28, 2046

The day warms. At her suit's seams, Penelope no longer feels a faint chill. It's midsummer at this planet's equator. By midday the temperature could reach 70 degrees Fahrenheit. She tilts her face to the sun and closes her eyes to its rays, like a seal basking. She hasn't seen seals in real life, only in books and on screens. With the sea it's the same. Seventeen years she spent underground in the Northern Refuge's white tunnels. David had designed it like that to keep the project secret, though Penelope wasn't sure from whom. On her trips up to the surface, Penelope saw no seashore, just spruce and fir, balsam and birch. Deer peeking from thickets. Cardinals in high branches. Water in lakes and swamps, not seas. It feels strange not to have seen the ocean when it has swallowed so much of their globe.

What she'd give for a sight of trees or deer or eagles. Anything other than red sand and burned sky. Back at the station, she loved the hydroponic gardens best, for their glimmer of green. Not that she visited much. The volunteers stayed in their quarters and kept to their strict routine. Agnes received the most walking privileges. The obstetrician said it was good for Agnes's baby to stretch her legs. The geneticist would arrive to escort her, shepherding her from pod to pod, letting her linger in the gardens or watch the grain's rapid spinning in the mill. A few times he let Penelope accompany them to hold Agnes's other arm when she was feeling weak. Steady now, he would say when she'd tilt, and Penelope would right her.

After a while the walks grew too difficult. When Winona's time came, Penelope hoped to accompany her on walks too, but the geneticist and obstetrician seemed to have forgotten about such things. By then their minds dwelt elsewhere. They weren't worried about exercise. Penelope missed the break in routine, the hellos from technicians, the glimpses into the labs. She never did see where they kept the guinea pigs. When she'd asked the geneticist, he'd waved off her request. Still under construction, he'd demurred.

When Penelope thinks of the fire, the guinea pigs hurt her most. She hates the image of their furry bodies crisping. She doesn't know why. She was happy to eat them when she could.

This hour she feels stronger. Her moon has steadied within her, a solid rock at her core. As though impatient for their journey's end, it rolls forward with her motion. Phobos and Deimos are still following them. Gabrielle won't look at them, but Penelope keeps sneaking glances backward. Earlier they looked like boys. Now, even from a distance, they look like men.

HOUR SIX

June 28, 2046

Noon approaches and, with it, heat. Penelope's armpits dampen, the underside of her breasts where they meld into her chest. Moisture coats her stomach's protuberance. Back at the airlock she'd stripped off her hospital gown so she could slip into the suit. Now she wishes she could strip her skin off too. She slurps water through a tube, but it doesn't help much. Even if she were healthy, a walk like this would take endurance. You are healthy, a small voice whispers. No, she responds. I'm not. Her child, her little moon, has sucked her strength, as she does oxygen from her suit.

Her thighs feel wobbly. She must sit down.

She eases herself onto a jut of land. Hold me fast, she tells the earth. But it's soil. She can't call it earth. Just like Mars has moons, but not *the* Moon. The objects closest to humans earned preference. What must it have felt like to name the world with simple terms? Earth. Moon. Sun. As though a single entity of each existed.

Penelope's mind wanders. She knows she is clutching a boulder. She knows her legs have failed her. She knows she is in trouble. But her brain plays tricks. She is a child, starting awake in the night's wee hours.

K lies damp beside her, sweat pearling on her skin. Her mother is asleep, but weeping. She mumbles something about the desert, and Penelope is afraid.

Around Penelope stretches the desert, devoid of joy. But can she call these dunes a desert when no water exists to define them as one? She is confused. She is not thinking straight.

Pain, Penelope's body tells her. Yes, she replies. The baby speaks in a sharp language, a red scribble from pubis to breastbone. She remembers how Gabrielle used to track her new dark line from cleft to navel. Maybe it's Gabrielle touching her, not the baby within. Is that you? Penelope asks. But their helmets are locked and Gabrielle can't hear. The man comes, Penelope recalls her mother mumbling. Penelope can see him. He has brought a twin. Four boots march toward her through the sand. I am afraid, Penelope says, and her lover's gloved hand appears. I will not leave you, Gabrielle tells her. But Gabrielle hasn't spoken. Her face is turned away.

Penelope's gut clenches. She is going to vomit. It roils her gut, scorches her esophagus. She braces herself for the blood it will bring. A red line, a red line, a red line. Then warmth.

What is this? her body asks, but she does not question it. Heat is spreading through her. Her gorge recedes. Her baby uncurls and returns to its lazy orbit. The trembling in her legs stops. She sucks air in and pushes it out. She is strong again. She is the Penelope who refuses to wait at home, who strikes out on her own journey. Fuck patience, she thinks. Let's go.

Gabrielle helps her stand. But Gabrielle is not alone. Six hands grip her arms and torso. Phobos and Deimos are holding her too. They hoist her up. It was Phobos and Deimos, she realizes. Not Gabrielle. They saw her crumple. They marched forward. They laid their palms upon her. Warmth came, and she could rise.

Penelope examines their faces, wide and empty as the moons after which they were named. Their blinks are rhythmic and indifferent. If Penelope didn't know who their mothers were, she'd have no way to tell. Agnes had mobile, often mocking expressions, but Phobos has none. Winona was patient like Deimos, but her eyes could sparkle, whereas his remain flat. What Penelope presumed from a distance is true. Phobos and Deimos are no longer boys. They are men, or something close. Despite their strangeness, they have saved her. Maybe she's been wrong to fear them. They might not be the monsters she thought they were.

Come on, she mouths to Gabrielle.

Gabrielle darts her eyes at Phobos and shakes her head. Penelope gestures at her belly and trusts her expression to communicate urgency. Gabrielle nods, but does not share her smile. When they resume walking, Gabrielle turns her back to Deimos and Phobos, as if pretending they do not exist. As before, they maintain a polite distance, though not nearly as great. Perhaps ten paces behind. Perhaps eight.

HOUR SEVEN

June 28, 2046

Their odd quartet presses on, Penelope and Gabrielle leading, Phobos and Deimos trailing. They now walk five paces behind the women. To conserve energy, neither Penelope nor Gabrielle attempts communication, though Penelope keeps peeking at her companion's profile.

They are not Agnes or Winona or Chantrea. They are Gabrielle and Penelope. Against all odds, they live.

Thinking about the other volunteers hurts. Penelope wishes she had known them better. She spoke to Winona—really spoke to her—only once. It was a short exchange, but Penelope remembers it clearly. The day was fresh, sunrise blooming in the east. The others had not yet stumbled from their pods, and she was running beside Winona on the treadmills. Through the wide window they could watch themselves turning toward the sun. How inexorable it felt, a grand dance of celestial bodies they could not control.

Once upon a time I was famous, Winona said, still running. Believe it or not.

We're famous now, Penelope replied. Probably everybody on Earth knew their names, at least those with communication devices. Histories would speak of them as heroines, women who saved humans from extinction.

A different famous, Winona said. More heroic.

Then Winona told her about her battle with the White Pirates. Her words painted the scene. The chilly ripples of the Great Lake Sea. The ships speckling the horizon, sails billowing. The pirates with their torches, their chants of pure blood, pure race. The fear gripping Winona's heart. Battle-ax in hand, a mere fifteen, the youngest of her tribe, forced to fight for survival.

What happened? Penelope asked. How did it end?

We had to kill them, Winona said, so they wouldn't kill us. We tried our best to be merciful. But it was war.

I thought people didn't fight anymore, Penelope said. I thought wars had finished.

In your world maybe, Winona said.

Do you think they will come again? she asked. She stopped running too.

Not here. Winona took a breath, turned pale, took another breath.

Is that why you chose this mission?

I didn't choose it, she said. Did you?

No, Penelope admitted, and anger lit up within her.

Penelope remembered how on their occasional nighttime forays to the surface, her mother would guide her chubby finger to locate the red star. That's your destiny, K would say. Penelope remembers Pa too, sitting in his wheelchair at the airstrip in the Northern Refuge, how he'd swiveled away before the plane had even taken off, as though it were a foregone conclusion. She imagined David on Winona's doorstep like a witch in a fairy tale, offering her parents riches in exchange for their child.

Penelope felt sticky, like she'd touched something she shouldn't have.

You're right, Penelope agreed. We didn't choose to come. But why do you stay?

We want the species to live, Winona replied. She had regained her color, her breathing grown steady. Even if our land dies.

Chantrea entered the gym and took the treadmill on Penelope's other side. Penelope didn't talk to Winona again, not in a way that mattered. The last time she saw Winona she was so drained of blood, so white, she could have been one of those pirates.

Penelope doesn't waste energy turning to look behind her. She knows what she'll see. Phobos and Deimos, bald and bland and unstoppable as the planet's circular motion. She would like to call them men, not moons. She would like to recognize Winona in Deimos, but the sole trait he shares is patience. Maybe that's enough.

We are your army now, she tells Winona's memory. We'll win this battle too.

HOUR EIGHT

June 28, 2046

They have stopped to rest. The women balance on a hard dune, their thighs touching. Phobos and Deimos have paused too, but remain standing. Penelope knows that on Earth, the stronger gravity would make this journey impossible for her. It would drain her too quickly. Although she might be more powerful than she thought. All those hours on the treadmill are paying off. When she spoke to K after her implantation, her mother praised Penelope for her strength, for continuing her exercise. In the past, she said, many women didn't. They were afraid of jarring the fetus. Afraid of blood spots. Miscarriage.

Miscarry is a funny word, Penelope thinks. To be unable to carry. Or to do it wrong. As though forming a human with the meat of one's body is merely a matter of carrying. If this were the case, Penelope could set her burden down, like a piece of luggage that had grown too heavy.

This morning at the station—before the fire—Penelope did consider setting everything down. She was in the examining room with the obstetrician. Brandon. He had called her in for a predawn visit. Why so early? she complained when the technician wheeled her in. We must be extra vigilant, Brandon insisted, waving the technician away. Then he slid his needle in, drained her blood, and injected something else. She sat up, rubbing her arm. Lie down, Brandon said, but she didn't want to. When she lay flat, her nausea got worse. Take me home, she told him. It was the first time she'd used the word *home* to mean their pod. Anything can become normal if it persists, she thought.

He was about to press the intercom for the technician when they heard a noise from the next room. A crash. A cry. Then silence. Penelope and Brandon looked at each other. Neither of them expected disaster. By that point they should have. Then they smelled smoke.

Penelope's first thought was Yes. Set this all ablaze. Burn me clean. Burn this out of me.

Then instinct took over. She leaped off the gurney, pushed Brandon aside, and ran, her belly misshapen and obscene. In the hallway she nearly collided with Gabrielle. Fire, Penelope yelled. Run. She and Gabrielle locked hands and together, they ran.

I saved you once, Penelope tells her unborn. Will you do the same for me?

HOUR NINE

June 28, 2046

Our tale continues, Penelope thinks. Behind them, the sun is arcing westward, casting their shadows forward. Penelope remembers her mother's tale, the one she called a history. She wrote it while pregnant with Penelope, months after arriving at the Northern Refuge. Penelope asked to read it, but K refused. Unless your father comes, she said. I gave it to him. Why did you give it away? Penelope asked. I thought it would do some good, her mother said. I thought it would at least bring him north. I sprinkled some pretty big clues in there. He should have understood what I meant. That you were coming and you were his. But it doesn't matter. It was nothing new. At this, K sighed. Just another story.

K reminds Penelope of Chantrea. K and Chantrea might have understood each other. Chantrea also kept a record, though not in words. A day after Penelope's implantation, Chantrea showed it to her. Maybe she was trying to make friends. Chantrea brought a plate from her pod, lidded to contain its contents.

Look, Chantrea said. Beneath the plastic lid, the plate's smooth surface held a filigreed design, intricately sketched in sand. Reds and blues. Blacks and yellows and whites.

Where'd you get the sand? Penelope asked.

The craft box, Chantrea replied. There's a ton of good stuff in there.

What is it? Penelope leaned closer.

A mandala, Chantrea said. I learned how to make one in the Reclaimed City, at the main temple. One of the nuns had come from the mountains. She taught me. See. Chantrea pointed to a swirl of green. There's me. And that's you. Her finger followed a red curlicue swirled with blue. With Gabrielle. She peered at Penelope, as though gauging her reaction. Penelope's face flushed, but she said nothing. Agnes is here. Chantrea leveled her finger at a white lotus. And Winona. Another lotus, but smaller.

What will you do with it? Penelope asked.

Destroy it.

Why?

Why not?

But what's the point of all this work? Penelope gestured at the mandala.

The work itself. Chantrea smiled, and her tight face loosened. Penelope saw then how beautiful she was, more beautiful than any of them. She felt ashamed she hadn't seen it before.

As she walks, Penelope considers her own record, the log she typed back at the station. She should have erased it. She meant to, but she had no time. It must have melted. Or does it still exist? Is it radioing her message into the void, the dark nothingness through which she traveled to get here? She can't imagine anyone listening. Penelope used to think she and the other volunteers were famous, but most people on Earth probably have no idea they're up here. It's not like they can read the news to find out.

Penelope glances behind. Deimos and Phobos are only a few paces behind. Phobos is smiling. No, wait. He is not. A problem with the angle. Phobos and Deimos do not smile. Penelope's sight blurs. She will not lie down again. She breathes. She takes another step. She can't imagine what they're thinking. She's never heard them speak. What can their thoughts look like, if they have no words with which to frame them?

HOUR TEN

June 28, 2046

They have reached a hill. It seems like a mountain, a wall stretching upward. How will we climb this? Penelope mouths through her helmet. Gabrielle points right. That way, her lips say. Her arm bends in a circle. This means they'll go around. Behind them the sun slips downward, seeking its date with the west. The day's sojourn is stretching into night. When darkness falls and the temperature plummets, Phobos and Deimos might protect them: circle their arms over them, lend them their heat. Penelope believes they could do this if they chose.

They turn and trudge on, four figures at a mountain's base, the two women in front, Phobos and Deimos following close behind. The sinking sun projects their shadows sideways, silhouettes that mimic their movements.

They are nearing a low dip in the hill when they spot an object. It is spindly and upright, metal glinting against sand. Gabrielle reaches it first. What is it? Penelope asks, but Gabrielle is not looking her way and so does not hear. Gabrielle nudges it with her boot, and then stands back. It's not rusted, for no water exists to spur corrosion, but it's sticky with dust. Poised on six legs, its neck extended, it looks like an animal.

Its feet are wheels and its head alert, as though sensing their intrusion. If Penelope squints, she can see a face, its camera a single eye. It must have snapped pictures and sent them speeding toward Earth. Perhaps some remain trapped within: images of dunes and cliffs, blue sunsets, nights furious with stars. Its own wheels rumbling over unknown territory, searching in vain for evidence of life.

It dwarfs Gabrielle, minimizing her humanity in a way the mountain to their left cannot. It doesn't belong to Red Star. No stenciled icon—that crimson starburst—exists to announce ownership. It's a dinosaur, a relic. It's like Risk or Monopoly or pennies. Or Gabrielle's city.

They have no time for antiques, leftovers from an era they didn't know. Gabrielle toes the metal creature once more as if expecting something. Movement. A voice. Acknowledgment. Penelope cannot know what she is thinking. When they reach the station, after they tug off their helmets, Penelope will ask. What were you thinking, she will say, those hours we traveled? I was thinking of you, she dreams Gabrielle will respond.

Stop, Penelope tells herself. Don't think of the future. We own the moment we're in. Nothing more.

HOURS ELEVEN AND TWELVE

June 28, 2046

Night is coming. The sun is setting behind them in an indigo blaze. High above the sky flames pink and orange and red. Before she arrived on this planet, Penelope learned about these sunsets, but the first one she saw still amazed her. She should have understood then that if the sunsets and sunrises were opposite here, other things would be different too.

Her little moon within is also turning. Pain jabs her diaphragm. She stops to catch her breath, but cannot. Gabrielle turns a worried face, lit by the sunset's splendor. A shape moves to Gabrielle's right. Phobos. He plods forward and holds his hands against Penelope's belly. She closes her eyes. This world disappears.

Penelope sees aspen, leaves flickering in a breeze. A lake rustling with cattails. A rabbit in a thicket. She hears a cardinal's liquid trill. A brown hand holds out a berry. The hand's palm is seamed and hard. The berry is scarlet, a downward cone with a leafed cap. A strawberry. She pops it in her mouth. Juice flows. Another, she demands. Another appears. Then another. She swallows each one. Summer has arrived. Green air. Sudden sun. Beyond this meadow, the fragrance of pine.

She has walked out of the woods into a clearing. An old woman leads her. The woman is small and straight, her eyes and mouth webbed with age. Her hair hangs down like gray moss. Penelope has seen such moss before, in her mother's books. Once upon a time, that moss hung from trees. Then the trees drowned.

Another berry, she cries, but the woman shakes her head. No more, this means.

The woman does not speak. She is quiet as the pines that circle the meadow. Penelope recognizes her. She is the woman from their northern legends, the one who wanders the forest and speaks in song. Sometimes— they say—she is an animal, sometimes a queen. Sometimes—K says— she is family, but will not explain what that means. Sometimes Pa dreams of her and wakes full of energy and plans. Penelope knows her from stories, but has never seen her. Now the woman walks beside her, patience radiating from her like light.

This is real, Penelope thinks. I am really seeing her. She knows this on some deep, true level, as she knows the truth of the dream she's had of the desert, the dream each member of her family has dreamed. Watching the woman now, Penelope sees she is neither animal nor queen. A leader yes, but nothing mythical. This old woman is exceptionally strong, but she is human. As human as Penelope.

They move into the pines. Shadows slide across their faces. A branch snaps. Stop, the woman's upraised hand tells her. In the bracken, a face appears. Long nose, brown fur, black eyes and muzzle. Nascent horns sprout from its head. Antlers, her mother's books have told her. Antlers, Penelope thinks, watching this creature.

She is silent as the woman, the trees. She holds her breath until it hurts, and then gently lets it go. Light speckles the ground. Penelope is warm and happy. She wants this moment to last. But a blue jay shouts, and the animal slips back into the woods. A white tail flicks. Stop, she says. But it is leaping away between the tall trunks. She could have stared into its black eyes for always.

I used to think my father was a deer, the old woman says. Her voice belongs to a child, lilting upward at its edges. But he wasn't, she says, and looks at Penelope.

What was he? she asks.

Just a man, the woman says.

Voices sound in the distance, and the woman turns her head. My people are calling, she says. You. Her eyes level with Penelope's. Keep walking.

Penelope wakes up. She's not sure whether she was sleeping or unconscious or dreaming or all three. She remembers the old woman she saw, but already the vision is fading. She knows she's cold. The sun has set. The baby has numbed within her. Some light clings to the sky's corners, but it is fading. She is standing, clutching her middle. Gabrielle's face is a dim shape behind her helmet's screen. Phobos and Deimos loom close. Don't leave me, she thinks. Don't fall behind. It's too dark to read Gabrielle's expression. Without them I may die, Penelope wants to tell her. Please let them stay.

Let's go, Penelope says instead. She's not sure exactly to whom she is speaking.

HOUR THIRTEEN

June 28, 2046

Darkness has fallen. Penelope senses the cold with her mind, not her skin. The suits are protecting them from the plummeting temperatures, but Penelope doesn't know how long that will last. She and Gabrielle have lit their helmets, and Penelope can hardly recognize her lover's face in the eerie glow cast across it.

Penelope has been lying to herself about the guinea pig lab. She did see it, this morning, during their escape. They were running so fast they nearly missed it. She spotted a wide window and a white space behind. Gabrielle banged into her when she stopped. Let's go, Gabrielle urged. One second, Penelope insisted. The lab was nothing like she'd imagined it. No artificial lawn. No free-roaming beasts. Instead it contained a stack of cages crammed so tight with animals they had no space to move. Penelope was so sorry she had eaten them. She wished she had found them earlier and released them in the dunes. Dying of radiation would have been awful, but at least they would have been free.

For one long second, she looked. Then Gabrielle pulled her arm. They ran. They could hear technicians screaming behind them. They could feel the heat from the flames. That's the exit, Gabrielle shouted. Hurry.

Pain is creeping upward like a vine. Penelope pauses, waiting for Phobos to catch up. In starlight's faint glow, she sees him move toward her. His big head is a white bulb in the dark. Penelope remembers this morning with Brandon the obstetrician. She can still smell the odor of disinfectant before fire caught hold in the next room and transformed the air to smoke. Is Bill still sleeping? Penelope asked. Who? Brandon said. The geneticist, she responded. Oh, he replied. You mean Bob. He's next door, with the babies. You're still calling them babies, she said. They're healthy—he passed her a lollipop, like he did every time, as though she were a little girl—developing at a good pace. They're already eating solid food. Isn't that wonderful? You must be kidding, Penelope said, but Brandon's face showed no expression.

He looked like Phobos, Penelope realizes now. Brandon the obstetrician was the fertilizer. This misshapen moon is his. And you his son, she whispers to the being that presses his palms against her. Her pain dissipates. Thank you, she tells Phobos. Of course, he does not respond.

HOUR FOURTEEN

June 28, 2046

Gabrielle has taken the lead, her suit glowing whitely against the darkened dunes. Penelope watches her receding, now and then, into the night. She struggles to keep up.

Penelope remembers her mother's instructions regarding love, the ones K offered on her thirteenth birthday, when she became a woman. K said they used to call it that, as though one had to bleed to grow up. Penelope knew what to do. She cleaned herself in the washroom, pulled on the necessary undergarment, bundled the sheets up for the cleaners. She didn't tell her mother, but when Penelope crawled into her bed that night for story time, K turned to her. Be careful, K said, whom you love. This can bind you to them.

Penelope knew she was talking about babies. She knew how they were made, what they could do to her. That's why her mother encouraged her to undertake this mission. Penelope sees it now. K wanted her to birth a baby without love. It was her way of protecting her. She wanted a future for her daughter different from her own.

Read me *Peter Pan*, Penelope asked that night. But her mother said no. That book is for children, she said. She opened another on her screen. This one is for you. That night they began *Jane Eyre*. It took them weeks to finish it, her mother's wistful voice curling around the words, but when they did, Penelope understood. Be careful whom you love, she told herself.

A month after her first blood, she questioned K about Pa's parents. Why doesn't anybody talk about them? she asked.

His mother was strange, K replied. That's all he's told me.

What about his father? Penelope asked.

I don't know, she said. I've asked too. He won't tell me.

Does he know? They were under the blankets with *Wuthering Heights* open on the screen. More love, K had said when they had started, and more hate too.

I'm not sure, her mother replied. Sometimes I think yes, sometimes no.

The next day Penelope went to her grandfather. She asked him straight out.

A bad man, Pa responded. That's all I know.

A bad seed, she suggested, because she'd heard it from a book. What if we're rotten? she asked Pa. What if we grew wrong from the start?

It's not that simple, he said.

By that time, Pa had moved reluctantly from roller board to wheelchair, and Penelope was sitting down, staring into his beautiful eyes. They were deep brown with flecks of yellow. His eyes had always reminded her of pictures she'd seen of Kentucky. The Kentucky deserts had the same colors.

We're more complicated than one bad seed, Pa said. Look at your mother.

Broken, Penelope thought.

Look at me, he urged.

A general without an army, she thought but did not say aloud.

Look at yourself, Pa said, and wheeled away to work on his designs. Her own pod, she realizes. That's what he was designing. The volunteers' entire wing in the Red Star station. The dining room, the gym, the bathing pods. Because he knew she loved it, he selected red for her duvet. Now those pods are gone, his dreams extinguished in a single explosion.

Phobos remains beside her. Penelope is afraid to let him fall behind. She needs his touch. From Gabrielle's averted face, Penelope can tell she doesn't like it. Maybe Gabrielle's right. Maybe he's a bad seed too. Maybe they all are.

What about you? Penelope pokes her stomach, prodding her little moon. Are you rotten?

In answer, a gentle kick. No, says this kick. I'm the last bit of the dream to remain.

Penelope wishes Pa and K could hear that.

I can still make you proud, she thinks. Just wait.

HOUR FIFTEEN

June 28, 2046

The horizon glows with an artificial radiance. The station, Gabrielle's lips tell her. Despite their fatigue, they begin to run as best they can. Their slow pace infuriates Penelope. She does not turn, but she can sense Phobos and Deimos quickening too.

The night is young but determined. The cold has begun to seep through Penelope's suit. Black dunes, black air. Frail illumination from their helmets, the distant station. Overhead a net studded with gems. Penelope sees Poseidon. Demeter. Orion, with his two dogs. But no pattern for the wife of Odysseus. Despite her loyalty and patience, Penelope cannot call a constellation her own. These heavens hold no space for her.

The station glimmers, a beacon at the planet's rim. Then it's gone. In the time it takes to glance at Gabrielle's opalescent profile behind plastic, the light vanishes. Shit, Penelope sees Gabrielle say. The station is gone. In its place spreads a blackness whose totality halts Penelope's breath. When her breathing resumes, her heartbeat feels persistent, yet crooked. Like Deimos and Phobos, she thinks. Like any malformed thing.

Penelope knows what this means. That darkness means a dust storm. Solar winds are kicking the dirt to a frenzy. She calms herself. It's okay, she tells Gabrielle, but Gabrielle cannot hear her. Her face points at the storm. Penelope tugs her arm until she turns. The wind won't be strong, Penelope tells Gabrielle, but can't be certain she understands. A stiff breeze, Penelope assures her. Run again, Penelope mouths. This time Gabrielle nods.

They run toward the storm. They have no choice. The other station lies there. We'll be okay, Penelope tells her baby. *Okay*, the baby echoes, *okay, okay*, until it sounds like nothing, like the wind's moaning, the stars winking out, blotted by blackness. *Okay*, Penelope hears it say, but it's not the baby. It's her heart beating, its two syllables, one soft, one hard.

Penelope is holding Gabrielle's hand, their thick gloves intertwined. She can hear her own breath rasping. She doesn't look behind her, but she knows Phobos and Deimos are keeping pace, their feet thudding their motherland. Keep up, Penelope urges them. She needs Phobos's hands. Her child cannot be born without his firm and pressing palms. Without them, she and it will die.

Hurry, her unborn screams, but that is the wind howling, black dust whipping past, speckling her helmet. Or are those clinging dots not dust at all? Is she puking blood when she believes she's breathing air? She will be Agnes, torn apart. She will be Winona, coughing her guts onto the ground.

You'll be okay, Penelope tells herself. The wind's not strong. A breeze. We can walk forward. We can survive this. But she hears screaming, a spiral that loops and loops, and why is she not running? Why is she on her knees in the frigid equatorial night? She needs to reach the station. Time vanishes. Come on, she shouts. But her baby says no. She tastes copper. She knows what is coming. Stop, Penelope tells the baby. No, it says. The time is now.

The storm is not black. It is red. Like fire. Like this planet's sand. Like the blanket under which Penelope learned to name love.

Go ahead then, Penelope tells her moon. Rise.

HOUR UNKNOWN

Day Unknown

Penelope wakes to trees. Have I been sleeping? she asks. Yes, a voice tells her. A woman bends over her. Penelope barely recognizes her without the helmet. It's me, Gabrielle says. Are there trees? Penelope asks. The smell is vivid and overpowering. A layered fragrance, rich with moisture. She pictures roots and earth. Not earth, she reminds herself, not anymore. Dirt.

Yes, Gabrielle says. Look up.

Penelope's eyes focus. She sees trunks. Bark. A lattice of green.

No. Penelope's mind jumbles. Black and red. Dust and fire. She is imagining this.

The trees are real, says Gabrielle.

What happened? Penelope asks. She is lying on a stretcher in a forest. Except it's not a real forest. The floor is white and tiled between its clumps of dirt. The roots sink below its surface. Above the treetops she sees a dome, also white. Somewhere, wind is moaning.

The storm will continue for days, Gabrielle says. Maybe weeks. But we made it.

Penelope feels too light. She has lost something. She's still swollen, but it feels different. Emptier.

Where's my baby? Penelope struggles to sit up.

Gabrielle presses a hand to her cheek. Rest, she says. It is safe. *She* is safe. We are safe. She begins to laugh.

Penelope's little moon has risen. Her baby is gone. Her baby is a daughter. Another woman, Penelope thinks, and her heart sinks.

Where is she? she demands. Gabrielle eases her back down. The sensation is as soothing as Phobos's hands. Penelope lets Gabrielle place her head on the pillow. Where are the children? she asks, but her voice has weakened. They're not children, her mind whispers.

Gone. Gabrielle's eyes tighten. In the storm. We lost them.

No. Fear leaps in Penelope's chest. She sits up again, but it hurts. Her middle has split and been sewn. She can feel the knots, wrenching skin to skin. We must find them, Penelope says. I need Phobos. He's the only one who can heal me. I'm sure of it.

He's gone. I'm sorry, Gabrielle murmurs, but she doesn't look it.

Dead?

We don't know. We can't track them.

We? Penelope asks. Who else is here?

Two men from our team have been living here, Gabrielle says. Tending the forest. Getting everything ready.

For the babies, Penelope says.

Gabrielle's eyes shift away. They were the ones who found us, she says. Tim and Tom. They spotted us on their screen and came out in the rover.

When Gabrielle says this, Penelope recalls the rover, a hand stretched down, harsh lights in the dark. A vehicle jostling over dunes. The unmistakable whoosh of an airlock. Where is my baby? she asks again.

Sleep, Gabrielle says. You can visit her tomorrow.

Penelope doesn't want to sleep. She wants to see her daughter, wants to search for Deimos and Phobos, wants to place her palms against these unbelievable trees, but she can't stop herself. She is spent. She closes her eyes and lowers herself into the darkness.

On the brink of unconsciousness, she whispers one more question. How big is she?

But Gabrielle has already left.

HOURS UNKNOWN

Days Unknown

Penelope wakes and sees green. The color of leaves, splotched white with daisies. Chantrea's here, she thinks. Chantrea must have wrapped her duvet around herself. You lived, Penelope tells her. You made it. But Chantrea shakes her head, and Penelope comes fully awake. She was dreaming. Around her tower pines and oaks, maples and birch. Vines twine underneath. Among the green, specks of color. Roses and black-eyed Susans and snowdrops. Mountain laurel. Daisies. Actual daisies. She is under the dome in Gabrielle's station. Chantrea is not here.

But Penelope knew she wouldn't be. She saw Chantrea at the Red Star station. She saw what happened to her. Chantrea had not shrouded herself in her duvet. She had not hidden in their quarters, hoping the fire would pass. She was not running beside or behind or beyond them. Chantrea had joined the guinea pigs. Penelope has been lying to herself about that too. She didn't want to remember. But Penelope did see her, when she and Gabrielle ran past, when she stopped to stare. Chantrea was in the lab among their cages. She was running around. Down on all fours, scampering. Scrabbling feet.

Penelope and Gabrielle tried to rescue Chantrea. They entered the lab. They pulled and beseeched. They dragged her kicking across the floor. But their noses scented fire, their hearts beat faster, and in their moment of distraction, Chantrea chomped down on their hands. First Penelope's, then Gabrielle's. Like a beast, she bit them. Like humans, they left her behind.

Don't look so sad, Gabrielle tells her. You're safe.

Gabrielle is bending over her bed. She looks older. There's more than a shadow of David in her face.

Where's Moon? Penelope asks. Her body is a ball of flame. She does not peep under her white gown. She does not need to see the stitches. She knows that she is a cobbled thing. Sewn up. Like Deimos and Phobos, she has become an object of someone's creation.

That's what you have called her? Gabrielle's eyebrows lift.

She's the original, Penelope says. She repeats the name to herself. Moon. Yes. That's her.

How fitting. Gabrielle's tone is bemused, as though humoring a child.

Penelope attempts to stand, but cannot get off the stretcher. Show me my daughter.

Gabrielle extends a hand. Penelope takes it. Her lover helps her to her feet, as solicitous as a doctor. Penelope doesn't like it. She's had enough of doctors. Did you deliver her? she asks.

I'm not skilled enough, Gabrielle says. That was Tom.

Is he another geneticist? Penelope asks.

Come see your baby, Gabrielle replies.

Gabrielle opens a hatch in the floor and beckons. With much difficulty, Penelope follows her down a ladder into a tunnel. Beneath the dome lies a tangle of tunnels, each one leading to a pod. No windows exist, but Penelope imagines the grainy layers of sediment pressing against the walls. Far above, in what could be day or night, solar winds tear at the surface. Phobos, she thinks. Deimos. My body hurts. Come find me. Make me strong again.

In a cozy pod piled with acrylic furs, Moon is waiting. A man is sitting beside her, rocking her gently in a cradle.

I'm Tim, says the man. Welcome.

Penelope approaches the cradle and gazes down at her daughter. Tiny nose, tiny mouth, tiny eyelids in a perfect face. Skin golden brown as Penelope's own. Like any newborn, she is peacefully, mercifully asleep. She is not already standing, staring blankly at her world as Phobos was mere days after birth. Penelope's daughter is neither big nor bland. She seems like a baby. Nothing more. Love for this small and ordinary creature fills Penelope. Her child is human, or close enough. Relief pricks Penelope's eyes with tears.

She holds out her arms. Tim wraps the blanket more snugly around Moon. Then he places the child—a miracle all her own—against Penelope's heart.

GABRIELLE AND PENELOPE are eating among the trees in the dome. Moon swings in her cradle by their table. Tim and Tom have elected to eat below, in one of the pods underground. We don't want to disturb you, they said.

Penelope forks up another piece of meat. They are dining on dried venison, softened and roasted to a semblance of tenderness. A treat, Gabrielle has called it, for our homecoming. Penelope does not argue this isn't her home. She knows what Gabrielle will say, because the small voice has said it already. It is your home now. Where else would you go?

What about Phobos and Deimos? Penelope asks. Have you found them?

Still searching, Gabrielle replies cheerfully. She picks up her glass.

Her water, like Penelope's, is tinted red to mimic wine. To new beginnings, she says.

To Moon, Penelope says and raises her own.

They clink glasses or try to, for they are plastic and make only a little tapping sound. But Moon opens her eyes. Her irises are blue, but her skin has begun to change, with shades of brown and pink and ebony and pale conflicting. Watching the various tones shift across Moon's body is disconcerting. Despite her baby's rapid gestation, Penelope assumed Moon was human the first time she saw her. Her daughter is not like Phobos and Deimos, but she's not the ordinary baby Penelope initially assumed her to be.

As though reading her thoughts, Gabrielle juts her chin toward Moon. Creepy, isn't it? she says. Like some weird metamorphosis. A chameleon from outer space.

Penelope looks more closely at her daughter, considering Gabrielle's words. No, she thinks, it's not creepy. It's amazing.

Moon seems to be a composite. Her skin's shifting colors tell a story. A fragment of Michelangelo exists in her. A piece of K, who once was Kaiser, leader of a floating city. Pa too, and Pa's mother, a woman Penelope never met. In her daughter's cells nestles her ancestors' DNA, but she is more than they were. K used to call Penelope the new breed. If K could see this baby, she would realize the absurdity of that statement. Moon is the one, not Penelope. Another breed, this child. Penelope's unease dissipates. In its place, a different feeling. Pride. As she stares at her daughter, her heart swells. Finally, a new thing.

THE NIGHT DRAWS CLOSE. Penelope and Gabrielle share a pod. Moon is snuggled in her cradle and they in their bed. They have shed their jumpsuits. Gabrielle lies delicate beside her. Penelope is knotted and raw, her breasts bloated with milk, her tummy tied tight with thread. Nonetheless they turn to each other and in the artificial glitter of this man-made place, they reach out hands. Penelope's palms to Gabrielle's hips. Gabrielle's thighs around her face. Penelope's mouth to the sweet seed within her. Beyond this moment they will create nothing. K was right. Loyalty and patience can have their rewards.

Before sleep Penelope musters courage. What will we do now? she asks.

Stay here, Gabrielle mumbles sleepily. For a time.

And then what? Penelope asks. Radio for help? Return to Earth?

Gabrielle suddenly looks more alert. That depends, she says.

On what?

On your baby. Gabrielle glances at Moon.

In her sleep, Moon emits a milky cry and then lapses into silence. The advice offered by the manuals they read at the station has proved useless. Penelope's baby faced no problem latching. Without hesitation, Moon tugged from her breast. In its purest form, Penelope's body flowed into hers.

What do you mean? Penelope asks.

Let's wait, Gabrielle says. And see.

What about Deimos and Phobos? she asks. Are we waiting for them?

Absolutely not, Gabrielle says. Those monsters.

They weren't so bad, Penelope insists. They kept me alive.

They killed Agnes. Probably Winona.

Not on purpose.

Penelope. Gabrielle traces her stitches with a gentle finger. Phobos and Deimos set the fire, she says. They attacked the geneticist. They started a fire in his lab. I don't know how, but they helped it spread. The Red Station exploded because of them.

Penelope sucks in a breath. It could be true. She was with Brandon when they heard noise in the geneticist's lab next door. Then they smelled smoke. Phobos and Deimos could have set the fire. How, Penelope does not know. But what if they did burn the station? She sees the guinea pigs banging into their cages. She sees Chantrea crawling on hands and knees. She sees Winona stretched cold on a slab, the second youngest of the Ojibwe tribe frying to nothing on a planet over thirty million miles away from the one she fought to save.

We had to let them go, Gabrielle insists.

Moon cries out again in her sleep, and Penelope gets out of bed to pick her up. With her baby's face pressed tight to her chest, Penelope walks her up and down. Gabrielle watches them, but Penelope avoids her eyes. She doesn't care what Gabrielle thinks. Even if Moon had emerged as tall and terrifying as the other Red Star babies, Penelope would have kept her. No matter what, she would have learned to love her.

At least Moon isn't a monster, Penelope says. Just new.

DAYTIME

June 35, 2046

Gabrielle has an apparently infinite store of food. For breakfast, she and Penelope are eating dehydrated eggs on dried wafers crafted to look like toast. Moon is still sleeping, snug in their pod. Penelope's nausea has returned, but she forces an egg down. You must be strong, she tells herself, for whatever comes next.

Trees on Mars, she says to Gabrielle. Who would've thought?

Gabrielle considers the oak across from their table. Incredible, isn't it? she says. The solar panels are particularly clever, I think. We use the generator during dust storms, but the sun holds the real power. Even if we disappeared, this place could continue. Before the collapse, a scientist at an American university designed this dome, she says. We have been very fortunate to put his design to use.

We're living in marvelous times, Penelope says.

They share a look, but whether it's one of glee or horror, Penelope is not certain. The wind's wail reaches them, like Catherine's ghost crying on the moors in *Wuthering Heights*. Penelope tries to eat another egg, but cannot. She doesn't like the way it wobbles.

Have you found Deimos and Phobos yet? She will keep asking.

Gabrielle slides another egg onto a wafer and pops it into her mouth. She chases it with water colored orange to resemble juice. Not a trace, she says. But don't worry about them. We have your child to think about now.

Penelope doesn't like the way she says it. If she can find a screen here, she'll try to contact her mother. K must know Red Star has exploded. The information would have found her somehow. She probably thinks Penelope is dead, that she burned too. When she calls, K will answer. She'll have to. She'll be thrilled her daughter is alive. Penelope can't wait to tell her about Moon. K will be so proud, so grateful the experiment is—despite everything—a success. This story has a happy ending, Penelope will announce in triumph. Yes, the small voice mocks, a happy ending.

IN THE AFTERNOON, the storm abates. Penelope hears the wind subside and the dust cease speckling the dome. She has lived so many days with the noise she misses it. Come see, Gabrielle says. She leads Penelope down a tunnel that curves around the dome's perimeter. Penelope's stitches pull at her skin. She must stop and breathe. Once. Twice. Her body is twanging with pain.

Gabrielle halts at a window. This is our only one, she says. I tucked it back here so we wouldn't be tempted to keep peeping outside. It's easier to be content, she adds, when you're not always looking toward the next horizon.

Dust clings to the window with static electricity. With a button's push, Gabrielle summons wipers to scrape it clean. See how peaceful, she says. Penelope is holding Moon. Gabrielle is holding her hand. They are a microscopic family in this galaxy studded with stones. They look. The dunes have settled and the sky has cleared, yellow as corn silk in the soft summer day. Gabrielle is right. It is beautiful.

Then Penelope sees it. A figure at the window's periphery. It is cresting a dune. It is tromping forward. Her chest flutters. Gabrielle's smile fades. The figure is not alone. Another one walks behind. Dust smears their jumpsuits. With their globular heads, they are unmistakable.

Phobos and Deimos.

The last time Penelope saw them they were young men. Now they seem something else.

This wasn't supposed to happen, Gabrielle says.

As they watch, the two figures march closer. Closer still. Neither Penelope nor Gabrielle speaks. Gabrielle drops Penelope's hand and clutches her own arms. Penelope tears her eyes from Phobos and Deimos and looks at Gabrielle. Her lips and cheeks have lost circulation, her knuckles whitened against her sleeves.

Gabrielle doesn't want Phobos and Deimos to return. That is clear. But what about Moon? Moon is no monster—may never be—but what if Gabrielle has been planning to lose her too? Penelope doesn't know. She realizes with a nasty jolt that she doesn't want to wait to find out.

Phobos and Deimos have nearly reached the dome. Their boots raise little puffs in the dirt. Penelope believes she can hear their footsteps, even in the sand. Penelope has dreamed this moment. So have her mother and grandfather. The man walking out of the desert has revealed himself, and he is this: two monsters whose faces show no expression at all. It is not the moment K and Pa expected. It is something more.

Penelope glances down at Moon. Her perfect eyelashes on her perfect lids. Her beautifully shifting skin. On their walk from the Red Star station, Phobos and Deimos healed Penelope. They helped her stay strong until her baby was born. Deimos and Phobos clearly want Moon to live. Phobos and Deimos can protect this baby—will protect her—from whatever is coming. With their help, Penelope will be able to rear her daughter to adulthood. She will see Moon grow into a woman, someone who can populate this planet with her own breed, one not seen before. If she lets Phobos and Deimos into the dome, Penelope can keep her family's dream alive.

She has no choice. When did she ever? Penelope backs away from Gabrielle and hurries down the tunnel before Gabrielle notices she's gone. Penelope reaches the tunnel with the exit. She moves toward the airlock. She positions her palm over the button. Phobos and Deimos will be right outside. She can feel it. They'll be waiting.

Please, come inside, she will say.

You have reached your story's end, she will tell these two giants.

EVA

KANSAS TO COLORADO, 2048

The marauders have destroyed everything. Or nearly everything. What they haven't destroyed, they've stolen. Eva's entire tent city, razed. And in August, with winter coming on. It's not the first time they have hit, but it's the worst. Last year they nabbed a few sheep, the year before their best milk cow. But those losses were sustainable.

The marauders must have been planning this awhile, Eva thinks. She toes the shards of a clay bowl in the mud. Its delicate markings tell her it's Marybeth's work. They've taken Marybeth too. Her friend from the days of yoga class and Sunday brunch. The pain of it clutches her heart, and then it lets go. She has lost other friends. The grief is familiar. So much she's had to relinquish out here. Not only here, but before, in Kansas City, the place she once called home. Paul, her heart reminds her. Kay. Hush, she says.

Other women are picking through the ruins. Eva can count ten women. No, eleven. Giselle rises from the rubble, clutching a cloth bundle. From this distance, it sounds like she's laughing, but Eva has lived long enough on the Kansas plains to recognize weeping when she hears it. She thought she saw one of the marauders galloping off with Alicia's baby, but she couldn't be sure. It's the sole baby born in the past ten years. Of course the marauders would take it.

They should have taken me, she thinks. I'm too old for this. Seventy-six years on this ball of dirt spinning through space. I should never have lived to see this.

When Eva was a kid, 2048 seemed an impossible year. As an adult, it's even more so.

One of the women steps over the shattered tent poles and through blowing bits of tarp toward her. It's Alicia. She's thirty, born in 2018, Year of the Collapse. She knew civilization in its final stages, when you could buy a blender at Target, but not spend spring break at Daytona. A survivor. Alicia has been an asset to the community, good at herding sheep, though some think a little flighty. For six months she disappeared, came back pregnant, wouldn't speak of the father. The others presumed a love match, assuming Alicia absconded with a hunter from a tribe outside Wichita.

Eva knew better. Shortly after Alicia's return, Eva stumbled upon her bathing at the creek. Hurriedly Alicia yanked her tunic over her head, but not before Eva saw the ladder of scars from buttocks to shoulder blades. Marauder trademarks. Alicia had not left their tent city by choice. She had been taken. How she'd escaped, Eva did not know. Little wonder they snatched the baby. It belonged to them.

"We can rebuild," Alicia tells her. They are standing together in the mud, a torn piece of tarp blowing against their shins. Alicia's right cheekbone looks dark and pulpy. Eva wonders what her own face looks like. Her neck feels tender where a marauder grabbed it. She smacked him away with a tent pole, but couldn't knock him unconscious. At least he lost interest in her, went howling after one of their mongrels, a rangy black-and-white dog named Radar. The worst are the marauders' nails. Grown tough and thick, each one filed to a nasty point. Poor Radar, Eva thinks.

"I don't know," she tells Alicia. "We've got no food. Not even grain. I saw them hauling away the barrels."

"We'll grow more wheat in the spring," Alicia says. Her profile reminds Eva of Paul's. It bears that same sharp strength, though in Alicia it asserts itself as pride rather than stubbornness.

Eva rests a hand on the younger woman's shoulder. "We are lucky to have you."

She hangs her head. "They took baby Edgar."

"I know." Eva pulls her close and presses her cheek to Alicia's head. "We would have had to send him to the tribes anyway when he came of age."

"Would we?" Alicia mutters back. Eva remembers the night three years ago this woman came to her tent, how boldly Alicia stripped her clothes off and clambered onto her. The press of Alicia's round breasts against Eva's withered ones, the deep slick between her legs. As leader, Eva has spent time with each of the women, but Alicia she remembers with the greatest thrill. The musky scent of her unwashed hair. Her yips, wild as the coyotes' they hear in the dark.

"Maybe not." Eva inhales the woman's scalp, feels that thrum within her. "Maybe so. No boys, we said."

Alicia moves away. "I think Edgar was really a girl." Her mouth turns down. Again, that echo of Paul. Go away, Eva tells her memories. Leave me alone. "We won't know now. I wonder if they've eaten him yet."

"Alicia. Go gently with yourself."

"I don't think I'll ever go gentle again." With that she walks away, leaving Eva with the broken clay bowl at her feet and the clouds overhead, threatening rain.

THAT NIGHT EVA CALLS A MEETING. Giselle and Alicia have erected a makeshift shelter of the broken tent poles and some scraps of tarp, but it's unsteady, creaking in the wind. The twelve who remain huddle under it, trying to ignore the rain that drips through the ragged plastic onto their faces. At their feet lie the cold remains of a rabbit someone managed to spear. One morsel per woman. They'll have to hunt more tomorrow.

Eva examines their faces. Half are as old as she, friends and acquaintances from Brookside whom she hauled with her when she fled. How absurd they must have appeared, sprinting through burning Kansas City in their yoga pants. But it was flee or die, or so it seemed. Eva is grateful for them, their loyalty, their link with her former self. Through their eyes, she can see herself as she once was: a woman with sleek hair and exfoliated skin, sipping an avocado smoothie and tilting her head back to laugh at their gossip. Impossible to believe that was her life, but she likes remembering who she used to be. It helps her appreciate how far she has come.

She's grateful for the younger women too, who have come stumbling across the Midwest plains toward their tents, starving for food or something else or both. Alicia appeared like that, leading a cow across the grasslands. She told them later she'd found it wandering around a farm near Peabody. House and barn burned to the ground. A few chicken feathers blowing in the yard. The cow mooing for someone to milk her. I have brought a gift, she said before collapsing from exhaustion.

"The question," Eva says, "is what do we do."

"What can we do?" asks Giselle. Her shorn hair is as gray as Eva's but her face less lined. In her past life, her husband was a hedge fund lawyer with a mansion in the Country Club District. All those expensive creams and gels really made a difference.

Eva brings one knee up and rests her chin on it. "We stay and try to rebuild. Hope they don't come back. Or we leave."

"Leave," Alicia says in a flat voice.

"But where?" Another younger woman leans forward. Fatima. Before air travel became difficult, her parents emigrated from Nigeria. Most of the women have discarded their traditions, but Fatima observes hers faithfully, unfurling a mat five times a day and bending to pray. Because of her, they've raised sheep and cows, not pigs. "Not back east."

"Nobody's going back east," says Eva. "Nor south."

"Going north would be dumb," Giselle says, "with winter coming."

"I hear it's good up there," pipes one woman. Lucy. A Brookside friend. "The government still gives a shit."

"What government?" asks Alicia.

"The American-Canadian one." Lucy picks up a stick and absent-mindedly pokes at the rabbit bones. "I don't know what they call it."

"Whatever it is, it's not ours," Eva says. "There's no government west of the Mississippi. Hasn't been for a decade. Maybe more. Not that having one seems to help."

They fall silent, remembering stories they have heard of the governments in the east.

"I don't want to go north." Alicia sits up straighter. A spark kindles in her eyes. "I don't give a fuck how much money they've got up there. I don't care if they've got rocket ships launching people to the moon. I don't want rules and leaders. I want to go west."

"Shall we take a vote?" Eva studies their expressions, but it's difficult to read them. Years of wind and weather have hardened their faces to masks. "All for staying?"

No hands go up.

"All for going west?"

The decision is unanimous. They look like eager schoolchildren clamoring with the answer. Satisfied, Eva leans back against one of the rickety tent poles. She can't wait for the morning, when they'll knock this crappy shelter over and point their bruised faces in a new direction. Kansas reeks of death.

THEY SET OFF AT DAWN, bringing the clothes on their backs and little else. Lucy has already fashioned a fresh bow and clutch of arrows from the saplings by the creek, and Fatima has strapped her knife to her belt and her spear to her back, but beyond that they carry nothing. Hunger chews at their stomachs, but they ignore it. They have been hungry before. They can bear it. The air is deceptively warm, almost springlike, and Eva allows herself a glimmer of hope. Maybe winter won't come this year. Sometimes it doesn't. One December blew so hot the creek dried up and they had to dig a well to drink. She wouldn't relish a drought, but a longer summer would be a welcome thing indeed.

Alicia walks by Eva's side, her sadness for her son leaking from her like sweat. Alicia is silent. They all are. None glance behind at their decimated city. They are accustomed to leaving things behind. Their hearts are tough muscles, clenching just to pump blood. As she walks, Eva pictures her heart toiling inside her chest. How much longer until it wearies and stops cold? How much longer must she tread this broken earth?

An hour into their journey, Lucy glimpses movement in the grass. She knocks an arrow into her bow, aims, and lets it fly. Whatever it is dies instantly. When they reach it, they see it's no rabbit. It's a cat, an orange one. Around its neck a tattered collar with a nameplate.

"Marmalade," reads Lucy.

They eat it anyway, slicing it open with Fatima's knife and tearing its flesh raw from its bones. No time to make a fire. The marauders could be watching them. To their left, a rusted gas station tilts on its cracked concrete island. They could be inside, peering through the grimy windows, their god-awful fingernails tapping with impatience on the sill.

"Hurry," Eva tells her women.

They swallow what they can, leave the rest for the crows, and keep moving. By late afternoon they know they've reached the marauders' border by the line of human bones circling the plain. Why didn't I leave Kansas before this? Eva wonders. We were here first, she used to insist. She and her women raised their tents, plowed their lands, dotted the grass with animals. No marauders would force them out. That's what she told them. Just a pissing contest, she thinks now. Holding hands, they step over the wall of bones. Eva tries not to look down, but she glimpses a skull with skin still clinging to it. Marybeth, she thinks. Quiet, she tells herself.

Once past the border, they relax. Fatima stops to pray. As they stand over her rhythmically rising and falling body, Giselle begins a melody deep in her throat. Lucy catches the tune and continues it. Eva hums too. Even Alicia joins in. Once she has finished praying, Fatima takes up the song. It's wordless but resonant. With the setting sun blazing into their eyes and the grasslands infinite around them, the women march forward, singing.

That's the end of the first day.

THEY TRAVEL. Eva loses track of time. These are happy days. They walk, they hunt, they eat, they walk again. They sleep under the stars. Sometimes they build a fire. Sometimes they don't. The weather holds. They pass no people, only vacant houses and gas stations, strip malls with signs faded and fallen. Their muscles ache, but it's pleasant, a slow burn. Rarely they speak. Often they sing. Giselle and Lucy hold hands. Alicia stays by Eva's side.

One afternoon outside Dodge City, a dust cloud rises to the south. They hunker down and prepare for a storm, but none comes. Instead the ground shakes and a dank stench rides on the wind. They stand up. They climb a grassy knoll to get a better view.

"Would you look at that?" Giselle marvels.

"Holy shit," Eva says. "I thought the pioneers killed them all."

The dust cloud is a tremendous herd of bison, galloping from south to north. As the women watch, the bison flow across a parking lot, past a defunct Dollar Tree and Famous Footwear and Wells Fargo, over a railroad crossing with busted barriers and dead lights. The dust rises and the earth thunders with their hooves. Their smell is incredible: woolly and dense and alive. The women watch breathless until the herd is gone.

"That was fucking awesome," Fatima says.

They press on, pulses pounding. If the bison have survived, so will they.

ANOTHER DAY, GISELLE SNIFFS THE WIND. "It's cold," she says. "Do you think we've hit Colorado yet?"

"Could be." Eva points at the horizon. A jagged line breaks the morning sky. "Those must be the Rockies."

"Is this west enough, you think?" asks Giselle.

"No," Alicia says. "I don't want to risk seeing Edgar." Her face darkens. "What they've done to him," she adds.

Lucy lays a hand on her arm. "They're behind you, child."

"Not far enough."

"How far are we going anyway?" Fatima asks.

"To the mountains," Eva says. Before they left, she decided. We will reach the Rockies, she told herself, and we will stop. This is the first time she has said it aloud.

"Not beyond?" Giselle squints into the distance. "We could reach the ocean."

"I've never seen it," Fatima says.

"Me neither." Lucy frowns. "I'm seventy-four years old and I haven't seen anything bigger than a lake."

"It's a fun idea," Eva says, "but nobody's crossing the Rockies in winter."

"Why?" Alicia says. "What could go wrong?"

It takes them a moment to realize she's joking. When they laugh, they do it as they sing, with abandon.

"Fine." Giselle kicks dirt onto the embers of their breakfast fire. This morning they ate rabbit, not cat. A good omen. "We'll cross in the summer. Whenever that is."

"I wonder how high the Pacific reaches," Lucy says.

"I wonder what a beach looks like in the Rocky Mountains," adds Fatima.

"I wonder if we can wear bikinis at the end of the world," says Alicia.

This time they do not laugh, but they smile, and even in the brisk wind, they feel good. They lace up their boots, and Lucy straps her bow and arrow to her back, Fatima her spear to hers. Eva burps up the taste of rabbit.

"Excuse me," she says, as in the old days at brunch.

As though she remembers their leisurely mornings of mimosas and eggs Benedict, Giselle considers her with softened eyes. This life, her eyes say, is a miracle.

THEY WALK ANOTHER TWO FULL DAYS and rest another two full nights until they reach the Rockies. Their entire journey they encountered no people, but at the mountains' foot they discover a tent city not so different from their own. They approach with their hands up, but the city's inhabitants don't seem to fear them. With open arms, the people stride through the dry grass toward Eva and her women.

"You have come home," says a man with dreads down to his knees.

"No marauders here," whispers Lucy.

"Look." Alicia points. "They have babies."

The plural is an exaggeration. Nevertheless, one woman does hold an infant in a sling. As they near the city, they can hear its plaintive wailing. Nothing has ever sounded so welcome.

THE DREADLOCKED MAN GIVES them bowls of cornmeal mush and tents of their own. The woman with the child shows them the path to the creek and hands them a bar of real soap with a faint *Ivory* scrolled across it.

"Where did you find this?" Alicia tilts the soap back and forth to examine the lettering.

"We ask," the woman replies, "and the universe responds."

Though Alicia says nothing, Eva can read the mockery in her eyes. Not just mockery, but hurt. The marauders must have picked baby Edgar's bones clean by now. They've probably crammed them in the border wall with the others. Eva wonders how many murdered children make up that wall. If I were a man, she wants to tell Alicia, I would help you make another one.

At the creek she washes Alicia's back, scrubbing the hard dirt from her skin with a tangle of grass and a sliver of the precious soap. The others are splashing and laughing downstream. The sun is directly overhead, and Eva can see the droplets sparkling on their bodies. This is too good, she thinks, all of this too good.

After they have bathed, she sits with Alicia on the bank, working her fingers slowly through her hair to pick out the tangles. The creek burbles at their feet, dappled with sunlight. The others have taken their clothes and left, Giselle mumbling sleepily about a nap.

"What was it like for you?" Alicia asks. She looks browner and smoother when clean. Eva untangles one long lock and drapes it over her left shoulder.

"What was what like?" she asks.

"When you lost your child?"

Her first urge is to laugh. What child, she could ask. But she knows better. Alicia has seen her body, its puckered stretch marks. She knows it's not just age that has dragged her breasts down and toughened her nipples. She could lie, but what's the point?

She sees Kay, with her fiery hair and flinty eyes. How obediently she used to swallow her Wellbutrin with the water Eva offered. The daughter she thought she could save.

"I didn't lose her," she says, her voice soft with pain. "I let her go."

"Tell me." Alicia does not turn around, but Eva can feel her watching her nonetheless.

"What's to tell?" The words emerge flat and dead as the memory. "She left Kansas City with her father. They were headed to New Orleans after the hurricanes. They thought they could build something in those filthy floods." The sound she makes is half snort, half sigh. "I didn't go with them."

"Why not?"

The knots in Alicia's hair are almost gone. Eva combs out the last one and then runs her fingers through the damp mass. It smells like soap and clean water. She used to be obsessed with such things. She used to think they mattered.

Eva leans forward and wraps her arms around Alicia, this young woman who has lost so much and yet persists. She is breathing deeply, her breasts swelling against Eva's arms, her heart tapping out its tiny tune.

"Why do we do anything?" she murmurs into Alicia's wet hair.

THAT EVENING THE TENT CITY holds a celebration for the newcomers. There is roast game and bitter wine, a series of mismatched instruments twanging a discordant but delightful melody. They have built a gigantic communal fire at the city's periphery, and they gather around it, lips shiny with grease from the rabbit and prairie dogs, eyes rolling wildly from the wine. Some dance to the music, some rock and clap. Eva and her women stick together, not ready to separate.

The dreadlocked man and the mother with child sit close to them, offering them more food, more drink. At their backs the Rockies stagger upward to the glittering sky. On the mountains' distant side rolls the Pacific Ocean, lapping at their base. How much longer, Eva thinks, until it rises higher, until it washes over us?

"Eat up," the mother tells Alicia. "Who knows what will remain tomorrow?"

"I thought you said the universe will provide," Alicia responds.

"I did?" The woman smiles, her eyes empty. The baby in her lap whimpers in its sleep.

Eva can sense Alicia is near laughter, and nudges Alicia with her knee. Be quiet, this knee says. Stay polite.

"We are grateful," the dreadlocked man says. "You have brought us a beautiful evening. All the stars are out. The planets too." He points upward. "There is Mars. The red star. I have heard tales."

Eva perks up. Paul used to talk about the red star. "What kinds of tales?"

"That we have made a journey," the man replies. "Humans have traveled there. They have begun a new thing."

"What kind of thing?" Eva asks.

"Uncertain." The man takes another swallow of wine. "Could be a footprint. Could be an entire society."

"Could be bullshit," Alicia says.

The man is not offended. "Could be," he agrees. "More wine?"

"Please." Eva takes the wineskin and drinks. It was bitter before, but now it tastes rotten. She swallows, but the taste lingers on her tongue. "Excuse me." She stands up. The side that was next to Alicia turns cold.

She weaves away from the fire, through the people, over a sleeping dog. She remembers the dog the marauders took. Radar, she thinks, poor little asshole. In the shadows beyond the gathering, she unties her trousers and squats. Above her that reddish twinkle.

Fuck you, she tells the dark, but she is talking to Paul. He was rotten as the wine. He had a dark spot within him, like a bruise deep inside a piece of fruit. He called it his dream, but to her it was a curse. She used to blame his mother, that bat-shit crazy child, but it wasn't her fault. It was Paul's. He was born with that rotten spot, but he didn't try to dig it out. He cultivated it. He let it consume him. And then it consumed their daughter. She can still see Kay's face pressed against the bus window as it pulled out of the station. Twelve years old and too proud to cry for her mother. Fuck you too, she tells Kay. I hope your father's dream is dead.

Eva stands and pulls up her trousers. The night sky is also rotten, punched and pummeled by stars. Later, in the musty shadows of their tent, she will pull Alicia close. Don't cry for your child, she will tell her. He would have left you anyway. He would have broken your heart.

MOON

MARS, 2073

For seven days, I lingered at the Red Star station. I'd intended to return to the dome by evening, but I wanted time to think before I faced the Uncles. I needed to formulate my refusal in a way that wouldn't hurt them. They had kept secrets from me, had lied to me, had sometimes been wrong. But they'd also raised me. They'd cared for me when no one else could.

During those seven days, I tried to honor my mother. I felt certain she was dead. Rest, I kept telling her memory. Be at peace. Her log had told me about sorrow, about horror and pain. She had loved a woman named Gabrielle. She had loved me. Despite everything, she had loved K and Pa. She deserved tribute. I thanked her for the determination she had bequeathed to me. I promised her I would not repeat the wrongs that had been done to her. I wrote her name in the sand and let the staticky breeze erase it.

On the seventh night, I traveled back to the dome. It looked bizarre and beautiful, a disembodied sphere floating in the darkness. Above it teetered our two moons, the ones after which the Red Star volunteers had named the Uncles. I hoped it was Penelope who had named me Moon.

I expected to find the Uncles asleep. I had planned to visit them in their pods and offer them a gentle, yet forceful no. But Uncle One was sitting on the ground in the dome, his legs stuck straight out. His face looked particularly vacant, his white eyes staring at no fixed point. Uncle Two was nowhere to be seen.

The forest is sick, Uncle One said when he saw me. He pointed at a patch of flowers. The rhododendrons are dying.

It was true. Their petals had browned, their leaves withered. Some had surrendered and toppled onto their beds of soil. The pine trees were also ailing. Rotten patches speckled each trunk, a damp dark fungus that reminded me of the burned station's blackened edges. When I gazed around me, I realized the snowdrops and maples and mountain laurel, every plant really, was near death.

What happened? I asked.

The outside air got in, he replied. I broke the doors on purpose. I wanted our two worlds to mix.

But they can't, I said quietly.

Uncle One patted the dirt next to him. Come sit by your Uncle, he said.

When I hesitated, he grinned. It was a real grin—a human one, with stretched lips and bared teeth. It occurred to me he had always known how to smile. Uncle Two probably had too. I couldn't understand why they had chosen not to reveal such expressions to me. Maybe if they had, they would have revealed more than tears and laughs and frowns, more than they wanted to.

Please, he said. Genuine sorrow creased his brow. I promise I won't bite.

I sat cross-legged across from him. "Tell me how my mother died," I said aloud.

At the sound, Uncle One flinched. Use your inside voice, he said.

Fine, I responded. Tell me.

He flexed his toes as though suddenly distracted.

Phobos, I urged.

His head snapped up. Don't call me that, he said.

Why not? I asked, leaning forward. Did you hate the ones who named you?

They hated me. His mouth turned down. Watching the movement of his face was disconcerting. His lip curled. They called us monsters, he said.

I shook out my hair's rough tumble. I don't feel like a monster, I said.

You're not. His eyes found me, and for the first time, I sensed his resentment. You were your mother's great hope, he spat. The new breed. Then, as quickly as he had grown angry, he softened. His voice wistful, he said, You're going to refuse us. You don't want to procreate. You don't want to build a civilization. I know that.

I'm sorry you're ill, I said. We can try to heal you.

I'm dying. He blinked at me, and I knew he was telling the truth. Your mother wrote about how quickly we grew, he said. Apparently, we shrink swiftly as well.

And that's why we came here? I asked.

I thought I could continue this. He gestured at the brightly lit dome, its wilting blossoms and torpid trees. I wanted to make something before I died. I wanted to continue you, he said. Your progeny might need oxygen. And so.

And so, I replied. I fingered one of the rhododendron leaves. At my touch, it crumbled. What happened to the humans? I asked.

His face became unreadable. They perished, he said.

Yes, but how? What burned the station? A dark thought bloomed. Was it you? I asked.

No, he said, that was Gabrielle, the Red Star leader. Some sort of explosive device.

How do you know? I asked. Did she tell you?

I could hear her think, Uncle One said. She was quite transparent. She knew her uncle's experiment had failed. We were not the babies she'd been expecting. She wanted to destroy us. The explosion was meant to be isolated to our lab, but the fire spread farther than she planned. I can imagine her relief when she saw Penelope running toward her. I suppose she'd gotten attached. So she saved her, and by default, you. Maybe Gabrielle thought you'd be different. But she didn't reckon on us.

I don't understand how you survived, I said, if she blew up your lab.

It turns out, he said, we can walk through fire.

Can I?

Let's not find out.

And so you walked here, I said. After the Red Star station burned. You and Uncle Two. I paused, trying to figure it out. Gabrielle too? With Penelope?

Uncle One's eyes twinkled, but I didn't know with what. Yes, he said.

Was Penelope still pregnant? I asked.

He nodded. You were born here, he said.

That's what Uncle Two meant when we found this place, I said. That I had come home. But what happened to them? I peered into his face, hoping it would reveal something. His eyes twinkled again. My dark thoughts unfurled, leaf by leaf, like a plant. Did you hurt them?

Uncle One smiled at the memory. Oh yes.

I could hardly get my next words out. What about my mother?

Uncle Two and I kept your mother strong on the walk here, he said. We wanted to make sure you were born healthy. We were curious— again, that unnerving grin—what you would look like.

But what happened after I was born? I prompted. What did you do to the humans?

I killed Gabrielle and the other two. A couple of men. They were annoying. But not Penelope. Uncle One flexed his toes again. That was Deimos, he said.

I caught my breath. Uncle Two, I said flatly. He killed my mother.

He loved you from the start, Uncle One said. He wanted you for his own.

I needed to find Uncle Two. I stood up, then paused, considering Uncle One's pale legs, longer than mine would ever grow. Why are you and I so different? I asked. Is it because of our fathers?

He waved that away. Our fathers had nothing to do with it. They were human as our mothers. No, my dear Moon, they simply bungled it. A bigger dose of radiation here, a smaller squirt of oxygen there. They wanted to make sure we'd survive in this atmosphere, but they didn't know what they were doing. People from Earth—he sneered—never do.

One more question.

One more, he agreed.

Why do you think they added so many cartoons to the screens? I asked.

Another smile flitted across his face. Those were for us, he said. To entertain us when we were children. His grin widened. But we were never quite children, were we?

I FOUND UNCLE Two asleep in his pod. I shook him and shook him, but he wouldn't wake. His breathing was raspy and labored, and an odor of decay was wafting from him. His formerly plump body looked shrunken. Gazing down at his wasted face, I wanted to hate him, but couldn't. I could only hate Uncle One for trying to coerce me into what had been forced upon my mother.

I lay down beside Uncle Two and pressed my back to his. His gasps were so noisy I had difficulty sleeping, but eventually I did. As I drifted off, I was grateful I wouldn't experience the nightmares my mother had. Creatures like me don't dream.

WHEN I WOKE THE NEXT MORNING, Uncle Two was dead, his body thinned to a husk. I bundled up his remains in his blanket and carried him to the dome. Uncle One was lying in the rotting garden, his breath rattling in his throat. His eyes were shut and his skin ashy, his limbs scattered around him as though he'd lost control of his body. I sat with him until his breath rattled to a stop and, with a small sigh, his body collapsed. I thought of his brother. I thought of the Red Star station. I thought of Gabrielle, who had sought to destroy us.

All the monsters are dead, I thought.

I bundled him in another blanket and hefted both Uncles on my back. I carried them out of the dome and into the dunes. On some unremarkable plain, I shrugged them off and left them to blow away with the wind. Uncle Two had murdered my mother, and Uncle One had let him. I owed them nothing.

THAT EVENING I SAT in the dome with the freshly charged screen in my lap. Without prompting, Ivy appeared. I could see her. At the sight, the confusion and pain of the past days dropped away. Here she is, I thought. My friend. Her eyes were black instead of icy pale like mine, and she was wearing clothes and seemed much tinier than I was, but we could have been related. I wanted to reach through the screen and touch her tough skin—lighter than mine—and her glossy hair and her grin, just this side of wicked.

"I got the video to work," she said. "Holy moly, look at you. You're naked."

"And you're not. Why didn't you refuse clothes?"

"Ha. Not an option here."

We paused, studying each other. The wonder of the moment expanded.

She broke the silence. "I was kind of hoping you'd look more like an alien."

I laughed. "I was hoping you would too."

"And I thought you'd be older. Your mother wrote that diary twenty-eight years ago."

"I'm in my fourteenth year."

"Oh." She smacked her forehead with her palm. "Right. My mom's boyfriend told me about years on Mars. Two for you, one for us. Still, you look awful young." Her eyes lit up. "Maybe that means you'll live twice as long."

I thought about this. The Uncles and I had been born within weeks of each other, but they had grown so quickly I used to think they were years and years older than I. Now they were dead, and I was not. Ivy might be right.

Behind Ivy I could see shadows and rounded edges. "Is that your tent?" I asked.

"Forget my tent," she said. "Come see Earth."

She brought the screen with her to what I presumed was outside. The day was ending there also.

"Your sunset's pink," I marveled. The colors were overwhelming. "So much green. That blue sky. Those are all tents?"

"Yeah." Ivy's face popped back into the screen. She rolled her eyes. "My mom would have hated it. We keep growing. People seem to like it here. They keep bringing us stories of other places."

"What kinds of stories?"

"Like what folks are doing to survive. The best one I've heard is about a city that floats on air. They say it's led by a legless man and a poet, that only artists live there. That they dance every night on the rooftops." Ivy did a spontaneous skip, as though the story delighted her. "I've heard also that they're rebuilding New York, but I'll believe that when I see it."

"What's a poet?"

"Someone who writes words mashed together to sound pretty. I like it. My favorite is my mom's poem about the bison. We have a ton of them. They stink, but they sound awesome when they're running."

I couldn't see any humans among the tents. "Where are all your people?"

"It's Big Fire night," she said. "They're off chanting."

"What's behind you?" I asked. Huge shapes rose up behind her, slanted with light.

"The Rockies. They're mountains. You have mountains on Mars?"

I nodded. "There are no trees on them though. What's behind your mountains?"

"The ocean." She filled the screen with her face. "That means water. Lots of water. They call it the Pacific. It used to cover thirty percent of the globe, but it's got to be more now. We think it's grown way closer."

I couldn't imagine all that water. Basins' and basins' worth. "Have you seen it?" I asked.

"You're funny. No. We don't go to see it. That's one of our things, like poetry's our thing. We wait for it to come to us."

"What about Mars?" I asked. "Will you come here someday?"

Her mouth twisted. "No freaky experiments?"

"No freaky experiments," I promised. I thought of the Uncles' desiccated forms, blown across the sands. You too, I thought. May you rest.

"A week ago, I would have laughed at you," Ivy said. "Rocket ships to Mars? No way. But I've been doing some digging while you were gone." Her eyes lit up. "I caught a signal, did some listening."

"And?" I prompted.

"It seems the Northern Refuge is still a thing. That's where your mom came from, right?"

I nodded.

"They're at it again," Ivy said. "I guess it takes a lot for people to give up on a mission to Mars."

My heart did a quick pitter-pat. To meet a human face-to-face. That would be something.

"So someday, maybe yes?"

"Someday maybe yes." Ivy grinned at me, and I grinned back, delighting in how wide my smile could spread. "It might take a while," she said. "But who knows? Maybe you could come visit me too." Behind her, the sun dipped below the mountains' rim. The sky's pink melted into purple. "You could meet Fatima," she said. "The last of my mother's friends. She checks on me sometimes, tells me about Alicia."

"Who's Alicia?"

"Right. Sorry." Her eyes misted, then cleared. "That was my mother. When she was alive, I called her by her name. Hey." She pointed at me. "I don't know your name."

"I'm Moon."

"Ha." Ivy skipped again. She seemed to enjoy being outside among the tents. "Of course that's your name. I'll howl at you," she said, "next time you're full." She pointed behind me. "What's that place you're in? What's with all those trees and stuff? I thought Mars was a desert."

"This is the dome. It's not mine." I gazed around me. Perhaps I could make it mine. I could clear out the rotten flowers and vines, uproot the shrubs and trees. I could make it clean and spare, more like the terrain

I had trekked before Uncle One decided we should become civilized. I would have the time. The Uncles had perished quickly, their life spans truncated. But if what Ivy said were true, I was going to live for many years to come.

Ivy seemed to read my thoughts. "Make that dome yours," she said. "That's what I did with the tent when my mom died. I moved the beds around and brought out her fancy tea set. The one she'd traded for. She said we'd use it for special occasions, but we never did. Now I drink water from it every day." Behind her head, the sky was deepening to indigo. One by one, the stars were coming out. "When you visit, I'll serve you a drink in one of the teacups. By then I bet I'll be old enough for wine."

"What else will we do?" I asked.

She shrugged. "I don't know. Hang out. Tell stories. I like telling stories."

"And not go see the ocean," I added.

"No." That wide and wonderful grin. "We won't need to. One day it'll come see us."

She began to walk then, taking the screen with her and naming the things I saw. A cooking pot. A dog. A candle with a crackling head of flame. I drank everything in. Before me I saw time stretching on, the days and years through which Ivy and I might travel, teaching each other what we knew. I could tell her about sandstorms and volcanoes, about the Uncles and the dome. Ivy could tell me more about her mother, about what family could truly mean.

The Uncles were gone. The Red Star volunteers. My mother. I had no family. But I felt neither afraid nor alone. I had a friend. I had a planet of my own. I had the possibility that one day, with the help of the Northern Refuge, Ivy and I would meet, would touch hands and mix our worlds.

This, I thought. This is enough.

SAMSON

KANSAS TO TEXAS, 1873–1925

A man named Samson kills seventeen buffalo one day, seven the next, eleven, six, twelve. He strips hides and severs tongues. Hams he carves hot from the carcasses, a bandanna shielding his nose from the stink. He and his fellows cart their load to Dodge City, cash in, return to the prairies. Blood burdens his days, but he does not falter. The nights drift with fire, roasted game, his body's odor, pungent as the earth that pillows his cheek. The fierce stars move him to tears.

He loves a young woman named Daisy, her hair as bright with flame as his. They share Irish roots too, and a fear of hunger. He is skinny and not tall, scarred within and without. He didn't think to find love, but she lends him her hand at the dance hall, and she is so small her eyes tilt far up to find his own.

For Christmas he buys her a ring, on New Year's Eve beds her in a rooming house where a squeak of springs is the least lonely cry. Three months later they travel to Texas, the wagon jolting their bones. The year is 1874. The buffalo are nearly gone, and the plains stink of slaughter and fresh hope. On a lonesome stretch of Panhandle ground, they build a dogtrot cabin and harbor two hounds to lie panting in the shaded dirt. Their tablecloth is checkered red and white, their kerosene lamp polished and gleaming. The lamp's lit circle contains their four hands, intertwined. In springtime he coaxes tendrils from the soil. Tomatoes and melons, snap beans and peas. They own cows and horses, some sheep. Daisy churns the cows' milk into butter Samson calls rich for the sweet sound of it.

The seasons turn, heavy as a man heaving over in bed. Near winter's widening mouth, Daisy births a son and dies. Samson names the son Charles, watches him grow tall and strong. Seven years after his birth, Charles disappears from the pasture. Despite Samson's best efforts, the boy does not return.

We will not speak of his time alone, the hounds that come and go in the breezeway between his house's two halves. Perhaps there is drink, tobacco. Perhaps women. Perhaps nothing but the solitary pounding of his fist upon a table.

In 1920, he marries a girl named Gertrude. She is twenty-five, blond, chunky, of German descent, which—given the recent war—they rarely discuss. He is sixty-seven, one side of his head a fossilized scar. When they lie down together, he is a dried riverbed, she a great offering of rain. Together they demolish the dogtrot cabin, erect a frame house, sow the soil with wheat. This land, Samson thinks, a great land.

On her twenty-sixth birthday, Gertrude delivers him a son. He does not say "another." To recall the first is to carve a runnel through his heart. They christen the boy Robert Henry, a solid name, one coined for a man of honor.

The boy grows up with straight legs and crooked eyes, though his father does not at first recognize the devil within. Samson dreams of the calves before they're born, of droughts years before they arrive, but he cannot envision his son's future, cannot see the woman he will rope like a cow and drag home, a woman from Mexico with damaged dreams of her own. He cannot predict the child—his granddaughter—this captive will birth one drunken day in 1963, a girl named Bea who will bear her father's son and name him a giant. A girl whose descendants will migrate through stars as her mother once did across Earth.

It is 1925 and Samson sees only his plump young wife in their porch's rocker, their four-year-old son chasing the chickens around the yard. He thinks of the crops he has grown, the animals he has raised, and remembers that day in his youth when he knelt to slit the throat of an orphaned buffalo calf.

He thinks now as he thought then, how good and kind is this country. This infant nation, so generous with its gifts. It would give you the stars if you asked. It would give you the Moon.

ACKNOWLEDGMENTS

Rarely is a book written in isolation. This one took a village.

I owe my place on this stage to Danya Kukafka and Michelle Brower, agents extraordinaire, who saw what this story could become and gave it a fighting chance. I will be forever grateful for your suggestion that I make this book "bigger and weirder," and for providing me with the editorial, intellectual, and emotional support to make that happen. With you, I am in the best of hands.

Tremendous thanks to my editor, the fearless Margaux Weisman, for loving this story from the start and giving Bea and Company a safe home at Viking with its incredible team of talented professionals. Your insightful feedback and attention to detail were exactly what these pages needed. They are so much better for knowing you. I am so much better for knowing you. It has been a joy to bring this book to life together.

Without the teachers in my life, I might have been a writer, but certainly not a very good one. I have endless gratitude for Catherine Arra, my very first writing teacher all the way back in high school. Thank you for letting me take your creative writing class (twice!) and for treating me as though I had something significant to say. You are the reason I am a writer and a teacher. I am honored to know you. To my wonderful mentor and friend, Helen Schulman, for lending a patient ear and wise guidance through my time at The New School and beyond. It is an exceptional feeling knowing you are in my corner. To the fabulous Tiphanie Yanique and Margot Livesey, thank you for your feedback on my drafts and your openness to what I was trying to do with this story. You encouraged me to be confident taking risks and to own my own voice.

I am deeply grateful to The New School's MFA program and to all I met there. What a talented, supportive, and welcoming community. I would not be where I am without you. I owe a great deal also to the writing conferences at Sewanee and Tin House, which provided me with the space to think about myself first and foremost as a writer and to connect with some of the most amazing and creative human beings I have met in this life.

So many people read drafts of this story as it toddled toward adulthood. Huge thanks especially to Brady Huggett, Tara Weinstein, and Anne Ray, for the multiple reads, perceptive feedback, and overall emotional support through this crazy process we call *writing*. Thank you also to Jecca Hutcheson for being the essential writer friend I know will read not just my work but also my anxiety-filled text messages. Thank you to Julie Goldberg and David DeGusta for reading my first whole draft, when I (foolishly) thought it was finished. And to the many others who read bits of this book in its infancy, true thanks for helping push it to the next level.

For giving me the space to write, thank you to the third floor of the Brooklyn Public Library's Central Branch. Your last table in the back helped give birth to the Floating City. I am indebted also to Schnabels' Woods for the cabin, the writing desk, and all the deer sightings I could ever hope for. Thank you as well to Matt Reeves from the Missouri Valley Room at the Kansas City Public Library for assisting with my research on children's hospitals and for showing me the joys of microfiche.

To my students at both the High School of Economics & Finance and Leadership & Public Service High School, thank you for reminding me to always think about the future. To my colleagues at these schools, thank you for your support. To Robin Dishner, a special thank you for acting as a sounding board for all my aesthetic concerns.

To my friends and family for the love and support, and especially to Martin Miller, for telling everybody you know about the book. I am so grateful I still have someone to call whenever I get good news. And to Madeline Graves, thank you for always cheering me on.

To my very unique parents, Sara Swan Miller and James Edward Swan, who gave me this life and the tools to navigate its treacherous waters. To my mother, for teaching me playfulness. To my father, for teaching me patience. To them both, for allowing me to be exactly who I was. How lucky I am to have known them.

And finally, to Pete Graves, partner in this wacky world for over twenty years. Thank you for carrying my backpack through that landslide in India. Thank you for reading this book in all its iterations. Thank you for the giant babies, and so much more.